By the same author

IN SOLITARY
THE NIGHT OF KADAR
SPLIT SECOND
GEMINI GOD
THEATRE OF TIMESMITHS
THE SONGBIRDS OF PAIN (*short stories*)
WITCHWATER COUNTRY
TREE MESSIAH (*poems*)
CLOUDROCK
SPIRAL WINDS
ABANDONATI
HIGHLANDER (*as Garry Douglas*)
IN THE HOLLOW OF THE DEEP-SEA WAVE
HUNTER'S MOON
MIDNIGHT'S SUN
IN THE COUNTRY OF TATTOOED MEN (*short stories*)
FROST DANCERS
HOGFOOT RIGHT AND BIRD-HANDS (*short stories*)
ANGEL
ARCHANGEL
HOUSE OF TRIBES
THE NAVIGATOR KINGS (BOOK I): THE ROOF OF
        VOYAGING
A MIDSUMMER'S NIGHTMARE

Books for children and young adults

THE WIZARD OF WOODWORLD
THE VOYAGE OF THE VIGILANCE
THE RAIN GHOST
THE THIRD DRAGON
DARK HILLS, HOLLOW CLOCKS (*short stories*)
THE DROWNERS
THE ELECTRIC KID
BILLY PINK'S PRIVATE DETECTIVE AGENCY
THE PHANTOM PIPER
THE BRONTË GIRLS
CYBERCATS
THE RAIDERS
THE GARGOYLE

THE
PRINCELY
FLOWER

THE
PRINCELY
FLOWER

THE PRINCELY FLOWER

Book II of
The Navigator Kings

Garry Kilworth

ORBIT

An *Orbit* Book

First published in Great Britain by Orbit 1997

Copyright © Garry Kilworth 1997

The moral right of the author has been asserted.

Map and illustrations by Wendy Leigh-James

A CIP catalogue record for this book
is available from the British Library.

ISBN 1 85723 469 3

Typeset in Sabon by M Rules
Printed and bound in Great Britain by Clays Ltd, St Ives plc

UK companies, institutions and other organisations wishing to make
bulk purchases of this or any other book
published by Little, Brown should contact their local
bookshop or the special sales department at the address below.
Tel 0171 911 8000. Fax 0171 911 8100.

Orbit
A Division of
Little, Brown and Company (UK)
Brettenham House
Lancaster Place
London WC2E 7EN

For Grace and John Chidlow

Contents

Author's Note

This is a work of fantasy fiction, based on the myths and legends of the Polynesian peoples and not an attempt to faithfully re-create the magnificent migrational voyages of those peoples. Other authors have done that, will do it again, far more accurately than I am able to do. This particular set of tales, within these pages, alters a piece of known geography, while hopefully retaining the internal logic of the story: my apologies to the country of New Zealand which has changed places with Britain. The gods of the Pacific region are many and diverse, some shared between many groups of islands, others specific to one set of islands or even to a single island. Their exact roles are confused and confusing, and no writer has yet managed to classify them to absolute clarity, though Jan Knappert's book is the best. Where possible I have used the universal Polynesian deities, but on rare occasion have used a god from a specific island or group for purposes of the story. Since the spelling of Polynesian gods and the Polynesian names for such ranks as 'priest' varies between island groups, I have had to make a choice, for example *Tangaroa* (Maori) for the god of the sea and *Kahuna* (Hawaiian) for priest. In short, for purposes of homogeneity I have taken liberties with the names of gods and with language.

For the facts behind the fiction I am indebted to the following works: *The Polynesians* by Peter Bellwood (Thames and Hudson); *Nomads of the Wind* by Peter Crawford (BBC); *Polynesian Seafaring and Navigation* by Richard Feinberg (The Kent State University Press); *Ancient Tahitian Canoes* by Commandant P. Jourdain (Société des Oceanistes Paris Dossier); *Pacific Mythology* by Jan Knappert (HarperCollins); that inspiring work, *Polynesian Seafaring* by Edward Dodd (Nautical Publishing Company Limited); *Aristocrats of the South Seas* by Alexander Russell (Robert Hale); the brilliant *Myths and Legends of the Polynesians* by Johannes C. Andersen (Harrap); and finally the two articles published back to back that sparked my imagination and began the story for me way back before I had even published my first novel, *The Isles of the Pacific* by Kenneth P. Emory, and *Wind, Wave, Star and Bird* by David Lewis (National Geographic Vol. 146 No. 6, December 1974).

My grateful thanks to Wendy Leigh-James, the design artist who provided me with a map of Oceania decorated with Polynesian symbols and motifs.

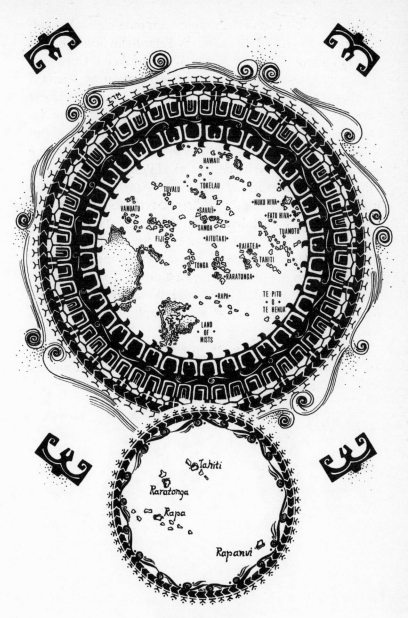

Oceania

Pantheon

Amai-te-rangi: A deity of the sky who angles for mortals on earth, pulling them up in baskets to devour them.

Ao: The God of Clouds.

Apu Hau: A god of storms, God of the Fierce Squall.

Apu Matangi: A god of storms, God of the Howling Rain.

Ara Tiotio: God of the Whirlwind and Tornado.

Aremata-rorua and Aremata-popoa: 'Long-wave' and 'Short-wave', two demons of the sea who destroy mariners.

Atua: An ancestor's spirit revered as a god.

Dakuwanga: The Shark-God, eater of lost souls.

Dengei: The Serpent-God, a judge in the Land of the Dead.

Hau Maringi: God of Mists and Fog.

Hine-nui-te-po: Goddess of the Night, of Darkness and Death. Hine is actually a universal goddess with many functions. She is represented with two heads, night and day. One of her functions is as patroness of arts and crafts. She loved *Tuna* the fish-man, out of whose head grew the first coconut.

Hine-te-ngaru-moana: The Lady of the Ocean Waves. Hine in her fish form.

Hine-tu-whenua: A benevolent goddess of the wind who blows vessels to their destination.

Hua-hega: The mother of the trickster demi-god Maui.

Hine-keha, Hine-uri: The Moon-Goddess, wife of Marama the Moon-God, whose forms are Hina-keha (bright moon) and Hine-uri (dark moon).

Io: The Supreme Being, the 'Old One', greatest of the gods who dwells in the sky above the sky, in the highest of the 12 upper worlds.

Kukailimoku: Hawaiian God of War.

Kuku Lau: Goddess of Mirages.

Lingadua: The One-armed God of Drums.

Limu: Guardian of the Dead.

Magantu: The Great White Shark, a monster fish able to swallow a pahi canoe whole.

Maomao: The Great Wind-God, father of the many storm-gods, including 'Howling Rainfall' and 'Fierce Squall'.

Marama: God of the Moon, husband of Hine-keha, Hine-uri.

Marikoriko: First woman and divine ancestor, wife of Tiki. She was fashioned by the Goddess of Mirages out of the noonday heatwaves.

Maui: The great Oceanian trickster hero, with powers which almost equal those of a god. Maui was born to Taranga, who wrapped the child in her hair and gave him to the sea-fairies. Maui is responsible for many things, including the birth of the myriad of islands in Oceania, the coconut, and the length of the day, which was once too short until Maui beat Ra with a stick and forced him to travel across the sky more slowly.

Milu: Ruler of the Underworld.

Moko: The Lizard-God.

Nangananga: Goddess of Punishment, who waits at the entrance to the Land of the Dead for bachelors.

Nareau: The Spider-God.

Nganga: The God of Sleet.

Oro: God of War and Peace, commander of the warrior hordes of the spirit world. In peacetime he is 'Oro with the spear down' but in war he is 'killer of men'. Patron of the Arioi.

Papa: Mother Earth, wife of Rangi, first woman.

Pele: Goddess of Fire and the Volcano.

Pere: Goddess of the Waters which surround Islands.

Ra: Tama Nui-te-ra, the Sun-god.

Rangi: God of the Upper Sky, originally coupled to his wife Papa, the Goddess of the Earth, but separated by their children, mainly Tane the God of Forests whose trees push the couple apart and provide a space between the brown earth and blue sky, to make room for creatures to walk and fly.

Rehua: The Star-God, son of Rangi and Papa, ancestor of the demi-god Maui.

Ro: A demi-god, wife of the trickster demi-god Maui, who became tired of his mischief and left him to live in the netherworld.

Rongo: God of Agriculture, Fruits and Cultivated Plants. Along with Tane and Tu he forms the creative unity, the Trinity, equal in essence but each with distinctly different attributes. They are responsible for making Man, in the image of Tane, out of pieces of earth fetched by Rongo and shaped, using his spittle as mortar, by Tu the Constructor. When they breathed over him, Man came to life.

Rongo-ma-tane: God of the Sweet Potato, staple diet of Oceanians.

Rongo-mai: God of Comets and Whales.

Ro'o: The Healer-God, whose curative chants were taught to men to help them drive out evil spirits which cause sickness.

Ruau-moko: Unborn God of Earthquakes, trapped in Papa's womb.

Samulayo: God of Death in Battle.

Tane: Son of Rangi the Sky God, and himself the God of artisans and boat builders. He is also the God of Light

(especially to underwater swimmers because to skin
divers light is where life is), the God of Artistic Beauty,
the God of the Forest, and Lord of the Fairies. As
Creator in one of his minor forms he is the God of
Hope.

Tangaroa: God of the Ocean, who breathes only twice in 24
hours, thus creating the tides.

Tawhaki: God of Thunder and Lightning. Tawhaki gives
birth to Uira (lightning) out of his armpits. Tawhaki is
also the God of Good Health, an artisan god particularly adept at building houses and plaiting decorative
mats.

Tawhiri-Matea: The Storm-God, leveller of forests, wave-
whipper.

Te Tuna: 'Long eel', a fish-god and vegetation-god. Tuna
lived in a tidal pool near the beach and one day Hine
went down to the pool to bathe. Tuna made love to her
while she did so and they lived for some time on the
ocean bed.

Tiki: The divine ancestor of all Oceanians who led his
people in their fleet to the first islands of Oceania.

Tikokura: A wave-god of monstrous size whose enormous
power and quick-flaring temper are to be greatly
feared.

Tini Rau: Lord of the Fishes.

Tui Tofua: God of all the sharks.

Ua: The Rain God, whose many sons and daughters, such
as 'long rains' and 'short rains' are responsible for
providing the earth with water.

Uira: Lightning (See Tawhaki).

Ulupoka: A minor god of evil, decapitated in a battle
amongst the gods and whose head now rolls along
beaches looking for victims.

Whatu: The God of Hail.

PART ONE

The leaping place of souls

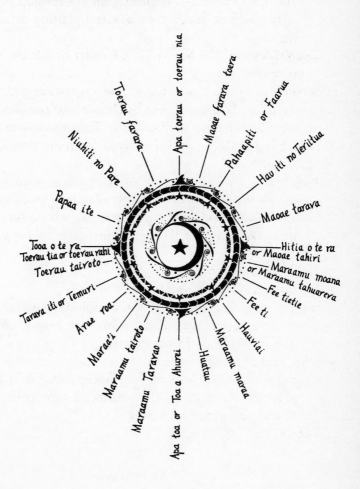

1

The Earthquake-God Ruau-moko turned unexpectedly in his mother's womb and woke Tikokura, who rose up out of a gentle ocean to form a giant angry face of water which swept over the surface towards a defenceless atoll.

The mouth of the Tikokura's face was a massive maw filled with white, foam-flecked teeth. The hidden eyes were sightless, blinded by fury, buried beneath heavy lids of water. The hair on the head of the wave was spindrift, terrible in its aspect, which trailed behind the broad expanse of Tikokura's brow.

On the beaches of the atoll, a ring of six islands, the fishermen and shellfish gatherers saw the tidal wave coming. Since the atoll was not more than six feet above sea level they knew that many, if not all of them, were about to drown.

'Tikokura's coming!' one of the women screamed. 'Save my children! Save my children!'

Birds flew up from the trees and beaches in a blast which momentarily filled the sky with black dots.

'I'm an old man, I can't run,' cried a white-hair in despair. 'Help me! Sons, daughters, help me!'

No one came to the elderly father's assistance, nor that of

the unfortunate mother, for there was nothing anyone could do, there was nowhere to run.

Some islanders were immediately resigned to the idea of death: as inhabitants of a low sandy atoll on which life was hard, where work filled almost every waking hour, and disasters were common, they were an unhappy group of people hammered into a dulled state of acceptance by misery, constant labour and deprivation.

A few, however, scuttled away for the palm trees, hoping to climb high enough to be out of the reach of Tikokura. They dropped their nets, without which they would probably die of starvation anyway, and ran for the scrubby patches of palm trees which were all but the only vegetation on the isles. In these few that unquenchable spark known as the will-to-live drove out all common sense and had them mindlessly attempting to cling on to their empty and worthless existence.

One or two, those lucky enough to own canoes, took to the boats.

No one questioned: *why?* Tikokura was a minor but unpredictable god, capable of destructive fury for no reason at all. His breast was full of bitterness; he preferred *hate* over all other emotions; he killed for the love of killing.

One young man already in an ocean-going canoe, a sea-faring warrior, a stranger merely touching the shores of the atoll briefly in order to replenish his water supplies, immediately turned his canoe and, unlike the islanders themselves, raced directly into the maw of the wave.

Those who saw this action were astounded. They wanted to call to the youth, warn him of the terrible consequences of his actions, turn him from his course. The warrior stood at his mast, however, a determined expression in his blue eyes, ready to do battle with the god of sudden waves.

He was a tall fair-skinned youth, out of whose partly shaven head protruded two dark-red twisted horns of hair

in the fashion of the Hivans. Indeed, the three solid bars
tattooed across the bridge of his nose, making his battle
expression one of the fiercest in Oceania, also proclaimed
him to be of the Hivan-peopled islands. In his right hand he
held a barbed spear, which he brandished in the face of the
oncoming god.

'Tikokura,' screamed the youth. 'My name is Kumiki, a
warrior of Nuku Hiva. These useless people have no temples,
or I would have sacrificed a pig or dog to you . . .'

The wave rushed onwards, seemingly unaffected by these
words.

'Let me ride over your head, Tikokura,' pleaded Kumiki,
'for you have no quarrel with me. I'm not one of these miserable wretches who scrape an existence from your back.
I'm Kumiki the Hivan, on a life-long quest to kill my own
father. I must live until my father lies at my feet, the blood
gushing forth from his throat, staining the coral of his
home isle. Spare me until that moment – *then* take my life,
if you must.'

Tikokura heard these words and knew then who was
Kumiki's father. He sympathised with the youth's mission,
for he had little love of his own people, let alone those
from an alien place. The wave-god's hate for mankind
would be better served by allowing this one Hivan warrior
to live, so that the youth could cause an untold misery and
upheaval amongst a distant island group. The boy was a
weapon, a spear in flight, and for the sake of bitterness it
was better not to knock him aside, but to let him fly
onwards to his target.

Kumiki saw the wave part before him, allowing him a
narrow passage over calm waters between tumultuous seas.
Once his canoe was through and he was safe the gap closed
and the wave continued on its relentless path towards the
hapless atoll. When it hit the outer reef it thundered over
the coral bed, drumming the island from a distance and
causing climbers to be shaken from the palms like insects.

They fell screaming to their deaths. Coconuts followed, raining on their twisted forms, pounding their bruised bodies into the coral dust.

Tikokura swept at last over the beaches and the islands, taking with him men, women and children, the force of his momentum gathering them up as a flood collects twigs. Flimsy huts disintegrated, fires were quenched in a brief hiss of steam, precious nets disappeared. The tops of palm trees, some bearing clinging mortals, were snapped like broom heads and washed away to unknown shores. Fishermen's boats were overturned, spilling out their occupants, who were instantly lost in the crashing, whirlwind foam of the breakers which tossed and tumbled over the small islands, grasping, crushing, destroying everything and anything which had been made or planted by human hand.

When the spilling torrent had finally rushed on, towards the horizon, the water left in its wake drained from the atoll, leaving the group of islands above the surface again.

Kumiki saw figures descending from the strongest and tallest of the palms, a few survivors climbing down to the wet coral dust, to stand and stare bleakly at the devastation that lay before their eyes. Everything they had ever owned had been torn from their grasp in a matter of moments. Their means of livelihood – their nets, their canoes, their scant crops – were all gone. All that was left were the flat islands themselves.

For the next few months, perhaps years, they would be scrabbling about in the lagoon searching for those shellfish which had not been ripped off rocks and carried away. They would be living on limpets and clams, seaweed and roots, fighting over the sparse numbers of coconuts, their only source of fresh drink since they had no wells. They would dwindle in numbers to eventually disappear completely as a people, until more exiles from the high islands began to land and populate the flat, uninteresting atoll – and the next wave came.

Kumiki turned his canoe in the direction of Arue roa on the windflower.

On his home isle of Nuku Hiva the eighteen-year-old Kumiki had left the girl who he hoped would one day be his wife. Her name was Miro and he loved her deeply. They had already made love in the sand and surf of the Hivan beaches, with others of their own age, since promiscuity and sexual licence among the unmarried was perfectly acceptable to Oceanians.

Once they were married, however, adultery was punishable by death, and she would be his alone to love and cherish.

It would not have been fair to have married her before he left, for he might never be able to return to Nuku Hiva. The sea might swallow him, the gods might take him, or a man might kill him, making the return trip impossible. Also, he had left her free to love whom she pleased, in a casual way, extracting only the promise that she would not marry another unless he, Kumiki, failed to return home within five years.

When Kumiki had asked for her promise, Miro had said, 'I shall never marry another – instead, if you do not return, I shall go to the leaping place of souls and end my life – for I know if you do not come back to me you must be dead.'

'Do not kill yourself,' he told her, knowing she meant to throw herself over the cliff where spurned and lost lovers ended their lives, 'for you can learn to love again.'

'Without you sharing my mat, dear Kumiki, I shall not want to live.'

This had disturbed Kumiki greatly. He did not want such a beautiful thing as the love between him and Miro to be stained with blood. It was enough they had loved for the short time given them until now. Still, he had every intention of returning to her, and no intention at all of allowing Tikokura to snatch his life, even after he had killed his father, despite what he had promised the wave-god in a moment of rashness.

Kumiki brooded on images of his father's death, once the pictures had re-entered his head.

The death of his birth-right father.

A brief inspection of Kumiki's skin would tell anyone that he was not of pure Hivan descent. From a distance he had sometimes been mistaken by strangers for an albino, or perhaps one of the Peerless Ones, the fair-skinned, fair-haired fairies of the mountains. Then, when he came closer and they noticed his hair, they changed their minds to believe him a goblin or demon. It was only when he was close enough to speak to them, and they recognised his tattoos, that they knew him to be a Hivan warrior from a princely family. A youth of noble lineage.

Kumiki had fair skin – fairer even than the pale Tongan, Samoan and Tahitian princes – and dark-reddish hair. Although adopted by a chief, his real father it might be thought was a supernatural creature. Yet Kumiki had been told a story which proved his real father nothing but a man – a man not from Oceania but from a land discovered by Kupe the Raiatean. A place called Land-of-Mists, where all men had white skins and blue eyes.

Kumiki's adopted father had told him that his real father had invaded their island with a band of warriors from Raiatea and had, in the course of that invasion, raped an innocent woman, who later died giving birth to Kumiki himself. Kumiki was the product of a savage outsider, a wild creature with none of the finer instincts of an Oceanian, no strong code of honour, no generosity of spirit.

The man known as Seumas possessed none of the traits which made men proud of themselves. He had not conducted himself with dignity after raiding Nuku Hiva, but had taken a woman by force in the troubled heat of the battle. This Seumas had not been able to control his basic urges at a time when he should have been glorifying Oro, the God of War, not slaking his lust in the dirt with a terrified woman.

Kumiki had been incensed when he heard what the boastful savage Seumas had done to his mother, even though it had resulted in his own birth. There and then he had resolved to seek out this foreign monster and kill him, first letting him know why he was going to die, then crushing his skull with a club. It was then Kumiki's intention to eat the head of Seumas, to steal his mana, and chew on his eyes and heart to humiliate him utterly.

Kumiki sighed as the wind drove the spray against his face, now set in the direction of Rarotonga.

'I can almost taste his brains,' whispered the youth, with longing in his voice. 'I can almost savour his eyes on my tongue at this very moment.'

There was a long way to go yet, however. Kumiki was no great navigator, no Kupe or Hiro, or even Karika. He was a youth who until the age of seventeen had sailed only in home waters. But sea-farers had come to his island, and he had talked long and hard with them, learning the ways of the open ocean, discovering the name and location of his enemy, gleaning the secrets of navigation on the high seas.

He had gathered together knowledge of the setting and rising stars in the roof of voyaging, the fanakenga and kaveinga; of waves, their sizes and shapes; of swells, rips, currents; of different types of wind; of seaweed and birds; of important cloud formations; of sounds and smells of distant land; of the colour of different running seas.

Still, he had no experience and would probably become lost at times. It would be enough to survive, *eventually* to track down his prey, murder him in cold blood, and laugh at those who tried to stop him.

It was all Kumiki could ask of his Tiki, the First Ancestor of all men, sitting now on the front of his ocean-going canoe. It was all he could wish of the demi-god Maui, the trickster whose body was held in thrall by the Hine-nui-te-po Goddess of Death, but whose spirit still roamed the world. It was all he could request of Tawhaki, the Great

God of Thunder and Lightning, of whom Kumiki wished to be a personal favourite.

'I shall leave his body to be picked clean by the reef fish,' snarled the horn-haired Hivan youth, the three solid bars of his tattoo twisting into a ferocious expression as he thought about his quarry. 'I shall throw his liver to the frigate birds and watch them tear it to pieces as they fight over the shreds.'

These juvenile and immature chants by the warrior, into the teeth of the wind, helped him maintain his courage in the face of the long, dangerous and arduous voyage. He was not cutting new pathways through the ocean, but following a memorised pattern of the swells, clouds, islands, reefs, rips and other navigational signs, given him by adventurers who had traversed the same route before him and had returned to pass on their knowledge. His fury at his real father helped him to overcome his fears of being lost, or of meeting monsters, or of being swallowed by gods.

'I hate him for his nothing-family!'

This was the main reason why Kumiki loathed his real father: because Seumas had left him no family line, no ancestors to revere. A community worshipped the gods, but an individual worshipped the spirits of his ancestors. Kumiki had no ancestors to look up to, to love and fear, to thank in times of plenty, of whom to beg forgiveness and food in times of want. Kumiki had no long genealogy to trot out in front of severe and intractable temple priests, no thousand names, no layers of generations which would make him proud. His name stopped with his blood-father, who had no *real* name, no name which meant 'son of the moon' or 'strong as a spear' but was just a jumble of worthless letters which when put together was pronounced 'Seumas'. There were of course ancestors on his mother's side, but these were so much less powerful.

'I'm coming for you, Seumas,' screamed Kumiki, his muscles rippling over the tautness of his chest as his hate fought to get out. 'I'm coming to eat your head, you lizard's tongue, you sperm of stone fish, you festering dog's intestines – I'm coming to tear the heart from under your ribs!'

And the words were swept away, over the vast reaches of the ocean, lost in a thousand miles of watery world, seeking the ear of the man they had once called 'the goblin'.

In the distance, a thousand miles away, a volcano erupted, spewing its red-and-white hot molten lava into the atmosphere in an immense spectacular pyrotechnical display. Kumiki took this breathtaking sight as a sign that Pele the Goddess of Fire and Volcano was on his side. The youth felt buoyed by the sight of redness covering the sky. This artificial sunset was Pele's stamp of approval on his mission.

Rarotonga has only two seasons: Winter and Breadfruit.

This was the Breadfruit season, a time of plenty.

Two thousand miles away from the voyaging youth, unaware that he had a son in the world, Seumas sat on his mat and contemplated his past. He was now in his early fifties, as was his wife Dorcha, and the pair were childless. Yet, that fact apart, they were not unhappy.

He had been happy on Rarotonga, an island which he had helped to find, and win. The two kings who ruled jointly had found a tribe in the interior, the remnants of an ancient race of people known as the Menehuna.

The Menehuna were wonderful masons and builders. It was the fairer-skinned Menehuna who had built the Toi's Road, which circled the island, and who had constructed the magnificent temple called Arai-te-tonga.

Over the years Seumas the Pict had gathered much mana unto himself. The young Oceanians regarded him as one of themselves, a distinguished citizen and warrior, full of honour.

It was true, too, that he looked very much like any other elder Rarotongan. Tattoos covered much of his torso, his arms and legs. His skin had been burned by the sun and stars into a rich mahogany colour. His pride and joy, his fiery hair, once plaited by Dorcha into a long red pigtail, had changed its hue. He was now an Oceanian in appearance as well as manner. Only his blue eyes gave any hint of his real origins.

'Seumas, don't sit in the sun too long,' warned Dorcha, her own black hair now streaked with white, 'you'll get one of your headaches.'

'Don't fuss over me, woman,' he grumbled. 'I like it here in the doorway.'

There was a dog named Dirk near his feet. All his dogs had been called Dirk, from the first faithful hound that he had owned in the country of Albainn, to this whelp that stared at him now, its brown eyes full of sorrow at having to laze away the day instead of running along the beaches with his master.

The shadows of day lengthened quickly, as they always do close to the equator, and soon it was dark. The sky above became a soft black imbedded with masses of bright stars. Hine-keha, the Moon Goddess, began smiling down on the island.

Dorcha had a fire going in the middle of the house, its smoke curling out through a hole in the roof, and Seumas went in and sat beside it.

While Seumas was serving them both the red snapper he had caught, cooked by Dorcha in a coconut sauce and garnished with a delicate seaweed, someone entered by the window.

'Hello, Kieto,' smiled Dorcha, 'you saw the smoke of our fire?'

Kieto's entrance by the window, instead of the door, was a gentle reminder that he was higher in rank than either of the house's occupants.

Kieto laughed. 'Since both Seumas and I are basket-sharers anyway, your rebuke has very little sting.'

Kieto was now a sturdy man in his mid-thirties, a strong warrior prince, the adopted son of Tangiia.

Kieto said, as he sat on the mat and was offered some fish, 'I've asked Boy-girl to join us. We need to talk about war, Seumas. The time is getting close.'

Shortly afterwards, the tall willowy figure of Boy-girl appeared in the doorway.

'At least someone comes in by the right entrance,' said Dorcha, with a sidelong glance at Kieto.

Boy-girl smiled at her hostess. The lean smooth Boy-girl had been born the seventh son of a family without girls and had been raised as a woman and as such she had great mana. Like Dorcha, Boy-girl was steeped in the occult.

'Come, Lei-o-mano,' said Boy-girl to a cockerel who followed her, 'heel, boy.'

Seumas growled, but said nothing.

This was Boy-girl's idea of a joke, to copy Seumas by training a rooster like a dog and have it follow her everywhere, even naming it after the Oceanian dagger.

The cockerel trotted in, running between Boy-girl's legs, and began pecking at unseen bits of food around the hearth, much to the consternation of Dirk, who kept looking at his master, then back at the bird, as if wondering when Seumas was going to toss this arrogant creature out into the night.

Boy-girl sat down between the two men, her decorative shells rattling as she did so.

Seumas shook his head as he stared at Boy-girl. 'Who would believe you're almost as old as me – you don't look as though you've added a year since we've been on Rarotonga.'

Boy-girl laughed, delighted at the compliment.

'Now,' said Kieto, 'to business. You have heard that the old king, Haari, is dying?'

What had once been an arduous and terrible journey, from Raiatea to Rarotonga, was now a flourishing shipping route. Consequently, news travelled between the islands too, keeping everyone informed.

Dorcha had now sat down and she said, 'I have heard this.'

'Well,' continued Kieto, 'one of the princes on the island is using the king's death as an excuse to form an expedition to find another island. He has no elder brother chasing him away, but he feels the island has grown too populous.'

'You're talking of Ru,' interrupted Seumas.

Kieto nodded. 'Prince Ru has persuaded his brothers and their wives to go with him in search of an island which he has seen in a vision. He knows the star in the roof of voyaging under which the island rests, and he proclaims that once he has seen it he will discover his new home. He has selected twenty royal maidens for his crew. These virgins have been chosen for virtue, strength and beauty – as the Great Sea-God Tangaroa has ordered in Ru's vision – and their purity and strength will ensure a safe voyage for the seafarers.'

Dorcha said, 'Yes, but what is all this to do with us?'

'You know my destiny, Dorcha – it is set in the heavens – to conquer the great island found by Kupe – the Land-of-Mists – the place from which you and Seumas were taken by us some decades ago. Of course I know your feelings about this.'

Seumas shook his head. 'There are wild tribes on those shores – a proud people.'

'In that case,' said Kieto, 'they must be subdued.'

Seumas smiled ruefully. 'I have given you two main reasons why you cannot win such a land – iron and horses – of which you have neither.'

'You don't understand the nature of the people you are planning to attack,' interrupted Dorcha. 'They make war against each other, but if a common enemy comes, the tribes will join together under one leader. "*I am against my cousin, but my cousin and I are against the stranger.*"'

'We will find a way,' Kieto said with confidence. 'It is why I have called this meeting. To talk to you of Ru's voyage. Boy-girl has been communing with her ancestors. As you know, the spirits of our forebears can see into the future and they tell Boy-girl that in the course of his voyage Ru will touch the shores of an island where giants roam. On that island is a gateway to another world. In that Otherworld is a nation of Oceanians called the Maori, a magnificent warrior race, who have colonised an island as great as Land-of-Mists – a country they call Aotearoa, or Land of the Long White Cloud.

'We must go and find these Maori, discover the secret of their success in war. We must learn their methods, their strategies, their tactics, and use this knowledge to conquer the Land-of-Mists. I know Albainn is your land, Seumas, and yours Dorcha, but this I also know – if we do not conquer the fair-skinned tribes of your country now, there will come a time when they will overrun *us*. We must do this thing, or our descendants will regret our faint-heartedness, and curse us for not taking our courage in our hands and striking first.'

Seumas understood all this, but nevertheless he was deeply troubled, as any man is whose loyalties are split.

2

Since King Tangiia and King Karika had founded their island domain, others had come in their canoes to swell the numbers of their subjects.

Tangiia chose, in the Tahitian-Raiatean way, to emphasise his divine origins. He was thus a very remote figure to the people, appearing mostly at night since commoners were obliged to sit with bowed heads when he passed.

It was lucky for them that he had not married his sister, instead of his beautiful cousin princess Kula, for then the commoners would have had to prostrate themselves.

Tangiia's servants carried him almost everywhere: his mana was so great that where he laid his foot became his property. Thus in order to disrupt daily lives as little as possible, and to allow the land to remain in the hands of commoners, Tangiia was only carried abroad during the night hours, when most of his subjects were asleep.

Karika, however, remained very much a man of the people. This was the Samoan custom. Samoan kings did not trace their line back to the gods, or if they did it was not made public knowledge. Karika was strong on dignity, could be stern and challenging, but did not stand on pomp.

From the Rarotongan commoner's point of view it might seem there was a king to despise and a king to love here, but each form of kingship brought with it certain rewards.

With King Tangiia's divine heritage came colourful ceremonies, music and dancing and a strong sense of religious fervour. He and his priests wore cloaks and helmets of brilliantly coloured feathers, while the Tangiia himself was resplendent in the scarlet sash which proclaimed his right of kingship. His royal canoe was a marvel of regal ornamentation and craftsmanship, heralded always by trumpeters, drummers and flautists of superior musical skills. His house, standing on the slopes of a mountain, was an architectural wonder. The people were immensely proud of such a haughty aristocrat.

Karika, on the other hand, remained very much a warrior king. He organised games and sports, was keen on bird hunting and fishing for bonito and albacore. He was not averse to removing his tapa bark shirt and helping in the fields. Karika introduced hunting with a hawk – Rarotonga's koputu fishing hawk – which was caught by lowering oneself down a cliff face, staring the bird unflinchingly in the eyes, then snatching it from its nest. If the hunter took his eyes from the raptor for a second, or gave way to the bird's piteous cries, the hawk dropped as a dead weight in free fall, opening its wings just before hitting the ground far below the edge of the cliffs. Karika was adept at capturing the koputu.

The people loved such a king as this too, and felt they were getting the best of both worlds.

Such an island then, with its two great kings and its unsurpassed landscape beauty, was bound to attract settlers from far and wide throughout all Oceania.

They came from Samoa, from Tonga, from the Tahitian group, from the Hivan Islands, and from many others. So many Tahitians arrived within the first year that two of Tahiti's oldest mountains also magically transported themselves, since they missed the company of their human friends, and became Rarotonga's Ikurangi and Te Atu Kura peaks. The basins where they once stood in Tahiti remain as a testament to their departure.

On the day Kieto's expedition was about to depart, the great adventurer Hiro arrived at the island on his weather-worn pahi.

Dorcha and Seumas went hurrying down to the beach, to see the seafaring hero, who almost rivalled Kupe in his wanderings, pass through the gap in the reef. Hiro had been to the far corners of the ocean, even to Hawaii. He had tales to tell which chilled his listeners to the pith.

Hiro was an important friend and visitor and King Tangiia broke his rule and appeared in daylight on the beach, carried high on his litter. Still only in his late thirties he was a fine figure of a man in his feather cloak and helmet, but necessarily pale and serious in aspect. His lovely wife Queen Kula, resplendent in her own right, accompanied him.

Along with Tangiia came his retinue: counsellors, priests, a masseur, guards, a storyteller, the jester, a wise man, his treasurer and his valet. Tangiia stood on his litter with wide arms, welcoming Hiro to the shores of Rarotonga, while a chosen warrior – one of Karika's personal bodyguards – made a show of pretending to attack the visitor with a spear, running forward, jabbing at the air, rolling his eyes up to show the whites, lolling his tongue, slapping his thigh, and distorting his features with furious grimaces and angry sneers.

Hiro reached the high-tide mark and was greeted by Karika, who rubbed noses with the adventurer, bidding him welcome.

The feasting and dancing began. Dogs, chickens and pigs were slaughtered, breadfruit pits were opened, pandanus leaves were laid down. Musicians fetched their instruments and played lively tunes, filling the island air with song. In the high green valleys of the bladed mountains, the birds rose and fell in clusters, wondering what the noise was about.

Kieto and Seumas managed to get Hiro on his own, by the fire later that night, and discussed their own plans with him.

'Have you come across an island where giants are said to walk about and command attention?' asked Kieto.

Hiro, broad-chested and tall, square-faced and hawk-nosed, with long flowing black hair and deep brown eyes, looked thoughtful.

'I have never been to such a place, but I have heard tell of it on my travels.'

Seumas said, 'Could we persuade you to come with us, lead our expedition?'

Hiro smiled, shaking his head. 'My path lies in the opposite direction. I hear that the island you speak of, which is called Rapanui, the navel of the world, lies just above Fee Tietie on the windflower from this island – but far off, so far away it must be in the corner of Oceania. I must sail Nuihiti no Pare on the windflower, or the gods will be displeased with me.'

'Why do the gods tell you to go in that direction?' asked Kieto. 'What is beyond Samoa?'

'I have to seek out an art form, called *writing*, which is like speech only silent.'

This was gobbledegook so far as Seumas was concerned.

'How can it be like talking, yet be silent? It doesn't make sense. Are you sure the gods are not having a joke with you? Which gods do you mean? If it's Maui, then you had better think again, Hiro, for you know what a trickster he is – that demi-god would lead you into Hine-te-nui-po's mouth.'

Hiro smiled and said, 'I cannot reveal which of the gods direct my path, but it is no trick. There is such a thing as *writing*, for I have heard the word on the wind, when the Great Wind-God Maomao blows from Nuihiti.

I must seek out this mystery and bring it back to my people.'

Hiro would be drawn no further than that and Seumas had to be satisfied with feeling that Hiro's journey would be a wasted one and that this *writing* would turn out to be silly pictures of some kind that did not talk at all.

The following morning, the pahi carrying Kieto's expedition set forth on the high seas. The expedition consisted of Kieto, Seumas, Dorcha, Rinto, Pungarehu (the killer of the Poukai bird), Polahiki, Boy-girl, Po'oi and the Farseeing-virgin, Kikamana. There was also a hired crew and the owner of the pahi on board.

Rinto was the son of the famous Manopa, right-hand man of Tangiia when that king had been struggling against the tyranny of his half-brother, Tutapu. Manopa had once saved the life of Seumas, even though the two were not basket-sharers in any sense and actively disliked each other. Manopa had died with the debt unpaid. Seumas therefore looked for an opportunity to save the life of Manopa's son, in order to discharge his obligation.

Kikamana was now an old woman, but still one of the most powerful priestesses in Oceania. Her knowledge of the occult was unsurpassed and her magic exceptional. Dorcha had learned much of her skill from Kikamana.

Polahiki was there on sufferance. A dirty, scarred and flea-bitten scrounger who stank of body odour and bad breath, this old Hivan fisherman invaded the space of others with all the sensitivity of a swamp hog. Polahiki had pestered Kieto night and day until at last the young navigator agreed to take the fisherman along with him. Polahiki said he was bored on Rarotonga and wanted to be out on the high seas once again. However, immediately the voyage began he started to complain that he was feeling sea-sick and home-sick and wanted the canoe to turn round and take him back. He only shut up when Seumas threatened to throw him overboard.

Po'oi was the son of Blind Kaho the navigator and Feeler-of-the-sea. The son was almost as adept as the father had been and Kieto had included him in the expedition for his great skill of knowing where the craft was in the ocean simply by testing the temperature of the water with his hand.

These, then, were the people chosen by Kieto to seek the legendary Maori nation, whose skill at war was unequalled, and whose mythical homeland could only be reached by a fairy gateway on an island somewhere far away, under the roof of voyaging.

Kieto followed a kaveinga to his birth place, the island of Raiatea, asking questions from time to time of the other navigators on board – Po'oi and Dorcha. Dorcha owned the only form of chart known to Oceanians, the shell-stick map, which she had fashioned from strips of criss-crossed bamboo studded with small cowries. The chart had been constructed on the first voyage between Raiatea and Rarotonga, and depicted the major navigational points – islands, setting and rising stars, reefs and rips – used on that original journey.

Halfway to Raiatea they sighted a magnificent flotilla of around one hundred and fifty pahi canoes coming towards them, heading in the opposite direction, with around eighty souls on board each of them. Seumas feared it might be an invasion fleet, on its way to conquer Rarotonga. He had never seen so many vessels in one group.

Polahiki said, 'If that's a war flotilla, I'm telling you now, I'm on *their* side.'

Po'oi replied scornfully, 'We know you'd betray each and every one of us, if it meant saving your own skin.'

'I'd betray my own mother,' agreed the incorrigible Polahiki. 'In fact, I did.'

'Well,' said Dorcha. 'If it is a war party they'll swarm over us straight away. We don't stand a chance of fighting or outrunning them. What are those colourful pennants they're flying? And they all have tall yellow sails. They don't look like war banners to me – they seem too stately for that. Best make friends with them.'

Kieto agreed with this plan and as the magnificent fleet approached he stood on the front of the pahi.

'Who are you?' called Keito. 'Where are you bound?'

A man stood on a high platform of the leading pahi, dressed in yellow and red leaves and wearing red body-markings.

He was a lofty, lean figure with a very handsome face. Droplets of water from the salt spray glinted in the sun-light like multi-coloured jewels on his muscular body. His hair was fashioned like two raven's wings, sweeping up from the sides of his head. Around his neck he wore a garland of hibiscus blooms and there were frangipani flowers decorating his ears.

He grinned broadly on hearing Keito's question, as if he could not believe his ears, and shook his head in amaze-ment. Instead of answering, he thrust forward one of his legs: an almost black limb which was literally covered in thick tattoos. The other leg was devoid of markings.

'So what?' said Seumas, mystified. 'So he's got a few tattoos!'

'Only on *one* leg,' breathed Boy-girl, suddenly coming to life. 'You know who that is?' Her voice was full of deep reverence, as if she had just encountered a god. 'Do you know to whom you are addressing your mundane remarks? We are indeed favoured of the gods. This is beyond every-thing.' As she spoke her voice rose to an excited high-pitched squeal, which grated on Seumas's nerves.

'So what's his name?' asked the Pict, wondering why he was so annoyed at Boy-girl's reaction. 'Tell us.'

'I don't know his name.'

They all stared in the direction of the white bow wave which preceded the yellow-sailed pahi.

Dorcha said, 'But you said you knew him?'

Boy-girl quivered visibly from head to toe.

'Know him? His name is not known to me, but his profession is. That man you see smiling at us is an exalted Painted Leg, one of the sacred ones. *A Painted Leg*. He's the leader of that group. Higher than a king – almost a demigod. You know what that means? It means that the fleet is the Arioi, sacrosanct to the Great God Oro.'

Now Seumas knew what Boy-girl meant, and was aware of the reasons for her great excitement. The Arioi was a unique society of dancers and singers, players and entertainers, who travelled Oceania building enormous stages on which to perform their various acts. There would be musicians and comedians amongst them, too, and other kinds of performers. There were seven grades of performer, the highest being the Avai-parai, the Painted Leg, and the lowest the novitiates, the Poo-faarearea, know as *flappers*.

Arioi shows included such diverse acts as histrionic orations, spear fighting, satirical plays, sparkling dialogues, chants on ancient history, laudatory songs of heroes and heroines, and provocative hura dances. The Arioi had sprung up from the Tahitian culture, in the years between Tangiia leaving Raiatea and the present day.

The Arioi had never visited Rarotonga before, it being a relatively new and small island. Seumas had heard of the troupe, but had not seen it. Now he and his wife were heading away from Rarotonga, it seemed the wonderful show was going to visit his home.

'Damn!' he said, disappointed. 'The one time they come to Rarotonga and we miss them!'

Now that the mighty fleet of travelling players was aware of another boat in the vicinity, the Arioi began dancing and singing in a lively manner, giving Kieto's expedition an unexpected treat out on the great ocean. The occupants of the six vessels behind the leader had locked their canoes together on the calm waters and were performing a hura dance. As the several pahi floated sedately by Kieto and his group, the Arioi drummers thundered out a fast rhythm on their log drums while women swished their grass skirts and men leapt and strutted.

The male dancers hopped and jigged around the swaying females, making lewd gestures with their hands and hips. When the shy 'maidens' retreated, the men followed them like rutting creatures of the wild, becoming more and more frenzied in their movements, their eyes rolling, their hands and feet flying. The music raced like hot blood through excited bodies, firing the dancers to a pitch which seemed to Seumas and Dorcha to be almost insane.

Boy-girl's cockerel ran up and down, crowing at the top of its voice, while Dirk barked excitedly, chasing the fiery feathered creature around the deck.

As the pahi drew alongside the male dancers leapt and bound up to the females with jerking bodies. Dorcha's eyes opened wide as she noticed that many of the extravagantly decorated men had erect penises jutting through their leafy kilts.

'Goodness,' she said, suddenly feeling hot and bothered. 'Do you see . . .'

It was true that the Oceanians were normally quite straitlaced when it came to exposing their genitals, going to great lengths to cover their private parts, yet on sacred occasions, such as when the Arioi danced, all their reserve was thrown to the winds and they became totally uninhibited.

In fact the dance in front of the expedition ended with one couple actually copulating to the encouragement of the other dancers, who showered them with flower petals.

'Yes, I see what you mean,' muttered Seumas primly, the priggish highland Pict coming out in him. 'Not very tasteful is it?'

'It's *wonderful*. It's a religious dance, you oaf,' said Boy-girl, who was obviously enjoying every minute. 'It's been blessed by the gods.'

'Well, we all know which gods they might be,' replied Seumas, his lips as tight as pahi sennit sheets. 'And we don't need to approve of them do we?'

The next two pahi had wrestlers on board, who were covered in coconut oil and struggled with one another, forming a tangle of bodies.

'And goodness knows *what's* going on under that lot,' cried Boy-girl, hot with excitement. 'For a few flower petals I'd swim over to them and join in.'

Next came the orators of ancient history and myth, chanting a song about Tawhaki's grandson, the great Rata:

'. . . one day the navigator king, Rata, began building a ship in which to make a voyage. As he went through the forest carrying his adze, with his men around him, he noticed a serpent struggling with a white bird.

'"Help me, O Rata!" cried the bird. "For I will perish under the coils of this terrible snake."

'Rata did not like to interfere with the natural order of the forest however, so he pretended not to hear and passed on.

'The next time Rata passed the spot the snake and the bird were still locked in an intense fight.

'The snake on seeing the sea-faring adventurer said, "This is a private battle, Rata – you should leave us alone." And Rata saw the justice in this remark, for the serpent was entitled to his prey, just as the birds were entitled to their insects.

'As he walked away, the bird cried, "If you aid me I shall help you finish your ship!" But Rata walked on, thinking that the bird was simply pulling lies out of the air in order to save itself from its fate.

'However, when he and his men reached the spot where they had previously felled the trees, there were none lying on the ground, but all were upright once again and growing tall.

'Angrily, Rata and his men felled more trees but this evening when they passed by the still battling snake and bird, Rata suddenly severed the snake in two, decapitating it, and the bird was able to escape the creature's coils.

'"Thank you," said the white bird, "you will not regret your actions, O Rata, for I am Ruru, King of the Birds, and I and my kind will assist you in your efforts to build a canoe. The trees you felled are in a magic wood and you will need my help to overcome the local sorcery."

'That night Ruru gathered together all the birds of the forest, who pecked and drilled at the felled trees, boring holes and stitching them together with sennit cord. Before morning a magnificent double-hulled canoe stood waiting for Rata and his men to carry it down to the sea. However, the sea was far away and the craft heavy, and finally it was the birds who with supreme effort managed to lift the pahi and fly it gently above the forest, to place it in the island's lagoon.

'"A pathway through the air for the ship," the birds had sung as they carried the pahi above the land. "A pathway of sweet-scented blossoms for the boat of Rata!"

'Rata set sail that evening, after thanking Ruru, but refusing to take a magician named Nganaoa with him.

'When the ship was out at sea a calabash floated along-side the craft which was taken aboard by one of the seamen.

'"Where are you going, O Rata, grandson of Tawhaki of the Thunder and Lightning?" said a voice from within the sealed calabash.

'"Where do you *wish* to go?" asked Rata.

'"To the Land of Moonlight, to seek my parents," replied the calabash.

'"What payment do you offer for your passage?" asked Rata.

'"I will look after your great sail."

'"There are mariners to do that work," replied Rata.

'"I will keep your hulls empty of seawater by bailing."

'"There are seamen for that job too. And the calabash is hollow, my friend. Why not sail to the Land of Moonlight in your own little craft."

'"Because I can't get out, without your help," replied the voice.

'"Then you are no use to me," replied Rata, "for a creature who can squeeze himself inside a calabash should surely be able to get out again without assistance."

'"Don't throw me overboard," cried the voice in panic. "I'll tell you what I will do – I'll protect you from three terrible monsters – the Gigantic Clam, the Ferocious Octopus and the Ship-swallowing Whale."

'Rata had heard of these awesome monsters and had entirely neglected to protect himself against them. He ordered that the calabash be opened. Out came Nganaoa, the magician.

'A few days later the craft was passing between two strange, fluted, white cliffs when they started to close on the vessel, hinged as they were below the surface.

'Rata cried, "It's the monstrous clam!"

'Nganaoa the magician immediately picked up a magic spear and with a spell on his lips threw the weapon down into the water. It struck the Gigantic Clam in a soft vulnerable area and the beast disappeared down to the depths of the ocean without closing around the great canoe.

'Several days later, a fantastic octopus, the size of which Rata had never seen before, came lashing over the surface of the sea, its tentacles flying and its mouth open and ready to devour the hapless mariners.

'Nganaoa flung a kotiate club, which passed through the flailing tentacles and struck the octopus a death blow on its bulbous temple.

'Next an enormous whale came rushing at them with its cavernous mouth wide open, ready to swallow the pahi and its crew whole. Nganaoa quickly seized two tall spears and jammed open the whale's jaws with the weapons, while chanting a sorcerer's song into the beast's face. The whale was defeated.

'"Well done!" cried Rata. "You have earned your passage, Nganaoa."

'But the magician did not need to seek further for his parents, for when he looked down the throat of the whale, he found them in its belly, trussed in sennit cords and waiting for their son to rescue them. Nganaoa made the whale vomit his parents by sticking a lighted stake down its throat. They fell on their son's neck, showering him with thanks.

'Rata, the great captain, navigator and king went on to discover many new islands, and to return to his homeland safe and happy with his successful voyages . . .'

The song drifted away on the breeze as the last few yellow-sailed and colourful-bannered pahi of the Arioi passed by Kieto's solitary craft. Soon the enormous flotilla was out of sight over the horizon and the still ocean, with its running cold currents carrying the craft, seemed a silent lonely place. Kieto disappeared into the deck hut with Kikamana to commune with his ancestors. Boy-girl went to sit in the bows of the double-hulled, twin-sailed canoe and dream of being a member of the elite Arioi herself.

Others drifted away to various parts of the boat, there being room to be alone on such a large craft with only half-a-dozen or so passengers and a crew of not more than twelve.

Dorcha tied a lead around Dirk's neck and left him lying by the mast, before taking Seumas by the arm.

'Where are we going?' whispered Seumas, bemused by her leading him to the stern of the vessel. 'What's going on? Have you something to tell me?'

Hidden by a sail from the rest of the passengers and the crew, Dorcha fumbled with her skirt, removing it. She then lifted Seumas's garment and pressed her hot body against his, making him open his eyes wide in astonishment.

'What's going on?' he whispered in her burning ear.

'If you don't know that by now,' she said hoarsely, 'you're less of a man than I thought you were, Seumas Black. *Cha toigh leam neach ach thusa,*' she added, slipping into Gaelic, as she often did when she was embarrassed by having to initiate a love-making. 'Come on, man, you couldn't witness a dance like that and still be soft down there.'

He wasn't 'soft down there' as it soon became apparent, but he was shocked to find that his wife of many years, a woman of fifty, was lustful and musty-breathed. He would have been startled had she been only twenty. She pushed him on his back and climbed on top of him, lowering herself on him.

'Is this right?' he moaned, wondering at the rush of pleasure, the electricity in his loins. 'It seems not to be proper to me.'

'Proper be damned,' she groaned. 'Just lie there and enjoy it – or not – I don't bloody care, so long as you stay stiff.'

So he did 'stay stiff' and he did enjoy it. In fact it was one of the most exciting love-makings he had ever experienced, even though he was grey-haired and fifty, and thought his time was past. And his wife, magnificent creature that she was, sat poker-backed moving rapidly up and down, her face and wild hair framed against the blood-red sky. When her orgasm came it seemed as if she were howling silently at the rising moon.

In the bows some sailor had begun welcoming the evening by beating the tai-moana, the Threnody-of-the-Ocean, a long drum carried by ocean-going canoes. The loving pair kept time with the beats, almost all the way, only overtaking the drummer at the very end of their session. Then they both lay there in each other's arms, glistening with sweat.

'By the gods, woman,' he whispered softly to her, as they drifted off into sleep, 'when I'm rich I'll *buy* the bloody Arioi and make them dance for us every night, so help me I will.'

And she laughed throatily into his ear.

3

Ao, the God of Clouds, was very important to seafarers in Oceania, for in the shapes and colours of the clouds the seamen recognised certain navigational signs. One particular cloud formation might indicate the presence of land beneath, another a dangerous reef below shallow water. Red clouds, grey clouds, white clouds, black clouds: all had significance when predicting future weather patterns. The reflection of sea colours, from lagoons and shallows, could be seen from several hundred miles away on the base of a cloud.

So, Ao knew of his standing amongst mariners, but he was not puffed up or arrogant. He could not afford to be, for he was subject to the whims of other gods, especially Maomao, the Great Wind-God, who blew Ao's children all over the sky.

Yet Ao had a certain power, being a close friend of one of the most powerful gods in the roof of voyaging.

Tawhaki, the God of Thunder and Lightning, who was greatly feared and respected both amongst the gods and amongst men, used Ao's clouds as hiding places.

One day Tawhaki asked Ao to take him down low, close to a vessel crossing the ocean from Rarotonga to Raiatea. Ao did as he was bid and Tawhaki was able to listen to the words of Kieto, who spoke of his intention to attack and subdue the peoples of the Land-of-Mists. Tawhaki knew the land of which Kieto spoke and he was not happy. Tawhaki was aware that there existed other gods, *different* gods, in the skies and earth of Land-of-Mists, and in the seas around Land-of-Mists. If Kieto went to war, then the Oceanian gods would have to do likewise.

'We shall have to battle these strange gods of that distant island,' Tawhaki told Ao, 'for the mortals take us where they go, and if Kieto goes to Land-of-Mists he will take the First Ancestor, Tiki, with him on the front of the canoes, and you and I, and all the other gods, will follow too. Those gods of that distant land will regard us as invaders and will attack us We shall have to war with them in their skies, under their seas, beneath their landscape.'

Ao replied, 'But we are such *powerful* gods, Tawhaki. There is the Goddess Pele, of the Volcano, shooting fire and molten rock with her mouth. There is Milu, Ruler of the Underworld. There is Ruau-moko, God of Earthquakes. There is Maomao, Tangaroa, Papa, Rangi, and so many others. Let us not forget Io, the Supreme One, who dwells in the highest of our twelve upper worlds, a hundred times more puissant and as remote from us as gods are from ordinary men.'

'Their gods are powerful too, the peoples of that land, and I foresee a long and weary war between us. Perhaps we shall win, but then again, we might lose. I think I might have to destroy Prince Kieto and his little band.'

'But what do Io and the other gods think?' asked the timid Ao, afraid of upsetting his superiors. 'Do they agree with you in this?'

Tawhaki growled in anger, his voice rumbling across the roof of voyaging.

'Io says the affairs of men are not our business, provided we are treated with respect and receive our due sacrifices.'

'Then should we not obey the Supreme One?'

'Not if it means the death of us, for what would he be to us then, but another fallen god!'

Ao realised now that Tawhaki was in rebellion against the highest order of the gods and he was a little afraid.

'And who do you have with you?' he asked. 'Who strides across the landscape, seascape and heavens beside the great Tawhaki, out of whose armpits comes the lightning, out of whose chest comes thunder? Who agrees with Tawhaki that Kieto must fail in his endeavours? Which of the gods is with you?'

'With *us*,' corrected Tawhaki. 'Why none, for they are all cowards where Io is concerned. Even Rongo and Tane refuse to brook the Father of the Gods. And Oro.'

'Not even the Atua? Even they are not with us? Tiki? Marikoriko? All the ancestor spirits? What about the demi-god, Maui? Surely, little Maui is with us?'

'Maui would help men make war on his grandmother if he thought it would be exciting,' snarled Tawhaki. 'And the ancestor spirits fear no mortal combat – they revel in it.

'And before you ask,' added Tawhaki, 'the beast-gods are also with Kieto – Dakuwanga the Shark-God, Dengei the Serpent-God, Moko the Lizard-God – they all revel in bloodshed and wish to feed on the dead souls that combat brings.'

'Then we are utterly alone.'

'Yes.'

In truth, Tawhaki *was* concerned by the prospect of a war with the gods of Land-of-Mists, but this was not his reason for wanting to destroy the Ru-Kieto expedition. In point of fact he was feeling jealous and spiteful. The island which Tangaroa was giving to Prince Ru of Raiatea was the very island Tawhaki had intended giving to an Hawaiian nobleman. It irked the God of Thunder and Lightning that Tangaroa had beaten him to it. Tangaroa, however, was much more powerful than Tawhaki, and there would be no use in the Thunder-God trying to overrule the Great Sea-God, master of all the oceans.

Ao would not countenance the idea of destroying Ru, so Tawhaki pretended it was Kieto he was after.

'Together we can crush this upstart Rarotongan,' Tawhaki growled. 'We can smash him.'

Ao saw then what he had let himself in for and he was very concerned for his own safety.

'Sneakily, then,' he said. 'We must do it with cunning and guile, not openly, with force.'

'Agreed,' muttered Tawhaki, 'but if we fail to do it on the sly, then I shall blast their pahi from the water with thunderbolts and lightning.'

'Oh dear,' murmured Ao, the gentle God of Clouds, regretting already that he was a close friend of the brashest and noisiest of all the Oceanian gods. 'I hope you won't have to do that, for Io will surely come to hear of it.'

'A last resort,' promised Tawhaki, striding out of the clouds and marching purposefully across the broad expanse of sky. 'Only as a last resort.'

Ao hoped so, or they would both find themselves standing on heaven's equivalent of earth's leaping place of souls.

Ragnu, once the high priest of King Tutapu of Raiatea and Borabora, now the high priest of the dying King Haari, waited in his dark Raiatean temple courtyard which stood next to Tapu-tapu atia, the Investiture Stone 'Most Sacred, Most Feared'. In this marae of Ragnu's stood an ahu, stained black with the blood of innocents, upon which the high priest, a kahuna of great power, had sacrificed men and used their kabu to work his sorcery. Even now he commanded souls, held them in thrall, and used them for his devious schemes, which were mostly designed to increase the power of the priest over the islanders.

Ragnu's hunched shape moved like a spider through the

stone-cold dimness of his temple bounds, muttering to the unfortunate captive souls, as they gathered in the corners of the ancient marae, their expressions of utter misery comforting to the priest.

'You serve me, you pathetic wretches, yet you are only of use for short-arm schemes. Once you leave my island, you scuttle down to Milu's Underworld and hide from me, out of reach of my magic. So, we cannot use you to destroy my Rarotongan enemies, can we, my wraiths, my wisps of mist? I have to trust instead one of my own kind, who are never to be wholly trusted.'

The dead souls, safe only from the ravenous Dakuwanga while they remained in Ragnu's thrall, wailed piteously.

'Yes, yes,' snarled the kahuna, 'I know you kabu are full of your own misfortunes, but what about *mine*? Almost twenty years ago Tangiia and his people – Kieto, Seumas and Dorcha included – made a fool out of me. They destroyed the finest king that ever sailed the ocean – my own Tutapu. Now they have come abroad again and must be ripe for my revenge. I will have it. I will have it. They must suffer pain and humiliation, just as I suffered. They must be brought down, humbled, stamped face-down into the red clay.'

The wooden temple gods stared broodingly from the chill shadows at the ranting priest as he paced the worn floors. Their thick noses, their hollow eyes, their brute-lipped mouths dripped with moisture and moss. They had seen death in multiples, witnessed the bones piled high on the ahu, beheld altars running with blood, watched organs eaten raw by novice priests craving power. The dark gods were steeped in death, it clung to them as a foul gas to a marsh, it permeated their porous forms. Death had weathered their shapes, eroded their spirits, turned them into coarse, jaded beings. They were sated, glutted with death. They had been corrupted and corroded by the atmosphere of death, which had rotted their timbers.

There was a noise outside the temple close and someone
peered through the curtains of vines that draped over a
doorway which led to the marae.

'Lord Ragnu?' a voice called, full of trepidation. 'Are
you there, o priest?'

The ancient, shrivelled figure of Ragnu, with its wizened
features and bright eyes, waited in the darkness, enjoying
the visitor's fear, savouring the man's terror. There was a
faint moan from the man. His legs seemed to buckle under
his own weight and it was obvious he was about to turn
and run. Ragnu came out of the shadows and confronted
him.

'You are here, Titopika.'

The man addressed as Titopika jumped visibly, but then
sighed in relief on seeing the priest.

'My lord – this place . . .'

'It worries you?'

'There are spirits here, ghosts, clinging to the walls like
spider's webs.'

Ragnu said, 'I am here to protect you.'

This remark did not appear to ease Titopika's apprehension. His eyes were switching back and forth in his skull
and his hands shook. Ragnu decided to light a torch, in
order to calm his man down a little, so he would concen-
trate on what was being said to him. There were the embers
of a fire in a clay bowl in the centre of the marae. Ragnu
took a brand and lit it from the charcoal, blowing on the
redness to create a flame. Once the place was lit Titopika
did indeed become calmer.

'You know why I have asked you here?' said Ragnu.

Titopika gave a final shudder and said, 'You wish me to
do something further for you?'

'You have made yourself a part of Prince Ru's expedition
with his family?'

'Yes, I obeyed the command you sent.'

'There is a party of six or seven Rarotongans who will

journey with him. They are at this moment on the high seas, on their way here. I have seen their crab-claw sails in my farseeing bowl. Amongst them is a man called Kieto. For some reason which I have failed to divine Kieto and his friends are accompanying Prince Ru on his search for a new island.'

'How is it you cannot find out?'

'I'm being blocked by another power – no doubt that damned high priestess Kikamana, with the help of the goblin Dorcha and that shred of whimsy, Boy-girl – which will not let me discover their reasons for going with Ru.'

'Oh. And what must I do?'

'You must ensure the destruction of this group. Do not enquire as to my motivation. It is enough for you that I wish them all dead. You must sabotage the whole expedition, if need be, but you must annihilate the Rarotongans.'

'Am I the person for this work?' quailed Titopika.

Ragnu studied the beautiful young man, seeing deeply handsome features and a finely wrought body.

'Yes, you are. Don't worry, I have a plan which will be acceptable to you. I understand you like women?'

'Doesn't every man?'

'Not in the quantities you do. But that is neither here nor there. If you do as I tell you, you will succeed.'

'And how is it to be accomplished?'

Ragnu said, 'I will tell you this before you leave. You are sure Ru has agreed to take you with him? What is your function on board his pahi?'

'I am to be the island's first resident priest, when he finds a new home for his family.'

'Good. Good.'

The young man was quiet for a while. He was considering the moral issue of what he was being asked to do. To destroy a group of Rarotongans was not of great serious concern to Titopika, but to sabotage the voyage of a prince blessed by the Great Sea-God Tangaroa was another thing altogether.

However, Titopika bore no love for Ru's family. They had refused to allow Ru's daughter, a puhi of great beauty, to marry Titopika's older brother. Titopika's family were almost commoners and that made the match unlikely, but the love was genuine and the result had been that Titopika's brother killed himself at the leaping place of souls.

So, Titopika had no qualms about destroying the Rarotongans and he bore a grudge against Ru's family which might one day have to be settled.

He was however afraid for himself for a number of reasons.

He was quite rightly and properly frightened of Tangaroa's wrath. And if he ruined the expedition completely he destroyed his own chances of becoming a high priest on a new Faraway Heaven. Finally, if he was on board the same craft he was being asked to wreck, why then it followed he was going down with it.

'What about me?' asked Titopika. 'How will I survive?'

'By special dispensation of our ancestors,' smiled Ragnu. 'The spirits of the dead will return you safely to this isle. I happen to know that Ru's expedition is not finding favour with certain gods and they wish him eliminated. Kieto is also under suspicion. Naturally as the agent of my scheme to destroy these two, you will be blessed by the gods and transported back to us here on Raiatea by the ghosts of our forefathers.'

'Are you certain of this?' whispered an elated Titopika. 'I will be kept from harm?'

Ragnu's eyes half closed as he smiled into the face of his spy and saboteur.

'You have my promise.'

PART TWO

'The valleys are thick with people'

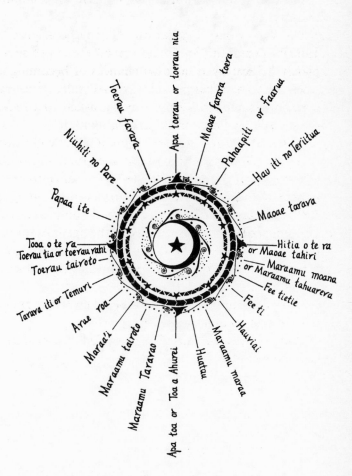

1

The arrival of Kieto's pahi at Raiatea coincided with the death of King Haari.

A messenger called 'the bird' was sent running around the island to proclaim 'King Haari is dead!' from every hill and every valley. Near relatives had immediately visited the house of the deceased king with gifts of cloth. The young men of the island prepared for the event known as 'the slaying of the ghosts' where they fought a battle with malignant spirits who would do harm to the king's soul on its way to heaven. The ghost-fighting was a serious dance in which young warriors struggled with unseen forces and were hopefully victorious, defeating the bad spirits before the king was wafted through the gateway into the place where his ancestors dwelt.

Even as the Rarotongan canoe entered the lagoon through a gap in the reef, there were people on the beach wailing and tearing their hair, and lacerating themselves with shark's teeth. The mourners, commoners and nobles alike, had dressed themselves in filthy floor mats and had daubed their skins with the ash from their fires to humiliate themselves. The sincerity of their grief was unquestionable.

One man had oiled his hair and as the Rarotongan pahi glided over the still surface of the lagoon, disturbing the fishes in the lime-green shallows, he set fire to his head to demonstrate the honesty of his penitence. Friends quickly doused the flames with sea water, but not before the poor fellow had suffered terrible burns to his scalp, face and neck.

Others were having fits, thrashing in the sand, throwing themselves bodily at tree trunks and rocks, to knock themselves unconscious. Yet others beat themselves with clubs, branches and sennit cord whips. It was a terrible if impressive sight and one which both Dorcha and Seumas found disturbing.

'Why do they do that?' asked Seumas of Kieto, appalled at the injuries the people were inflicting on their own bodies. 'Surely they can show others that their grief is genuine without such mutilation?'

'They do it to stop even more terrible things happening to them and their families.'

'Explain.'

'Well, as you know, a king or chief is close to the gods – when a king dies the gods are very upset. The great ones and the king's powerful ancestor spirits start to ask questions like, "Is anyone responsible for this death? Is it a necessary death?" Thus the people are afraid they are going to be held responsible. Were they neglectful of their duties to deities? Was there something they could have done to keep their king alive? Did they pray enough, offer large enough sacrifices while he was ill, do enough to drive out the demons which eventually took his life? All these questions worry the people, so they try to prove to the priests and the gods that they are so distressed by the king's death that they could not possibly have been in any way to blame for it.'

Seumas shook his head slowly. 'And what if the gods do decide someone was responsible?'

'Some terrible catastrophe might occur – a volcano might erupt, a great wave come, or the earth might shake.'

Po'oi added. 'They are not *just* considering the gods, but also the king's spirit. It will be angry that the body has not been able to hold on to it. It's possible the king's sau will go insane and cause untold damage, if not placated in some way, if not calmed and pacified by the solemnity of mourning.'

Once again, Seumas felt like an outsider in this world which had adopted them. There were times when Seumas considered himself an Oceanian through and through; times when he believed he had been on the islands for so long that he had become part of them; times when he saw no difference between himself and someone like Kieto or Po'oi. This was not one of them. Now he felt like the alien he actually was, witnessing strange and unfathomable rites, as different from the people around him as a fish was from a dog.

'I think I understand,' he said to Po'oi and Kieto, so as not to hurt their feelings.

'Understand?' grumbled the smelly Polahiki, coming up alongside Seumas and leaning on his shoulder. 'You understand *nothing*. Even I do not understand. Look at those stupid fools, hurting themselves.' Polahiki picked his nose as he spoke and wiped the mucus from his finger on his soiled loin cloth. 'Do they think a god is going to send a bolt of lightning because one old fool's heart stops beating?'

Seumas winced and pushed Polahiki away from him.

'Why are you so different to them?' he asked the dirty fisherman. 'You think your fleas will protect you?'

Polahiki grinned, revealing a mouthful of black teeth.

'I don't believe in these things as deeply as do most people. There may be gods, or there may not be – who cares? They've never shown themselves to me. I've never visited them. We get on famously by ignoring each other. The gods don't bother Polahiki and Polahiki doesn't give an owl's hoot for the gods. That's the way it should be.'

'Perhaps you're not worth it?'

The fisherman spat on the deck and grinned again.

'Perhaps, but I think the secret is – I don't believe in them, so they don't exist for me. I'm safe from beings who don't exist. I live in a bubble of unbelief. A *dirty* bubble, but who cares, it's my private bubble.' He laughed again.

Despite his loathing of the man Seumas felt there was something profound in what the fisherman was saying. He couldn't altogether dispute it. What if it were true?

'It sounds too easy,' he said. 'Too easy a trick.'

Polahiki grimaced now and his expression went deadly serious. 'You think so? Try it.'

And Seumas knew the man was right. It was not easy to stop believing. You could tell yourself something wasn't true, didn't exist, but deep down you felt afraid that you were wrong, that there was a supernatural force, omniscient and omnipotent, ready to crush you like a ripe breadfruit. His doubt must have showed on his face, because Polahiki nodded.

'See?' said the fisherman. 'Not easy at all.'

Seumas turned his attention to the island itself now, as they cruised into the shallows. He took hold of Dorcha's hand, called to Dirk, and the three of them jumped from the deck of the canoe and waded ashore together. Once on the beach, they stood and stared at the scene around them. Raiatea had been their home for seven years after they had been abducted by Kupe and his crew, taken from the shores of Albainn and carried away against their will. It had been the making of them, as individuals.

The sand on the beach was warm beneath their bare feet. A soft breeze gently stroked their shoulders. It felt good. Coconut palms curved over them, laden with nuts in various stages of ripeness. There were the scents of bananas and ti-lilies in the air, and the rustling sound of fields of sugar cane leaves fell like waves upon their ears.

Orange drala blooms, their shape and colour attempting to fool hungry parrots into believing they were also birds of spectacular hue, and not flowers at all, hung with many beaks from dangling stems.

Overhead the birds, sooty rails, wheeled and cruised on the thermals. Small fish like silver darts sprayed into the air from the shallow water near them, raining back into the lagoon again, as they were chased by some large predator hidden beneath. The green-ridged mountain before them was wearing an hibiscus shrub behind its unmarried ear.

Seumas put his arm around Dorcha. He inhaled the perfume of wild ginger sap which she wore on her skin and deep in her dark hair. He felt her hug him close and she kissed his cheek. It was as if they had come home.

Suddenly the foliage parted and two men stood before the couple. There was a look of indignation on the features of the intruders. Dorcha recognised them before Seumas did.

'Rian? Ti-ti?' she said, guardedly. 'How are you both?'

It was Rian who spoke. He had always been the belligerent twin brother. He was the one with the temper.

'What is our wife doing with her arm around another man?' cried Rian. 'You adulterous woman!'

Dorcha gasped. She had been away from the island for two decades and had almost forgotten that she was actually still married to these twin brothers who were as one in the eyes of the commoner's law. Now she had been to bed with another man. It suddenly struck her that this was a serious matter. Adultery was punishable by death, if the injured party requested such a sentence.

'Rian,' she said, 'I can't believe you're still interested in me. Surely you and Ti-ti have taken another wife? It's been almost twenty years.'

'We have taken no new bride,' Ti-ti interrupted. 'We have been waiting for our lawful wife to return.'

There was a hollow laugh from the Pict, who had thus far kept his peace, but now felt the situation was becoming ludicrous.

'Oh sure,' cried Seumas, 'you've had the dinner on the table for twenty years, waiting for her to walk through the door.'

Rian stepped forward, anger in his eyes. 'You mock us? You are an adulterer too! I shall see to it the judge chooses a very painful death for you, goblin!'

The tone in his voice made Dirk snarl. The dog took a couple of paces forward. Rian went pale and Ti-ti actually turned and ran back into the rainforest, to hide.

'You keep that hound away from me,' whispered Rian, pulling a shark-toothed club from his waistband. 'I'll kill it.'

'Not if he kills you first,' snapped Seumas. 'And as for this other thing, this judgement, I know the law as well as you, Rian. You can bring us in front of a judge, but listen to this – I'll opt for a trial by single combat. I'll take it out of the hands of men and put it in the hands of the gods. Remember what happened the last time we fought? This time I'll split your skull open. I'll leave your brains on the coral dust. I'll cut out your liver and throw it to the dog here, so help me. Then I'll do the same to your brother. Bear that in mind before you run whining to the priests.'

Ti-ti, hidden somewhere in the forest, gave out a cry of fear as he heard these words.

'Rian,' he called. 'Leave him alone.'

Rian ignored Ti-ti, saying to Seumas instead, 'My brother is a coward – I'm not afraid of you, goblin.'

Dorcha intervened here. 'Rian,' she said, 'why do you want to hurt me?'

'Because you went to the man we all hated!'

'But if you have him executed, then I shall be executed too. We are adulterers together, he and I. Do you want me to die in the hands of the priests?'

'If it has to be . . .'

'No,' screamed Ti-ti, from the bushes. 'Not her. You promised not her.'

Dorcha whispered to Seumas, 'The little one always loved me much more than the big one.'

Then to Rian, she said, 'You know if you have me killed, then your brother will never forgive you.'

Rian faltered now, glancing back into the forest.

'He will – in time he will.'

'I *won't*,' shrieked Ti-ti. 'I'll kill you myself if you hurt her. You promised it would only be *him*. I'll cut your throat while you sleep, brother. I'll poison your drinks. I'll rub deadly fungus into your meat.'

Boy-girl had now come up the beach, where the group was standing amongst the debris of the high-tide mark, where copra, dead leaves and driftwood formed a ragged line.

'What's going on?' she said. 'Seumas? Dorcha? What is this silly man brandishing a club for?'

Seumas said, 'He wants to kill two adulterers.'

Boy-girl raised one eyebrow. 'You two?' she said.

'Yes,' snarled Rian. 'And I won't brook interference from you, Boy-girl.'

The tall, elegant Boy-girl brushed away some locks of hair from her forehead, making her shell-decorations jingle. She stared down imperiously at Rian. Then she wet a finger and wiped it slowly down the flinching Rian's cheek, while he stood mesmerised by those dark eyes of hers.

Boy-girl said softly, 'My, my, Rian. Here you are, willing to call people adulterers, when you and I . . . but that was so long ago, wasn't it? Still, you *were* married to Dorcha at that time. You know, that sounds awfully silly, accusing someone of doing something you've done yourself, doesn't it? We could *all* be in serious trouble, couldn't we?'

Dorcha looked sharply at Rian, then at Boy-girl, while a groan came from Ti-ti, still hidden in the forest.

'I – I . . .' began Rian, looking confused.

'Yes, *you*, you naughty man. You and I, that is – remember – behind the breadfruit pits? And what about that virgin youth you used to desire, the sweet boy who used to tread the breadfruit? – yes you did – you told me so – did you ever manage to steal his chastity?'

'I – never . . .'

'Oh, I'm sure you did, you big liar you.'

Rian looked broken. He dropped the club and turned dazedly to stumble away, into the rainforest. He was shaking his head as he left to join his brother, but his eyes showed how unsure he was of himself. It was almost as if an argument were raging inside his skull.

Seumas heaved a sigh of relief. Dirk began to relax. Dorcha was still staring fixedly at Boy-girl, her head on one side. Finally she spoke to Boy-girl.

'Did he really – you and Rian, I mean?'

'What *do* you mean?' smiled Boy-girl, her cockerel brushing against her ankles and darting its head at Dirk.

'Well,' said Dorcha, 'you could be hypnotising him – I know that trick of yours.'

Boy-girl let out a tinkling laugh, before walking away, saying over her shoulder, 'You'll never know, will you? Even if I tell you one thing, you'll still wonder whether it was the other. Don't lose sleep over it, Dorcha. Rian isn't worth it. You have your chosen man, now. Worry about *him*. I've still got plenty of time to get my sticky fingers on his sweetmeats too – and I will, if you're not careful.'

'Never,' snarled Seumas, giving a little shudder. 'Not me, Boy-girl. And take this damn chicken with you. It keeps bothering my hound.'

'You leave my cock out of this,' called Boy-girl in that infuriating way she had which made Seumas so uncomfortable. 'You're always trying to get your hands on it.'

'Why do you always do that?' shouted the exasperated Pict. 'I wish you wouldn't use that kind of double-talk. Listen, I don't like you that way. I've told you a million times.'

'Oh *you*,' laughed Boy-girl, from halfway down the

beach. 'You don't think *you* would have any say in the matter, do you? You're just a shell to be played with, a flower to be plucked. No one takes *your* opinion seriously. When I want you, I'll just take you, Seumas.'

Seumas snarled again. 'She's been saying that ever since she met me, damn it,' he growled. 'I won't have it. Of course I've got something to say in the matter.'

Dorcha laughed and took his arm again. 'You really think so? You're still hard and strong, Seumas – a warrior through and through – but you're no match for Boy-girl. She could eat you alive. Don't even imagine you could do anything to prevent it. She has thousands of years of experience, in comparison to yours, when it comes to sexual matters.'

'Has she, by the gods!' muttered the ruffled Seumas, peeved by the fact that he was being laughed at. 'Has she?'

'Thousands of years. And what she can't get by any other means, she can certainly get by hypnotism and magic. You'd be like a little fluffy chicken in her hands. You'd be helpless. It's a good thing I'm here to protect you from that jaded libertine, isn't it? Or you'd end up being her slave.'

'Damned rubbish,' said the uncomfortable Seumas, walking off with Dirk at his heels. 'You talk so much non-sense, the pair of you. And I'll have that bloody rooster of hers in a stew one of these days – feed it to Dirk.'

'She's been promising to do the same to your dog,' said Dorcha, laughing. 'I'd watch out, the pair of you.'

The new king was crowned within the confines of Taputapu-atia, with the ancestor spirits looking on, and the gods smiling benevolently. The old heroes and demi-gods were also in attendance, standing in the shadows, to watch the donning of the red girdle. The sacred red girdle, maru-ura, a section added for each king, told the story of Haari's reign and many others before him. The scarlet feathers were woven into cloth and formed a genealogy and history of the kings: their work, their accomplishments in war, their enemies and friends, their wives, their sons and daughters, their achievements in peace time.

Early that morning the people had come from their houses and lined the route to Tapu-tapu-atia, while great canoes from other islands entered through the holy channel, the first one bearing the God Oro, the commander of the spirit world warriors. Like the other ocean-going craft, this one carried gifts for the new king, of fruits, and livestock, honey and fish.

There were sacrifices too.

Towards the end of the colourful ceremony the new king walked into the lagoon, and two grey shapes came from outside the reef, to rub against him, one side, and the other. Even the sharks of the ocean were loyal to the successor of Haari, as they had been to the old king. People saw this happen, or believed they did, which Polahiki would say was the same thing.

Then the king dressed again with great solemnity, and was presented with his fan of frigate bird feathers, his royal spear, and his mace of office, a wondrously carved stick.

Later, the feasting began, and it was here that Seumas and Kieto managed to talk to Prince Ru. Ru was not one of the new king's basket-sharers, so they found him sitting at one of the smaller fires away from the rest of the nobles. The prince, in his thirty-fifth year, listened to what Kieto had to say. He explained why he was leaving Raiatea.

'The valleys are thick with people,' he said, 'and I have been shown a star by the gods. Under that star lies the island that will provide us with a new home.'

'Will you take us with you?' asked Kieto.

Ru seemed puzzled. 'But the star I seek, the island home, hangs over the seas around Rarotonga. My new island is somewhere near your own island. Why do you come all this way back to Raiatea, just to make the return journey to Rarotonga?'

Kieto glanced at Seumas, before replying. 'Our priests have looked at your voyage through the mists of time. They have seen, vaguely, how you are swept off course by events you will be unable to control. During your wanderings, similar to those experienced by our people under Prince Tangiia when we were seeking a new Faraway Heaven, you will touch an island called Rapanui. The island of the giants.'

They saw Ru's eyes narrow in the firelight.

'I have heard of this place, from fishermen and adventurers who were blown off course. No one has ever disembarked on that island and lived to tell of it. It is far away, thousands of miles from my destination.'

'Will you take us? What have you got to lose if you *don't* sail to Rapanui, but go directly to the island under your star? The problem will be ours, not yours. We could assist your crew with their work.'

Ru shook his head determinedly. 'My crew, as you must have heard, consists of twenty royal virgins – puhi chosen for their virtue, strength and beauty. This was a command from the gods, from Tangaroa himself, if I am to succeed in my mission. The maidens will be my mariners. Already my brothers and their wives are afraid of the long sea voyage. I have promised them that the Great Sea-God himself has given his word that we will reach our destination, provided we follow his instructions.'

'We can cook, can't we?' said Kieto. 'We can sew. We can make fires, twist fibres into sennit, make mats. There are a multitude of tasks to be carried out on board, which don't involve handling the great canoe.'

'If your party comes with me, it will be as passengers, but I am of the mind that if I don't take you on board perhaps we will not be diverted to this island called Rapanui?'

'I think you know that what has been seen by the kahuna will come to pass, whoever is on board your pahi.'

Ru nodded thoughtfully, before saying by way of dismissal, 'I shall give you my answer in the morning. The name of my canoe is Te Pau-ariki . . .'

'The Princely Flower,' murmured Seumas, as the pair walked away from the fire. 'A very pretty name for a craft which has such a gruelling, difficult task ahead of it.'

'No doubt this too came as instruction from the gods,' replied Kieto. 'They are quite particular when they inform their adventurers of the details.'

'Do I detect a note of sarcasm?'

'I do not,' said Kieto, 'see why Ru should consider himself chosen of the gods, that's all.'

Seumas laughed. 'By damn – you're jealous!'

Kieto looked uncomfortable. 'I'm not, but I think our mission has far more importance. Why wasn't I given instructions from the gods! Why did I have to use priests to find out where I was going?'

'You forget – you *were* chosen – to conquer the land of my birth. If you have a few difficulties in doing that, I'm not going to call the gods unreasonable.'

Kieto grunted a little petulantly at this remark.

At that moment someone came along the edge-of-the-forest path, walking towards the great fire in the darkness.

'Out of the way,' snarled the man, 'I am a tapu.'

The figure was dressed splendidly in a cloak of feathers, a beautiful helmet, and carried a staff which proclaimed him to be a high priest. As a high priest he was indeed taboo to the touch, if not to the sight. Seumas stared at the features of the priest in the flickering light of the many fires, and recognition filtered through to his memory.

'Why,' he said, 'if it isn't Ragnu, the man we whipped like a dog some twenty years ago!'

Ragnu stared into the face of Seumas, clearly not recognising him for a while. Then the old priest nodded and smiled grimly. 'The goblin! Well, well. I would have taken you for an Oceanian, if it hadn't been for one or two tattoos on your body. And this I suppose is Kieto, full grown and looking only a little less like the runt in a litter of rats?'

'Still insulting people, Ragnu?' remarked Kieto, unimpressed. 'Have you nothing better to do?'

'Yes, I have a king to attend, if you would now step aside. I would hate my mana to be the cause of some illness, or even death.'

'Well, isn't that the truth?' murmured Seumas, in a deeply sarcastic tone.

The two men did as they were asked however and watched the kahuna stalk off, into the night, between the many fires. Seumas noticed that as he passed each fire the people sitting around it fell silent for a few moments, until he had gone. It seemed he was still feared, probably still hated, yet he held the highest priesthood in the land.

'I've often wondered,' said Seumas, to Dorcha later, 'what that man wants out of life. He's next to the king, despite being defeated alongside Tutapu at the battle at Rarotonga, yet he still seems to crave something. He knows he can't be king himself, he hasn't the blood line, so what else is he after?'

'Eternal life,' replied Dorcha, instantly. 'It's what every man wants, once he has all the earthly power he can get. Ragnu is probably directing all his energies, all his magic, towards making himself immortal.'

Boy-girl, sitting on the far side of the fire, said, 'To do that he has to eliminate all his enemies – take vengeance on those whom he has sworn to destroy. That's a long, arduous task, and one fraught with dangers and difficulties. I might wish him all good luck in his enterprise – if we weren't among the number he has to punish before achieving such an end.'

Kieto said, 'We have to mind our backs while we're here – I suggest we sleep on the pahi and set a watch.'

'You're afraid of that old man?' sniffed Seumas.

'I'm afraid of the power he wields,' Kieto said. 'And you would be too, Seumas, if you were sensible.'

'I've never been sensible,' Seumas said. 'It's saved my life on many occasions.'

'I doubt it,' Polahiki growled. 'Anyway, I'm in no danger – I was on Ragnu's side in that battle. I only swapped sides when Tutapu started losing.'

Dorcha grinned and said, 'And me.'

'In that case,' Kieto said, 'you two can take the first watch, because you have nothing to fear.'

Polahiki's face fell and Dorcha laughed, saying to him, 'Don't worry, fisherman, I'll do it alone. I don't want to spend the early hours picking nits from my hair after sitting next to you. You can sleep on the shore.'

Polahiki stared at the main fire, where Ragnu sat next to the new king.

'No,' replied Polahiki, after a moment's hesitation, 'I think I'll sleep on the ship. Maybe Ragnu didn't like the idea of me changing sides in the middle of the battle. I'll stay among friends, I think.'

Seumas growled, 'Friends? You've got to be mocking us, fisherman. No one here likes you.'

Having seen his enemies again, Ragnu was full of anger. He still intended carrying out his main plan, of sabotaging the voyage of *The Princely Flower*, but there was a longing in him for the quick death of the goblin, Seumas. Now that they had come face to face again, Ragnu was filled with repugnance, that this creature from beyond Oceania, should be living amongst them as if he too were a proper man like any other on the islands.

'His very presence on the soil of Faraway Heaven is an affront to the gods,' whispered Ragnu to himself. 'I must remove this vile creature from our society. I would be thanked by kings and commoners alike. He lives on us like a leech, flouts our conventions, and has his own strange code of honour. I will do it tonight, while he is within my reach.'

When the ceremony for the new king was over, Ragnu did not return to the marae at Most Sacred, Most Feared. Instead, while the nobles were getting drunk on kava he stole a pig from a pen outside one of their houses. He stifled its squeals, holding it tightly under his arm. He entered the hinterland jungle. In the darkness, with only the starlight to show him the way, Ragnu found a narrow winding path up through the green gorges, to a cave on the steep hillside.

A tapu had been placed on the cave many years ago, by Ragnu himself, who had hung wicker sharks over the entrance, warning any casual passerby, hunter or gatherer, that it was forbidden to enter this place on pain of a horrible death.

Once inside the cave, Ragnu lit a torch with a set of flints, then prepared his magic herbs and potions. First he drank several of the potions, to protect himself from the spirit world, taking care also to mark his own skin with certain symbols of which only priests of high rank had knowledge.

The walls of the cave were already hung with various objects – heads and hair of men and animals, strange idols made of clay and feathers, sharks' teeth, whalebones, dried skins of barracuda – which served to keep any visiting spirits from going berserk. Ghosts were highly strung beings, whose sanity was close to the edge, and in calling them one risked mindless destruction.

Down below, in the villages, the sacred drums were still beating, even though the new king had retired. The adulation of the people was not suppressed by lack of sleep. They would be sounding their praises, with shell trumpets, wooden flutes, and other instruments, throughout the next few days. Ragnu used the rhythm of the drums to chant a fangu, summoning ghosts from the well of darkness, calling on them to assist him.

First, he took some nail parings, dried skin and hair from a bamboo tube, where they had been for many years.

They had once belonged to Seumas, stolen from the floor of his hut when he was not at home. Ragnu had many such grisly collections, gathered in secret, once belonging to every important person on Raiatea and Borabora. These scrapings assisted him in his gruesome tasks of murder and spell-making. When you had some part of your enemy's body, you had your enemy's likes and dislikes, strengths and weaknesses, imprinted on his bodily parts, waiting to be revealed.

'Now we shall find out what will draw the Pict from the safety of his pahi,' murmured Ragnu.

He placed the body parts in a clay pan and heated them over a fire, weaving a spell at the same time. Taking a live owl from a cage he cut its throat and allowed its blood to squirt on to the parings. Next, he tossed various magic powders into the pan, and into the fire, releasing and searching through odours that had been imbedded in the hair and nails from long ago. The smells came one after the other, as Ragnu unlocked the secrets of Seumas's impregnated tissues. Finally, he found an aroma he believed would be irresistible to the Pict and captured the gas in several foot-long bamboo tubes.

He then took the pig and ritually slaughtered the animal, frying its heart in a bowl, offering the sacrifice to his own atua, asking his ancestor spirits to help him fashion a puata. Eventually, the smell of the blood and the fragrance of the herbs brought a powerful ghost into Ragnu's presence and this being promised him a puata. The ghost smelled foul – of rotting tissue and polluted earth – and once the promise had been extracted the priest wanted rid of the creature.

Ragnu thanked the spirit, profusely, sparing no compliments for dead souls are not immune to flattery and eat it like breadfruit. It took some time to persuade the atua to leave, for having confronted a mortal, it wanted to stay and talk. Eventually, however, the ghost went through the eye-socket of a human skull, hanging on the cave wall, and took its stench with it, back to its own personal hell.

'Now we have the power, we make the *thing*,' murmured Ragnu.

He was, by this time, shaking with exhaustion and fear. Oh yes, he told himself, he was frightened. He was afraid, but he was also very excited. What he was about to do was fashion a living monster out of clay and twigs, out of leaves and wicker: a dangerous creature, very strong, very big, but very stupid.

It would be able to talk, and though a beast walk on its hind legs, but it would need special guidance to its target, or it might rush off into the forest and prey on Raiateans for centuries to come.

Thus, Ragnu was agitated by what he was about to do: by the idea and the act of fashioning a supernatural creature.

Out in the forest Ragnu surrounded himself with ti'i. These wooden idols had a two-fold purpose: to protect the magician and to assist him with his magic.

A karakia was chanted into the blackness of the trees.

A whirlwind came, hurtling out of the darkness, carrying with it masses of twigs and leaves. It wrenched turf from the ground, moss and bark from logs, reedy stems and willowy saplings. First a cage of wicker was formed into a shape not unlike a boar standing on its hind legs, but much bigger than that beast – a *giant* boar. Onto the wickerwork was daubed a mixture of clay, twigs and leaves, until the towering shape was solid. Two curved branches stripped of their bark, white and smooth, formed the boar-man's tusks. A monstrous head with great ears and small eyes was seated on the torso. Rocks formed the boar's feet and dried grasses its shaggy hair. It was a boar, but a *mockery* of the real thing, a parody standing on two legs, over a head taller than the priest.

Yet it was a terrifying mud-wood statue: it drove fear into the priest's heart like a stake.

The final fangu came out as a hoarse whisper from the sorcerer's lips.

> 'O Rongo, *breathe life into this creation,*
> *Make it your own creature, a thing of the night,*
> *Out of the ancient memory of the forest itself,*
> *A thing conceived in a time before men,*
> *A monster of an older earth –*
> *O Rongo, breathe your breath into this clay.'*

And Rongo the Great Plant-God did as he was requested and made flesh of vegetable and put air into leafy lungs.

For a moment nothing occurred and Ragnu almost decided that his spells had not worked properly.

Then the incredible happened.

The tall, muscled monster boar moved some steps towards the priest on its hind legs, a little ungainly at first, but becoming surefooted with each pace. Legs covered in coarse hair grew stronger and less clumsy with every second. A great belly, overhanging a tiny set of genitals, swayed with the motion. Only around the navel and nipples were there no bristles: the rest was dark bushy whiskers. The boar's cheeks hung in flaccid folds of loose flesh.

The priest saw its tiny eyes flicker. A large flattened snout dribbled mucus onto the mossy floor. The creature's slitted mouth opened. Rows of strong-looking teeth were revealed between the bases of the sweeping tusks.

Stinking hot breath struck Ragnu on the cheek.

'Yes,' muttered Ragnu, his heart racing beneath his ribcage. 'It is *alive.*'

'I-am-alive,' said a dull, torpid voice.

The puata seemed too sluggish of mind to attempt an attack on the priest, but Ragnu was taking no risks and remained well within the circle of ti'i.

Ragnu issued his instructions to the creature, which swayed under the starlight, occasionally blinking.

'Have you got that?' asked Ragnu, hopefully.

'What?' growled the boar in a listless tone. 'Got what?'

'You stupid oaf,' muttered the impatient Ragnu, who once again explained his plan, slowly and carefully, hoping that at least a little would be absorbed by the immensely obtuse creature with whom he was placing this task.

Finally, all was ready: monster and man took the path to the beach.

On board the hired pahi the Rarotongans slept, while the waves curled along the outer reef, falling with a rhythmic booming sound upon the drum of coral. The moonlight glittered on the rearing waters as they reached upwards, then fell crashing on their faces: gleamed on the milky foam that washed back over the channelled lips of the reef, back into the broad ocean.

Beyond the sleepy island, the heart of which still throbbed with its own sacred sounds, the wide waters of Oceania would have been quite still if it were not for the footsteps of invisible fairies running over its surface: a million of them, playing their fairy games around the early-houred watch. The dancing wavelets and small lights had beguiled the dozy Polahiki, who was now draped over the steering oar, as fast asleep as those whom he was supposed to guard.

Far in the distance, where the dark sea met the dark sky, little gods laughed at the schemes of devious men.

Seumas woke with a start and sniffed the air.

'Is it?' he muttered, sitting up and sniffing again. 'By the gods, I think it is!'

He stirred himself. Dorcha had kept the first watch and had handed over to the lousy Polahiki. She had then crept under the blanket with her husband. Seumas now shook her and she tried to open her eyes without success.

'What is it?' she murmured.

'Haggis!' said Seumas, excitedly. 'I can smell haggis cooking – really. Take a whiff.'

'Don't be foolish,' grumbled Dorcha in a sleepy voice. 'Leave me alone.'

Seumas saw that he wasn't going to get her to stir.

'Suit yourself,' he said. 'I'm going to get me some haggis – someone knows how to cook on this island.'

So saying he walked to the side and slipped into the warm waters of the lagoon. They were like a tepid bath, soothing away his tiredness. He swam slowly towards the beach, trying to ascertain which direction held the source of that wonderful aroma. When he reached the shallows, he stood and let the water drain from his body, before wading to the beach.

'Where is it coming from?' he muttered to himself. 'Hell, my stomach is ready for some of that.'

The aroma seemed to be issuing from the direction of the forest, so he followed a path in the starlight. At one point, he stopped and stared behind him, thinking he was being followed. When no one was forthcoming, he continued his search for the fire on which the haggis was being boiled.

The trees closed in around him, causing the path to dis-appear beneath his feet, but Seumas had been on this island for seven years, he knew the ways like he knew himself. There were no dangerous creatures – no snakes or savage beasts in the forest – so there was nothing for him to fear. Only the birds were disturbed by his thrashing along the path and they simply moved on their roosts to a shadier part of the tree.

'Where are you, where are you?' muttered Seumas.

Once more he heard the crack of a twig behind him, turned and stared, but again no persons revealed them-selves. In his belt Seumas had his lei-o-mano and he felt he could handle any attempt at an attack, should it come.

He walked on.

Finally, he came to a clearing within which was an old disused hut, its palm-leaf roof collapsed at one corner, its walls running with roaches. A dark doorway beckoned as the smell seemed to be coming from within the hut.

'A secret cook,' murmured the Pict, for the first time thinking rationally and suspecting something was wrong. 'Why would someone come right out here to boil a haggis? Where would they get a haggis in the first place? I must be going mad.'

He drew his lei-o-mano, wishing he had thought to carry a patu club, and went through the doorway.

Inside the hut, on the floor illuminated by starlight coming through the broken roof, were several tubes of bamboo.

'What the hell . . .?' he began.

Just at that moment a tall huge beast came charging out of the dark corner of the hut, struck him and bowled him off his feet, sending him flying backwards through the doorway. His lei-o-mano went sailing from his hand to land somewhere in the bushes. The brute who had collided with him using its chest and shoulders now stood snorting and bellowing above his supine form, glaring down at him with wet-pebble eyes.

'Shit!' muttered Seumas, staring up at the monster.

The tusks of the beast gleamed in the starlight as the creature dribbled down their curves. Seumas saw the mouth open slightly and knew a blow was coming. He rolled aside just as a hoof smashed into the spot where his head had been.

Seumas was chilled by the strength of the stamp, which raised a great divot and penetrated the earth. This was no ordinary creature, no boar taught to walk on its hind legs. This was a product of the occult, a supernatural being dragged out of some hellish place not fit for the eyes of mortals, and thrust into the real world. The fear coursed through Seumas, who in his fright reverted to Gaelic.

'*Tha e cho laidir agus a bhitheas e!*' he cried, exclaiming at the beast's brawn.

The boar took a step back at these words, as if they had startled it.

'What-say-you-human?' it boomed, dully. 'What-words-make-you?'

'Arrrgghhh!' screamed Seumas, on hearing the brute talk, more terrified by this aspect of the situation than any other, 'You speak, you fiend!'

'I-kill-you,' intoned the boar. 'Now.'

'*Ann an comhairle nan aingidh,*' shouted Seumas, trying to push himself backwards into the forest with his feet. 'Go talk to some other poor man.'

The puata put his hooves over his ears on hearing the strange language again, as if the words hurt his head.

'Say-not,' he boomed. 'Speak-no-ugly-speakings.'

Seumas tried to get to his feet, desperately thinking of something else to say in Gaelic, since doing so clearly confused the creature. As he got to his feet however, the monster charged at him, its head lowered, its great tusks pointed at the Pict's chest. Seumas tried to scramble out of the way and was caught on the right shoulder, pierced by a tusk, then flung against a tree by the momentum of the brute's charge.

'I-kill-you,' boomed the puata.

'You've already said that,' gasped Seumas. 'Now do it, you thing of the mist. *De'n cheo.* I'm caught between tree and rock. *Tha bi eader a' chlach agus a' chraobb.*'

'Arrrrghhhh!' cried the beast, much as Seumas had done on hearing it speak. 'Say-not, say-not.'

It charged again, and would have trampled over the body of Seumas, had not a black shape come out of the darkness like a winged demon and buried its teeth into the throat of the puata, hanging there, snarling, rending the flesh.

Seumas recognised the demon instantly. It was Dirk III,

sired by Dirk I, out of Dirk II. His hound had followed him into the lagoon, up from the beach, but had not approached before because it knew it had not been given permission for this walk in the night forest. Now though, the master was in danger, and it had come running to the attack.

'GAAAA!' cried the boar, its throat tearing open, spilling out twigs and dirt from within.

It tried to shake the dog loose, and pounded it with its forelegs, but once Dirk had his teeth into something they met and locked and there was no way the beast was going to get rid of its attacker by simply shaking and striking it. This the brute realised, even in its stupidity, and it ran at a tree intending to crush the dog against a hardwood trunk.

Seumas leapt to his feet now, grabbed a thick branch, and struck the puata across the back of its hind legs. It fell crashing to the forest floor with Dirk still gamely seeking a better hold on its throat. Seumas brought his club down hard on the creature's skull several times, smashing it open.

More dirt spilled out.

Seumas jumped on the puata's belly and, turning, struck it between the legs, splitting it to the navel.

Once the brute had started to crumble it was broken apart remarkably easily, as if one small crack in its façade had been enough to cause weaknesses to radiate throughout its whole frame. Dirk worried the top half of the beast, tearing and ripping chunks away with his teeth, while Seumas continued to smash the lower half apart with the branch. When Seumas paused to begin pounding the head, the beast's mouth opened for the last time and out of its torn throat came the feeble words, 'Hit-not.'

'Sorry, friend,' said Seumas, 'you've been used.'

He hammered with the branch-club and scattered the fragments of the head amongst the trees, and it was over. There was a wooden tusk here, a leafy ribcage there, something which might have been an eye lying in the dust.

Seumas kicked at the dead leaves and twigs, strewing them still further.

'Damn beastie,' he muttered. 'Where the hell did you come from?'

Since there was no answer from the creature, Seumas decided it was not in his interests to remain in the forest.

The Pict gave his dog a hug and stroked him, telling him what a hero he was.

'Boy-girl's blasted chicken couldn't do that, now could it?'

Dirk wagged his tail in appreciation of the praise. Seumas then staggered away, along the forest path. His wounded shoulder was hurting him badly. He made it back down to the beach safely, with his faithful Dirk trotting by his side.

When he entered the waters of the lagoon, the salt both stung and did his injuries good. He was not seriously hurt, but his wounds did not heal as well these days as they had done when he had been a young man. Dirk swam beside him, head high, nose well out of the ripples, eyes bright with the satisfaction of having saved his master from almost certain death.

Back on the ship, Kieto was awake and standing watch.

'Where have you been?' asked Kieto.

'Fighting boars made of rubbish,' muttered Seumas. 'I'll explain later.'

'You want a compress on that wound.'

'In the morning,' said Seumas.

He crawled under the blanket next to Dorcha, slipped an arm around her waist, and was almost asleep, when he heard her murmur sleepily, 'Where have you been, lover?'

'Chasing haggis,' he replied.

2

Kumiki sighted Rarotonga on the horizon and almost wept with relief. Since he had left the shores of Nuku Hiva, to search for his father the demon called Seumas, he had been through much. The loneliness of being at sea without company had almost turned him mad. He had not only been having terrible dreams at night, but during the day too, while he was awake. They were acted out in front of him, on the platform of his double-hulled canoe, and he was afraid they were terrible portents of things to come. Yesterday, Maui and Ro themselves had appeared before him and acted out the story of when they had changed heads:

Maui had been summoned by the gods to discuss with him some mischief for which he had been responsible. Perhaps they intended to punish him? No one knows that part of the story, for it took place in heaven. What mortals do know is that the person who brought him the message to accompany her to heaven was Ro, who had been Maui's wife until she became disenchanted with his tricks and had gone to live in the netherworld.

'I shall come with you,' said Maui, 'but I must avoid a certain village on the way, for there are people there who plan to attack and hurt me.'

Ro led the way, but ignored Maui's pleas not to pass through the area where there were men who wanted to harm him, for she knew he was capable of avoiding such an attack and wanted to see how he would do it.

When they were outside the village where these men lived, Maui turned to Ro and said, 'Give me your head.'

'No,' replied Ro, 'for how can I find the way to where the gods dwell without a head?'

'You shall have mine,' said Maui.

And so, after more arguments, Maui finally persuaded Ro to exchange heads with him and the pair of them walked through the village. Just as they were emerging from the other side, a gang of men pounced on Ro and dragged her off, while Maui made his escape into the rainforest. There he waited for Ro. Indeed she appeared some time later.

The pair exchanged heads again and Maui asked, 'What happened?'

'It was just as you said,' replied Ro. 'They tied me to a stake to burn me, pulled away my garments, and were amazed and frightened to find that I was female.

'They said, "Has Maui become a woman? What magic is this? We are men of a tribe which does not harm women!" And so they let me go.'

Maui laughed again. 'I knew this was so – they would not hurt a female – now they will forget the tricks I played on them and leave me alone.'

This scene had been played through on the deck of the canoe the previous morning and Kumiki's brain was still reeling with the images which had been dancing before his eyes. It was as if it had all been real – Maui, Ro, the village, the ambush, the rainforest – and these people, these things, had actually stood on the front of Kumiki's deck.

Yet he knew he was feverish from lack of good fresh water, and the solitude had plucked and tweaked at his mind.

The reason he had needed to mix seawater too heavily with his fresh water, thus not only making it unpalatable, but dangerous to his sanity, was because of the last island he had stopped at.

The island had looked innocent enough, but in fact it proved to be the home of some terrible spirits. While collecting drinking coconuts Kumiki was chased by a spirit known as the putuperereko, a monster with huge testicles who devoured people when he could catch them.

Kumiki was a fast runner however, and managed to outdistance the putuperereko, but dropped all his coconuts in the chase. When he went back for them later, feeling it was safe, he came across a beautiful creature who attempted to seduce him.

Remembering in time that this was a strange island he was on, home of peculiar spirits, he recalled that there was a spirit called a tarogolo who seduced people of the opposite sex and when it had them in their power, killed them by cutting up their genitals. When he refused to lie with the creature, it screamed at him with foul words, and its face became distorted.

With a half-coconut shell held between his legs, to protect his valuable private parts, Kumiki had run back to the shoreline and boarded his canoe. The island was clearly enchanted by horrible creatures. Despite the fact that he had only three drinking coconuts on board, Kumiki set sail and left the region as fast as the wind would carry him.

Thus he had to mix his fresh drink with largish quantities of seawater, which might have brought on the hallucinations. To cure himself of these daytime dreams, Kumiki had invoked the Healer-God, Ro'o, whose chants had been taught to men to help them drive out the bad spirits which cause illness and death. Ro'o had now helped him by bringing him to his destination, Rarotonga.

Before he entered the lagoon, Kumiki prepared himself for war. He put on his feathered helmet, took up his kotiate club in one hand, and a spear in the other. He had no cloak to put on, but he squared his muscled shoulders and wore a ferocious expression, his tongue lolling out, his eyes swivelling up occasionally to show only the whites. He knew the three solid bars tattooed across his face made him look fierce. He was also aware that his Hivan hairstyle, the two horns jutting from an otherwise bald pate, frightened his enemies. He had his terrible battle cry ready in his throat.

Since he knew Oro, the Great War-God, would not come to the aid of a youth about to go into single combat, for Oro commanded armies not individuals, Kumiki asked his ancestors to invoke the Goddess of Volcanoes, Pele, to assist him by permitting him to spit fire. Kumiki did not think this too much to ask.

He tried spitting flames once or twice, with no success, though thought that perhaps Pele might be waiting to give him fire to cough up in the heat of the battle.

When Kumiki's canoe drifted around a corner of the island he was amazed to see a whole fleet of ships anchored in the lagoon. A hundred at least: perhaps two? They jostled each other in the rippling waters, their sails folded away somewhere, leaving their masts to fence each other in the wind. Kumiki wondered if some king were visiting, from Samoa, or Tonga, or perhaps even Tahiti? He tried to not let it influence him in any way. He was here to kill a man. That must be paramount in his mind.

When he reached the beach, it was crowded with people. Some were singing, some were dancing, others were telling jokes, doing somersaults, acting the buffoon. Kumiki was a little daunted by this, but was determined to carry his plan through. He swelled his chest like a hero should and took up a fighting stance on the hot sands.

'Where is the demon they call Seumas?' he cried. 'I shall slay him in single combat.'

To his annoyance, hardly anyone took notice of his words, still carrying on with their leaping and prancing, their chattering and running through the musical scales. One or two gave him an uninterested sidelong glance. The nearest man to him said, 'Oh, very good – not bad at all – but you'll need to sharpen up those accents.'

'Bring out the Seumas creature,' screamed Kumiki at the top of his voice. 'Let me see the fiend I am to kill!'

'That's *much* better,' said the other man. 'I can hear the Hivan warrior in that one. Needs just a *little* more venom. Just a teeny bit more fire. Who are you anyway? Want to join the ghost dancers, do you?'

Frustrated, Kumiki stamped his foot. 'I am Kumiki, son of Seumas the goblin, whom I am about to kill – if someone will take the trouble to find him for me.'

The man stroked his chin. 'Seumas, Seumas – oh, yes, I know, I've heard of him – the Pict. Oh, he's not here at the moment. You'll have to work up another act if you want to join the Arioi. Seumas has gone on a long ocean voyage in search of an island.'

Kumiki almost wept. 'A voyage?'

'So I hear from the locals. He's joined with Ru, the Raiatean prince. They'll be gone – oh, ever so long. Chances are they'll never come back again. You know what these adventurers are like. They'll brave the world, but they're as vulnerable as the next man. I shouldn't be surprised if he drowns or gets eaten by sea monsters.'

Kumiki sat down on the beach and hung his head. His enemy was not on the island. All that time, all that courage, wasted. Kumiki had made the journey of a lifetime, alone across vast tracts of dangerous ocean, and all for nothing. The demon was not here. He was off somewhere on one of his jaunts, raping women no doubt, pillaging innocent islands, tearing down graven images and flouting the gods. Seumas was with Prince Ru on a voyage to nowhere, out of reach of Kumiki's club and spear.

'It's not fair,' sobbed the youth. 'I have come so far – so far – and all for nothing.'

'Where have you come from?' asked the man, who appeared to be some sort of dancer. 'Tell me, boy?'

'From Nuku Hiva,' sighed Kumiki.

'Wow, that's impressive,' replied the man, squatting down near him 'Look, my name's Ramoro.' He didn't ask Kumiki *his* name for that would have been extremely impolite. Kumiki might be someone famous and you were expected to know famous people by their aura. Instead he simply waited for Kumiki to tell him.

Kumiki stared at the man's face and saw by his tattoos and the way he arranged the flowers in his hair that he preferred men to women when it came to love-making.

'I'm Kumiki,' he said at last. 'I'm on a mission to kill my father, Seumas.'

'Wow!' said the other delightedly, 'that's impressive too. I've never heard of anything like that. But you'll be disappointed. As I said, Seumas the Pict is not here. He and his wife have gone with Kieto to join Ru's voyage.'

'And no one knows where Ru is bound?'

'That's it. What are you going to do now?'

'After I get a drink of water?' said Kumiki, realising that his mouth was lined with a white crust. 'I don't know. Wait here for Seumas? Go home? I don't know.'

'Come on, boy, let's get you something to drink,' said Ramoro, taking his hand. 'And you needn't worry about me trying to seduce you. I've already got a lover.'

'I wasn't worried,' lied the Hivan youth.

After he had drunk a refreshing coconut full of water, sipping it carefully to prevent stomach pains, Kumiki stared about him at the activities on the beach. It seemed a sort of controlled chaos, with people practising all sorts of skills. And very interesting skills they were too. Kumiki liked the noise and colour of the scene. It filled him with excitement. Who were these people? They clearly did not belong to Rarotonga, for Ramoro had called the islanders 'locals'. Then Kumiki remembered the word Ramoro had used.

'The Arioi?' he asked. 'Did you say the Arioi?'

'Yes,' laughed Ramoro. 'I'm one of the dancers. My best friend is a singer – he has a divine voice. He's as beautiful as Kopu, the Morning Star, and I love him very much. We joined the Arioi together, two years ago.'

'The *Arioi*,' breathed Kumiki. 'I've never seen it before. When I was a boy,' he gabbled, 'very young, I wanted to run away to join the Arioi. It was the dream of all my friends, to take to the seas with you people.'

Ramoro laughed again. 'It's the dream of every young man or woman – those with any imagination. And who can blame them? This is a wonderful life, travelling from island to island, being praised for our performances, enjoying the best of everything, having no other responsibilities except to the company. I adore it. I wouldn't change places with anyone in Oceania.'

'Nor would I, if I were a member of the Arioi. I would like to be a Painted Leg. That's what I would like to be.'

'Oh, *that's* all?' said Ramoro, amused by the boyish enthusiasm and reverence in Kumiki's tone. 'Just a Painted Leg.'

Kumiki nodded and looked serious. 'Well, I know that's very ambitious. I know a Painted Leg is, well, the *first* rank amongst you Arioi. But *someone's* got to be there, haven't they? And I think I've got a lot of talent. I'm sure I have.'

Over the next few days Ramoro explained to Kumiki what he would have to do if he were to join the Arioi.

'You need to have a talent, of course – what can you do? Sing? Dance?'

'No, not really.'

'What about clowning? We have one man who dresses up like a baby and rolls around the floor making baby noises. What about doing something like that?'

Kumiki screwed his face up in disgust. 'That sounds demeaning and humiliating.'

'All right, it's not amongst the more highly regarded of our performances, I admit – but how about spear fighting, or wrestling?'

Kumiki nodded enthusiastically. 'I'm quite good at wrestling. I'm very strong.'

'Good. We'll try to get you in as a wrestler. Now what you have to do sometime in the next few days is attract a lot of attention to yourself, to show you're not afraid of audiences. The normal way is to dress yourself in brilliant yellow and red leaves, paint yourself all over with dyes, stick leaves and mud to yourself, and act as if you're absolutely crazy. When people look at you, spring in front of them and behave as if you're deranged.'

'Do I have to?' asked the unhappy Kumiki. 'Couldn't I just go and say I wanted to join?'

'You'd be laughed and jeered all the way back to Nuku Hiva. You've got to prove to everyone that you don't care what people think of you. You've got to prove you'll do *anything*, go to any lengths, to become a member of the Arioi.'

Kumiki sighed. 'Well, if I *have* to.'

He did as Ramoro said, he painted himself to look like a madman and decorated himself with leaves and twigs. There were leaves sprouting from his nose and ears, stuck to his chest with mud, sticking out of his waistband. There were twigs entangled with his hair. There was a broken branch poking like an erect penis from his skirt. A bunch of feathers trailed from a cord around his waist. Grass was stuck to his underarms like hair.

He jumped out on people, leapt into rings of talking elders, made noises like a chicken being strangled, rolled his eyes, burbled his lips, snorted like a pig. He hooted and shrieked, he danced like a maniac, he fell down and gibbered. One night he leapt into a huge basin of warm soup and pretended to swim, splashing startled onlookers and causing havoc.

In short, he looked and acted crazy.

Within a week he was asked to join the Arioi as a wrestler. He sold his canoe, joined the performances, and by the time the troupe was ready to sail away from Rarotonga, Kumiki had small circles tattooed on his ankles, denoting he was an Ohemara and in the sixth class – one up from a flapper.

He was as proud as Io.

PART THREE

God of all the sharks

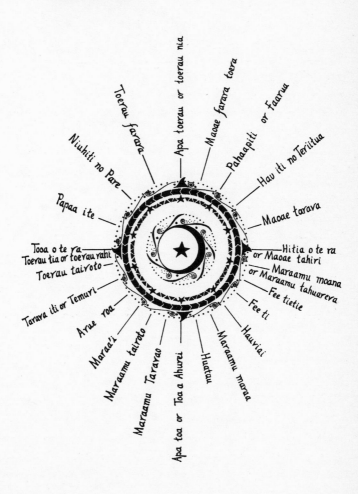

1

The Princely Flower set sail from Raiatea, bound for Maraamu tairoto on the windflower.

Seumas did not discover for sure exactly what or who was behind the attack by the puata. If he had not been woken in the middle of the night, but had smelled haggis during the more sane daylight hours, he would have been extremely suspicious. The night hours and a sleepy head however lulled one into accepting things at face value.

Seumas had many old enemies, as well as friends on the island, and it could have been any one of them. Rian and Ti-ti might have paid a priest. Or it could have been Ragnu. He was in no doubt that he had been lured away from their pahi, to face the puata, but he could prove nothing.

'Best let it lie,' said Dorcha. 'We're leaving this place in any case. It's not our island any more.'

She and Seumas had been bothered by the presence of Rian and Ti-ti and were glad to be out of their sight. The two brothers had not openly attacked them again, but had often stood with smouldering eyes some way off, watching Dorcha. Seumas had wanted to bash their heads together and probably would have done if not prevented by Dorcha.

The Scot was aware she and Seumas had technically broken the law and the brothers could have caused a lot of trouble for them had the pair not been divided in their opinion over the matter. Ti-ti was the gentler of the two and did not want Dorcha to come to any harm, though the same gentle soul would have been delighted had Seumas been skinned alive and hung up in the noonday sun for the ants to eat.

'I'm certain sure those two paid a priest to make that creature out of clay and twigs,' grumbled Seumas, 'then lured me away from the pahi with the smell of cooking haggis.'

He sighed as he recalled the aroma, thinking how good it would have been if the smell had led him to a pot over a fire, and a friendly Raiatean ready with a spoon.

Most of the rest of the party had gone abroad on the island, and on nearby Borabora, visiting relatives.

Polahiki was one exception, since his home was somewhere in the Hivan islands, but Kikamana had found her sister, and Boy-girl her parents. Po'oi had also visited his brothers and sisters, who were scattered over the island. Pungarehu had cousins who wished to make a fuss of him, people who lived in the hills: he managed to reach them, stay a short while, then had to make the long trek back to the coast.

Rinto, son of Manopa, had hardly stepped off the chartered pahi onto Raiatea. The place had been his father's home, not his, and this was his first time on the island. Unidentifiable cousins, aunts, and various other relatives, all of whom were unrecognisable to Rinto, kept coming up to him and telling him he looked just like his father. Strangers to him. They rubbed noses with him, hugged him, called him Manopa's boy, made him feel extremely uncomfortable. Rinto was glad they were on their way. He didn't like people he didn't even know touching his body, making him squirm with embarrassment inside.

Prince Ru was in sole charge of the craft, a single pahi with only his extended family and a few other passengers on board, besides the contingent from Rarotonga. Although technically Ru was entitled to call himself king, once he had set sail, he told his crew and passengers he would remain a prince until he found the island he was seeking.

'There would be problems with mana on board and I will not *feel* I am a king until I have an island under my feet.'

Ru was a navigator prince of great renown, known throughout the Tahitian Islands as one of the best pathfinders in Oceania. For this voyage to find his family a new home he had obeyed the gods and crewed his vessel with twenty virgins, who now worked the sails, rived the ropes and bailed the water from the twin hulls. They were magnificent women, strong yet lithe and comely. With frangipani and hibiscus blooms behind their ears, they sang at their work as they steered the ship towards an invisible point on the horizon, following the swell beneath the craft.

Seumas couldn't take his eyes off them at first.

'If you stretch your neck any further, your head will fall off,' remarked Dorcha, drily. 'I'd be very careful, laddie.'

'Looking at what?' he feigned innocence. 'Oh, *them*? I was just interested in the way they do the work, that's all. Very efficient lasses, every one of them. Very efficient. Up with the sails, down with the sails . . .'

'It's not their competence at sailing which attracts, you dirty old man. You just mind yourself.'

He laughed and shook his head, knowing that very little passed Dorcha by.

'They're forbidden taro, anyway,' said Seumas. 'Nono nuts, that's what they are. Apart from anything else, Ru would execute any man who touched one of those maidens, since it would bring him into direct conflict with the gods.' Seumas sighed, adding, 'It's part of their attraction – that they are unobtainable.'

'Would you like me to make *myself* unobtainable,' Dorcha said, arching an eyebrow. 'It's easily done, you know.'

He slipped a tattooed arm around her waist and grinned at her.

'You're desirable, whether you're out of bounds or not, lassie. I could eat you for breakfast, dinner and supper, so I could.'

'Mind it stays that way, *laddie*,' she said.

Another passenger, a handsome Raiatean man, witnessed this banter with an amused expression on his features. Dorcha knew his name was Titopika, but was ignorant of the reason for him being on the voyage.

He said he was a novice tohunga, a priest specialising in removing taboos from people and places – a purifier of tapu – and in touch with the spirits of the air, sea and earth, having knowledge of their language. A tohunga is necessary to any new Oceanian society, because he is qualified to perform funeral rites. Dorcha assumed this young man was going to the new island to set up his own temple. Promotion would be quicker at a new location. Raiatea itself had priests by the several dozens. Competition for top places was fierce and nepotism was rife.

'What are you laughing at?' asked Dorcha, already uncomfortable with the feeling of claustrophobia a voyage on a craft induces. 'Can't we talk in private?'

'I'm sorry,' said the man, not at all put out by her tone. 'It was rude of me.'

Seumas said, 'Take no notice of her – she gets touchy unless she's got a mountain range to stare at.'

'I'll remember that. Do forgive me. I meant no offence.'

Dorcha relented under this barrage of profuse apologies and told the man it was all right.

He smiled and left them to their personal chores.

Tawhaki hid in a cloud Ao sent to him and after roaming the skies for some time finally came across Tui Tofua, God of all the sharks. Tui Tofua was not a relative or even a friend of Dakuwanga, who was the Shark-God who ate sau, the souls which were lost on their way to the Land of the Dead. Dakuwanga was a spirit-shark dwelling in the ether, while Tui Tofua was in human shape and commanded all the real sharks in the real ocean.

Tawhaki asked a favour of Tui Tofua, who hated human beings and saw them only as food for his sharks. He asked that Tui Tofua's sharks do a service for him. Tui Tofua asked what that service might be and when Tawhaki told him, the God of all the sharks agreed to assist the God of Thunder and Lightning.

A multitude of sharks gathered under *The Princely Flower* and no matter how hard the crew pulled on the steering oar, or set the sails with Maomao's wind behind them, the vessel persisted in following a different bearing to the one Ru had set. With sharks under the two hulls, jammed there, it was impossible to control the course of the pahi. The sharks took them off their chosen route and into unknown waters.

It took the combined efforts of Dorcha, Kikamana and Boy-girl, each chanting their own powerful fangu, to rid the pahi of the sharks. Gradually, as the chants worked their spells, the fish left. Finally, the craft was free again and the royal maiden on the steering oar asked Ru for a direction.

Even Seumas, who was no navigator, could see that the shapes of the waves were all wrong. They were in some part of the ocean where the sea birds were strange and the clouds had no real definition. The colour of the water was a dark blue, almost black, indicating great depths. There was no te lapa to give guidance under the surface and a strange calmness had beset them, accompanied by sweltering days and restless nights.

Tui Tofua would surely be punished for what he had done with *The Princely Flower*, when Tangaroa caught up with him. In the meantime the pahi was becalmed on sultry seas, a hot sun pressing itself down on the necks and backs of the seafarers. The crew had little to do but wait for the wind, for which Ru sent prayers daily, bound for the ears of Maomao.

Seumas rose one night in the stillness to fetch a drink from a gourd lying in a cooling tank forward. As he picked his way amongst sleeping bodies that tossed and turned in the hot inert air, he heard a quick rustling movement from the direction of one of the hulls. Seumas reached the halved water gourd and dipped the wooden ladle for a drink. A moment later the young man known as Titopika appeared to come away from the port hull.

He came up short against Seumas, visibly jumped, and then hurriedly tried to find a lost composure. Clearly Seumas had startled Titopika with his presence, but it was not surprising to find more than one person at the drinking water on such a night. Possibly Titopika had been half-asleep and unready.

'I – er – would like a drink, if you've finished with that ladle.'

'Sorry,' said Seumas, 'did I frighten you?'

'No,' replied the other in an unexpectedly irritable tone. 'I just didn't think to see anyone about at this hour.'

'So I *did* surprise you.'

Titopika looked huffy. 'If you insist. Now may I have a drink of water, or are you going to hold onto that ladle all night?'

Seumas handed over the ladle without another word, but there was something about the man's manner which interested him. It was as if Titopika had been caught doing something illegal. Had he been stealing rations? Not this early in the voyage surely? Yesterday they had caught several albacore using 'ouma fish as bait. The albacore were huge and there was more than enough to feed the whole vessel for many days, so even the strongest appetite could not be suffering at that precise moment.

Perhaps Titopika had smuggled kava on board? Or had a store of honey? It was all most intriguing.

When the young man had finished his drink of water and had gone away to his bed, Seumas went to the area of the vessel from which he thought he had seen Titopika emerge. It had seemed to be on the very edge of the deck, just where it met the port hull. Seumas felt around, under the boards, seeking a hiding place, but found nothing. Refusing to give up on the puzzle he looked further afield.

In the hull itself, some of the crew were sleeping: royal virgins swathed in pareu, curled up together in the bottom like litters of newly born pups. Seumas stared at the dark shapes lying on pandanus mats in the shallow swilling water at the bottom of the hull, trying to keep cool. There seemed to be nothing untoward there: no obvious place to cache illicit food.

Suddenly he was aware of a set of brown eyes on his face. He stared into the features of one of the women, whom he appeared to have woken. She looked frightened. It seemed she might scream any moment. His skin prickled with apprehension.

'It's all right,' Seumas whispered. 'I'm not going to do anything – I was just looking – just looking for something,' he finished lamely, aware of how feeble it sounded. 'Nothing to get alarmed about.'

The woman continued to stare unblinkingly at him and eventually he crawled away. The incident remained in his mind as mildly disturbing, but there was nothing to substantiate his feelings that Titopika had been up to something unauthorised. When he saw the young man the next day, there was nothing with which to confront him, but it was significant that Titopika would not look him in the eye, and passed by him close to the pandanus mat sail without a glance.

Ru's pahi lazily approached an island which seemed to move as the mist drifted over it, revealing now a mountain, now a valley, now a forest. People on board had smelled sweet potatoes cooking and knew the island was inhabited. As Oceanians they loved sweet potatoes, sacred to Rongo, and had long since eaten all those on board. As Oceanians they would brave any strange island to replenish their depleted stores.

'Be careful,' Seumas warned Ru. 'Remember what happened to me when I chased the smell of cooking haggis.'

'That was different,' Kieto interrupted. 'Your haggis food is back in your own homeland, Land-of-Mists, while sweet potatoes are to be found over the whole of Oceania.'

Yet, as they approached the island in the early evening through a narrow gap in a dead coral reef, grey and depressing, both Dorcha and Boy-girl reported seeing things dancing on the water behind the pahi. It was as if they had gone blindly into a trap and their captors were rejoicing at having caught the prey. Dorcha said she wouldn't have been surprised to see the pincers of coral snap shut behind them.

'What did you see?' asked Ru of Dorcha.

'I can't be sure exactly,' replied Dorcha. 'Perhaps nothing at all? Maybe a mirage. I just caught movements out of the corner of my eye. They flashed silver, like fish, but they weren't fish, of that I'm certain. I got the impression of – of human-like forms.'

'Ponaturi,' stated Ru with conviction. 'Sea-fairies. This is an enchanted place.'

Ru explained that the Ponaturi lived in the divide between the visible and the invisible world. One caught them in the glimmering light of a dawn, or in the last stray wispy tails of a disappearing sun. 'You think you see them, perhaps you do – but you can't be sure.' They were bright shadows that flitted past the corner of the eye, as they soared through the glooms of twilight, of too tenuous a nature to be completely discernible – but tangible enough to attack humans.

Seumas asked, 'Are the Ponaturi like the Tipairu, the Peerless Ones?'

'No – the Tipairu are gentle creatures, who love their dancing. The Ponaturi are savage sea-fairies who live in hordes, more willing to fight than dance. Once they latch on to a vessel, they won't let it go until all the seafarers are dead. Their chant is:

"Scent, scent,
Odour, odour,
My food is man,
My drink is blood."'

Polahiki gave out a low moan of fear.

'The hero Rata slew them in great numbers,' continued Ru, 'using deadly karakia chants as well as physical force. We must keep our weapons handy – we may need them. Where's Kikamana, our priestess? Dorcha the Scot? And that young tohunga?'

Kikamana, Dorcha and Titopika came before Ru.

'I want you three to protect us from the Ponaturi when we have to leave here,' he said. 'Can you do it? We're not a large enough force to beat the Ponaturi on purely physical terms. They'll swarm all over us.'

Kikamana said, 'For the karakia to be effective we need human bones to beat together, preferably those of an ancient warrior hero. Otherwise the karakia will be slow to work. We are not carrying such a cargo.'

Boy-girl took Polahiki by the hair and pushed him forward.

'We could kill this otherwise worthless specimen and use *his* bones as drumsticks.'

'True,' argued Seumas, 'Polahiki has done nothing so far – it's his chance to be useful.'

'You leave me alone!' screeched the terrified fisherman. 'Who catches your fish for you?'

'I think we do that ourselves,' Boy-girl said. 'You eat anything you catch.'

Boy-girl's cockerel ran up to Polahiki and began pecking around his feet. The fisherman had become so agitated he was dislodging some of his lice and other tiny parasites which infested his body. They were falling to the deck, to be devoured by the colourful rooster pet of Boy-girl.

The Farseeing-virgin interrupted. 'I'm afraid this is serious. We do need the bones if we're to escape a battle with the Ponaturi. Rata's tohungas used the bones of Wahieroa.'

Seumas said, 'We could search this island for graves – I'm not above grave-robbing if my life's at stake. I doubt we'll find a hero in a place like this, but if we don't do something we'll be trapped in this lagoon while those sea-fairies wait for us on the other side of the reef. What do you say, Kieto?'

'I don't like the idea of robbing graves. Our ancestors, and perhaps even the gods, would not approve of such a thing. But if we scour the caves on that ugly-looking mountain, we might find some bones. I see no signs of civilisation here – this is a primitive place. There are islands where they do not bury their dead, but pile the bones in some cave.'

'Isn't that the same as stealing from a grave?' said Dorcha. 'I can't see much difference.'

'The difference is that the bones will not have been subject to funeral rites,' replied Titopika. 'They will not be so powerful, their mana will have dwindled, but Kieto's right – we're more likely to find bones in a cave than anywhere else.'

A three-person team was chosen to go ashore to search for the bones. These were Seumas, Dorcha and Kikamana. Ru was taking Pungarehu and Po'oi to look for sweet potatoes. All the others were to remain on board the pahi, which floated on a scummy tideless stretch of lagoon where the flies and other insects were persistently annoying. Rotten stumps of palm trees projected from the water under which lifeless coral was corroding and filling the lagoon with grey sludge.

Polahiki was attempting to fish, but the only thing he was catching in that dull, torpid water were moray eels with thick slimy skins.

'The goddess Pere has deserted this place,' he moaned. 'She has left it to stagnate.'

Those remaining on board prayed to Tiki to protect them from the onslaught of the Ponaturi fairies, while their captain and pathfinder was on the island. Ru had assured them the sea-fairies would not attack while the ship was anchored in the lagoon, but a little trust in Tiki did not harm. The First Ancestor's wooden face remained impassive as he imbibed the prayers, glad to be of some comfort to his many descendants.

When the party of six reached the beach, they followed a trail of coconut shells and fruit skins up the beach to a village just inside the rainforest pale. There they found a listless, apathetic tribe, who seemed to be living in a state divided between fear and boredom. They poured out their misfortunes to the visitors, complaining of everything and anything, and finished by telling Ru not to send anyone into the middle of the island because no one had ever managed to come back alive.

'All the best land is there,' moaned the chief. 'We could grow better crops, if it weren't for the fact that a monster lives on the mountain. It eats anyone who ventures into the hinterland.'

'A monster?' queried Ru. 'What kind?'

'What kind is your *fear*?' asked the chief, rhetorically. 'It is a taniwha whose name is Hotu-puku.'

'I have heard of this noxious monster. And the lagoon – why is that dying?'

The chief replied, 'Tipua. The Ponaturi allow them to come and feed on the coral and weed. Without weed and coral there are no fish.'

Ru nodded. 'We need some human bones to escape the Ponaturi – can you let us have some?'

'We would if we had any ourselves. Most of our people are taken by the taniwha, but the Tipua also carry away the dead in the middle of the night, to feast on the rotting flesh. We have no graves, no corpses, no bones. Our ancestors haunt us nightly, keeping us awake and in fear, because their bodies have been treated so badly after death.'

Ru turned to Dorcha, Seumas and Kikamana.

'Well, do you still want to go into the high country?'

'We had no choice before,' said the Farseeing-virgin. 'And even less now, if we want to escape from this place.'

'Off you go then – and good luck.'

The three went out of the village on an overgrown path which led into the jungle of the foothills. Seumas was glad they had Kikamana with them, for though he considered himself a good warrior, and Dorcha also a fighter, the high priestess had powerful mana – much stronger than any they owned themselves – and this would be useful if they came up against a monster.

'What kind of monster did he say it was?' he asked Kikamana.

'It is the colour of your fear,' replied that kahuna. 'If you fear cockroaches, then be prepared for the mother of all cockroaches. With me, it is lizards.'

Dorcha shuddered. 'Snakes,' she said. 'I hate snakes.'

'Women,' said Seumas. 'It's women that terrify me.'

Dorcha shot him a look, but Kikamana, who was unused to humour in serious situations, stared at Seumas in surprise.

'Really – you fear women?'

'Actually,' said Dorcha, 'he's only terrified of one woman and if he doesn't behave himself you'll soon see why.'

Kikamana was still bewildered, but decided to let the matter drop, since she didn't seem to be getting anywhere.

They made their way inland, up the gradually sloping ground, until they came to a steeper climb. Here the jungle thinned out to become rainforest, and after that more open

country, with bushes and bamboo, rather than tall trees. All
the while they sought caves to investigate. When they found
them they went inside cautiously, discovering most of them
empty. Just occasionally there were the bones of birds, or a
ceiling covered in bats, but no human skeletons.

Finally they approached an enormous cave which
stretched like a mouth under the brow of a cliff. There was
something in the aspect of the cave which warned all three
that this was probably the home of the taniwha Hotu-
puku. In any case they were on their guard for a meeting
with the monster. Seumas asked the other two if they had
any plan.

Kikamana said, 'We could entice it from the cave then
bring magic to bear on its size. A karakia might be effective
in shrinking it, whatever it looks like to each one of us.
However, as you both know, we have no ancient bones to
ensure the effectiveness of the chant.'

Seumas shuddered. 'Put our faith in a fangu chant, without sacred bones? You must be crazy. I couldn't do that.'

'Well, what then?' asked Dorcha. 'Give us an alternative.'

Seumas looked around him. They were standing on the
edge of thick jungle. There was a clear grassy slope ahead
of them, leading up to the cave and the tall cliffs. To either
side the land fell away as steep escarpments. If the monster
came on foot, it would have to run down the narrow slope
and follow them into the dark undergrowth beneath the
dense canopy of the trees, where vines and branches hung
thick as curtains.

Of course, it might have the ability to fly, depending on
what each of them saw it as, but then they would be safe in
the jungle, below the path of its flight.

'I suggest we make snares out of the vines,' he told the two
women. 'Then when we have nooses around its neck . . .'

'Or *necks*,' said Kikamana.

'. . . or necks,' added Seumas, giving Kikamana a sidelong glance. 'When it's securely roped we kill it with clubs

and spears. We'll probably need the help of others.'

Kikamana said, 'It will only complicate matters if there are more people here – it means more variation to the shape of the monster. However, it sounds a reasonable plan. Dorcha and I shall protect ourselves with a karakia. What will you do?'

Seumas said, 'A good warrior doesn't need a magic chant – I'll face the monster without it.'

'Fine, then let's make the nooses.'

They set to work, tugging out the blades of cabbage-trees and twisting them into ropes, the vines being a little stiff to knot and use for snares. They were already armed. Kikamana had a carved rib-bone of a whale, which had been shaved into a sword. Seumas had a short wooden cleaver. Dorcha carried a long-handled club with a serrated hardwood edge on one side and shark's teeth down the other. All three held a spear each.

The ropes made from the ti fronds were hung amongst the vines, disguised as normal growth amongst the trees, their nooses hanging limply ready to be filled. The ends were fixed to tree trunks or stakes hammered into the ground with rocks. The knots were draped with blossoms and wild flowers to hide their presence and this was so well achieved that birds used the loops of the snares as perch swings from which to make their calls.

In the mid-afternoon they were ready to take on the tani-wha and each of them prepared their nerves for the coming ordeal.

'I shall call the monster down,' said Kikamana. 'It is my privilege as a kahuna.'

'Help yourself,' said Seumas, with a gesture.

'Likewise,' Dorcha added.

Kikamana, that magnificent priestess, left them to walk up to the opaque orifice of the mountain which pushed earth and rock apart in a cracked grin. The two Albannachs watched her progress with hearts beating rapidly faster, camouflaged by the slats of sunlight that shafted the canopy. They had the unenviable task of pulling the nooses tight if the monster's head (or heads) did not automatically do so.

Kikamana was about halfway up the slope when a blast of bats came from the cave, millions of them, blackening the air for a few moments. Then the taniwha's foul breath came hissing from the mouth of the cave. She smelled its rank odour and felt the damp warmth of it on her cheek. Then suddenly, there it was, the taniwha Hotu-puku, its fierce great head filling the entrance to its den, its burning eyes like two suns glaring down at her. It was indeed the head of a giant lizard, as Kikamana had expected; having explored herself thoroughly during many years of meditation she knew her own fears intimately. She shook in apprehension.

'Moko!' she cried. 'Lord of the Lizards, protect me from one of your deviants!'

The God of the Lizards made no obvious reply, nor had she really expected one, not having prepared the way to his ears with sacrifices and prayers.

Kikamana was absolutely terrified by the scaly beast before her, as Hotu-puku emerged from the cave. She witnessed its spear-like crest and the dreadful forest of spines protruding from its head and back. Its head jerked back and forth in the manner of reptiles as its tail pounded the earth in the cave behind it. A flat belly slid with a rumbling sound along the ground, dragging loose rocks and broken limbs of trees along beneath it. Those loose scales which dropped from its sides as it scraped through the cave mouth fell like turtle shells to the ground to shatter on the stones. A long tongue flicked in and out of its horrible split jaws, lapping the shrubs around the terror-stricken priestess as she fought for the will to move.

'Kikamana,' shrieked Dorcha's voice behind her, 'run away from the snake – quickly, quickly.'

But still those baleful eyes held her as the hot musty breath engulfed her own and made it difficult for her to breathe or think, fogging her reason with the lack of fresh air. Hotu-puku's mouth opened, revealing a blood-red interior which disappeared into a black throat. A hissing roar issued from this region, blasting the kahuna's ears.

'Look out, look out, the taniwha is upon you!' yelled Dorcha. 'Run away Kikamana!'

Finally, as the ridged spiny giant began to run forward, its claws thumping the moss-covered earth, Kikamana found some youthful strength in her tired old body and turned on trembling limbs to run.

When she reached the safety of the trees, skipping neatly through the loops of the snares like a little girl, she found that Seumas had fled, leaving just the two women to deal with the monster.

On it came, its head appearing halfway up the tall trees at the pale of the forest, then its forelegs entered, and one was caught within the snares. Kikamana slashed at an anchor rope with her whale-bone sword, releasing a tethered young tree to which the noose was tied.

A double-noose tightened around Hotu-puku's throat, which drew even tighter as the monster thrashed in its coils. At the same time the one snared foreleg was raised off the ground by the sprung tree, causing the beast to unbalance, while the second foreleg frantically clawed at a nearby trunk tearing the bark from the bole in one complete strip. A tail lashed the hill behind Hotu-puku, the spines ripping the turf to pieces and raining soil and grit upon the broad leaves of the undergrowth, adding to the noise and confusion.

'Kill it, kill it,' shrieked a wide-eyed Dorcha, clearly almost stupefied by terror.

She did not remain transfixed however and ran forward to slash at the monster's throat with her tooth-edge club, ripping the loose skin open where it flapped as the taniwha tossed and jerked its head. A foam-flecked mouth sprayed the women as they fought to bring the creature to its knees, splattering and drenching them in disgusting fluids that plastered their hair to their skulls and blinded them with its acidic properties.

'Get its legs,' cried Kikamana. 'Chop at its ankles.'

'What legs?' shrieked the Scot. 'I can't see any. Snakes don't have legs.'

Kikamana drove her whale-bone sword up into the sagging skin of the underjaw, pinning the beast's mandible to the roof of its mouth.

Kikamana then took up her spear and forced it hard into Hotu-puku's belly, spilling hot, thick steaming juices onto the floor of the jungle. Then the brave priestess went for neck and upper torso, stabbing with her long spear, piercing lungs and heart. Each time she struck the creature let out a shrill wail which was both pathetic and horrifying in its tone.

In the meantime Dorcha, emboldened by their success, chopped at the taniwha's head with her club, trying to split its skull and causing great wounds to its eyes, as it convulsed and moaned under the onslaught of the two warrior women.

Its hideous head gradually sank to the earth, as the stranglehold of the double-noose around its neck tightened further, stemming all oxygen to its body. The spear went in repeatedly, the club struck at kidneys, liver, and other vital organs, until with a final forlorn sigh Hotu-puku delivered itself up unto death and was rolled sideways to hang there by the springiness of the tree to which its foreleg was attached.

The women let fall their weapons and hugged each other. Both were pouring sweat and showed signs of their ordeal in their lank hair and limp muscles. When they were able to, they let go of one another and went to a nearby pool to bathe away their grime, to help relax, and to wash the monster's phlegm and spittle from their skin and clothes. Their own blood besmirched their garments too, where they had scratched and cut themselves in the mêlée. They went back to survey their kill.

'What do you see?' asked Kikamana of the Scot.

'A snake,' answered Dorcha, shuddering. 'What do you see?'

'A giant lizard, bristling with poisonous spikes. A scaly monster of a thing. I wonder what Seumas saw that terrified him so much? He must have run all the way back to the village, judging by the speed at which he left.'

Dorcha shook her head. 'He'll be so ashamed, I know he will. Poor Seumas. He'll never live it down.'

'There's no shame attached to it. Either one of us might have turned and run too. I'm sure I would have done, in the beginning, except I was frozen to the spot. Had we enough sense, we would have done exactly the same. There's only a split second between so-called cowardice and bravery – his survival instinct is obviously stronger than mine, that's all. He should be proud of that fact.'

Dorcha said with a sigh, 'He won't see it that way – he'll curse himself for being afraid, he'll hate himself for leaving us to do what he will see as his work, he'll despise himself for running when women stood and fought. It'll be a long time before he stops loathing himself for this act.'

Returning to more practical matters, Kikamana said, 'I think we ought to disembowel the monster, to make sure of its death. We don't want it resurrecting itself once we leave it. Magical monsters have a habit of reviving and returning to avenge their own deaths.'

So the two women set to work once more. They began by sawing open the belly with the shark-toothed club, spilling out the liver and lights, scattering them amongst the forest ferns. They removed the heart and burned it on a fire and broke open the skull with rocks to drain it of brains. Finally they came to the stomach, opening it with knives of obsidian and sharp mussel shells. They cut through the layers of fat and through the folds of muscle, until they had opened the sac, to reveal a horrible and disgusting sight.

Whole bodies of men, women and children fell out, some severed in the middle, some without arms or legs. There were also piles of greenstone weapons, hardwood clubs and lei-o-mano. A great variety of body ornaments were clustered in heaps, from shell brooches to wooden amulets to necklaces of bones and teeth. There were garments and cloaks of every kind, including flax war-cloaks woven with dogs' tails and embroidered with parrots' feathers, so thick they were impervious to the strong juices of the beast's stomach. There were cloaks of white dogskin with fine borders and others of rich red kula feathers. Piles of old bones, steaming with enzymes, dropped to the ground.

All these the women gathered in a great mound, to collect later when they returned with more people.

It was a treasure trove, but more importantly, amongst the fresh victims were the ancient bones of distant ancestors, which Kikamana assembled in a cloak ready for use against the Ponaturi. There were legbones and armbones which could be used as drumsticks to beat on old skulls.

'That's enough then,' said Kikamana. 'We must make our way back to the village.'

They cut out the taniwha's tongue to carry with them as proof of its death.

On the path back to the village they met Seumas cowering behind a rock.

'What happened?' he cried, hugging Dorcha to his breast, clearly in a state of shock. 'I thought you were both dead.'

She was both pleased and touched that the first thing he thought to do was take hold of her, glad that she was safe, and did not immediately whine about his own cowardice.

'We destroyed the monster,' she said. 'It went exactly as

you planned it. You should congratulate yourself for a brilliant scheme which worked. Otherwise I think we should all be dead,' she added generously.

'No,' he said, hanging his head, 'the credit all goes to you – to both of you. I turned and ran, coward that I am, but it was impossible for me to stand. I could not. What I saw was invincible – the thing which terrifies me most in the whole world. I still could not have fought it, even were it to happen again right here on this very turf. I would still turn and run, I'm ashamed to say. But there, it's done, and I must live with my shame.'

Kikamana said, 'I blame no man for being quick enough to preserve himself in the face of his worst nightmare. You must know that it is no shame for an Oceanian warrior to turn and run at any point in the battle? It is accepted that a good warrior is fleet of foot too. He is expected to be ferocious when he stands and fights, but is applauded if when he flees he outruns the enemy chasing him. That is our way.'

'But it isn't the Albannach way. A man who flees the field is a coward and deserves death. I have dishonoured my name.'

'You'll get over it,' said Dorcha, grimly. 'I want no man of mine pining for his honour so much it puts him into the grave. That's a weakling for you – not a man who runs – but a man who can't face up to his failures. Yes, you damn well failed, you running Pict, but you'll have to live with it. I'll only think the more of you, if you do. It's love's way.'

He hugged her neck with his arm, a tall man gripping a short woman, one strong in body, the other in spirit – but both strong in mind. He wanted to argue with her, tell her he should by rights go and hang himself from the nearest tree, that this was the only honourable way out for a real man, but he knew she was right, that it was harder to stand and fight with his own inadequacies.

'All right, woman, I won't mention it again, so long as

you don't. If you bring it up in some argument in the future, I swear I'll kill one of us, you hear.'

'Agreed,' she said, and smiled. He was her man, strong in spirit too. Not as strong as her, but close. 'Now let's get down to the village and tell them we've killed the monster. We've got the bones we need too, to fight the sea-fairies. It's been a successful day.'

As they made their way along the path, the women asked him what he had seen, when the taniwha emerged from the cave.

'You'll *never* know,' he said to Kikamana, 'but I may tell Dorcha later, when I feel more myself.'

And they had to be satisfied with that, staring at the man's muscled back, as he strode ahead of them, eager to be done with this place where his weakness had over-whelmed him.

2

While *The Princely Flower* was at rest within the reef, Tawhaki plotted his next move against the expedition, calling on his old friend Tawhiri-Matea the Storm-God, the smiter of trees, the lasher of waves. Tawhiri-Matea had little respect for mortals and though he was aware that Io would be angry with him for assisting Tawhaki, the Storm-God was thirsty for human lives.

'You must wait for the canoe to leave the waters of the enchanted island,' said Tawhaki, 'then strike.'

'It shall be as you say, Thunder-God,' replied the brutal god of storms. 'I taste death on my teeth.'

While the party of six were on shore some of those left behind on the pahi were becoming impatient. Titopika spoke to Polahiki, saying that he feared something had happened to Ru, Kikamana, Seumas and the others, and that they should go and search for them, to see if they needed help.

Polahiki scratched his sores, picked at his scabs, and replied, 'You sure we should? We've been told to stay here.'

'That was not an order to be taken literally. After all, if something *has* happened to the shore party, we can't just sail away and leave them here, can we? They might still be alive, trapped in some cave, or locked up in cages. Who can tell what dangers there are on that island. I say we take some men and go over there to look for them.'

'All right,' said the fisherman, licking his salt-encrusted lips. 'I could do with a drink of cool fresh water. Let's go and speak with Kieto.'

Titopika shook his head. 'Leave Kieto out of this – he's not as flexible as we are. He's rigid enough to follow Ru's orders to the letter. We'll just take a canoe and go and look for them ourselves. What do you say?'

Polahiki was not stupid and soon realised that Titopika had his own reasons for wanting to do this thing, but on the other hand the fisherman had no love for anyone on board the pahi, he was desperately thirsty for some good clean water and he had a naturally belligerent and rebellious nature, which of course was why Titopika had chosen to persuade him.

'All right,' he said, 'but I'm not paddling all that way in a dugout. It's too much like hard work. You get one more man and I'll come with you.'

Titopika went off and found a cousin of Ru, a man of twenty years named Kiaru, who was jealous of the fame of his older relation. The thought of disobeying Ru's orders both scared and excited Kiaru, who wanted his own name to be as revered as that of his noble cousin. Titopika tempted the young man with visions of him as the saviour of the expedition.

'We should take the initiative then?' said Kiaru. 'After all, orders are for the guidance of wise men and for fools to follow to the letter.'

'We need to weigh up the circumstances of the situation and act accordingly,' confirmed Titopika. 'It seems to me that Ru and the other five have been gone far too long. If they're not in any danger, why aren't they on their way back to us? We would see their dugout on the lagoon.'

The young man Kiaru stared at the dull grey waters of the lagoon, empty of any craft.

'Let us go now,' he said to Titopika, 'while Kieto is at rest in the deck hut.'

The three men armed themselves, two in order to protect themselves should they meet with hostile forces, the third with more sinister intentions.

Titopika hoped to be able to find Prince Ru on his own once they were on the island. The six already there would be gathering stores – sweet potatoes and breadfruit mainly – and Titopika meant to sneak up on Ru. If and when he did, Titopika was going to kill the prince, quietly and efficiently. Ragnu had said this would not be possible on the pahi during a voyage, with so many people in so small a space, but out there on an island it was a very workable plan. The undergrowth in the rainforest was often thick enough to hide men from one another's sight, even though they were but a few paces apart.

Ragnu's long-term plan for the destruction of the expedition was proceeding gradually, according to that priest's intricate and devious scheme, but it was a slow process and this was a much quicker way of bringing the voyage to an end. With their navigator prince gone one of the several brothers of Ru would take over command. Ru's brothers had no love for the Rarotongans and could be persuaded to put them ashore somewhere, on a deserted island, where they would rot and die. Ragnu would be delighted by such an end for his enemies – and of course the pahi would be there to carry Titopika to the new island, where he could one day become a great kahuna like Ragnu.

The dugout slid away from the pahi before the warning could be given and they were halfway across the lagoon when the shout came from an enraged Kieto.

'Come back,' cried Kieto. 'What are you playing at?'

But the three men knew Kieto could not follow, since there were only two dugouts on the pahi, and both were now in use.

Kiaru looked anxiously back at the ocean-going canoe.

'Don't worry,' soothed Titopika, 'he'll thank you when you rescue your cousin and bring him back safe and well.'

Polahiki sniffed and lay back in the canoe as if he were on a leisurely boating trip to visit an aunt.

'Personally, I couldn't care less whether Kieto snaps a gut and goes spinning off in space.' He picked his nose and spat to emphasise his carelessness. 'Just keep paddling, boy, don't worry about nits like *him.*'

But Kiaru was still a little worried. 'Kieto has a great deal of mana. He sailed with the great Kupe to the Land-of-Mists when he was but seven years of age. He is not a man to be dismissed lightly.'

'Yes, his mana is strong, but we are doing the right thing,' said Titopika, thinking he would have to sacrifice this finicky youth once the main job had been done. The young man's disposition was too particular. 'Kieto is too much the seafarer to understand what dangers lurk on the land.'

Kiaru had to be satisfied with this explanation and paddled harder to reach the shore, while the other two discussed which way they would go once they reached the beach.

They landed on the dingy sands and took the path into the rainforest. Soon the three men met with a fork. They argued as to which way they should take and Titopika won. The party struck off left, away from the density of the jungle.

Despite the fact that they had taken the easier path it was humid and unpleasant under the rainforest canopy and storm flies stuck to the sweat on their skin. The dank smells of areas always in shadow assailed their nostrils and in one place there was a danger of quicksand, when Kiaru sank to his thighs and had to be extracted by the other two.

'Where are we going?' grumbled Polahiki. 'We don't seem to be getting anywhere.'

'Listen,' said Titopika, 'I hear running water!'

They carried on, following the narrow path, until they reached a stream just at the point where the foliage met the beach.

'We've come to an inlet,' Kiaru said. 'It cuts deeply into the island. We'll need a canoe to cross this.'

Titopika was now beginning to realise he had chosen the wrong track and that they should have taken the *right* path at the point where it forked.

'Let's drink and then turn back,' he said. 'We haven't come too far in the wrong direction.'

All three fell to their knees to slake their thirst on the crystal waters which tumbled down from the hilly interior. As they refreshed themselves they heard twittering noises, as if people were imitating birds, coming from the beach hidden behind the water-edge shrubs and plants. It was almost a musical sound, yet at the same time irritating. Titopika went down on his stomach and wormed his way through the shrubbery to see what kind of creature would make such peculiar chatter.

The sight which met his eyes was truly wondrous and made him gasp in astonishment.

Landing on the beach from the clouds were a dozen winged women, fairies from regions in the sky, all of them naked and beautiful, with pearl-coloured skins and silvery hair. They were uniformly two-thirds as tall as Titopika, a man of average height, and their limbs were slender and pretty. The hair which fell from their heads was long and straight, dropping to their ankles, and it shone like the waters of a lake caught in the bright sunlight. Their eyes were magenta and as cruel and deep as an ocean trench. Heart-shaped faces, with small sweet mouths, perfectly shaped noses and tiny abalone ears, captivated the watching Titopika, as the fairies clustered around the pool formed by the stream as it flowed onto the beach.

Even as he watched the entrancing creatures, Titopika sensed a ruthlessness about these beings, who he was sure would think nothing of taking a man's life. There was about them an air of strangeness beyond their mere physical forms, an alienness as far from a mortal as the moon was from the earth. It made him shiver with apprehension.

By this time the other two had crawled to where he was lying and they two were staring open-mouthed at the fairies whose figures no mortal eye should ever behold.

'Look – look what they're doing,' whispered the enthralled Kiaru.

As the three men stared the women removed their white wings and these they left above the high-tide mark, amongst the shards of broken shells tossed up by the ocean, before plunging joyously into the pool to wash themselves and play in the cool water. Their games were sexual yet at the same time innocent, and all three men felt red-hot knives of lust burning in their loins. These women were incredibly desirable and at that moment Titopika would have gladly passed over a kingdom for just one hour lying with the fairies on the warm sands of the bay.

'Quickly,' he whispered to the others, 'here's our chance to destroy Ru. If we can steal those wings the fairies will do anything to get them back. I shall take as my price for the return of the wings, the death of Prince Ru.'

'No!' said Kiaru, sharply. 'I did not come to harm Ru – I came to rescue him.'

'Fool,' hissed Titopika, 'do you want to be a king or a prince's doormat for the rest of your life? Don't you realise the power these fairies can give us? We can become legends – think about it! This is a chance that comes along once in a thousand years. We can be masters of the world!'

Kiaru wriggled with uncertainty in the sand. The idea of being so powerful that no one could touch him was stunning. He was afraid of what Ru might do to him, if he went against his brother, but as Titopika had inferred the three of them would wield so much puissance Ru would not be able to do anything. Kiaru would be in a position to crush all his enemies, stand tall and proud amongst his kin, and rule with bamboo rod.

The vision was all too tempting and he crawled forward to where he could reach for the wings, pulling them gently one by one into the shrubs and passing them back to Titopika and Polahiki.

The two older men worked with quickened breath, well aware of the horrible fate they would suffer were they detected in the act. Their lives would not be worth a pinch of sand. They gathered the soft white wings into three piles. When all were safely in their keeping, they took one bundle each and ran into the rainforest, to hide them under a bush. They covered the fairies' wings with fresh grasses, to camouflage them in case the now wingless women were to search the forest.

As the men returned to the beach, they heard a high piercing wail which threatened to split their eardrums.

'Oh – oh – oh,' cried Polahiki, his spirit shattering under the shrillness of that cry. 'They're coming for us!'

With that the fisherman ran off, back along the track down which they had come, eager to escape the wrath of the sky-fairies with wicked eyes that held promises of torture beyond that which any normal man can suffer, let alone a Hivan coward.

'What shall we do?' whispered Kiaru, who had gone as pale and grey as dead coral.

'You go back and protect the wings,' ordered Titopika. 'I'll speak with the fairies.'

Kiaru did as he was bid, trotting back to the hiding place, glad to let the tohunga deal with the delicate but vicious women against whom the men had committed a terrible sin. Such creatures would tear off a man's genitals with their slim pretty fingers, or suck out his eyes with their sweet lips, or blow into his mouth with their perfect noses until his chest exploded. The word *compassion* was not in their vocabulary.

With his heart pounding Titopika stepped out onto the beach to find the fairy women tugging on their breasts and wrenching at their long hair. Some were screeching in torment as they sought their lost property along the high-tide mark, while others clawed at the sand, digging holes at random, believing their precious wings might have been buried by envious crabs. Any live creatures which were unfortunate enough to be in their way, they crushed or stamped into the ground. The barbarism of their actions drove fear into Titopika and he almost turned and ran away like Polahiki, but managed to fight his panic into a small corner of his mind and there control it.

'Stop,' he cried to the fairies. 'I know where your wings are – they shall be returned to you.'

One creature with little pointed teeth came running up to him, screaming, 'Where? Where? Where?'

'They were taken by the birds,' lied the tohunga, 'and hidden in the bushes. I – I shall need payment for my services – payment in kind. If you agree, I'll lead you to the wings immediately.'

'Payment? What payment?' chorused the women. 'You wish to enjoy our bodies? You wish to make us love you?'

'No, no – that is, the thought is as delightful as you are all beautiful – but I have a more urgent need. There is a prince somewhere on this island, a noble from Raiatea. I want you to tear him to pieces and throw him to the sharks. If you do this, I'll tell you where your wings are hidden . . .'

At that moment a shadow passed over Titopika: that of a great bird. The tohunga looked up and so did the fairies. The man let out a gasp of astonishment as he recognised Kiaru, who had attached a pair of white-feathered wings to his back and was now flying over the lagoon.

'Kiaru!' shouted Titopika.

Kiaru was not only flying away from the island, but he carried the other sets of wings under his arms.

'Come back,' yelled Titopika. 'Where are you going?'

'I'm flying home,' came back the reply on the wind. 'I shall be famous . . .'

Titopika watched the young man sweep low over the waves. He did not seem to be able to get any height. Then he reached the outer reef. As he passed over the wide lip of coral, the ocean's waves crashed against it sending up spume and salt spray, which drenched him. Suddenly, his wings seemed to peel away from his body, and drifted downwards like falling leaves. Kiaru fell with them, hitting the surface with a splash. He could not hold on to the other sets of wings and they floated away from him on the surface of the sea.

On seeing Kiaru fall the fairies let out shrill cries and dived into the lagoon to swim out to fetch their precious wings.

While this was happening, Kiaru seemed to be striving in the rollers, thrashing and flailing with his arms. Titopika knew him to be a good swimmer and could not understand the reason for the youth's struggle. Did he have the cramps? Was a shark attacking him? Then Titopika noticed thick white stems, like headless flowers, growing around the young man. What was that? Surely not? But, yes, they were tiny arms, reaching up out of the water to grip Kiaru around the waist and head. The distant cousin of Prince Ru was then pulled down, to some awful fate below the waves, and never surfaced again.

'Ponaturi!' cried Titopika, shuddering. 'The sea-fairies have taken him.'

In the meantime the sky-fairies had reached their wings and were attaching them to their shoulders.

Titopika made off quickly, into the forest, aware that Kiaru was being torn to pieces somewhere on the ocean bed.

He ran all the way back to where the path forked: ran almost into the face of Ru.

'What are you doing here?' demanded Ru. 'I ordered all passengers to remain on the pahi.'

'It's your cousin, Kiaru,' gasped Titopika, pointing back along the path. 'He's been taken by fairies.' The tohunga then realised he had better not tell Ru the whole truth. 'Some sky-fairies came and took him away, up into the clouds. Others were after Polahiki and myself, but we split up and escaped. At least, I *think* the fisherman escaped.'

'My cousin, Kiaru?'

'Gone,' cried Titopika. 'I tried to save him but they wrenched him from my arms. They were savage creatures with terrible claws. I did my best, but I couldn't keep them from him. There were too many. Ask Polahiki.'

Prince Ru's expression was uncompromising. 'You disobeyed my order to remain on the craft. This is what happens when discipline breaks down. You shall be punished.'

Titopika's back straightened and his voice took on a harder note. 'No one punishes me – not even a prince. I did what I did for the common good. You were gone too long. We thought you had been attacked and were captured – or dead. Were we supposed to wait for ever? I think not. We are not children without initiative, or a will of our own.'

Ru conceded that the shore party had been longer than anticipated.

'Yet you should have obeyed my orders. I left Kieto in charge. Why did he not organise you?'

'Kieto was asleep. I did not wake him because it was unnecessary. I am quite capable of organising a rescue party without the help of a Raiatean.'

'Yet you lost my cousin.'

Titopika thought it prudent to hang his head for a moment, then he looked the prince in the eyes again.

'True, and if I could undo that part, I would, but this is a dangerous island. One can't prepare for every eventuality.

Accidents will occur on voyages such as ours. Lives will be lost. We will be lucky indeed if Kiaru is the last person to forfeit his life to our great adventure.'

Ru nodded, thoughtfully. 'I shall be lenient,' he said, 'but if you disobey my orders again, I shall have you flogged and dragged behind the pahi in shark-infested waters. Is there anything of my cousin to recover?'

'Nothing – he was torn to pieces in the air and the remnants cast down into the sea.'

'Then let us be done with this island now.'

Titopika allowed Prince Ru to pass him, carrying sweet potatoes in a tapa cloth sack. Not for the first time did Titopika regret he was not an expert in the art of makutu, or 'killing by thought' which had been the gift of very few Oceanian priests in the long august history of the ocean islands.

Other members of the shore party went by, each carrying fruit, drinking coconuts or breadfruit. Finally, Seumas brought up the rear with another sack, this one bulging with sharper objects.

'Bones,' grunted the Pict, as he passed the tohunga. 'Bones of ancient warriors taken from the stomach of a monster.'

'A monster?' whispered Titopika.

'A taniwha, killed by Dorcha and Kikamana.'

'And you?'

Seumas scowled and said sourly. 'I had little to do with it.'

There's a story there, thought Titopika, allowing Seumas to pass and tagging on the end of the single file. And as for the mighty Prince Ru, second son of a second son. He shall be lenient, shall he? How gracious he is in his mercy. How free with his compassion. I would like to give him a second mouth, with which to dispense his generosity to us lowly minions, a mouth below that which he already owns. I would like to slit his throat and watch him bubble out his lofty proclamations through blisters of blood. Indeed, I am quickly arriving at the conclusion that it might come to that shortly.

At that moment, a face leered at the tohunga from within the rotten recesses of a hollow tree. There was a creature there. It had long knotted arms and legs with which it pressed the sides of the wooden chimney, to hold itself halfway up inside the twisted bole. Its complexion was green, its features hideously ugly, and the consistency of fungi.

An enormous phallus and pendulous scrotum swung between its spread legs. A tongue came out, as long as a man's arm, to rasp in the face of the startled tohunga. Then it licked, stripping off a piece of Titopika's facial skin with its sandstone-rough texture. Rheumy eyes stared triumphantly as Titopika whined, then stumbled, badly shaken by the experience.

'A lipsipsip,' croaked Titopika, wondering why the gods were not happy with him today.

'What?' asked Seumas, turning to face him. 'Did you say something.'

'Tree-dwarves. I saw a tree-dwarf.'

'Well, don't shout it out, or everyone will want one,' joked the Pict.

Titopika was in no mood for such jests and might have struck Seumas had not the lipsipsip let out a monstrous fart that echoed in his hollow trunk and once again startled the priest.

'This is an evil place,' muttered Titopika, heaving because of the stench, 'and I shall be glad to be out of it.'

When they reached the shoreline they found only one dugout. Polahiki had taken the other one to get back to the pahi. They managed to cram in this small canoe however, since no one was willing to remain behind to wait for a second trip. When they reached the pahi they found Polahiki there.

'Took your time,' said the fisherman, standing by the

pandanus hut, eating mashed breadfruit out of a banana leaf with his fingers. 'I've been back ages.'

'You deserted me,' growled Titopika.

'You mean, when you led us into that den of fairies? Too right, I did,' snorted the fisherman. 'And you watch your tone – there are too many secrets on this canoe to start using accusing tones with people.'

'What secrets?' asked Ru, suspiciously.

'That's for me to know and you to find out.'

'Don't tempt me,' said the prince. 'I haven't burned the soles of someone's feet for a long time.'

Polahiki looked put out by this and went to another part of the pahi, to lie under the umbrella of a lo lop palm leaf. Titopika decided to let the whole thing drop. The fisherman was right. If he, Titopika, started taking Polahiki to task, revelations might follow, and things would be none too comfortable for the tohunga. Better to leave things as they were and continue with the long-term plan, which *was* making progress, if a little slowly.

Ru was now making an inventory of their stores. They had only one dog left which had recently been on heat and had been made pregnant by Dirk, who was called a 'libertine and profligate' in Gaelic by Dorcha as a result. It seemed sensible to keep this animal until they reached their destination island, in order to breed her puppies. There were three pigs, which would be used as sacrifices as well as for food. Also, there were over three dozen chickens, which provided eggs and some meat for the basket.

The vegetable larder had now been restocked with pandanus fruit, green bananas, yam, taro pudding and sweet potatoes. Ru had been given turtle eggs and turtle meat by the villagers, as a gift for the people who had slain the taniwha. From the old stores they still had plenty of hard poi, dried breadfruit, dried bananas, sugarcane, arrowroot flour, nyali nuts and coconuts in various stages. There was also plenty of dried skipjack and akule reef fish.

As for fresh fish, Polahiki and one or two others would provide. Unfortunately, they had no shark-callers on board, like the great Aputua who had sailed with Prince Tangiia, but the number of people on board was not great, and the odd hammerhead or grey shark was caught without the need of callers. Turtle kebabs would fill any menu that was short of fish or meat, and there was always jellyfish, cuttle-fish and other surface sealife to gather in the trailing nets as they went.

'We must now make a sacrifice to the Great Sea-God Tangaroa,' ordered Ru, 'before we go out to battle the sea-fairies.'

Every member on board the pahi took part in the prayers, worship of the gods being a group activity. Afterwards, individuals went to various parts of the pahi to pray to their own ancestor spirits for victory and a safe voyage.

One or two called on the demi-gods, such as Maui, or his sister Hine-uri (the dark form of the moon), though not the two together for Maui's sister had been angry with her brother since the time Maui had changed her husband Ira-waru into a dog, for eating the bait which Maui wanted for his fishing hook.

Ru ordered his virgin crew to raise the sails of the pahi, one on either mast. The pandanus mats filled with wind. Then Ru put on his cloak of feathers, and his feathered helmet, took up a patu club in one hand and a spear in the other.

Others armed themselves, all except Kikamana the kahuna, Titopika the tohunga, and Dorcha with her occult powers: these three held the bones found in the belly of the taniwha and would beat them together while chanting karakia. The three magicians had surrounded themselves with Ti'i to protect them from the sea-fairies while the battle raged around them and also to assist them in their spells.

Seumas had a wahaika club which he would wield double-handed, while Dirk guarded his back.

'Let go the anchor!' cried Ru.

This done the vessel lurched forward, skimming over the slick grey waters of the enchanted lagoon and out into the open sea.

Immediately the pahi had crossed over the reef the sea began to boil with silver-grey bodies as the Ponaturi rose up in their hordes to attack *The Princely Flower*.

PART FOUR

People of the
darkness

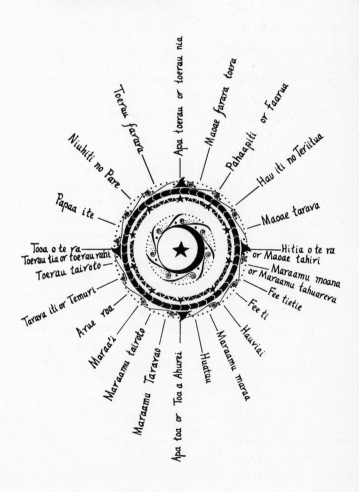

1

By the time the Arioi fleet arrived in Tonga, having been to Fiji and Samoa, Kumiki was a Hua, an Arioi of the fourth class. On his shoulders he proudly displayed the tattooed figures which denoted his rank. His friend, Ramoro, was also a Hua, and thus Kumiki had caught him up and intended to pass him by and become at least an Otiore, a second-class Arioi. Since Ramoro was not an ambitious man, this feverish ride to the top was not a hindrance to their friendship.

'You have done wonders, my friend, especially for a Hivan,' said Ramoro. 'Especially for a man with dark-red hair and a pale skin.' He was not speaking out of bitterness, but was genuinely happy for his comrade.

The truth was the Arioi was essentially Tahitian and ninety-five per cent of its players were from the Tahitian island group. Men and women from other island groups were permitted to join, but they were regarded as slightly inferior to the Tahitians, whose culture was full of colour and light, wonderful ceremonies, and the splendour and opulence of a wealthy, divine kingship.

Only such islands as Tahiti or Hawaii, with their love of display and their reverence of dancing, acting and games, could have produced the Arioi. The Tongans were pirates and sea raiders, the Samoans were too starchy and conservative and the Fijians were too fond of fighting to find time to develop such a marvellous troupe. Other island groups were either too remote, or too small, or just too busy living ordinary lives.

Indeed, Kumiki's home, the Hivan islands, had a smaller, looser circle of travelling players than the Arioi, called the Hoki, a wandering set of musicians, poets and dancers. But whereas the Arioi were a revered semi-religious group said to be of divine origin, the Hoki were despised by their own warrior nation as being effete and effeminate.

Hawaii could have produced an Arioi Society, but those islands were far off and though seafarers had touched their shores, all that came back were stories of wonderful courts, glittering ceremonies, and wild wars. The Hawaiians loved gambling too. They were a bright people: creative. Their temples were full of wicker images, marvellously interwoven with thousands of tiny feathers, the hideous mouths of which were doubled-looped, like a figure eight on its side.

So, Kumiki's pride in rising so quickly amongst the ranks of the Tahitian players was evident in his whole demeanour. This did him no harm, for its artistes were expected to be fine strutting characters, different from ordinary people.

The fleet of three hundred ships approached Heketa on the tip of Tongatapu. They made sure their yellow sails were in evidence in order to ensure that the fierce Tongans, eaters of men, would not mistake them for an invasion fleet. The singing and dancing, which never really stopped even on a long voyage, increased in fervour and energy.

'I must be at my drums,' said Kumiki to Ramoro. 'You go to your dancing.'

Kumiki had found his niche. After trying almost everything from wrestling to poetry, he had discovered in himself a talent for drumming. He was becoming a superb percussion musician, whose flying sticks were studied in awe by the less able drummers of the Arioi. Whence this natural skill had derived Kumiki had no idea, but his household deity was now Lingadua, the God of Drummers, whose single arm equalled a thousand mortal limbs in its ability to produce frenetic rhythms.

Kumiki knew there was more to drumming than just producing superb rolls, sustained highly imaginative rhythms and inventing new patterns. One had to be a showman too. In this Kumiki excelled, dressing himself dramatically in black tapa cloth, and using athletic movements. His fitness was essential to his act, since he did somersaults, high leaps, and handsprings when leaping from drum to drum. He had an assistant now, a woman named Linloa, who tossed him drumsticks and changed his instruments at crucial times during his act, and indeed made suggestions for enhancing his performance.

Linloa was a Harotea, a third-class dancer in her own right, and she was in love with Kumiki.

As the fleet approached the beach the Tu'i Tonga, the lord of the islands, was waiting in his chair. His mana was great since he was ruler of one of the most feared fleets in the whole of Oceania. The Tongans believed themselves to be superior people, warriors first and last, and even though they owned no large trees (their land being coral reef islands and not heavily forested) they had managed to pillage the wood they needed from neighbouring Fiji to build the fiercest navy on the ocean. They were raiders, and sometimes mercenaries when Samoan or Fijian chiefs needed support, and other island groups fearfully kept watch for the Tongan canoes, hoping never to see them appear in their waters.

The Arioi landed on the beach and the dancers and flautists leapt ashore to entertain the king, while the others were left to unload the equipment and stores.

'You carry the big drum,' ordered Kumiki to Linloa, 'while I get the smaller ones ashore.'

Linloa did as she was bid, but when she jumped down into the surf carrying the large drum, a Tongan man rushed forward and tried to take it from her.

'We do not allow women to do the hard work,' he admonished Kumiki. 'Women are delicate creatures to be cherished and protected.'

'Release that drum,' ordered Kumiki, 'it is a valuable instrument. I am not a Tongan, I am a Hivan. This woman is not a Tongan, she is a Tahitian. You will therefore allow us to be the judge of whether she should carry the drum or not.'

The man scowled darkly. 'You may not be Tongans, Redhair, but you are on our soil. You are expected to respect our customs while you are here, or there may be trouble.'

'I respect your customs,' replied Kumiki, leaping down into the surf and striding onto the beach. 'I would not dream of asking one of your women to help me with my drums. This lady is trained in drum-carrying. She is an expert. In her hands what would be a heavy load for a man, is light and easy, for she has the knack of carrying drums. In fact, you could say she is the top drum-carrier in all of Oceania.'

The man's eyes narrowed. He was tall and lean, with supple movements. In his hand he carried a patu club.

'You are making fun of me, Hivan. Be careful. I do not take insults lightly.'

'I should think not. Insults are heavy things to carry. Much heavier than drums. I always ask Linloa to bear my insults. They're far too weighty for me.'

The man's eyes opened wide in anger and he drew back his paddle club to strike Kumiki. However, a shout came from behind him and he stayed his hand. One of the island's nobles had intervened.

'Tuloa, these people are our guests!' cried the noble.

The warrior lowered the raised weapon, but stared hard

at Kumiki. There was the strong suggestion in that stare which carried a message of a future meeting. Kumiki shrugged and shook his head slowly. Tuloa walked away.

'Funny ideas these people have,' muttered Kumiki to Ramoro and Linloa later, as they sat around a fire in the darkness. 'Where do they get these peculiar notions about women from? Hivan females are almost as strong as the men.'

Ramoro said, 'It is just their way. Who's to argue with them? They are a ferocious people.'

'So are we Hivans,' replied Kumiki, proudly, 'but our women work in the fields, carry water from the streams and do all kinds of heavy tasks. Why should they not? I think the arrogance of these Tongans is hard to bear. Have you ever been treated with such lofty disdain before in your life?'

Linloa poked the fire with a twig. She had eaten on reef fish and coconut and was feeling pleasant. Later Kumiki would make love with her. She felt no resentment towards him for treating her as a servant, but she could also see the Tongan point of view. Why should they not refuse to let their women do heavy manual labour? Every woman here was a princess.

'I don't think they mean any harm,' she said. 'It's just their way – they're a proud people. I – I think the women look very pretty, don't you, Kumiki? They don't have rough hands from digging and their complexions are softer, since they seem to stay out of the sun more.'

'Well, crazy ideas or not, that Tuloa had better keep out of my way, or I'll show him who is the great warrior,' promised Kumiki.

'You Hivans,' remarked the impressed Ramoro. 'You're just as strong-headed as the Tongans.'

The next day the whole troupe was engaged in building the mighty stage, as long as seventy men lying toe to head, on which most of their performances would take place.

Some of the Tongans assisted in building the stage. Both Kumiki and Linloa were engaged in carrying planks, strapping together posts, and fitting joints. While they worked storytellers entertained them, with tales of Pele the Fire-thrusting Goddess of Volcanoes, Maui and his tricks, Tawhaki, Rata, and other gods and demi-gods.

Kumiki and Linloa heard the story of Hutu, the man whose love had died, who went into the Underworld to fetch her back again:

'You know of the Underworld', began the storyteller, 'for it exists under our feet. You will recall the time Maui pulled up one of his house posts and looked down the hole. Maui was amazed to see his ancestors below, carrying on their daily tasks in the life beyond this one.

'So it was then, that Hutu, a young nobleman, but not of very high birth, was playing darts near the house of a puhi, a high-born virgin, whose tapu was so strong there was not a man in the land noble enough to be her husband. The pahi's name was Pare, and she dwelt alone in a beautiful house set aside for her use only and protected by three sets of palisades.

'Pare wanted for nothing material. There were plaited flax mats on the floors of her dwelling, made white by boiling. Its rooms were scented with the fragrance of kopuru moss and karetu grass, and perfume from kawakawa and tarata. Her clothes were wonderful cloaks with black borders and long black thrums, some made from the hair of dogs' tails plaited into the thick strong selvage.

'However, she was a puhi, and it seemed would never marry, and for this reason she was dreadfully unhappy. She saw only high-ranking servants, who gave her food, and the birds of the garden. In this garden she wandered during the day, weeping for the unknown lover she could never meet.

'Now one of the darts thrown by the youth Hutu, who was a handsome and intelligent young man, passed through the gate of Pare's house. He went to the fence and called to whoever was in the garden to return his dart. Pare looked through a crack in the fence and saw the beautiful young man and fell instantly in love with him. She tossed him back his dart and then cried, "I have formed an affection for you. Come into my house."

'Hutu, however, was afraid, for he knew this house belonged to a puhi and he knew the punishment for attempting to consort with a virgin of so high a rank.

'"I cannot," he said. "I am a stranger here and must obey the customs of your people."

'So he went away, troubled in heart and mind, and later the tribal elders came for him to execute him, for Pare had died in the night of sorrow, and they blamed Hutu for her death.

'When they took him to see the body Hutu was struck by her amazing beauty, and when he remembered her voice he too was overcome by sorrow.

'"Leave her body here," he said, "for I shall make the journey into the Underworld and retrieve her spirit."

'So saying he chanted a karakia taught him by a tohunga and when he rose he walked down into Te Reinga, the Land of the Dead, where Hine-nui-te-po sits as guardian. On reaching her, Hutu told her his story and the goddess took pity on him and pointed to the path used by the spirits of dogs when they journeyed to the Underworld. Hutu then gave her a mere of greenstone, a jewel which pleased her, and she then allowed him to use the path for the souls of men. She prepared him a basket of Ngaro, in case he became hungry in the Underworld, but Hutu was eager only for the soul of Pare and did not eat.

'When Hutu reached the Land of the Dead he asked for Pare and was shown to a village. Pare was still upset with Hutu though and even now he had come to fetch her from

the Underworld, she would not come out to see him. So
Hutu organised some games amongst his ancestors, who
delighted in the sports they had left behind them in the
real world. While Hutu was throwing darts, he let one fly
purposely through the doorway of Pare's house where it
stuck to the wall. She laughed on seeing his dart again and
came out to meet him. They hugged and rubbed noses and
professed their love for one another.

'Soon it was time for Hutu and Pare to return to the real
world, but the path back to life was so complicated and
tangled that it was impossible to retrace one's journey.
Hutu however had an idea. He asked his ancestors to bend
down the tallest palm tree near the village and tie it with
ropes. When they had done this he took Pare on his shoulders, climbed into the bushy head of the coconut palm and
ordered the severing of the rope. Hutu and Pare were catapulted towards the roof of the Underworld, where Hutu
gripped the turf and roots of this world and finally hauled
himself and his new bride into the light.

'When Hutu returned with Pare the people said he was a
great man, of considerable mana, and allowed the couple to
live together as husband and wife.

'And that is the story of Hutu and Pare.'

The platform was completed in a day and that evening the
performances began. Tongans from all over the islands
came in their canoes to witness the dancing, the wrestling,
the tumbling, and to listen to the poets, the musicians, the
songs. Once again Kumiki astounded the audience with his
phenomenal skill on the drums, leaping from small drum to
large drum, from log drum to skin drum, pounding out
natural and artificial rhythms. Even the Tu'i Tonga was
impressed and asked to meet this young man with the pale
skin and dark red hair. Kumiki went before the Tu'i Tonga,
careful to keep his head lower than the king's, staying at a
safe distance from the king's mana.

'You are my special guest here,' said the Tu'i Tonga. 'You may have what you wish – food, female company, any present you choose for yourself, it shall be yours.'

'Thank you, my lord,' said Kumiki, his heart full.

Of course there were several other 'special guests' of the Tu'i Tonga, who had pleased the king with their performances, but none so gratified as Kumiki. That night he slept with a local girl who giggled and kept him awake, while unknown to him Linloa spent a miserable night lying alone.

Tuloa the Tongan who had formed an enmity for Kumiki cursed his luck, for he could no longer kill Kumiki with a group of his friends as he had planned earlier, without falling foul of his king. A special guest was protected by the king's decree and if anything untoward happened to Kumiki while he was in Tonga, those responsible would answer to the king's personal guard.

'If I ever see him again,' snarled the thwarted Tuloa, 'I swear I shall cut out his liver.'

His ancestors sympathised deeply, but what could they do?

The sea-fairies came in silvery-skinned hordes, attempting to swamp *The Princely Flower* with their vile bodies, but the crew and passengers beat them back with clubs, and chopped off their gripping fingers with sharp shells, while Boy-girl, Kikamana, Dorcha and Titopika sat one on each corner of the pahi and clashed the bones together and chanted karakia.

During the battle three of *The Princely Flower*'s passengers were dragged overboard. They died screaming in the mass of fairy bodies, torn apart before the eyes of the rest of the mortals. The Ponaturi were merciless once they had you in their strong hands. They stripped the flesh from your bones quicker than barracuda and left the sea stained red with clouds of blood. They pulled arms from sockets, legs from joints, opened the abdomen with their sharp talons, devoured the pieces even as they fought for more human bodies to rip and tear. One creature was chewing on the flap of a dead man's cheek when Seumas severed its head from its body with his kotiate club.

As the fairy's head floated away on a pool of ambergris its jaws continued to masticate mechanically, out of habit.

The canoe ploughed through the water, helped by Maomao's wind, and gradually the Ponaturi began to fall back. The deck was littered with their finger-claws, their crushed skulls floated on the waves of the sea. Their sundered limbs and fingers wriggled like silver fish, attempting to rejoin their bodies.

One or two fairies kept their grip on the craft. They gnashed their teeth, and thrashed their clawed limbs, but to no avail; *The Princely Flower* was soon surging forward over the surface of the ocean, out into sweeter waters. A few more hacks from clubs and adzes and the last Ponaturi slipped away.

'Well done, my comrades,' cried Ru. 'We have escaped the clutches of those horrible creatures. Now we must set sail for Rarotongan waters again.'

Even as he spoke the wind picked up in strength, but it was not a wind of Maomao's making, it was a false wind created by Tawhiri-Matea. The Storm-God had brought with him two of his brothers, Apu Hau, God of the Fierce Squall, and Apu Mantangi, God of the Howling Rain. They began to lash the pahi canoe furiously, creating a chaos of white and dark. Forest-high waves rose around the canoe, which was suddenly very small in the midst of the fury generated by the three gods.

The twenty virgins, strong and able, worked at the rigging and the sails. Seumas and the other passengers crowded into the deck hut, keeping out of the way of the busy maidens. Ru stood by the mast, directing his crew, sometimes managing the steering oar himself, at other times lending a hand with a slack or wayward sheet. The women worked tirelessly, their purity assisting their stamina, magnificent in their efforts.

Divested of their garments, which tended to get tangled in ropes and other equipment, the rain whipped at the skins of the naked maidens, ran in rivulets down their backs and breasts, streamed from their brows, soaked their long hair which plastered itself to their shapely forms. If the situation had not been so precarious, Seumas might have been lost in sexual fantasies, as he watched these beautiful nude females plying their sailing skills. Instead he was appalled by the severity of the storm, and was simply glad they were mariners whose mastery of their trade was keeping the pahi from plunging into the ocean depths.

Lightning flashed – Uira darting from the armpits of a watching Tawhaki – illuminating the turbulent darkness. Lithe bodies gleamed in the brilliance. Then the thunder crashed, punching the belly of the sky, robbing Rangi of wind for a moment. Colours patterned the leaping waters, running like live creatures over the dark hills of the sea. Hollows appeared in front of the pahi as the ocean sucked in its stomach.

Try as they might though, the storm brothers could not sink the pahi with its proficient crew, and gradually they tired. First Apu Hau, God of the Fierce Squall, began to flag, he being the one who expended the most energy in the shortest time. He left to go and sleep. Then Apu Mantangi, God of the Howling Rain, ceased his screaming. Finally, the leveller of forests, the lasher of waves, Tawhiri-Matea, could no longer find the strength to stir the ocean, and he too sought a haven of rest. Tawhaki had to be satisfied with the thought that *The Princely Flower* had been flung even further into unknown waters, and that Captain Ru would be well and truly lost.

The first thing Ru did was thank his crew for their expert seamanship. Then he offered prayers of thanks to Tiki, for his part in seeing them through the storm. Finally the whole pahi offered prayers to Tangaroa, who had not swallowed them despite the opportunity, but was still their patron.

Ru did his best to find the right stars that night, but the kaveinga were unknown to him. He sought any local te lapa beneath the waves without success. The shape of the waves, the direction of the swell, meant nothing to him. They had gone well off the edge of Dorcha's bamboo and shell chart, so this was of no use to them. Even the fixed stars, the fanakenga, were in strange positions and of little assistance to him in his navigating. The constellations were little help – Ru found Ara Toru, the Path of Three, and Te Rua Tangata, the Double Man, but they were on the edge of the sky and not in a familiar position.

The morning brought a little more success. Po'oi had inherited his father's skill, that of the Feelers-of-the-sea, and found the waters warmer than deep ocean would suggest. There was a cloud in the distance: the kind of cloud which hangs over a mountain peak. In the briny there was driftwood and in the skies some red-footed boobies. Land was nearby.

'Even though this atoll is in the wrong part of the ocean,' said Ru as they approached the ring of low islands, 'we may settle here if things are as we wish them.'

There were eight long islands in the circle. Around the whole atoll was a ring of coral, making for a massive lagoon in the centre, but each island also had its own reef and its own lagoon facing the ocean. Between the islands there were either tidal sweeps of deep water or a ridge of coral just below some shallow water which could be used as a pathway.

In the middle of the atoll's lagoon was a greater island, making the ninth in the whole group. Thus there were eight elongated islands coming from a central round body. Ru, or some other member of the party, might have guessed what this place was from the mere shape of the landscape.

'This seems like a good place,' said Ru, smelling the

fragrance of sandalwood on the breeze. 'A low set of islands, but with some large trees.'

They rode the breakers over the reef, to enter the outer lagoon of the largest outer island, and all seemed well enough. However, as they approached the beach they saw what they first thought were millions of crabs. On closer inspection, these turned out not to be crustaceans, but spiders. The nearer they drew to the strand, the thicker seemed the number of spiders. Every conceivable type of arachnid seemed to live on that shore, from tiny creatures with minuscule spinnerets, to massive weighty lumps with large unsegmented bodies.

'Ugghh.' Dorcha shuddered. 'I can't stand them.'

'Look at them,' said Boy-girl, equally uncomfortable. 'All different kinds. There are some with yellow-and-black legs – big ones – I hate those. And the red bulbous ones. And some with long hair. My cockerel, Lei-o-mano, can have a feast. Millions of them. What is this place?'

Kikamana said, 'This must be the earthly home of Nareau, the Spider-God. See, they're all over the trunks of the trees and there are nests of them in the palm leaves. Look at those webs – thousands of them – hanging between the fronds.'

'I am not stepping ashore here,' said Dorcha in a determined voice. 'I refuse to go amongst those – those creatures.'

Ru ordered the sounding of the tai-moana, the ship's long drum, to scare the spiders from the beach. Indeed, this worked, for when the drum was sounded the spiders scuttled away, into the hinterland, leaving the sands clear. Dorcha still refused to leave the canoe, but Seumas went with the landing party, accompanied by Dirk, who had been kept tied while the vessel had been at anchor off the island of the taniwha. The dog was restless and needed a good run. Dirk was not frightened of spiders, of course, and delighted in chasing some of the bigger ones up the trunks of trees, leaving him to bark at them.

Seumas was secretly pleased that both Kikamana and Dorcha were too frightened to step ashore amongst the spiders. It gave him a chance to prove himself again, retrieve a little of his lost honour and dignity, left behind on the island of the taniwha. He said nothing to the two women, but held his head high, kept his face grave, and stepped ashore without a falter.

The two women and Boy-girl, along with half the crew and passengers, male and female, waded the shallows of the lagoon searching for shellfish while the shore party went on its way. There were no spiders to bother them in the water. There were deadly stone fish, whose poisonous spines could kill within a minute or two, toothed moray eels as thick as a man's thigh and smoky sting rays that hid in the grey coral dust. These they would brave – but not spiders. They gathered the bounty of the ocean: cones, spires, conches, cowries, turbans, combs, razors and other molluscs, risking death in unknown shallows.

Ru stayed with the canoe, to await the shore party's report when they returned. The leader of the shore party was Pungarehu, the man who had killed the Poukai bird on the voyage with Tangiia. He stayed close to Seumas, being an old friend. They fought their way forward with difficulty, through the sometimes thick nets of webs that were spread between trees.

As they neared the centre of the island the spiders became bigger and uglier, until they were the size of small pigs. The arachnids stared with their four pairs of compound eyes, their several jaws working like mechanical devices.

Some would stand their ground, while others rushed away into the undergrowth, timid creatures on spindly legs.

They lit torches with a flint, partly because it was dark under the canopy, and partly to keep away the spiders.

They entered a large clearing with soft green light falling on the surface of a still pool.

'Look out,' cried Pungarehu, shouting a warning to Seumas. 'On your left flank!'

Seumas turned to see a giant black spider charging at him like a wild boar, bearing down on him with terrifying speed on its eight bamboo-like legs. Seumas saw the jaws working and salivating, and knew he might lose a limb if he was not quick. The rest of the party including Dirk scattered, running for the trees, unsure of whether or not they would meet equally horrifying spiders inside the woods and rocks.

The Pict stepped to one side and swung his club, bringing the weapon down with great force onto the spider's back. The creature buckled in the middle, as if made of tree bark, and spilled its innards on the mossy floor. Out of its stomach poured thousands of tiny white spiders, which swarmed over Seumas, biting him with the severity of wasp stings. They seemed to be going for his earholes and nostrils, trying to enter his body by his several orifices.

'Ow, ow!' the Pict yelled, slapping at them.

Pungarehu came rushing back out of the trees, carrying a torch of dry grass. He ran it quickly over Seumas's body, not lingering long enough to burn him, but ensuring that the spiders either frizzled or ran. Some became tangled in the Pict's long hair and Pungarehu removed these like someone picking lice from their friend's head. They bit his fingers, making him yell too. Dirk did not come out of hiding until all the white spiders had disappeared.

'A lot of help you were,' yelled Seumas at the dog. 'Get on with you.'

Dirk cowered and slunk ahead, aware that his cowardice was unworthy of him.

They caught up with the rest of the party, who had by now lit more brands. It was the most effective way of removing the cobwebs from their path and keeping the spiders at bay. Compound eyes shone from the darkness of the trees. Millions of them. The spiders watched but kept their distance, secure in the knowledge that this island was their home, a sanctuary of Nareau the Spider-God, the weaver of sticky silken ropes on which he hung mortals like pendulum weights. When Seumas looked up through the canopy, he saw thousands more of the tinier spiders, using threads like kites to carry themselves along on the breeze. They seemed to be heading towards the anchored canoe.

'I hope those women don't take over the ship and run,' he muttered to Pungarehu. 'I wouldn't want to be stranded on *this* place for very long.'

Finally the group reached a central clearing in the island where they were surprised to see a long hut raised on stilts, as long as a hundred men laid toe to head, and very wide. It was made of the trunks of trees plugged along the gaps with mud. There were no windows and no visible doors. The roof was thatched more sturdily than usual. It looked for all the world as if this were a solid structure, with no entrances.

'What do you think it is?' asked Seumas. 'A store house of some kind?'

'That's what it looks like,' remarked one of the crew, a tall woman carrying a spear. 'But I've never seen a store house that size before. Either this place has a large population hidden away somewhere . . .'

'Or it's a land of giants,' muttered Pungarehu, looking around him nervously.

They went forward to inspect the hut and found some tightly fitting trap doors underneath. There were no handles however, with which to open these doors, as one might expect. Moreover, there were steps leading down from them, as if this was a place to enter and leave, rather than allow dried foodstuffs to spill out into sacks or some other kind of container.

Carvings adorned the exterior of the long house, of moons, stars, comets and meteors. There was the figure of Hine-nui-te-po, Lady of Darkness, on one end of the hut and Hine-uri, the goddess of the dark phase of the moon, on the other end. Black dye covered the whole building, even underneath. The space beneath the hut was hidden by dark flaps of cloth pinned to the edges of the floor.

'This is very puzzling,' remarked Pungarehu.

Darkness had begun to sweep in swiftly, as it does in tropical regions, where the sun drops down behind the wall of the ocean like a hawk stooping for its prey. Soon the torches were needed for something other than keeping spiders at bay. No sooner had the light disappeared, than the trap doors began to open beneath the hut. The shore party retreated to the trees, quickly snuffed their brands because they would surely be seen, and there they waited to see what or who would emerge from this long house in the middle of spider country.

The people who came out – if they could be called real people – were pallid and wan creatures. They drifted over the ground rather than walked, like evening ghosts. They carried no lamps or brands, yet they seemed able to see their way without difficulty in starlight. Once outside, it was as if they had just woken from a long sleep. They stretched and yawned, then stared at the sky as if watching the dawn come up, while they slaked their thirst from gourds which hung from lines on trees.

Pungarehu, Seumas and the others watched hidden in the trees, curious as to the nature of these strange people.

The children came out of the long house and almost immediately began playing games, in the way that children do, probably having been eager to be out for some time now. They played hunt the shoe, blind man's buff, played with spinning tops and various other games which seem universal amongst the young. The older female children juggled expertly with kukui nuts, while others stood around and chanted rhymes until a nut was dropped.

No rough games were begun, however, such as the ball games played on Rarotonga and Raiatea, in which women and men sometimes broke limbs in the scramble to get the ball over the goal line, especially since there was no limit on the number of players.

Curiously, no fires were lit and the wan people seemed to keep to the shadows of the hut. There was no moon but there was the starlight, though even this seemed too bright for the islanders. They shaded their eyes when they crossed open ground, as one might do in intense tropical sunlight. Some of the shore party began to wonder whether they were witnessing the activities of creatures from the spirit world. Yet the local people seemed simply blanched rather than insubstantial: their movements were not the motions of ethereal creatures.

Although there were no open flames, umu were used, and the smell of roast pork, baked chicken and edible rat came wafting over to the group in the trees, making their stomachs churn in anticipation of a feast. Eventually Pungarehu decided they should make their presence known to the islanders, before they were discovered accidentally. The group stepped out of the trees.

'Hello,' cried Pungarehu. 'We are visitors here – can we share your food?'

The result of this call was electrifying. All movement amongst the wan people stopped immediately. If someone had dropped dead on the spot the response would probably not have been different. Then the children took to their heels, running towards the hut. Some of the adults too, made off. The braver ones stood their ground while Pungarehu and Seumas approached, leaving the rest of the party on the tree line.

They went first to an old man, who stood quaking by an umu.

'Sir,' said Pungarehu politely, 'forgive the intrusion. We are not hostile. We are seafarers lost on the wide ocean and have come across your island by sheer chance. Is it possible to sit and talk with you?'

Once the old man had been assured he would not be harmed, he seemed to settle down a little. He called to others, younger men and women, who now approached the pair cautiously. Although Pungarehu and Seumas carried arms, there were no weapons of war in evidence amongst the wan people, and Seumas wondered if they were an entirely peaceful people. Perhaps they did not even hunt, but took their meat entirely from domestic livestock?

The first question the old man asked was a strange one.

'Are you day-people?' he said.

'Day-people?' questioned Pungarehu. 'What do you mean by that?'

'Do you go abroad during the light hours?'

'Of course we do,' said Pungarehu. 'Doesn't everyone?'

The old man and some of the others shook their heads.

'We do not. We are the people of the darkness. Our bodies dissolve in strong light.'

Seumas doubted the truth of this last statement, though he was quite sure the old man believed it to be the truth. The Pict felt that perhaps these people had got into the habit of staying out of the sunlight for some reason and now *believed* the light would harm them. Back in the old country of Albainn there had been an eremite who entered a cave in the mountains. He lived on worms and fungi, and bits and pieces brought to him by outsiders. After a few months he convinced himself that he could not go out of the cave again, telling visitors that his body would fall to pieces in the open air.

This was surely much the same situation. Perhaps these people had been driven into their hut as a means of protection and had grown dependent on the darkness? That seemed more likely than the bizarre idea that they would disappear if struck by the sun's rays.

'Would you like to eat with us?' asked one of the young men. 'Tell us news of the outside world. Because of what we are we cannot travel like you day-people. We would be honoured to have you share at our baskets.'

Pungarehu accepted on behalf of the whole shore party.

They were led to the area beneath the stilted hut. A flap was rolled up to allow them entrance. When they were all underneath, the black flap was dropped again leaving them in complete darkness. Seumas was suddenly suspicious of their situation. A panic began to rise in his throat. Nothing but blackness all around: no sense of who lay where. The whole shore party could be slaughtered here, where they could not see. There was no room to manoeuvre. Claustrophobia overwhelmed him. He drew his dagger and took up a fighting stance, wondering from which direction in the blackness the attack might come.

'Pungarehu! Are you still here? Hello! What's happening? Are we being attacked? To me, Pungarehu! To me, man. Here, here. Hello?'

2

Seumas felt a hand descend on his shoulder.

'What?' he cried, jumping.

'It's all right,' came back the voice of Pungarehu. 'It's me. Once your eyes get used to the darkness, it'll be fine. I don't think these people trust us. They don't like the light – and having lived in the darkness for so long, they can see quite plainly in it.'

Seumas was not happy. 'The feeling's mutual. I don't trust them, either. And I don't like being surrounded by people I don't trust in a dark, confined place.'

'They have no weapons,' reminded Pungarehu. 'If they try anything, we can give as good as we get. Just settle down and try to get some rest.'

Pungarehu was the leader of the shore party, so Seumas did as he was told. After a while his eyes did indeed get a little more used to the darkness and he saw shapes moving around, carrying platters of food. He stayed on the alert, expecting an attack at any moment. He had his club and would use it if he had to. Pungarehu was not so concerned and was tucking into fruit and vegetables.

'Keep your wits about you, man,' whispered Seumas, wondering if the right leader for the shore party had been chosen. This is not a good time to relax.'

But Pungarehu had his eyes on one of the local women and he waved Seumas away impatiently.

'Stop worrying,' he said. 'I've got one hand on my club.'

Seumas snarled, 'Which club is that, man? The one between your legs?'

Pungarehu ignored this remark.

Seumas was given a plate of banana porridge, but he scraped it away surreptitiously, fearing poison. All the while, he was aware of being watched intently. Perhaps these people might be without weapons, but they could fall on him in numbers and beat him to death with their fists, or strangle him in the dark. To Seumas the situation was highly volatile.

While he was eating something struck him as extremely odd and he asked one of his hosts warily, 'Why are there no spiders in here? Elsewhere, the island's covered in them.'

'You must not have seen the carvings of Nareau which surround our village area. The Spider-God keeps his creatures from our house. We are not afraid of spiders, but they get into everything – into the soup and sticky fruit – so it's best they remain outside the village.'

'I quite agree. I wish we'd done the same thing,' said Seumas, but the man failed to hear the irony in his tone.

When the meat came round, Seumas's appetite got the better of him. He asked, 'Is that pork or dog? I don't eat dog meat.'

'Pork,' came the reply. 'Here, smell.'

Having smelled he decided to trust to the God Rongo that it was not poisoned.

It was indeed succulent pork, roasted crisp and even, and pungent with the odour of singed bristles.

The women, as in most Oceanian societies, did not eat with the men, but sat in their own group. They were not allowed pork or dog meat, only fish and shellfish. It was a taboo which Dorcha did not mind respecting, since she had never much cared for meat anyway. Occasionally she had deliberately eaten with the men, to show them that they were not special, but since she was a strange person from the Land-of-Mists she had been allowed to get away with it. When she and Seumas were alone together, she ate with him as a matter of course.

Seumas found the pork running with the hot fatty juices of the roasted pig. It was delicious. The first taste, for a long time, was delectable. Pork fat dribbled down his chin, onto his chest. He discovered the joint was stuffed with wild herbs and wild bananas. There was fermented poi on the side. Baked yams to follow. Fresh spring water was available to wash it all down. He ate until he was near bursting. Then he rolled over and unfortunately fell asleep, having had an exhausting day getting to the night-people's village.

He woke much later to find a figure wielding a weapon standing over him. Seumas reached quickly for his own club and was about to swing it up at the crotch of the man who threatened him, when he saw it was Pungarehu. He gave a shout of annoyance at having nearly crippled his friend.

'What is it? Why are you standing over me like that? You crazy fool, I almost killed you.'

Pungarehu sounded distracted.

'They've run back to their long house. I think they have weapons there. We should get back to the ship.'

Pungarehu threw back the flap and sunlight flooded in, hurting Seumas's eyes.

'It's morning,' said Seumas. 'They can't follow us in the light, can they? I don't understand it? Why didn't they kill us while we were asleep if they wanted to?'

'We didn't sleep,' said Pungarehu, indicating some of the shore party. 'They turned nasty just before the dawn, but we couldn't wake those of you who ate the pork. It must have been something in the herb stuffing. Some of us avoided eating that, since it was the obvious place to put a poison or a drug, in something with a strong overpowering taste.'

Seumas felt guilty. 'What happened next?'

'We stood over you,' said a young Raiatean. 'We stood around you, guarding you with our weapons. They shouted and waved their fists at us for a while. Then the dawn came and they had to go up into their long hut.'

Seumas was still bewildered. 'But why did they turn nasty all of a sudden? I mean, they could have attacked us when we first came into the darkness. I still don't understand.'

The young man glanced towards a spot on the ground. It was where Pungarehu had been sitting beside one of the local women when Seumas fell asleep. There appeared to be two depressions in the sand, quite close together. Looking up at Pungarehu now, he knew that the leader of the shore party had been indiscreet, had made love to one of the night people.

'Pungarehu, what have you done?' said Seumas.

Pungarehu looked angry. 'None of your business.'

'Of course it's my business. You've put the shore party in jeopardy. You knew these people did not trust us, were watching us like night hawks, yet you took one of their women? That's madness. They'll slaughter us now. Couldn't you curb your lust for one night?' growled Seumas, furiously.

The killer of the Poukai Bird looked shame-faced. 'I – I couldn't help myself. She is so beautiful. My arm was touching hers – soft, delicate skin against mine – I could smell her hair – it was driving me crazy, Seumas. We – we began by exploring each other secretly with our hands – and it led to more – and soon she came to sit on – on my lap, and she had nothing on under her loin cloth . . .' Pungarehu groaned.

'I don't want to hear any more,' growled Seumas.

The night-people had had to go into their lightless long house, but once the darkness came they would no doubt fall on the intruders and attempt to slaughter them. The shore party started back, battling their way through spiders once more and eventually reached the lagoon. Seumas found to his relief that they had not panicked and sailed away, but had dutifully waited for the shore party to return with their news.

Pungarehu made his report to Ru while Seumas sought out Dorcha, who was gathering shellfish and anemones in the lagoon. He found her lifting a rock with a hooked stick. A moray eel shot out from under it, snaking through the shallows to look for a new hiding place. Under the rock was a murex shell with occupant, which Dorcha popped into her basket.

'Oh, you're back,' she said, giving him a peck on the cheek. 'And what was my fine brave Pictish warrior doing out all night? Did you find people? Were there any women? I can smell pork fat on your breath. You've been feasting on piggies. Did you get drunk too? Was there any kava?'

'Not drunk, no. There was no booze. People, yes.'

She stared at him. 'Beautiful women?'

'To some they may have *seemed* beautiful, but to me, who has beauty at his fingertips in the form of a lovely Scots lass, why they were turtles by comparison.'

'Bletherer!'

'It's true. They couldn't hold a candle to you, my love. Besides, they were a sort of ghostly hue. Not my type at all. I like my beauty substantial.'

'And the other men and women? Did they think these people unattractive?'

'I can't vouch for all of them. I know Pungarehu slept with one of them. We're going to have to leave here as soon as we can because of it.'

'Pungarehu? The fool.'

'Yes, you'd think he had more sense, wouldn't you?'

'Men's brains are in their loins,' snorted Dorcha. 'I don't

think I'm really surprised at all. Are you sure you didn't bed one too? You look guilty.'

'I'm looking guilty because I was asleep while all this was happening. If I'd stayed awake I might have prevented it.'

She touched his cheek. 'I believe you, Pictish man. You're more sensible than most of them. Didn't used to be, but then you're older now. Wiser. And more handsome.'

'Now who's blethering?'

Dorcha bent to pick up a money cowrie. 'What are they like, these local women?'

'Strange as snow in summer. The men too. They hate the light. I think they believe daylight would melt them. It was only the coming of the dawn that saved us from attack.'

Seumas explained what had happened to them. Dorcha shuddered at the bit about the huge spider and acknowledged that she could not have stood her ground in the face of such a horror. Seumas knew better, however, since she had been attacked by the thing she feared the most – a giant snake – and had remained to support the Farseeing-virgin Kikamana. When he told her about the night-people, she was intrigued.

'You mean they *never* go out into the light?'

'Never,' confirmed Seumas. 'They think they would dissolve in the sun.'

'Hmmm, I'm inclined to believe what you said before, that they've been avoiding it for so long they've forgotten why. If one or the other of them disappears occasionally, when they go out into the light, it's probably because they're blinded and get lost in the forest. Probably get eaten by *spiders*. Ugghhhh. Anyway, you're all back safe and sound.'

'Safe and sound,' confirmed Seumas. 'You were right about the feasting though – we were fed like kings. I don't suppose they've had visitors in a long time. They were most hospitable at first – until one of their virgins was breached.'

When Ru heard about the strange night-people he

wanted to sail immediately. Pungarehu admitted he had violated the spider islanders' trust, but begged to be allowed one more visit to the long house, alone. It was obvious to most of the passengers and crew of the pahi by now that Pungarehu had found a soul mate amongst the weird people of the island. He made no secret of it.

Ru said he would wait until midnight only, then he would set sail, even if Pungarehu was not on board.

Seumas, Kieto and Boy-girl, basket-sharers, sat talking about it in the early evening. They still remained on the pahi because of the spiders. It was true that familiarity bred contempt, for Boy-girl was no longer afraid to go ashore. But the spiders got into everything, including human orifices, and it was unpleasant to sit around in a place where eight-legged nuisances were crawling all over you.

There was still the occasional attack by bigger spiders, whose bites were no doubt quite virulent, all spiders being poisonous by nature. Some of the littler arachnids floated out on threads, but a quick once over with a swat and the canoe was clear.

So, the three friends remained on board the pahi, and now sat around a low fire talking. They had their weapons in their hands, as did all the other people on board, expecting an attack from the strange night people. Seumas had strung his bow and had a quiver of arrows.

Pungarehu had gone to abduct his pale woman. Seumas had wisely decided not to accompany him, but he felt guilty about it. Pungarehu had said it was best he went alone. He had left a secret message with his paramour, telling her to meet him in the forest, once darkness fell. Pungarehu would meet her and they would run together towards the waiting pahi.

Seumas wondered at the wisdom of Ru, allowing this kidnapping to happen, but admitted privately to Dorcha that he still did not know these Oceanians whom he now called friends.

'What's it going to come to?' asked Boy-girl, in her throaty tones. 'I mean, it's all right if he just wants *sex*, but what if he's fallen in love with the creature?'

Seumas was never very comfortable talking about sexual matters with Boy-girl, who professed she wanted to experience the Pict's body more than anything else in the world.

Kieto replied, 'Yes, I know what you mean.'

'I think he should just stick it to her and then wave bye-bye,' sniffed Boy-girl, twirling one of her many dangling ribbons around her forefinger. 'What do you think, Seumas?'

Seumas felt uncomfortable with the question.

'Me? Oh, I don't know. Ask somebody else.'

'No, come on – do you think he should just—'

'Look, Boy-girl,' said Seumas hotly, 'you know how I feel about these matters. I don't believe in sex for its own sake. I think it has to have a spiritual side to it. You have to be in love with someone to make it work properly.'

'You didn't think that when you first came to us.' Boy-girl sniffed again. 'You went through about twenty of our Raiatean maidens, just like that! I was absolutely amazed at your virility and capacity for sexual variety. You had no shame. I mean, twenty, in as many days. I think you set a record. Even we Oceanians, advanced as we are in sexual matters, thought that was a bit extreme. Were you in love with *all* of them?'

'That was different,' snapped Seumas, glowering. 'I was – I was very young in those days – irresponsible. And I was trying to teach Dorcha a lesson. After all, the first thing she did when she got to Raiatea was marry those stupid brothers.'

Kieto took up the teasing too, now that Boy-girl had Seumas on the run. 'Oh, so you didn't actually *enjoy* those women? You did it just to spite Dorcha. It must have been tough for you, making love when you didn't want to. Did you have problems with your potency?'

Seumas's manhood was now at stake. 'I don't say I didn't *want* to. I'm just saying it's much more pleasurable doing it with someone you're in love with.'

Boy-girl was grinning now. She smoothed out the skirt which covered her long lean legs. 'Better leave him alone now, Kieto, or we'll be getting challenged to single combat before the night's out. You know what he's like when it comes to sex. He's thoroughly inhibited.'

'I am not,' cried Seumas.

But the matter was dropped by mutual consent and they got to talking about their expedition to reach the Maori in the Otherworld beyond the Rapanui cave.

'We must be getting close to the island of the giants now,' Kieto said. 'Ru never expected to come this way, but as it was foretold to us, we have been pulled and pushed over the ocean by sharks, storms and all manner of strange winds and currents, until we are truly in unknown waters. Soon we shall step foot on Rapanui and our search for the cave begins. Are you both ready?'

'I'm ready,' Seumas replied.

'So am I,' replied Boy-girl.

The three friends clasped hands.

Seumas sometimes wondered if he should start to feel he was getting too old for this kind of adventure. His hair had begun now to turn silvery-white. He oiled it, making the excuse to Dorcha that he liked to smell fragrant for her, to darken it. Most of the skin on his shoulders was tattooed now, with sweeping lines of dark blue and black, which made the grey of his hair stand out more. His chest too, was covered with zig-zag lines, like the patterns on mats, and the nipples were the centre of great whorls which covered his hard pectral muscles. There were other lines which led to his thighs, where the serious tattooing began again, covering most of his thickly muscled legs. The crisp white bodily hair stood out in contrast to the candle-nut powder imbedded in his skin.

Yet, when he really thought about it, the great Kupe was an old man of seventy before he gave up long sea voyages. King Tangiia's father, once ruler of Raiatea and Borabora, was an old man before he stopped testing himself on the ocean. Why, so long as the air was clean, the sea was warm and the skies were bright blue, why not seek adventure? It wasn't as if Seumas was trying to be young again. He didn't mind being old. But he would mind being put out to grass, like a veteran donkey.

At around midnight there was a shout from the beach. Seumas and everyone else leapt to their feet, weapons in hand. Soon Pungarehu came paddling furiously towards them in a dugout canoe, a delicate pale figure in the boat with him. The pair were being pursued by about a hundred ghostly warriors, with slings in their hands.

The night people first let fly from the beach, showering the water around the dugout with rocks and stones. Then they rushed to canoes, hidden in the foliage by the shore, to pursue Pungarehu on water.

Ru had already ordered his virgins to raise the sails and the pahi strained at anchor ropes, ready to leap forwards like a flying fish being chased by a shark.

The air was full of yells and threats, as Pungarehu finally reached the pahi and almost threw his abducted bride on board, where she was grasped by Ru. A stone struck Seumas on the shoulder, painfully. He saw that it had come from a spectre with a slingshot, standing up in the bows of a pursuing canoe. He fitted an arrow to his bow and fired at the man, hitting him in the foot, seeing with satisfaction that he fell back amongst those paddling his craft, thus disrupting their progress.

'Let's get out of here!' cried Ru. 'Let go the anchors!'

The order was obeyed and the pahi shot forwards, over the reef, and away from the island of spiders. Behind them they left shouting, screaming warriors, who wanted blood.

The islanders were to be disappointed.

Once they were out at sea, one of the two huts on the pahi's deck was converted. This hut had no windows. During the day it was to be occupied by Pungarehu's new wife, Wiama, who would lay under a thick blanket of pandanus leaves inside its walls.

For the first day or so the scabby Polahiki hung around the edges of the hut, hoping to be shut in with Wiama, not because he wanted her sexually, or because he was curious about what she did locked up in there all day long. He wanted to be shut in because no one could open the door during the day and he would not have to do any chores. Pungarehu chased him away saying that if he caught him hanging around the hut again, he would personally throw him overboard, where the fisherman could get all the rest and quiet he needed – for a whole eternity.

Wiama came out at night, a waif whose skin was almost luminous. Seumas could see the framework of her bones. On a full moon she stayed in the shadows. She claimed that Hine-keha's face was too brilliant for her, and blinded her. Wiama had made the penultimate sacrifice for love. She risked death on a daily basis, simply to be with her new husband, Pungarehu. She was fascinating to the rest of the people on board. You could see a taper through her hand. Her eyes were so pale they were almost white. Her skin was a network of blue veins and arteries, crazing her porcelain skin. Everyone saw her as some kind of fragile spirit who would one day simply shatter like a bird's egg before their eyes.

PART FIVE

Island of Giants

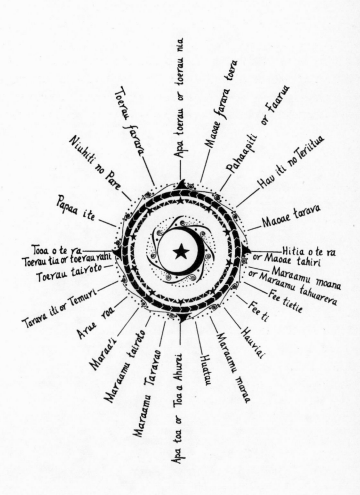

Toerau farara

Apa toerau or toerau nia

Maoae farara toera

Pahaapiti or faarua

Niuhiti no Pare

Hau iti no Teriitua

Papaa ite

Maoae tarava

Tooa o te ra

Hitia o te ra
or Maoae tahiri

Toerau tia or toerau rahi

Maraamu moana
or Maraamu tahuareva

Toerau tairoto

Fee tietie

Tarava iti or Temuri

Fee ti

Arue roa

Hauviai

Maraa'i

Maraamu maraa

Maraamu tairoto

Huatau

Maraamu Tararao

Apa toa or Toa a Ahurei

1

While resting at the spider islands, Ru had found and shaved a new mast to replace one damaged in the storm. There was a good wind behind them in the form of the goddess Hine-tu-whenua, whose benevolence was ever bountiful. The ship was heading in the direction of Fee tietie on the windflower, but since Ru did not know where they were on the vast face of the ocean, it was impossible to tell whether they would reach a destination. Polahiki was as usual despondent and negative, telling everyone they were going to their doom.

'The fish in these waters are strange. I think we're going to sail for ever and not find land.'

And indeed, it seemed that way. They appeared to be in a particularly empty quarter of the great ocean. Each day they searched the sky for cloud formations which would indicate land beneath them and found nothing but puffs of white and endless blue. At night the roof of voyaging kept its secrets close to its breast. Gradually they ate through their stores, until food was dangerously low. Water too, was becoming a problem, though there was some rain during the nights.

Ru stood at the mast, day in, day out, staring at the distant horizon. Occasionally Kuku Lau would try to fool him with a false image, an island shimmering in the heat waves, but Ru was a navigator with much experience and did not allow his wishful thinking to overwhelm his senses. Occasionally too, they would be given hope in the form of a white flush of surf in the distance, only to find rips or flocks of seabirds.

One evening Ru held a meeting with Kieto, Seumas, Dorcha, Kikamana and Boy-girl. He asked for their opinion on the situation.

Kikamana said, 'There are signs in Tiki's face that all is not well on board. Nor can I reach Tangaroa in my dreams. The Great Sea-God has abandoned us.'

Ru said, 'This he would not do unless he was displeased with us for some reason. Do you think it is Wiama? Perhaps Pungarehu should never have taken her from that island? Maybe her presence on board is making Tangaroa angry.'

Kikamana shook her head. 'No, things started going wrong before she came on board. It is something more deep-rooted and less obvious than that. We have broken some command.'

'Well, I can't think what that is,' said Ru, irritably.

Seumas suggested they keep a watch between them, and they agreed, but since none of them knew what to look for it was a very unrewarding business.

Things became even worse. The wind died down: Hine-tu-whenua deserted them. One of Ru's relations disappeared one morning, hooked up into the clouds by Amai-te-rangi, the fisher of people. Ua sent no more rain for many days and they began to seriously thirst. There was a herb they could put in the seawater to make it palatable, but one could only drink a certain amount of salty water before retching it up. Dakuwanga was seen swimming in the mist between the earth and sky, waiting to devour any sau which came his way. The kabu of the man lost to Amai-te-rangi was witnessed floating like a balepa over the roof of voyaging one night, giving everyone the chills.

'We are surely going to die soon,' said Polahiki. 'I have never been on a voyage where the gods hated me so much.'

One night Ru dreamed he visited Limu, the Guardian of the Dead, in his vast wooden palace beneath the ocean. Ru passed through the Land of the Dead without incident, as one does in a dream, seeing neither the terrible Nangananga, nor the Ruler of the Underworld, Milu. When he reached the palace of carved and polished woods, he found it surrounded by guardian lizards feeding on flies, which seemed strange to Ru since they were below the waves and one does not find insects like flies under the water. The lizards allowed him to enter the huge halls of the palace and Ru went straight to the heart, where he was told the god Limu was waiting to give him audience.

Inside, the palace was magnificent, with hundreds of huge pillars of wood supporting a high roof, and beautiful wooden floors and ceilings, covered in carvings of men, fish, birds and other forms of the natural world.

There were balconies reaching up into the misty heights of square towers, tier on tier of them, all filled with curious spirits of the dead, waiting for an audience with Limu. They peered down in resentment on the intruding Ru, who seemed to be jumping ahead of them in the order of things. None spoke to him however, nor tried to bar his progress through the sweeping wooden arches, for the lizards kept watch on their behaviour, and fiercely ejected any soul that caused upset.

Finally Ru came to a darkened room with a wooden throne ten times the height of a man. The throne was decorated with skulls and bones, and masks of men with long tongues, and lizards, and other representations of the dead. On this seat sat the Guardian of the Dead, who told Ru he had been petitioned by Tiki, the First Ancestor, and his wife Marikoriko, First Woman, to give Ru due warning of the consequences of his circumstances.

'If you do not sort out your troubles soon,' said Limu, 'you will end up here.'

'Is there no alternative?' asked Ru. 'I do not think we are going to discover the source of our problem. We have tried and nothing comes to light. I hate to think I have led my people to their deaths.'

'I could arrange for you to land on the Islands of Eternal Souls,' Limu said. 'On Lotophagoi there is singing and dancing – happiness – for ever.'

Ru said, 'It would seem that this would be no different from death.'

'It is death of a kind,' agreed Limu. 'All that is left to you is to make a discovery on your ship.'

Ru then left the palace and travelled up towards the stars, where the Oceanian Star-God Rehua sat in the tenth heaven at a place called Te Putahi Nui O Rehua, The Great Crossroads of Rehua. It was from here that Kaitangata, the beloved son of Rehua, fell one evening. The blood from his fall washed over the sky and now forms the colourful sunrises and sunsets.

Ru was not allowed to enter the tenth heaven, where only one more heaven would have separated him from the Supreme Being, Io, in the twelfth and topmost heaven. No mortal has ever been that close to the highest deity and Ru was to be no exception. He had to shout to Rehua from below, to ask him if he could help.

Rehua replied, 'I can only tell you this — it is in the dark hours when you break your word to Tangaroa.'

'I, break my word? How is this?'

'I can tell you no more,' said Rehua, sparkling with a thousand stars, dazzling Ru with blazes of brilliant light, scintillating in his aura of cold fire. 'The rest you must discover for yourself.'

While Rehua was speaking, Mareikura, heavenly angels

and attendants of Io, were passing by Ru and brushing him with their ethereal forms. These creatures were the Supreme Being's special envoys, carrying messages between the highest deity and the other gods of Oceania. Where they touched Ru's skin they left a smudge of precious glittering stardust.

Ru left the Crossroads to the Stars, and returned to his own body, sleeping on *The Princely Flower*. He was convinced now that Wiamu was their problem, for Rehua had stipulated that the disobedience occurred during the dark hours, which was the only time Wiamu was abroad. Ru waited until night, then demanded she be brought before him.

'You must be the perpetrator of our difficulties,' Ru said, 'for you are the only one who does not sleep through the night, but has the freedom to do as you choose while others are not so alert.'

'This is not quite true,' whispered Wiamu in his ear, taking up her defence. 'There are others who do not sleep.'

'Who are they?' demanded Ru, quietly. 'Tell me their names!'

'Better I should show you,' Wiamu said, softly.

She rose and crossed the deck to the starboard hut, the one used by her during the day. There she took hold of a large piece of tapa cloth and under Ru's gaze, whipped it away. Underneath were two naked bodies, struggling together in the throes of love. One was Titopika, the tohunga, the other was one of the crew of twenty virgins, plainly no longer a maid.

Ru let out a loud cry. No wonder his voyage had slipped from Tangaroa's favour. The Great Sea-God had demanded but one condition for his assistance, that virgins only were used as mariners to sail the craft. Here was one of his crew, her maidenhead taken by a priest who should himself be chaste. This was in flagrant violation of his orders and those of the Great Sea-God, Tangaroa, whose very breath was law on the ocean.

Ru ran to his bed on the deck and snatched up a weapon, a club made of nokonoko. He rushed back to the fornicating pair, intending to dash out their brains. Others had been roused from their beds and had gathered around the guilty couple, staring down at them as they slipped from each other and tried to cover their nakedness. As Ru raised the club over the woman's head, Seumas reached out and gripped it, holding it fast.

'You dare to touch a prince?' cried the stricken Ru, the source of whose mana was great nobility.

'I don't touch your head,' said Seumas, 'nor even your arm – only your club. I can't allow you to murder this woman. It's not her fault. It's *his*. He seduced the maiden. I remember now, seeing him sneak back and forth across the deck at night. I thought it was for drinking water, but he was obviously visiting this woman. He has used his magic to make her his slave.'

Ru managed to control his anguished spirit for long enough to be able to speak with Seumas and a hastily formed council, while the Titopika and the woman dressed.

Ru said to the council, 'Seumas has said the woman was seduced, but not against her will, or she would have reported Titopika's actions.'

'She is a young woman, without experience in these matters,' Kieto agreed. 'Yes, she has done wrong, by disobeying your orders, Prince Ru, but her wrong is *nothing* beside his. Titopika has done this thing, perhaps with the intention of sabotaging the expedition? I have no doubt it was deliberate.'

'You think it was done on purpose?' Ru cried, incensed. 'Why would a young priest do such a thing?'

By this time Titopika had been brought before him and spoke in his own defence.

'I am only a novice priest. I am Ragnu's agent. He told me what to do. I was afraid of him.'

Kikamana said, 'Once you were on the voyage, what did you need to fear? Ragnu's arm is not that long.'

'So you believe,' snorted Titopika. 'I think otherwise. I have seen the punishments he hands out to those who fail to do his bidding. I have seen men's souls in torment, their bodies signifying nothing, yet they scream for mercy. Ragnu is a very powerful priest, a kahuna with magic which can reach a thousand miles—'

'If he's that powerful,' snorted Seumas, 'why bother with creatures like you – why not just sink us with his magic?'

'I am not a man with great mana, like Ru, and I'm not protected by the gods.'

This was true. A kahuna, no matter how powerful, would not openly be able to sabotage an expedition led by such a man as Ru, whose actions had been guided by the gods. Such destruction would have to be done furtively, out of sight of any deity, so that it might seem an accident, or weakness of human nature. The gods were very disparaging about the frailty of mortal will and would not look too closely at any reason for failure which seemed to spring from mankind's deficiencies.

'Get out of my sight,' said Ru to Titopika. 'I shall consider how to deal with you later.'

Once Titopika had taken himself to another part of the canoe, where he would be guarded by some of Ru's relatives, Ru put his mind to the problem of rectifying their situation.

'We must make a sacrifice to Tangaroa,' he said. 'I would like it to be Titopika, but his soul is stained with dishonour and as such he is not a worthy sacrifice. Instead, it will have to be either another person on board, or at the very least a deserving animal. We wish no harm to come to any member of this expedition and we have no domestic livestock left.'

Seumas suddenly realised all eyes were on him and Dorcha, and he leapt to his feet as it dawned on him where Ru's hints were leading.

'No,' he said, 'I absolutely forbid it!'

Kieto said, 'We know how you feel, Seumas, but if we don't do something we shall all die anyway.'

'Think of another way,' cried Seumas, putting an arm around the neck of his dog, Dirk. 'Dorcha, help me.'

Dorcha said, 'Give us until dawn, Ru. If we can't think of anything else, then you'll have to go ahead. At least give my husband until the sun rises.'

'Until morning,' agreed Ru. 'If Seumas has no other answer, then we shall sacrifice his dog. In the meantime, I have to replace the crew member, or we shall still be in violation of Tangaroa's command.'

'You're not going to execute her?'

'No – I'm going to marry her to Titopika. They deserve each other. But more importantly, do we have any more strong, healthy maidens on board? I need an able female virgin to man my ship, or we shall founder in these doldrums for ever. Do we have such a woman amongst us – one who is not a child – who can replace the wayward maid?'

There was silence amongst the council for a moment, then one voice spoke up.

'Yes, we do.'

It was Kikamana, the priestess, personal kahuna to King Tangiia of Rarotonga.

'You?' murmured the prince. 'Of *course*.'

He did not ask if he could trust her. If Kikamana said she was still a virgin, then it was so. One did not question a kahuna of her status. Though in her fading years, her spirit was as pure and unblemished as that of a newly born infant. Kikamana, old in age, but young in her virtue: chaste as a high mountain spring. Her body unviolated, her soul and integrity flawless, she was the perfect replacement for the fallen maiden.

'So be it,' stated Prince Ru.

*

Titopika was married to the young woman the next day. She clung to him possessively, while he himself exhibited nothing but an air of boredom. Seumas wanted to reach out and bash their heads together, believing them to be as stupid as each other.

A close watch was kept on Titopika after this. Ru had warned that any further attempts to impede the expedition would result in the death of the spy. Most thought it a miracle that Ru had not slit his throat and thrown him overboard already.

In the night Seumas had come up with what he believed to be a solution to his problem. Dirk was his dog, raised by him, trained by him. He would not allow his dog to be killed. There would be no ritual sacrifice.

Seumas told Dorcha what he was about to do and her eyes widened in astonishment.

'You're either mad or stupid. You can't love a dog *that* much. Give him up.'

'No,' replied Seumas, determinedly, 'I will not. It has nothing to do with being fond of an animal,' he added, grimly. 'Dirk is my responsibility. If you take on the responsibility for a life, you do everything possible to see that life is preserved. Nothing to do with sentiment at all. I feel nothing of that sort for the dog – he's a good hunter, quick and obedient, and he would die for me – but I am without the kind of silly emotions you're talking about.'

Dorcha raised an eyebrow. 'Are you indeed? I know you, Seumas, you're my man. When you were in love with me and couldn't have me, you were sentiment from your toes to your eyeballs. I used to see you mooning around the beach, staring at my hut. It turned me off my dinner.'

'A dog is not a woman,' he stated, flatly. 'And in any case, I didn't moon around after you. You must have imagined things – that's your vanity working there, lassie. I did nothing of the sort. I was simply—'

'Responsible for my welfare?' she interrupted.

'In a way, yes. It was because of me you'd been taken from Albainn, so of course I felt I had to protect you.'

'What a bletherer,' she said. 'Look, man, you can't risk your life for a scruffy *cù*,' she used the Gaelic word for dog, in order to get through to him, 'so come to your senses.'

'My mind's set,' he replied. 'I won't have it changed by a woman.'

'Oh, no, a woman couldn't influence you, could she – but a bloody dog can. Preserve us!'

That day there was a clear sky like a blue bowl over the curving ocean. There was a swell on the seascape, but the waves were small – 'licking waves' Dorcha called them – and a brisk following wind filled the pandanus mat sails sending the great pahi shooting like a small váa fishing canoe over the surface. Fairy terns from some nearby island, which Ru sought in vain to locate, skimmed through the air above them.

In a clay bowl on the deck a small fire was going and some cooking was in progress. A mother and her small daughter, relatives of Ru, were baking taro. From the hulls came the ever present sound of the bailers as the crew removed the water which constantly seeped through the stitched planks caulked with vegetable and shark oils.

Despite the calm weather the women were working hard, getting the most out of the sails, using the steering oar to its best advantage. The salt spray glistened on their teak skins, which had grown darker since they had begun the long voyage. A new Oceanian infant was as fair-skinned as any baby Dorcha and Seumas could produce. It was the constant exposure to sun and the elements which turned an Oceanian's naturally pale skin a darker hue. Many noble women never went into the sunlight and retained an ivory complexion for their whole lives.

The twenty virgins, Kikamana now amongst their number, were becoming weathered and brown, but were still no less attractive for all that. They were a beautiful people altogether, thought Seumas, the men and the women, with their muscular lithe bodies and long black hair, with their handsome features and dark eyes. Very handsome. No wonder they were so vain.

'Well?' said Ru. 'Have you come to a decision?'

Boy-girl and Kieto stared from behind Ru at their basket-sharer, Seumas, also waiting for his answer.

'I suggest,' said Seumas, evenly, 'rather than slaughtering my dog, in which I have invested many years of patient training, that we sacrifice a great white shark.'

Ru frowned and shook his head, as if there were water in his ears from swimming.

'A great white shark?'

'Yes.'

'But,' said Ru, 'we don't have a great white shark, we only have a dog.'

'Then we must catch one,' replied Seumas. 'We must drag some bait behind the pahi and catch a great white.'

Boy-girl, as puzzled as Ru, intervened here.

'But we have no meat to use as bait – you know that, Seumas. A fish will not do. It needs to be a chunk of bloody meat.'

'There is meat walking around on the deck right now,' Seumas pointed out.

Polahiki shook his head and said, 'If you're talking about rats, we ate the last one two days ago. There are no more rats on board. I've looked in all the hollow bamboos and amongst the vegetables – everywhere that they hide. I admit they are devious creatures, good at squeezing into small places, but we've definitely eaten the last one. I had some myself.'

'You had it *all* yourself,' grumbled one of the women passengers. 'I saw you eat it half raw.'

Seumas said calmly, 'I meant two-legged meat.'

Kieto took a sharp intake of breath. Others had stopped their tasks to listen now. Ru frowned again.

'I think I know what you mean, Seumas. Titopika! We should use the new husband as bait?'

Titopika heard this and came striding over the deck.

'Goblin! You have always hated me, haven't you? This is your revenge, is it? Because I am Ragnu's creature? Have pity, man, on someone who has been ill employed.'

'I did not mean to use you.'

After Seumas had made this remark all eyes swung naturally to where the dirty fisherman, Polahiki, sat peeling his scabs and scratching his lice bites.

'Me?' cried Polahiki, leaping to his feet. 'Oh yes, pick on a poor defenceless fisherman, who's only trying to do his best. That's typical. Naturally because I'm a Hivan I'm fair game, to be pushed around, bullied and persecuted, just to satisfy some cruel—'

'Oh shut up,' Seumas said, wearily, 'I meant *me* – I will be the bait. Make some cuts on my legs so that I trail blood, put me out on a line, and when the great white comes, make sure you harpoon him before he gets my feet. That's all.'

There was stunned silence around the Albannach as passengers and crew digested this extraordinary suggestion. One or two glanced at Dorcha, to gauge her reaction, but realised she already knew what Seumas was going to say. Boy-girl gave Seumas a tragic look.

'Oh, *no*,' she said. 'Not for a *dog*. Here, let's use Titopika after all? He's the cause of all our troubles anyway. Let's use him as the bait.'

Titopika said nothing, his lips tightening, but his new bride clung to him and started to weep. Seumas called Titopika to him. The fake priest roughly pushed away his distressed bride and walked up to face Seumas.

Seumas said, 'Are you really a full tohunga?'

'No – I was hoping to be – but Ragnu has destroyed all that for me.'

'But you know how to slow-bleed a man?'

Titopika and a number of others around him looked puzzled.

'Yes.'

Seumas handed him a sharp-bladed shellknife.

'Then you can cut my ankles for me, man, so that I leak, but not gush blood. Can you do that?'

Titopika smiled, nodded, and took the knife.

'No!' cried Boy-girl. 'He'll cripple you.'

Titopika looked scorn upon the unhappy Boy-girl.

'I shall do as I was asked and no more. Do you take me for an idiot? If I cut him any more than necessary, you can feed me to the great white and have done with it.'

Boy-girl looked at Dorcha, who said, 'I trust him – in this anyway. If my husband is such a fool to go through with this, he needs to be sure he won't bleed to death before noon. Cut him, Titopika.'

Ru, once he saw that Seumas meant what he said, had his crew make ready a harness of sennit, with a trailing rope. Then some bamboo logs were lashed together to make a small raft on which Seumas would lie, his legs dragging behind him in the water. Dirk looked on, bemused by all this activity around his master, wondering whether or not to attack the man with the knife, who was making thin incisions on his master's ankles. Seumas, in the harness, was lowered off the back of the pahi on the small raft, which rode the water like one of those boards which Hawaiian's used to ride the booming surf.

Kikamana beat together the bones she had used to drive off the Ponaturi, and chanted a karakia, while Boy-girl threw some magic stones into the sea to attract their quarry:

'O, great shark of the seas,
Great white hunter of lesser hunters,
Here is the bait for you to devour,
Blood draining like a sunset drains from the sky,

Clouding the waters, bringing frenzy to your senses,
Come and take him – if you can!'

The karakia over, Kikamana picked up a thick bamboo
harpoon with a whalebone barb on the end and stood with
the others, waiting for the great white to come to take the
bait.

'Let us hope Magantu, the monster who can swallow a
pahi whole, does not take the scent of the blood,' whispered Po'oi, the son of old Kaho. 'If Magantu comes, then
we shall all be bait and snapped up pretty quickly.'

'Stop trying to put cheer into our hearts,' moaned Rinto.
'We're happy enough as it is.'

Seumas skimmed the waves behind the canoe, a thin red
trail of smoke in the water behind him. The wash occasionally went over his head, making him splutter and snort.
It was difficult to discern his feelings from his face, on
which he deliberately kept the wooden expression of a
suffering Pict.

Seumas's greying hair flowed behind him like the kelp
tresses of the female who dwelt in the monstrous seas far
below the islands, in that foggy, misty and dark ocean – the
frozen sea of pia, with its mountainous waves – where she
lived with a deceitful creature called the sea-elephant, who
dived to great depths and was hidden from hunters by her
long mane.

After some time, when no great white appeared, Dorcha
had Titopika cut her own ankles and took some sponges,
soaking them in her blood then throwing them overboard.
Others began to do the same. Seumas began to look chilled
and miserable, unable to keep his expression bleak any
longer. More blood-soaked sponges were thrown into the
sea. There was a danger of tiger sharks coming to take the
bait, instead of a great white, but this was not spoken of,
for tiger sharks were not worthy sacrifices to the Great
Sea-God, Tangaroa. Only a great white would do.

The day dragged on and Seumas appeared to be growing weaker, through exposure and loss of blood.

Suddenly Po'oi, having climbed the mast to get a good sighting, yelled excitedly, 'Here he comes! The great white shark of the seas!'

A dark fin was seen cutting through the water, approaching Seumas at right angles.

'Pull him in!' shrieked Dorcha, grabbing the taut line.

'Not yet,' murmured Boy-girl, gently taking her hand from the line. 'We might lose the fish if you take him in too early – just a little while longer.'

The tail of the shark flicked above the surface and Dorcha could see the black fringe. She was astonished at the length of the beast. It was a monster. It could surely swallow Seumas *and* the surf raft whole in one bite. The dorsal fin sliced through the waves with amazing speed, as the great white began to circumnavigate the pahi, its circles growing tighter with each revolution. Soon it was cruising just two body lengths away from Seumas, whose face was once again impassive.

Ru said, 'Pull him in – gradually.'

'No, no, *quickly*,' said Dorcha, her heart in her throat.

Those on the line took no notice of her, but did as they were told by Ru, taking in the raft and Seumas by slow degrees, with the great white decreasing his circles all the time, being drawn in closer to the waiting harpoons and nooses.

'The rope's fraying,' cried Dorcha. 'It's snapping!'

'Slowly, slowly,' murmured Ru, ignoring her. 'Easy, easy.'

To Dorcha it seemed to take a year before the gentle bump of the raft on the back of the pahi was heard. Seumas remained where he was, waiting for the moment when the great white turned in the water as he must to take his prey, his mouth being on the underside of his monstrous head. In that moment the softer underbelly of the shark was exposed. Seumas was snatched literally from the crescent mouth with its saw-tooth jaws. Then the harpoons flashed in, seven of them burying their barbed points in the shark's belly.

There was much yelling and calling from the harpooners, amongst whom was Ru himself.

'Hold him, hold him!'

'Watch it – his skin's like sandstone!'

'The mouth, the mouth – keep away from the mouth.'

The great fish thrashed once against the side of the canoe and immediately four of the harpoons broke or came out. The owners of the other three held on grimly, waiting for the tail to thrash again. When the tail showed, a noose was swiftly thrown around it by Polahiki, the expert, the man who had killed more sharks than any other aboard. Once that was tightened another went on, and another. They had him now and let go the harpoon lines, so that the great white was dragged along behind the pahi, half as long as the ship itself, a burden on the sails.

'Oh laddie,' said Dorcha, her eyes afire and her expression a mixture of anger and relief. 'You are the most bone-headed Pict I have ever had the misfortune to – to marry.'

Seumas grinned sheepishly at his fretful wife, while Dirk wagged his tail and nuzzled his neck, as if the dog knew his master had saved his life at the risk of his own.

Dorcha wiped Seumas down, drying his body, then set about putting ointment on his cuts. Tenderly he did the same with hers, kissing her now and then on the soles of her feet, licking the salt from between her toes to make her mad, blissful in the knowledge that she loved him fiercely.

Occasionally he whispered in her ear as they were ministering to each other, things which must be secret between a husband and wife of middle age, gradually bringing a smile to her face, sometimes allowing her to punch his arm when he became too outrageous in his suggestions. To Seumas it was worth the risking of his life, to find himself so close to her again, as when they were young and freshly in love.

2

Tangaroa was aware that some god or gods, either to spite him or the humans on board the pahi, was doing their best to ensure *The Princely Flower* did not reach its destination. It was a puzzle that Tangaroa could not solve at this time, since the perpetrator kept himself or herself hidden. And well they should, for Io himself had proclaimed the voyage to be worthy.

The Great Sea-God had not searched too hard for this interfering god, since he himself of late had been misdirecting the canoe. It was not spite on Tangaroa's part, but punishment for those on board not adhering to his strict orders. Now things had improved and he had been propitiated.

Tangaroa watched the great white shark being dragged on board the pahi, taking up half the ocean-going canoe's length. The shark was ritually slaughtered, offerings were made to the Great Sea-God. Tangaroa was gratified and appeased. Now that the situation on board had been rectified, with regard to his instructions, he saw no reason to delay the pahi any longer. First, however, the ship would need to call in to an island, to replenish its supplies.

The nearest landfall was an island called Rapanui.

*

After the sacrifice and the feasting on the great white, most of those on board fell into a deep sleep. Wiama almost came out of her hut, thinking that it was nightfall, but was warned by her lover Pungarehu not to open the door. Pungarehu had heard her stirring behind the walls of the hut and though he was waiting impatiently to see her he was terrified she would leave the hut too early and destroy herself.

When indeed it was dark, the waif left her hut. She fell into her lover's arms. The pair of them went to the front of the canoe to sit and watch the darkness flowing over them from the direction of Apa toa on the windflower.

'I have missed you, my love,' said Pungarehu. 'The day is long without you, even though I sleep to pass the time.'

'You *must* sleep then,' she said, 'for you would get no rest otherwise. You must regulate your hours to mine, for you do not dissolve in the darkness, as I do in the light.'

Pungarehu saw the logic of this, though he was growing increasingly upset with their need to part during the day.

'I could come into your hut with you.'

She smiled and touched his cheek with a hand as translucent as a bubble shell that floats on the ocean waves. 'Then we should both get no sleep at all.'

'Please, let me stay with you in your hut tomorrow?'

Wiama sighed and considered this request. The truth was, she liked Pungarehu to be on the outside of the hut, so that he could protect her from accidents, or possibly even deliberate attempts to harm her. While he was out there he could stop anyone going near to the deck hut. There might be those who might forget that she was in there and absently open the door in search for stores. There might be those who were jealous of Pungarehu for some reason and who sought to harm him by destroying her. It was best he remained on the outside, while she was on the inside, in order to control access.

'It's best . . .'

'Please?' he murmured into her ear, delicate as a nautilus, with such deep longing that she could not resist him.

'All right,' she said. 'Just for one day.'

'Tomorrow?' he cried.

'Tomorrow.'

Back on Raiatea, in the temple at Tapu-tapu atia, Ragnu was pacing the floor in fury. He had used his far-seeing devices and was aware that his agent on board *The Princely Flower* had failed him. At first he had wanted to destroy the young man, but once he had calmed his fury was no longer directed towards Titopika, whose efforts at destroying the pahi had not in Ragnu's estimation been worthy of a high priest's spy.

The irony of the situation was not lost on Ragnu either. His machinations had actually contributed to the successful outcome of Kieto's expedition. The Rarotongans were about to land on Rapanui and would undoubtedly discover the passage to the Otherworld which they sought. This was due in part to Titopika's seduction of one of the crew and Tangaroa's subsequent misdirecting of *The Princely Flower*.

A white-bellied sea eagle had been despatched, with a calabash in its claws, to seek out the vessel and to deliver the container to Titopika. There were symbols scratched on the calabash, which Titopika would recognise as the product of Ragnu's hand. These symbols would also lead the young man to believe that there was poison in the calabash, to be administered to the enemies of the kahuna of Raiatea.

There was something far more deadly inside the container, however, but less reliable.

Ragnu's difficulty had been in the numbers of his enemies. It was unlikely that Titopika would be able to poison everyone on board the pahi. Even a delayed-action poison might not be imbibed by all the passengers and crew. Then there was the problem of Titopika himself. Ragnu did not wish *anyone* to survive the voyage, including his agent, who would have a hold on the kahuna for the rest of his life. The new king would not be pleased to learn his cousin Ru had been murdered by his own high priest and supposed guardian of the noble families.

It was possible of course, that the bird would not make it, that some accident or incident would befall the raptor. He could do nothing now but wait for the outcome and hope that his booby trap managed to destroy the whole contingent aboard *The Princely Flower*.

In the meantime, Ragnu prepared himself for a new sacrifice to his ancestor-spirits, who were waiting to be appeased by the death of Seumas, Kieto and the other original members of the Tangiia expedition to Rarotonga.

'A young boy, I think,' murmured the priest. 'I'm sure my great-grandfathers would appreciate some roast long pig.'

Tomorrow he would lead the other priests of the island in a gathering to honour the Great Creator-God, Rongo, god of all things growing. These gatherings were now the only times Ragnu had the opportunity of meeting other ordinary people, for his mana was so great now that it almost equalled that of a king. If his shadow should fall on a commoner, that man might die. Power had its bad side, in that he was a lonely old man, too lofty for the masses and too sinister for the nobles. They were all aware of his great mastery of the occult and were afraid of him, commoner and nobleman alike.

He was a friendless old man, bitter and cold, with nothing to take pleasure in except the deaths of his enemies.

When morning came there was deep mist over the sea. Hau Maringi, God of Mists and Fog, had decided it was a day in which to cast his cloak over the ocean. *The Princely Flower* entered this bank of sea fog, sliding over a still sea, and cruised on into its heart. The crew paddled in the absence of wind, to take their craft through the vaporous barrier, and out on the other side, while Ru stood at the mast.

'Listen!' he cried, after a time. 'Hold the paddles.'

The women rowers did as they were asked. Seumas strained his ears. He was rewarded with the faint sound of waves dashing themselves on rocks. There was land somewhere around, but the fog disguised the direction.

'Which way?' he asked Ru.

Ru, whose navigator's ears were more tuned to such sounds than a warrior from Albainn, pointed.

'That way,' he announced. 'Paddlers, follow the direction of my finger.'

The women did as they were bid. Seumas and Dorcha, and the rest of the passengers from Rarotonga – Po'oi, Rinto, Boy-girl, Kikamana, Kieto and Polahiki – all crowded onto the front of the craft. Pungarehu was inside the second deck hut with his new wife, Wiama, enjoying a honeymoon. He and Wiama heard all the scuffling outside and called to ask what was the matter.

'An island,' cried Polahiki, excitedly. 'We're approaching an island.'

Suddenly, the mists cleared, and there indeed was the source of the breakers: a high volcanic island. The scene was dramatic. Before them lay a heavily wooded land, rising from a small sandy bay directly in front of them, to the rim of an enormous crater. In some places the heads of giants appeared above the trees. They had either red or white bodies, but all had red topknots on their heads. These figures with their distinctive features, their long heads and long noses, dominated the landscape. The red giants had long ears, the white giants short ears. Several of these creatures were moving, as if along paths through the forest.

'Do you see that?' breathed Seumas. 'A land of giants.'

'Rapanui!' confirmed Dorcha. 'I shall add it to my shell chart tonight, relative to the stars in the roof of voyaging. We have found the place we were looking for.'

On hearing this, Ru interrupted angrily, 'But this is not *our* destination. You said we would be taken here and I hoped you were wrong. Are you sure you did not use your magic to take us off course and to this godforsaken place?'

Kikamana, whose magic it would have been if anyone's, replied, 'If we could have used magic to guide a canoe here we would have had no need of you, Prince Ru. We would have come to this place ourselves directly from Rarotonga. We are here because it was foretold that *The Princely Flower* would touch these shores. It is part of your destiny, part of our destiny, and unavoidable.'

Ru seemed to be satisfied with this answer.

As the canoe entered the bay and cruised slowly towards the sandy cove a man burst from the treeline. He was tall and thin with an aquiline nose and long ears, not like an Oceanian but with the appearance of the giants, and he was running as if pursued by someone. Every few moments he darted a look over his shoulder in a terrified manner, sometimes stumbling when he did so, as if he expected those chasing him to emerge from the forest.

'Do you think a giant is after him?' whispered Polahiki. 'He looks as if demons are on his trail.'

Indeed, at the next moment a group of warriors, heavily tattooed with claw marks, stripes and bars, came hurtling out of the forest. They were dressed in dried grass skirts, with long grass leggings, and carried spears with huge obsidian points. Their appearance was ferocious and terrifying. Their frenzied manner, wild hair and grass garments, and their sinister body markings, were all obviously designed to make them appear diabolic in the eyes of the uninitiated. Skulls hung from belts of what looked like human hair. Necklaces of dried body parts decorated throats. Bones dangled from locks of hair.

Seumas for one had no doubt this was a barbarous death cult. He had known them before, both in Oceania and in the land of his birth. He knew their ways: dark and savage ceremonies taking place in the dead of night, victims speechless with terror, fear ruling the communities in which such cults operated.

One of the warriors pointed to the fleeing man and they set off in pursuit of him, over the rocky ground towards the beach.

The fugitive looked up and suddenly saw the pahi, gave a frantic wave, and set off towards the canoe. His hunters followed, yelling and screaming at him. They seemed determined he should not escape. Ru realised that his ship was being placed in a dangerous situation and ordered crew and passengers to arm themselves, which they did with alacrity.

Soon the man with the long ears was close enough to be heard, and he yelled out in absolute terror, 'Birdmen!'

'Birdmen?' said Seumas. 'What does he mean?'

The chasing warriors were near to their quarry now, as he splashed through the shallows, only a short distance from the pahi. They let loose their spears, throwing the short-shafted weapons at the back of their target. The first four missed their mark, but the fifth struck the desperate man squarely in the back, its large stone head probably smashing through his spine, the point coming out of his abdomen.

The sixth spear seemed to be lifted by a strange gust of wind, which carried it over the heads of those on the deck of *The Princely Flower*, to bury its point in the wall of the second deck hut.

Blood gushed from the wound, as the fugitive managed to stagger another few paces, before he slid down into the water. The waves rippled over his head and the water around him became scarlet and smoky. The grass-covered warriors on the beach, the 'Birdmen' as the dying victim had called them, gave out screeches of triumph, like raptors who have caught their prey. Then they were off, running up to the woods again, yelling insults over their shoulders at those on the deck of the canoe.

'What do you think of that?' said Po'oi in an awed voice.
'We witnessed a manhunt in our first few moments. This is
not a happy island. He knew they were going to show him
no mercy. I'm sure if we had harboured him, they would
have attacked us too. They looked a very fierce clan.'

'I think you're right,' said Seumas, grimly. 'They looked
like marauders. When he said "Birdmen" I think he meant
birds of prey. Did you see those claw tattoos? They were no
ordinary symbols – they were the mark of the pirate.'

Polahiki turned his back on the island and said, 'Perhaps
we should leave here now?'

After he had turned he noticed the spear sticking out of
the wall of the second deck hut. He was amazed at the size
of the spearhead, which was more like a long knife.
Rushing over to it, he grasped the haft. A shout came from
within the hut, a command *not* to remove the spear, but
Polahiki was already in the process of pulling it out. There
followed a scream which chilled the blood of every person
on board. Then came the sound of weeping and the beating
of fists on the deck.

Next, to the amazement and horror of all, the door to
the hut flew open and Pungarehu appeared. His hands
were cupped and full of golden dust, like fine beach sand,
which blew away on the stiff offshore breeze. Tears were
streaming down his face. He uttered one word which said
everything.

'Wiama!'

Polahiki backed away from the ravaged face of
Pungarehu, the stranger's spear still in his hand.

'It wasn't my fault,' cried the fisherman. 'Don't come
near me – I'll kill you. I didn't know. You called too late.
Don't look at me like that. Somebody hold him!'

Dorcha walked into the hut and stared at the walls.
There was a hole left by the removed spear. Through this
hole came a thin but brilliant piercing ray of sunlight. The
Scot imagined it must have struck Wiama in the chest, as

she lay with her lover on the deck, for there were two depressions in the straw. One of these two imprints was glittering with golden dust. The shaft of light illuminated a spot one third down this indentation. The waif had been mortally wounded by a javelin of sunlight, as solid to her frail body as the point of a real spear.

Outside, they were trying to comfort the distressed Pungarehu, who cursed Polahiki with every sobbing breath, until finally it was Seumas who intervened.

'Stop your oaths, man, do you not realise? It was the wind which carried that spear into the wall of the hut. No ordinary wind, for they are heavy weapons, not meant for throwing but for jabbing at close quarters. If Polahiki had not removed the spear I'm sure it would have been blown out by the wind.'

'The wind?' said Pungarehu, fighting against his tears still. 'What has the wind to do with it?'

'There is a god of the wind, is there not?' explained Seumas. 'His name is Maomao? I seem to remember a priest telling you that Maomao was angry with you and had promised to make you sorry. Yes? Yes, you remember. You are the killer of the Poukai bird, the giant bird under the protection of Maomao – I was with you man – I helped you kill the creature. This is the Great Wind-God's punishment for slaying the Poukai. You killed the giant bird with a stone axe, broke its wings first, then its jaws and skull. Remember?'

Pungarehu stared at his friend's face and knew this to be true. His wife, the beautiful and delicate Wiama, was the innocent victim of a long-standing dispute between a god and a man. Now the debt had been repaid, the man was no longer under threat – but the price had been unbearably high.

3

A meeting was held between the Rarotongans and the Raiateans. It was decided that Kieto and his Rarotongans would go out into the island, to search for the entrance to the kingdom of the Maori tribes. Ru and the Raiateans would stay with the canoe, replenish supplies, and defend their position against any attack from either the Birdmen or warriors from any other clan on the island, the giants included.

'Once we have supplies on board, we may anchor a good way offshore,' explained Ru. 'We must be in a position to sail away out of reach of any war fleet. But we will not leave you for good. Come to this beach and light five small fires in a straight row, the length of a man's arm between them, and if we're out on the ocean we shall come for you.'

'How long will you wait?' asked Kieto.

'One month at the longest. If you do not return within that time, we shall assume you are all dead.'

Kieto nodded. 'That's fair.'

'May your ancestors smile on your expedition,' said Ru, to the Rarotongans.

They nodded gravely and each sent up a prayer to Tiki, the First Ancestor, even Dorcha and Seumas. Besides the two Albannachs and Kieto there were Kikamana, Polahiki,

Boy-girl and Rinto, son of Manopa. Po'oi and Pungarehu were to remain behind with the vessel. The former because he was unwell with some digestive complaint and the latter because he was still grieving over the loss of his bride and not in his right senses.

Heavily armed, the group set off into the interior of the island, hoping to find a person or tribe friendly enough to help them with the location of the magical cave.

When they reached the forest and entered it they felt a little more secure. At least the trees masked their movements. Out on open ground they were vulnerable to attack from the Birdmen, who both Seumas and Kieto felt would return with more warriors. Ru was no fool though and would not risk *The Princely Flower* in any foolish gesture of honour. The prince would weigh up the consequences and act accordingly. He was the right kind of hero to have in such circumstances: neither rash nor given to stupidity or temper. The ship, at least, was safe.

Polahiki, as usual, dragged his feet and complained the whole time about the amount of walking he was having to do, but Kieto would not wait for any stragglers and the fisherman was having to keep up with the rest of the party.

It was only a short while before they came upon one of the giants, this one obviously without movement, for it was lying flat on its back, its massive topknot missing. They studied its strange long ears and enigmatic expression. The giant had been *painted* red, and its eyes were white coral with red pupils.

Kieto went forward and touched the creature, which appeared either dead or dormant.

He withdrew his hand quickly, then tentatively touched the still form again.

'What is it?' asked Seumas.

'Stone,' said Kieto. 'It's made of stone.'

He chipped at its face with his club.

'Yes, solid stone.'

'Did it turn to rock when it died, do you think?' asked Rinto.

'Look at the size of it,' muttered Kieto. Even just the head was three times his height. 'I hope we don't meet one of the living ones.'

Polahiki said, hopefully, 'Maybe those we saw were being moved by humans? We couldn't see their legs for the trees, if you remember.'

'I saw one turn and look behind it, and bend and stoop to pick something up – could men make it do that?'

'No, I suppose not,' replied an unhappy Polahiki.

The group continued along a path, which eventually led to a village of distinctive houses. Kieto told his group to stay hidden until they had observed the natives for a while. This they did and were soon rewarded as they watched people moving around the village. Their appearance was not like that of the victim of the Birdmen, but Oceanian, but they were not dressed for battle, nor did their tattoos give the same impression of hostility as those of the Birdman cult.

Finally, Kieto judged it right to call softly from the shadow of the forest to one of the villagers, a young girl fetching water from a surface pool. She was a sad-looking spindley creature who hummed to herself softly. The water container was a third the size of herself.

'Child!' he called. 'Come here.'

The girl looked up, gave a startled yell, and ran back into the village, shouting, 'Long ears! Long ears!'

Almost immediately warriors came running from the houses, brandishing spears and clubs, yelling their heads off.

Kieto said, 'Steady   don't fight unless we have to.'

When the shouting warriors of the village were a few yards away, the leader suddenly stopped and stared. Others gradually came to a halt behind him. One young man, whose battle fear had made him blind to all about him except the need to kill, continued his screaming charge but was deliberately tripped by one of the more experienced men of his village, sending him sprawling in the dust.

'What was the girl saying?' asked the front man. 'These are short ears like us – but new to the island, yes?'

This question was directed at Kieto, who nodded his head.

'We have landed here in order to replenish our supplies, but so far have seen nothing but a horrible murder.'

The leader of the party stuck his spear head first into the ground and the other villagers copied him.

'You have come at a bad time,' said the man. 'There is a war on, between the Long Ears and the Short Ears. In ordinary times visitors are welcome, to fill their water gourds and gather drinking coconuts, fruit and vegetables for their voyage, though we see few such sea-farers on the Navel of the World.

'Now, though, the smell of blood is in the air night and day. There are many bad men around, who will kill anyone, whoever they might be.'

'War tends to do that to people,' agreed Kieto.

Seumas said, 'These bad men – would they be called *Birdmen?*'

The village leader nodded. 'You have seen some of the Short-Eared warriors of this clan? They are as dangerous as the Long Ears . . .'

'What about the giants?' asked Kikamana. 'Are the living ones made of stone too?'

'Living? Dead?' said the man. 'These are strange times. Some move, but are they living? Some are motionless, but are they dead? Who can tell, but the sorcerers.'

'Why are they painted different colours?' Kikamana queried.

'The red stone giants are on the side of the Long Ears, the white ones with the short ears are on our side. Sorcerers on both sides work to control the giants. Some give them the power of movement, while others seek out new spells in order to turn them back into solid stone again. The giants fight each other, try to crush enemy villages, cause much damage. No one seems to be winning except Hine-nui-te-po.'

'In war she is always the winner,' Kieto said.

'Come into our village,' said the leader, 'and take of refreshments. If we can help you, we will. I hope we can show we are not entirely devoid of hospitality, even though our island is torn apart in these dark times.'

The group of seven were led into the village where there was a temple with its marae. There were also several ahu around, some stained black with blood, others clean. Kieto asked why there were so many altars and was told that some were platforms where giants had stood, when they were dead stone.

Seumas, like others with him, retained a firm grip on his weapons, in case they were being lured into a position which they would have to fight their way out of. It would not be the first time warriors pretended to be friendly in order to slaughter their guests.

'We have recently killed a Long Ear,' said the leader of the warriors, who appeared to be an ariki of some kind. 'We still have some of the meat left – liver and thigh mostly.'

'Don't you have any pork?' asked Kieto. 'We are not used to eating human flesh.'

'Pork?' said the chief. 'What is that?'

And, looking around them, the Rarotongans realised there were no hogs to be seen, only chickens. It appeared that these people did not have pigs, nor dogs.

Seumas was glad he had left Dirk behind on the pahi, or the locals might have killed him for fear he was a demon. So, if they wanted red meat, they would have to eat people. The thought turned the stomach of the Pict.

'Just fruit for me,' said Seumas, quickly, still not over his first experience of long pig on a Hivan island. 'I've promised Rongo I would remain his faithful servant for three months, since a coconut struck me on the shoulder and not on the head.'

There were a few raised eyebrows at this hastily contrived excuse not to eat the liver of a human.

Seumas added quickly, 'It could have killed me, if it had hit my head – I owe my life to Rongo. He obviously steered the coconut away from a death blow.'

Kieto shook his head sadly.

Dorcha did not protest because she knew that as a woman she would not be offered meat. She and Kikamana would have to eat apart from the men, as was the tradition. It would be interesting to see what the natives would do with Boy-girl, who was a woman in appearance, but still possessed a man's genitals.

Boy-girl took one look at the half-cooked flesh of a roasted human being carried to the mats on wooden platters and promptly sat herself down with the women.

'These two,' said the chief, pointing first at Dorcha and then at Seumas, 'there's something curious about them. They have unusual eyes. And their hair is different. They have strange faces.'

'They are not Oceanians by birth,' Kieto replied, 'but they are now our basket-sharers.'

'I see,' said the chief.

He sat down on a mat and gestured for the Rarotongans to do the same. Food was being brought by women and placed in front of the men. Then a basket of fruit and fish was taken to the women. Polahiki dived in without any ceremony and began chewing some of the liver and thigh meat, while Seumas kept to breadfruit paste and taro, along with some dried fish. The rest of the Rarotongans, not cannibals by tradition, picked a little at the meat, then settled down comfortably with the rest of the fare. The villagers did not mind that their meat was being spurned by most of the newcomers, since it meant more for them.

'So,' said the chief, 'you are from a distant island?'

'Rarotonga.'

'And who is chief there?'

'We have two kings who rule jointly and peacefully – King Karika who came from Samoa and our own King Tangiia who came from Raiatea. We have only settled the island in the last several years. Rarotonga is a long way from this island, which we believe is called Rapanui?'

'This is correct,' said the chief, human fat dribbling down his chin. 'Rapanui is the name of our island, and the king who first found it was called Hotu Matua, who taught us how to make these beautiful houses. Hotu Matua is our most revered ancestor and he will deliver us from these Long Ears.'

'When did the Long Ears first come?'

The chief shrugged. 'Perhaps they were here when Hotu Matua landed?'

He did not seem inclined to speak any further on the subject and Kieto wisely dropped it.

However, the chief went on to say, 'Yes, Rapanui we call our home, but it should be called Blood Island at the present time. There have been too many deaths – massacres of whole villages – and we do not know where it will end. You would do well to leave quickly. Things here have degenerated into a dark swirling chaos. Men are not in their right minds.'

'Thank you for your advice, but we are looking for a cave, the gateway to another world. I was told it would be on this island. Do you know of such a place.'

The chief looked about him nervously and shook his head.

'On this island there are many, many caves.'

Kieto was disappointed with this reply and the chief saw that he had been the source of unhappiness to one of his guests.

'I think I know of a man who could tell you the answer

to your problem,' the chief said, by way of reparation. 'He is a great sorcerer – but he is a Long Ear.'

'Tell me his name?' asked Kieto.

'His name is Tapu Tao.'

'And where does he live?'

'In the mountains.'

At that moment there was a crashing sound from the jungle path and on looking up, Kieto and his group saw the head and shoulders of a red stone giant parting the crest of the trees.

'Look out!' cried Kieto, leaping to his feet.

The earth shook with a 'thump, thump, thump' as the giant continued its progress towards the village. Its top-knot, which was of red sandstone and had not needed painting, perched on its head like a strange-looking hat. Its expression seemed more monstrous for being blank and lifeless, than if it had shown fury or lust. The coral eyes with their red pupils were penetrating. Heavy arms swung pendulum-like from the giant's shoulders. Its head made grinding noises, rock rubbing against rock, as it turned this way and that.

Kieto and the others were unsure what to do and looked to the villagers for some sort of guidance. Should they run? Should they attempt to hide? The natives however showed little enough fear, but appeared to have urgent tasks to perform. They were alert and primed for something. Splitting into two groups which went to different sides of the village they gave the impression of being annoyed rather than scared.

The giant came on, its gait ungainly but seemingly determined, into the village. Its right foot crushed a house to matchwood under fifty tons of solid rock. Its left foot squashed a chicken run, killing some of the livestock and sending the rest fleeing and squawking. Here the giant stopped and paused for a moment, turning its great head with its topknot balanced on its crown, the squealing, grating sound making the Rarotongans cover their ears. It was an appalling noise that set the teeth on edge. The massive stone man then started to move again, into the heart of the village.

As he did so, ropes suddenly sprang up criss-crossing the village, strung between the tops of tall trees with strong thick buttresses. The lines caught on the topknot of the colossus and strained as the giant continued his progress. The monster seemed unaware of the net of ropes, or did not care, and continued to walk forward while the lines stretched. One or two of the thickly woven ropes snapped like cord, whipping away and lashing the treetops on either side of the village. Gradually, however, the red topknot began to slide backwards, held by those lines which remained. The tops of the two great trees to which the lines were attached bent like bows under the strain.

Finally, as the huge stone man took another step forward, his topknot was dragged off, several tons of it falling to the ground, the thump of the impact causing the baked earth to shudder so hard it threw people off their feet.

The losing of its topknot was obviously a magical trigger which robbed the giant of its power of movement. The legs of the colossus slammed together like stone gates, closing and welding into one single pillar. Its head locked in the forward position. Its arms crashed to its sides. Chips of stone flew in all directions. Dust billowed from the armpits. Its nipples, standing proud, quivered.

The giant's momentum so suddenly checked caused the monolithic creature to fall forwards like a massive felled tree.

'Look out!' cried Kikamana.

The group scattered, heading away from the direction of the fall and into the trees. The local people dropped to the ground where they stood. They were wise in the ways of falling giants. The newcomers were not so knowledgeable.

This impact was tremendous.

The visitors, some still caught in the act of running, were catapulted into the air.

Trees were shaken from their roots by the hammer blow. Houses, outbuildings and stalls leapt and rattled their hardwood joints. Around the village the whole forest had gone remarkably quiet, with not a bird sound to break the silence. The stone giant had been defeated by some prior knowledge of its vulnerability. It lay face down in the dust, next to its topknot, obviously unable to stir.

The villagers then jumped to their feet and ran to the fallen idol. There was a joyous shout and they began to beat the inert statue with stone axes, hammers and other implements, as if it were capable of feeling their blows. They spat and urinated on its head. Children ran up and down the spine and old women attacked the creature's feet, throwing mud cakes onto the soles so that they stuck there. Cockerels were encouraged to climb on the topknot, to crow.

It was bedlam.

Kieto motioned for his party to move on, since they were having trouble getting any sense out of the villagers.

The group entered the forest once more, heading inland towards the mountains.

Kieto decided they should avoid any other villages, since even hospitality would slow them up. Everywhere they went they came across the signs of war. There were areas of burnt scrubland and deserted houses. Every so often they met with fences, corrals where domestic livestock had been penned, which had been torn down. Occasionally they stumbled on a corpse, a pile of fresh bones, or skulls in a heap. Dead animals and birds littered clearings in the forest.

'War is such a waste,' said Seumas. 'And here we are preparing for a new one.'

He meant the war Kieto was planning to take to the Albainn, which Kieto insisted was inevitable.

'That's not a war we can avoid – anyway, I prefer to call it a conquest. It is in our destiny to conquer the whole of Land-of-Mists. I keep telling you this, but you don't believe me, Seumas. Why is that *The Princely Flower* was driven on to the shores of this unhappy island, when Prince Ru wanted to search the seas around Rarotonga? Destiny, my friend.'

Seumas looked at Dorcha, who shook her head in sympathy with his point of view. But there was nothing they could do about it. It did seem an inevitable course; now that Albainn had been discovered the Oceanians had to conquer it.

At one point they were on the rim of an extinct volcano crater and looking down could see a light swathe of green reeds in the collected water below. They passed an unfinished stone giant, half-hewn from the rock, as tall as twelve men standing on one another's shoulders. Not far from this was a rock covered in strange symbols, pictures of a kind they had not seen before, as if they were intended to be informative signs.

'This is a strange place,' said Boy-girl with a shudder. 'It arouses the curiosity in my womanly instincts, but at the same time my manly intuition tells me to run back to the pahi and get away from here as fast as I can.'

They reached the foot of the mountains by the early evening and made camp in a low valley. Behind them were the rainforests, down to the shores. In front of them fantastic bladed green mountains, like shards of flint or frozen sea waves, thrown up by volcanic action into mysterious shapes. Here they refreshed themselves with rainwater which had gathered in natural rock bowls. When night fell, and the spirits of the landscape were abroad, they fell in with their learned fears of the supernatural, and where their knowledge of the island was limited they invented, allowed their imaginations creative licence. It was not difficult to find something to be afraid of, on an island which was steeped in dark wars and mysticism.

Also, they were physically cold, for this was an island nearer to the frozen seas than their own: a near sub-tropical climate with a different flora to Rarotonga. The temperature dropped when Ra took his golden face down below the skyline. Cool winds swept down from those sharp heights above them.

'We should have brought blankets,' said Dorcha, shivering. 'Why can't we have a fire?'

'Because it's dangerous,' Kieto replied. 'A fire can be seen for many miles. Even though we're in a valley it might reflect on any tall rocks around us.'

So Dorcha, who had been raised until her womanhood in a land which froze solid for four months of the year at least, had to suffer the indignities of a cooler climate than Rarotonga.

Seumas mentioned this fact to her.

'In Albainn I had a cat-skin shawl to keep me warm during the day and a wolf-skin blanket at night. Anyway, I've been living under a hot sun for most of my life now – my blood is thinner. That other life was a thousand years ago.'

'It does seem a long time ago – so far in the past it's become a faded memory.'

'Well, if Kieto has his way, we'll be going back again soon, though I'm not sure I want to.'

They woke the next morning, chilled and eager to walk again to get warm. However, they soon found their muscles were still stiff from the walking they had done the previous day. The trouble was, they were not accustomed to hiking over long distances: they were seafarers, not land travellers. Even when at home on Rarotonga, they had little need to walk far. So the trek began to tell on their tempers, fraying them at the edges, and they began to snap and snipe at one another.

Around noon they came across an elderly male with a

bundle of sticks on his back twice his own height. The elder and his burden were going in the same direction up the mountain path, but he was moving so much slower than Kieto and his party. They saw that though he was bent, he was actually quite tall and lean. His ear lobes were long and hung low. Catching up with the old man, they confronted him, Kieto throwing questions in his face.

'Where are you going?'

The old man glared, not in the least confounded.

'To my village, weevil brain. Now if you'll step aside? This stack is heavy.'

'Can you not see we are short eared?' said Kieto. 'Are you not afraid we will kill you?'

'Well, if you're going to do it, do it *now*, because I'm old and tired and don't want to carry this load a step further if I've only got a short while to live. After all, I collect the wood to make a fire to cook myself a meal in order to keep myself alive. If I'm to die very shortly, then my labour is all for nothing and I might as well rest until the end comes.'

Kieto smiled at this speech.

'We're not going to kill you.'

'Then get out of the way, hog's turd, so that I can be about my business.'

'Look,' interrupted an exasperated Polahiki, 'we're new-comers to the island, having only arrived just yesterday and we want to find a man named Tapu Tao. We were told he's a Long Ear. Where can we find him?'

'I don't know.'

'You don't know him?'

'I didn't say that, you flea-bitten fool, I said I don't know where you can find him. Everyone knows Tapu Tao, but no one knows where to find him. He's a hermit. He lives up in the mountains.'

Seumas said, 'I thought we were in the mountains?'

'No – higher up. Up there!'

The old man's bony finger pointed dramatically to the peaks of the sharp, bladed mountains, where the hawks and high birds circled. Up there amongst the damp misty regions alpine flowers clung gingerly to precipitous ledges and overhanging crags. There an Oceanian rat would have difficulty in finding a wide enough path. Polahiki groaned. Seumas's heart sank. It seemed impossible. The ways were too steep, the escarpments too sharp. Perhaps the Pict could do it alone, but Kieto would never allow that, in case something happened to him.

This was turning into a nightmare journey.

'This is crazy,' said Boy-girl. 'I can't climb up there – I'd die.'

'That goes for the rest of us,' muttered Dorcha, 'except maybe my husband, who used to collect fulmar birds for their oil from such places, but that was when he was young.'

'We're never going to find this cave,' moaned Rinto.

'What cave?' asked the old man, apparently entertained by the idea that he had been the cause of so much consternation amongst these Short Ears.

He had divested himself of his huge bundle now and was staring from one face to another with a half-smile on his face.

'We are seeking the cave to an Otherworld, where the Maori dwell,' said Kikamana.

'Oh, *that* cave,' replied the old man, reaching down for his bundle again.

Seumas grabbed the stack himself, to help load it on the old man's back, and found it extraordinarily heavy. In fact he could not lift it on his own. Rinto lent a hand.

When the burden was in place again, resting like a house on the old man's spine, Seumas said, 'When you said *that* cave, it sounded as if you knew it yourself.'

'I do,' replied the old man, walking on with painfully slow steps. 'All of our elders know where it is.'

'Could you share your knowledge with us?' asked Boy-girl. 'Or do we have to be Long-Eared elders?'

'Yes and no.'

'Yes and no what?'

'Yes, I could share it with you and no, you don't have to be an elder of my people.'

Boy-girl looked significantly at Kieto.

They waited, but nothing more was forthcoming.

Finally Kieto said, 'Will you tell us?'

The old man paused in his stride.

'I might do, but I have to get this bundle to the top of this path. It's heavy.'

'*Very* heavy,' muttered Seumas.

'Why don't we carry it up there for you,' suggested Kikamana, 'and you can explain to us where to find the cave as we walk?'

The bundle of sticks hit the floor with a thump as the old man let go of the carrying strap.

'What a good idea,' he said, smiling.

So they split the bundle into four and Seumas, Polahiki, Rinto and Kieto took a stack each, leaving the women to walk one either side of the old man. He seemed to enjoy their company more than that of the men, who trailed on behind, the bundles being heavy enough even though a quarter of what had rested on the old man's back. Boy-girl walked on ahead, like a tatterdemalion leading a parade, waving away the clouds of insects that infested the rockside grasses.

The women spoke low and earnestly to the old man, who took great delight in the touches he received on his arms every so often, and occasionally patted a shoulder in return. When they reached the top of the winding path, where they found a cave with an old woman sitting hunched over a tiny fire of dried bird's dung, they had all the information they needed. The old woman wanted to know what in the name of Ara Tiotio was going on and they left their informant to face a barrage of abuse for being so long with the wood.

The group descended the mountain again, happy to have found the location of the entrance to the Otherworld.

According to the old man the cave was actually only accessible from the sea and the party had to get down to the shore. 'There are high cliffs,' the old man had told them, 'so you can't get to it from above, but the water is actually quite shallow – too shallow for your ocean-going canoe. You'll have to find some outriggerless canoes and paddle into the cave.'

In fact, the cave entrance was on the other side of the island to where the pahi was anchored. Kieto had decided they would borrow some canoes from the locals and hopefully return them at a later date. There were seven of them altogether, so they would need at least two canoes.

As they descended from the mountain they could see the island below them littered with stone giants, both white and red, some standing on ahu, others clumping around the landscape. The moving ones had their topknots in place, the motionless ones had their topknots missing. Here and there too, was the smoke from burning villages. Great areas of forest had been shorn. Deserted villages, some in ruins, were like patches on the ground. It was an eerie scene. This was Rapanui, land of stone carvers, going through a bad time in its history.

PART SIX

The Armies of the Dead

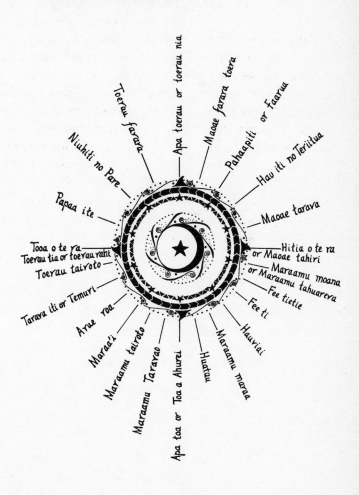

Toerau farara

Niuhiti no Pare

Papaa ite

Tooa o te ra
Toerau tia or toerau rahi

Toerau tairoto

Tarava iti or Temuri

Arue roa

Maraa'i

Maraamu tairoto

Maraamu Taravao

Apa toa or Toa a Ahurei

Huatau

Maraamu maraa

Hauviai

Fee ti

Fee tietie

Maraamu moana
or Maraamu tahuareva

Hitia o te ra
or Maoae tahiri

Maoae tarava

Hau iti no Teriitua

Pahaapiti or Faarua

Maoae farara toera

Apa toerau or toerau nia

1

The group travelled over hills and through valleys, using the trees high plants for cover, until they came to a grassy clearing which they had to cross to reach the fringe of forest which ran along the shoreline. They had just started over this open patch of ground, when a long-eared red giant appeared out of the trees to their left. It had obviously seen them and began striding towards them.

'Look out!' cried Polahiki. 'Kieto, do we stand or run? Which way shall we go?'

The obvious course of action was to take flight – men could not fight stone giants with puny wooden clubs and spears – but for the moment Kieto was indecisive.

'Quick man,' said Seumas. 'Make a decision!'

Although the stone giant was awkward in movement, the sheer length of its strides brought him almost upon the group. Then suddenly, it stopped, and turned its grating head towards the forest. It seemed to be listening for something.

'What's the matter with it?' asked Dorcha.

Her question was answered by the trees parting again and another giant emerging, this time a white giant with short ears.

The two monoliths stood and stared at each other with

baleful eyes. Their split peg legs had no feet on the bottoms, which meant they walked as if on stilts. Although they tried to stand on one spot, they in fact had to totter this way and that to keep their balance. No sound came from their big-lipped mouths, which remained sealed. Only in the way their heads swivelled did the Rarotongans, tiny by comparison, feel there was any hostility expressed.

Then as if by some given signal, the colossi moved towards one another, clearly ready to do battle. The humans were about to witness single combat between two massive stone giants: a spectacle they wished to observe from a place of safety. They felt vulnerable and exposed out in the clearing.

'Quickly,' cried Kieto, firm at last. 'To that rock over-hang over there – let's get out of their way.'

The mortals ran across the grassy area to the shallow cave pointed out by Kieto and crowded underneath. The red giant's head swivelled on its shoulders, making that horrible grating sound again, and observed their progress. While he was doing so the white giant struck him a terrible blow on the shoulder.

Chips of stone whined through the air as part of the red giant's collar shattered. Bits of gravel came zinging from the fist of the white giant too. The flying fragments hit the cliff around the rock overhang in a hail of stone splinters. Had the group of humans been exposed, they would have been cut to pieces by the blast. As it was, they clustered behind their rock shield, hoping the giants would destroy one another.

The red giant now turned on his opponent, charging with his damaged shoulder. They met like two mountains clashing together, making the ground shudder with the impact of their collision. The white giant developed a fissure down the left side of his body: the humans heard the ear-splitting sound of the stone cracking. It was like a cry of agony.

The force of the blow had not only damaged the white giant, but his opponent too. In the meantime the shattered white monolith had been in the act of swinging his free fist at the topknot of his antagonist, only to make contact with the arm of the red giant blocking his blow. Instead of hitting the topknot, he struck the red giant's wrist, snapping off the ruddy statue's hand and sending it spinning and crashing into the forest, felling several trees.

Miraculously, the topknots of both giants remained in place, as if attached to their heads by more than gravity.

'The red one is winning,' groaned Polahiki. 'Look at that crack down the white giant – he's falling apart.'

'But the red giant has lost a hand now,' said Seumas, hopefully. 'Maybe he'll turn and run?'

But neither monster stone image seemed ready to yield. Both of them appeared stubbornly ready to fight until they crumbled to sand. They might have been made of hate instead of stone, the way they swung their arms at one another's topknots. It was a strange combat, silent of battle cries, but noisy with the clash and crack of stone on stone.

A red nose went whizzing past the rock overhang, to ricochet with a humming sound off a boulder. This loss of his olfactory organ seemed to spur the red giant to more drastic action for he suddenly head-butted his opponent just below the ear, endangering the safety of his own topknot, but managing to destabilise the balance of the white giant. The white giant's earlobe fell to the earth and buried itself in the moss. A hunk of rusty chin followed the descent of this lump of anatomy as the white giant's elbow came up under a red jaw.

'Have you ever seen anything like it?' whispered Rinto, the youngest member of the group.

'No,' said Dorcha, 'and I don't want to ever again. I wish the white giant would finish off that red devil, so that we could be on our way . . .'

Her words turned out to be the death knell of the white

giant, for at that moment his peg leg accidentally found a hole in the turf and he went flying backwards to land in a sitting position. He struggled to get off his backside, but his noseless assailant picked up an enormous boulder, as big as a house, between his right hand and his left wrist stump. He threw this chunk of moraine full force at the white giant's face. The force of the blow rattled his head. At last the topknot toppled to the earth and rolled away down a slope. The white giant immediately became immobile and rigid as a pinnacle.

'Now we've had it,' moaned the pessimistic Polahiki. 'That red oaf will come for us next. He'll make fish meal of us within a few moments.'

However, the cardinal giant seemed more intent on turning his blanched foe into gravel before taking care of any other matter. He began pounding the head and torso of the white giant, steadily, almost rhythmically, with his broken arm. His stone victim began to shatter and break, chunks falling off easily now that he could no longer ride with the blows. The ochre giant was not satisfied even with this and seemed intent on reducing his conquered adversary to powder. Blow on blow rained down on the unfortunate and helpless Short Ear, while in the meantime the humans managed to sneak away around the base of the cliff, into the long grasses on the far side of the clearing.

Seumas, the last in the line, looked back to see the red giant holding the white giant's sundered head in his good hand, about to pitch it into a long slope which led to a bog. The deed was done and the head rolled like a pale massive cheese down the gradient. The red giant's ochre face was as expressionless as ever, but the Pict got the feeling that the victor of the contest was experiencing a moment of triumph as he watched his enemy's pate sink slowly in the morass.

'By the gods,' Seumas muttered, 'those creatures might not have any hearts, but they have a taste for winning.'

The Pict was right. Just as Seumas turned to follow Rinto, the last but one in the line, the giant saw him. An ochre hand reached down for a missile. Before the grasses closed around Seumas a triangular stone nose zinged past his ear. It buried itself deep in the nape of Rinto's neck. Rinto fell to the ground without a murmur, dead before he struck earth. Seumas was in turn astonished at the speed at which it had happened, then shocked to the core by the tragedy.

He quickly examined his friend, but it was clear there was no life in him. Seumas could do nothing. Stepping over the body of Manopa's son, he caught up with the others, knowing if they waited they would become further victims of the red giant's callous enmity. When the group was far enough away from the scene, Seumas called softly to Kieto.

'We've lost one man.'

Kieto, at the head of the line, turned and stared.

'Rinto?' he said. 'We'll wait until he catches up.'

'No, you don't understand,' murmured Seumas, as the others were looking at the path behind him. 'He's dead. Killed by a stone. The red giant threw his own nose. It struck Rinto at the base of the skull. He's lying back there.'

'We have to fetch his body,' Kikamana said. 'We have to give him a burial ceremony.'

Kieto stared at Seumas, a look of comprehension entering his eyes, and he shook his head.

'No, Seumas is right. The giant's back there and anyway, we can't carry Rinto into the Otherworld and home again. He's lost to us. We have to go on without him.'

'You can't,' snapped Kikamana. 'His father was a hero. Rinto deserves to join his family. Without a ceremony his sau will be at the mercy of Dakuwanga.'

Kieto replied, 'You think he will get past Nangananga? Better his soul is swallowed by the Shark-God than be left to rot inside the womb of that foul goddess.'

'What's the difference?' sniffed Polahiki. 'One end or the other.'

It was true, Rinto was a bachelor and had not the protection given to priests and virgins. He had no excuse for being single. Kikamana might give him a fake wife, a doll, to carry with him down the purple path to Milu's land, but these artifacts seldom fooled the monstrous goddess who waited beyond the entrance to the Underworld. Rinto would be stuffed up inside Nangananga's womb with all the other bachelors, a hell within a hell, for the rest of eternity.

Behind them came the sounds of the giant crashing around in the forest, looking for their trail. Kikamana shook her head sadly and realised that more of them would die if they went looking for Rinto. It was true he would be a burden on them, heavy to carry, and jeopardise their mission. They had to go on and Rinto's sau would need to see to itself.

'On then,' ordered Kieto.

The group continued down towards the shoreline. Once there they followed the coast until they came across a village similar to the one they had first encountered. There were marauders at work there though, pillaging and burning houses. These were tall men, whose ear lobes had been stretched by some method and hung down long and loose.

Down on the beach some of the invaders, who had obviously arrived in their own narrow canoes, were busy smashing holes in the bottoms of their enemies' boats. Their own vessels were grouped on the sand at some distance from the village. Kieto and his party took the opportunity to seize two of the Long Ears' canoes and paddle them out into the sea. They were spotted when one of the wreckers looked up and gave a shout.

Four canoes set out in pursuit. The lead canoe was fast and covered distance quickly. The other three were strung out behind this speedy crew.

'Here we go!' muttered Seumas, gripping hold of his

whalebone club and placing it in his lap. 'If they catch up to us, you carry on paddling, Dorcha.'

'Who are you handing out orders to, laddie?' she muttered. 'I'll do what I think best.'

Seumas sighed, knowing his spirited wife would do exactly what she believed to be necessary, without thought for her own protection. It was what he would do himself of course, but then he was a man and she a woman. Since she had left Albainn however, the difference between them meant little to her. It was really only at meals or in bed that their genders were obvious and even then Seumas sometimes became confused.

In Seumas and Dorcha's canoe was Polahiki. The other three, Kikamana, Boy-girl and Kieto, were in the lead canoe. The three in front had weapons to hand and looked ready to defend themselves at a moment's notice.

Polahiki who only needed the flimsiest of excuses to stop paddling, which was hard work, dropped his oar and felt around in the bottom of the canoe. He found what he was looking for and gave a shout of triumph. It was a canoe breaker, carried on all Oceanian war craft: a lump of volcanic rock lashed to the end of a sennit rope. Polahiki was a fisherman, skilled in the art of flinging heavy nets, having to be accurate enough to hit shoals of fish as they flashed by a boat. He began swinging the canoe breaker round his head in every increasing circles.

The lead canoe of the Long Ears drew closer and closer. Spears began to plop into the water around Seumas. Stones from sling shots sang around his head. He could not turn and throw back because it was an awkward movement returning spear throws from a front canoe: he might overturn his own boat. Besides, Polahiki was in the way, still whirling the canoe breaker around his head.

'Hurry up,' he snapped, irritably. 'What are you waiting for, man?'

'Patience, patience,' muttered Polahiki, his dirty arms

swinging the plumbline around in widening steady circles. 'I need to be sure . . .'

A spear thudded into the rim of the canoe.

'For the love of the gods,' moaned Seumas. 'Throw the damn thing.

At that moment Polahiki let go the line. The weight of the volcanic stone carried it sailing through the air. It smashed into the bows of the lead Long Ear canoe, just on the waterline: a perfect shot. The damaged canoe was flooded immediately, seawater gushing through the gaping hole in the front. Warriors yelled excitedly, diving overboard. One of them, a strong swimmer, tried chasing after his assailant. Polahiki showed him a filthy backside, knowing the man could never catch up.

The second war canoe did not pause to pick up the men in the water, as expected. They left that to the third and fourth boats. Since they were quite close to their quarry now, rescue attempts could be left to stragglers. This was a tactic quite unanticipated by the Hivan fisherman and he sat down and began paddling furiously.

'They're still coming,' he cried.

The second Long Ear's canoe also began to gain on Seumas and his party, having five men at the paddles. Kieto looked back, saw what was happening, and made a brilliant naval decision. There was only a canoe length between his vessel and Seumas's. However, the distance between the lead Long Ear canoe and his two remaining companion craft was widening.

Kieto ordered Kikamana and Boy-girl to turn the canoe round and they began heading back towards the oncoming Long Ears. Seumas was at first puzzled, then realised what was happening. It was now two canoes against one. Seumas shouted orders to Polahiki and Dorcha and they too swung their canoe back to face the Long Ears. The Long Ears glanced behind them and began to understand the quandary they were in. They had no support.

'We don't want to fight you,' cried Kieto, as the two Rarotongan crews approached the enemy canoe. 'Turn back and we'll let you go.'

There was a snarl from the leader of the Long Ear's canoe and he leapt from his vessel's bows towards the nearest of his enemy: the Pict.

Seumas, despite his age, was blindingly fast. He dropped his paddle, snatched up the whalebone wahaika club resting across his knees and struck the leaping man all in one smooth movement. The body hit the side of the boat, rocked it dangerously, then slid into the water.

There followed a short period of inactivity. Everyone was trying to assess the situation and decide what to do next. The man in the water was bleeding but not unconscious. With one injured shoulder, he struggled to reach his own canoe again.

One of the Long Ears then stood up and shouted. His arm came up as he pointed. Hammerheads were homing in on the bloody swimmer. The predators were incredibly swift, flashing grey and white through the water. In less than a moment they were on their prey. The Long Ears tried to drag their man out of the water, but a hammerhead shark had gripped him by the legs and was shaking him as a dog shakes a rag. No sound came from his throat, but the victim's eyes were wide with pain and fear. Seumas guessed the Long Ear's voice was locked tight by the terror which must have been surging through his brain.

The hammerheads won the tug of war. There was nothing anyone could do. Hammerheads are infamously tenacious and persistent. The victim was dragged under the canoe, out of the grip of his comrades, and the water around became a furious flurry of lashing fish forms with log-like heads, swilling blood and pieces of floating meat.

Seumas signalled to Kieto and the two Rarotongan canoes slipped away, out towards the big waves, leaving the Long Ears to garner what they could of their comrade. The

sun was going down behind the horizon, Ra had finished
his task for the day, and the light was fading rapidly.
Phosphorescent light danced on the waters in the gloaming.
The paddlers reflected on the day's events, each lost in
images of red and white giants, the untimely death of a
comrade and hammerhead sharks tearing human flesh.

Fortunately Hine-keha was at her brightest. The two
canoes slipped under the brow of the sea-facing cliffs, passing cave on cave, and eventually found the one they were
looking for with striations around the mouth. Seumas was
carrying a fire-making stick, Polahiki the block, and
Kikamana and Dorcha the brands. Soon they had torches
in their hands and entered the cave, paddling slowly and
warily, their flitting shadows acting out different lives on
the walls of the tunnel to the Otherworld.

The water in the cave seemed to go deep into the heart of
the island, before they could beach the canoes. It was here
the tunnel widened to a cavern. They dragged the two
canoes up on to the grey sand and began walking, surrounded by stalactites and stalagmites. Above them there
was a black, moving ceiling, as they disturbed millions of
roosting bats. It was an eerie and claustrophobic journey
for the Oceanians, though the two Albannachs felt curiously at home: they had experienced such places in the
land of their birth.

The cavern grew ever wider and wider, until they seemed
to be walking in a wide landscape, but still the sky and
horizons remained rock, from which emanated a soft grey-
green light. There were thousands upon thousands of
moths in the air and on the ground. Why these creatures
were in such abundance was a mystery, but they appeared
to be multiplying all the time.

'We don't need the brands any more,' said Kieto, indicating the strange light. 'Best put them out.'

They snuffed the torches and left them where they would

be found on the return journey. They had another problem now, however, which they had not anticipated. With each step they took they were vaguely aware of a growing hunger, which they could not satisfy. There was water in pools, but no food, and the party began to experience ravenous cravings for nourishment. They also had to keep stopping for sleep, becoming tired again after only a hundred paces or so once they woke up. It was a confusing and upsetting episode.

'What's happening?' asked Kieto of Kikamana. 'It's not that long since we last ate. Why do I feel starved? Why do we have to stop and drink every few paces? Why do we need so much rest? I don't understand it.'

Kikamana looked about her at the undulating rocky landscape and shook her head.

'I think – I think something is happening to time in here. It goes by much more quickly. It's as if a day is passing with every two or three hundred steps we take. If we continue, we'll starve to death. Look at Polahiki. He's lost weight since we entered the cave. And me. We all have.'

'If we turn back,' asked Polahiki, 'will we reverse what's happening to us?'

Seumas growled, 'We're not going back, Polahiki. Get that out of your head. We've come this far and I for one am curious about what lies at the end of our journey.'

'Me too,' said Dorcha. 'I want to meet the Maori.'

'What if I go back on my own,' said the belligerent fisherman. 'What then?'

'Off you go then,' said Kieto, with a wave of his hand. 'But if you take a canoe, we'll hunt you down and kill you ourselves. But don't let us stop you.'

Polahiki gave his leader a sour look and said no more on the matter.

The party continued for a while, growing steadily weaker with malnutrition, until suddenly Polahiki began grabbing handfuls of moths, scraping them off the floor, and stuffing them in his mouth. The others, famished, followed suit. The six of them now scooped moths from the ground, grabbed them from the air, and crammed them into their mouths. No words were spoken, they simply knew they had to eat something. Sometimes, with a handfuls of moths from the floor came red clay and this was eaten along with the lepidopterous insects, helping to fill the huge cavity in their stomachs.

Seumas had to take mouthfuls of water to wash down the dusty, dry creatures, some still wriggling as they descended his oesophagus. Their wings stuck to his teeth and the roof of his mouth, their antennae tickled his throat. He felt it was a disgusting thing to be doing, but he was so hungry he could not help himself. It was either this or eat one another.

After a while they all sat down, a little pale around the corners of the mouth, and Kieto spoke to them.

'Let's hope we get to the end of this journey soon – I don't think I could do that again.'

'You'll do it,' said Kikamana, 'if you have to.'

When they had rested, for they were extremely tired, they continued their journey.

They came to a shallow river flowing over a rocky bed. It struck Seumas that the stone walls of the cavern had moved back. This was probably the largest part of the whole cave system, the centre of their journey. They were now at the heart of the monstrous cavern, with its echoes, its moths and bats, its spikes of lime. The river, however, appeared to be some sort of boundary line, because as they began wading over to the other side, the party began to see visions, hear sounds, which must have originated in the preternatural world.

'Do you see them?' whispered Seumas to Dorcha.

Dorcha nodded. 'Kikamana, what are they?'

There were translucent men and women, all very tall and straight, marching a foot above the surface of the river.

They moved in ranks and files, fifty wide, thousands long, relentlessly towards the six Rarotongans. The figures were humming some kind of marching tune and carried torches in their hands, but the flames did not illuminate the cavern, they burned with an uncanny light whose rays went no further than the face of the carrier. At their head was a leader, who moaned incessantly in hollow, emotionless tones, 'Kill them, kill them, kill them.'

'The armies of the dead,' replied Kikamana, softly. 'Quickly take off your clothes. Lie down in the water.'

No one thought to argue with the priestess, who knew about the culture of the Dead. They tore off their skirts and lay down on the pebbles and rocks in the water, letting it trickle over their backs, keeping their noses just above the surface, and waited apprehensively for the spectres to pass by.

Over their bodies marched the armies of the dead, the ghostly feet not far above their heads. Seumas found the whole experience ghastly. He shook, both with fear and the chilling waters of the river. Grisly men and women with dark sunken eyes, sallow skins and vacuous voices tramped above him, creating in him a feeling of grey sickness and horror. They seemed endless too, these great battalions of spectres, while Seumas just longed for the last line to pass over, and be gone.

Suddenly, Polahiki stood up and tried to run, screeching at the top of his voice.

'I can't stand it. I can't stand it.'

He managed to reach the rocky shore, but appeared to fall there, and be held by an unseen force. The troops now ceased humming their dreadful monotonous tune and followed their leader in chanting, 'Kill him, kill him, kill him . . .'

The line of marchers weaved towards the spot where Polahiki was lying, wretched and quivering with terror. They stretched out grisly hands, on the end of grisly arms, as if to welcome him into their ranks. They pursed their grisly lips, ready to kiss his cheeks, while blowing foul gases down their grisly nostrils. Their sunken eyes glowed with an acquisitive light. He was theirs. It seemed they were going to lift him up like a child of the departed, carry him off, take him to their asylum. Polahiki was gibbering with fright, making the horrible whimpering noises that Dirk made in his sleep.

Then one of the marchers cried out in louder tones that overrode the chanting, 'Leave him. He is mine. Touch him not. He is mine.' This was repeated a dozen times over.

On hearing this call the armies of the dead turned back into their straight line again, gliding over the surface of the river, leaving Polahiki still sobbing and gasping on the bank. For reasons yet unknown to Seumas, the Hivan fisherman was safe. Yet it had seemed that he had been doomed until that single voice had cried above the chanting, 'Leave him. He is mine . . .'

Finally, the last battalion of the army of the dead passed over the group and they were able to rise and dress.

Polahiki joined them again, considerably shaken, but probably no less so than the others. They all took some time to recover from the experience, which had bitten into their minds and souls with cold teeth. They began walking again, Seumas and Kieto taking the front position. Dorcha deliberately remained at the back, so that she could speak with the priestess.

'Why was he saved?' asked Dorcha of Kikamana.

'Polahiki? He will probably tell you that.'

The fisherman nodded. 'My father,' he said. 'My father was in the ranks of the dead. It was he who told them to leave me alone.' Polahiki's eyes appeared to mist over a little. 'When I left my home isle, my father was still alive. He must have since died.'

'I'm sorry,' Dorcha said, though she could not bring herself to touch the fisherman, whose unwashed body and dirty habits revolted her. 'You must be grieving.'

'No,' said Polahiki, candidly. 'I never liked him much. He used to beat me as a child. In fact, I hated him. I'm glad he's dead. I hope it was very painful. I hope he trod on a stonefish and died in agony. It would be too much if he just died quietly in his sleep.'

Dorcha was shocked by this speech.

'Then why did he save you?'

'Well, I never did anything to *him*. He probably thinks I had a wonderful childhood. He probably thinks I revere him for drumming his knowledge into me. He probably thinks he was a good teacher, strict and firm. In fact he was a cruel monster. I remember the bamboo cane swishing down on my bare back and legs, while he beat some piece of useless wisdom into me. It didn't occur to him that I would forget what he was telling me and remember only the pain. He thought it was the only way to learn things, since that's the method *his* father used.'

'Your grandfather.'

'Yes – he was an old bastard too. I hated his guts as well.'

There didn't seem to be much Dorcha could say to this and she joined her husband up front. They were coming to a narrow place now, where the light had undergone yet another change. Here the rock walls of the cavern were much closer together and had dark shadows at their bases. The group could hear movements amongst the shadows, but could see nothing.

'What is it?' asked Seumas of Kikamana. 'Monsters?'

'Demons,' replied the priestess, firmly. 'We will need a karakia.' She took some bones from her waistband and began to beat them together, chanting a fangu as she walked. The others followed after her, keeping well to the middle of the cavern.

Suddenly, out of the shadows came showers of stones and rocks, striking the Rarotongans.

'Don't run,' cried Kikamana, breaking her chanting for a moment. 'Walk.'

The others did as they were told, but the missiles were extremely painful. At the same time the hidden demons began hooting and jeering at them, challenging them to do battle, calling them cowards, saying they were poor specimens of human beings. Seumas gripped his club. Dorcha grabbed his wrist.

'No,' she said, as the stones rained on them. 'Follow Kikamana's lead.'

As if running this gauntlet were not enough they came to an even narrower passage, where the walls were slamming together in an irregular fashion. It meant they would have to run a short stretch at the risk of being crushed to breadfruit pulp. Such a daunting prospect once again had Polahiki complaining, as rocks struck him on the back and head, opening the festering sores which seemed to be so much a part of his life.

'Now this?' cried Seumas, more irritated than afraid. 'Do we make a dash, or what?'

Once again the knowledge of the kahuna, Kikamana, was necessary to their survival.

PART SEVEN

Land of the Long White Cloud

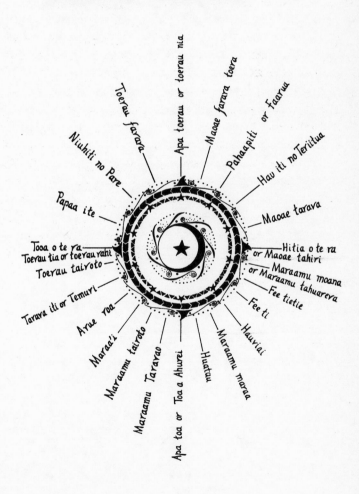

1

Kikamana ordered every member of the party to find some large stones, as big as they were able to carry. The demons in the shadows seemed to have run out of ammunition now and were watching the humans with bright eyes. There was no more hooting and shouting, just curiosity. The demons wanted to see what would happen when a mortal was caught between the slamming cliffs.

'They spurt,' said one.

'Squish and spurt,' muttered another. 'You see.'

'They crack too,' murmured a third. 'They squish, spurt and crack – like a ripe fruit with a kernel.'

Polahiki threw a wicked glance in the direction of these creatures, but said nothing.

Kikamana said, 'Select hard rock, if you can – not sandstone, or limestone, or anything too soft.'

This they did. There was nothing as tough and brittle as flint in the enormous cavern, but there were chunks of gneiss. These they gathered at the entrance to the clashing cliffs. When they had accumulated as many as they could find, Kikamana told them what they must do.

'When the cliffs draw back, we must throw as many of these rocks as possible inside, so that when the walls slam together the next time, hopefully they will jam them wide enough apart to create a tunnel.'

So, they waited for the cliffs to smash together, then when they drew back there was frantic activity to roll and throw boulders into the gap. They had about three-quarters of their load within the space, when the cliffs slammed together again. Some of the rocks were crushed, smaller ones on the edge, but essentially a gap was created. When the cliffs drew back again, the group filed through at a rapid pace.

Boy-girl, Polahiki, Kieto and Dorcha made it through before the next coming-together of the cavern's savagely mating walls. Seumas and Kikamana were caught towards the end of the passage. The cliffs managed to smash more rocks this time, narrowing the gap considerably. If Seumas had stretched his arms out either side, he would have touched the walls. However, they would surely get to the end before the *next* blow.

Seumas was about to step out to safety when the cliffs unexpectedly shut again. This time he was actually grazed on one side of his body and had but a finger's-length to spare on the other. Kikamana was not far behind him. The walls drew back. Seumas leapt out.

Again, it was only a moment after they had drawn back, that the cliffs smashed together again, as if determined to trap at least *one* victim. Kikamana was in there, as the walls met with a thunderous sound, causing the floor to vibrate. Boy-girl screamed. Every member of the party imagined the priestess was blood-and-bone paste on the faces of the two cliffs.

The walls drew back again, and miraculously Kikamana came on through, stumbling out to freedom.

'You're alive?' cried Boy-girl. 'You must be the greatest kahuna of all time!'

'Not so great,' said Kikamana, getting back her breath. 'There are hollows on the cliff faces. I just happened to be opposite one. Very lucky.'

'Not lucky,' said Kieto. 'You are beloved of the gods, Kikamana. If it had been one of us, we would have been crushed.'

The slamming cliffs appeared to be their final obstacle in the great cavern, which now began to narrow again to the size of a normal cave. A breeze was felt. There was an opening, somewhere ahead, into another world. Every member of the party gathered their mental strengths, ready to face this fresh challenge. They all had their own ideas on what the new world would be like.

The light of the sun was in their eyes and they followed it.

Seumas was the third to step out into the Otherworld. The light dazzled him for a while, but when he was able to look around him he saw a landscape of undulating grasslands beyond an area of bubbling hot springs and tall hissing geysers. This did not appear to be small-island terrain, but more on the scale of his homeland Albainn, and its attached neighbour, Engaland. This was a big country, with a vast blue sky above, and elongated clouds that stretched like lazy giant sheep over the heavens.

Seumas heard a sound next to him and turned to see an enthralled Kieto.

'Aotearoa,' breathed Kieto in wonder. 'Land of the Long White Cloud.'

'Land of the Maori,' Seumas said.

'Yes, land of the great Maori warrior race, whose fame has reached our world through the dreams and the visions of kahunas. We must be cautious here, for we are out of our own place and things will be different – customs, manners, perhaps even gods? Who knows, we may be the first of our people to come here?'

Kikamana looked about her in awe. 'I have often dreamed of this land, during trances and fevers, when my mind was able to reach out beyond our own world. It is larger and more beautiful than I imagined. See, in the distance, the blue ridges of mountains. And here, beyond this hill, the spouting hot waters shooting up into the air like quick-growing trees. This is a land of contrasts, the very hot and the very cold.'

'Cold?' said Polahiki.

Kikamana said, 'I have seen a coldness beyond belief, in its high places – there it becomes so cold the rain falls as white powder and the water hardens to stone.'

'This is surely not true?' argued Polahiki. 'Hard water? And rain like dust?'

'It is true,' Dorcha confirmed. 'These things are called snow and ice. We have them in our land, the birthplace of Seumas and myself. Snow and ice, made from rain and still water. Snow settles on the land and turns everything pure white, muffles it in a cold powdery coat. Lakes and ponds ice over and turn hard as stone. They make for wicked winters, when everything freezes, and mind and body go numb.'

The other members of the party shook their heads, as if it was all too much for them. They stared around them at the magnificent rolling landscape, leading as Kikamana had said, to the distant ranges of mountains. On the grassy hill where they stood they were able to see the hot springs surrounded by simmering pools of lava. Hissing, yellow-edged holes sent out a pungent gas which stung their eyes and nostrils. Steam drifted over the landscape in rising veils, making the scenery quite mystical to Rarotongan eyes.

Despite the warning of cold weather, Polahiki was much impressed with this new land. All his life he had lived on boats or small islands and now here was a land, perhaps an island, perhaps not, which stretched as far as the eye could see. It was an ocean of grass and trees. Surely this was a place where one could settle in comfort, fishing in a calm lake instead of a vast sea, where there was so much land one might build a house and never have to see another human being again?

There was something of the eremite in Polahiki.

Around the hot springs were ferns as tall as many coconut palms, decorated with butterflies and birds. There were rainforests in the distance, dark green and moody. There were valley pockets thick with rotting vegetation and nets of vines, and littered with fallen and leaning trees. It was a richly layered land, full of life, with a cooler climate than they were used to, but with more shades of green to its covering. The travellers had no doubt of the wealth of the country in which they found themselves: it was evident in its every aspect.

Kieto scanned the horizon and eventually found the sight for which he was looking.

'Smoke,' he said, pointing. 'We must head in that direction.'

The party set off, with Kieto at their head.

Polahiki asked of Boy-girl, 'How do we know these people, these Maori, won't be hostile?'

'I expect they will be,' replied Boy-girl, cheerfully. 'Kieto will be disappointed if they're not. After all, that's what we've come here for, to meet a warrior nation.'

The answer did nothing for Polahiki's worries, except to reinforce them.

Pathfinding a broad landscape was a little like navigating on the ocean, except there were more markers. Kieto dropped down into a valley and followed a braided river the width of which astonished him. Everything was so much larger here in the Land of the Long White Cloud. The river led him in the general direction of the smoke he had seen and he guessed the makers of that smoke would not be too far from a source of fresh water.

As evening fell on the broad land, they began to approach the place where they had seen the smoke. Now they could see the lights of the fires. Kieto had decided on a bold entrance, since they did not have a great deal of time and they had to make contact with Maori soon. Ru would only wait for a month off the coast of Rapanui.

It was true that Kikamana was with the exploratory party, and she was a member of Ru's crew, but no doubt Ru would find himself another virgin to take her place from amongst the Short Ears if he found it necessary to do so.

Kieto and the group came to a bend in the mighty river. At that moment there was a yell from a Maori sentry. A hundred warriors leapt to their feet and came charging down a slope in a tight formation which looked like a solid unit.

'Don't touch your weapons,' warned Kieto. 'Stand your ground.'

Seumas was itching to draw his club, but he did as he was ordered and hoped they would not be subject to the worst.

When the Maori saw that there were only six intruders, three of them women, they broke formation. The front ranks of the Maori stamped forward, step by step, with lolling tongues, distorted mouths and rolled-up eyes to show the whites. At the same time they sang a harsh song which sent shivers of fear through the newcomers. This was a terrifying spectacle and Polahiki turned to run – would have done so had not Boy-girl grabbed him by the arm and held him there.

By the dying light of the sun the visitors could see that the Maori had tattooed their faces, a custom which was repugnant to Kieto's people. It was true Hivans had tattoos on their faces, back in their old world, but not people from the Tahitian group of islands. Hivan tattoos tended to be straight bars and lines, whereas these Maori faces bore fantastic designs which followed the contours of their cheeks and mouths, around the eyes, on the brow. There were curlicues and whorls on the chin and down the nose the spine of a fish with spreading bones, and circles within circles, maze leading into maze on either side.

One man now came forward, brandishing a spear, his face twisted into a demonic expression. His legs in a wide stance, he stamped the ground, chanting oaths. With the spear he jabbed the air before him, continually.

Kieto cried, 'Brave warriors of the Maori, we come in peace. We are from a distant island. Give us your hospitality.'

The words had their effect. The warrior in front became less aggressive in his pose. He stared hard at the group. Finally he slapped his thigh and called.

'You are ship-wrecked here?'

'We are Rarotongans,' said Kieto. 'We have come to find the Maori tribes!'

'We are the Maori,' replied the warrior. 'Come with us.'

They were surrounded by the warriors and led towards the campfires. Seumas realised, as they approached the fires, that there were many more warriors than they had first imagined. There were several hundred men around the fires. This was no village either, but the camp of a force on the move.

The group was the object of curious interest as they were led through the camp by those who had captured them. Finally they were brought before a standing man who was flanked by two carved wooden posts stuck into the ground. The carving was of such superior quality that Seumas almost reached out and touched the posts. These he knew were staff-gods, probably ancestors-gods, and it would not have been wise to defile them with a stranger's hand. Nevertheless, he was impressed by the sheer craft of the artist, who must surely have been a genius.

'I am Chief Tuwhakapau,' said the tall stately figure between the posts. 'Where are you going?'

Seumas knew immediately why the chief did not ask who they were or where they were *from*. It might be that they were famous Oceanians and therefore to ask who they were would reveal ignorance in the chief. If they were notable men he would be expected to know who they were on sight. So, good manners dictated that he should not ask them their names, nor their homeland, but their destination only, since of this he could not be expected to have fore-knowledge.

'We are Rarotongans,' said Kieto, 'but from an Otherworld, out of the cave by the hot springs.' He named each of the party in turn. 'We come to learn of warfare from the masters of war, the great Maori race, O king.'

The chief stared at this motley group and suddenly grinned. His warriors laughed to see him smiling. Kieto and the others joined in the mirth. Then the man spoke again.

'You must not call me king, for the Maori do not have kings, we have only chiefs. We are not puffed-up Tahitians, with so much mana that we cannot walk among our own people. We are fighters—'

'That's why we have come to see you,' said Seumas, interrupting.

Heads turned to look at this new speaker. The Maori chief stepped forward and looked into Seumas's eyes, studied his hair, then stepped back again. He nodded.

'A Captain Cooker,' he said. 'You come from King George?'

Seumas did not know what to say to this, since it meant nothing to him.

'A Captain Cooker?' he asked at last, when the silence became unbearable. 'What is that?'

'You are a man from the tall ships,' said the Maori. 'You come with guns?'

Seumas looked helplessly at Kikamana. She was the one with the knowledge of this land. She was the one who should know what *guns* and *tall ships* were.

Kikamana said, 'I am a priestess. You must know we are from the Otherworld. We do not have such things as King Georgers and Captain Cookers there. You must forgive us for our ignorance. This man comes from Land-of-Mists, and his wife here, the same. Their land is without a sun.'

'Just the same,' nodded the Maori. 'Just the same as Captain Cook.'

'I do not know this Captain Cook,' said Seumas, evenly, 'and I have no king called George. My king is called Tangiia.'

The chief looked startled at this.

'You know the ancestor heroes?'

'Where we come from, Tangiia is no ancestor, but is alive and well.'

'Then,' said the chief, clearly impressed, 'you are from Hawaiki, the Old Homeland, where we all began!'

'What is he talking about?' Seumas asked Kieto, quietly.

'Hawaiki, the cradle of our people. Some say Raiatea was once Hawaiki, but no one really knows. It is the beginning and the end. A sacred land whence the earliest of our fathers and mothers emerged.'

'Hawaiki,' murmured the chief, this time a little more suspiciously. 'If you are from Hawaiki, then you must either be gods or ancestors.'

'Neither,' replied Kieto, 'but from *another* Hawaiki. Just as a palm overhanging a lake has an image in the water, a reflection of itself, so we come from a world which is the image of this world. Yet the lake ripples with the wind and so the two palms, the one on the bank and the one on the water, are not *exactly* the same, but have some differences. So it is with the two worlds, which are remote from each other, and similar in appearance. Without one, the other would not exist however, and each has its own importance in its own time.'

'What my leader here says is true,' Seumas confirmed. 'We can talk of reflections, or shadows, or the great ocean and the roof of voyaging. There are many examples.'

The chief nodded thoughtfully.

At this point Seumas felt he should not put himself forward any more and excused himself and stepped into the background, leaving Kieto and Kikamana to speak to the chief. Afterwards, when they were around a camp fire, not far from the Maori and under guard, they spoke amongst themselves.

'These people do not trust us yet,' explained Kieto, 'so they put a watch on us. But I believe they will let us take part in the battle. It's the only way we will get to fully understand their strategy and tactics. In the meantime, we must study their ways, try to understand them.'

Dorcha said, 'First I would like to understand what this place is and what it means to us. Seumas and I are completely confused with all this talk of King George and Captain Cook. Do you know who they are, Kikamana?'

The priestess shook her head. 'No, I have never heard of them, but what you must understand is that this world roughly mirrors our own. In this world there is probably a Kikamana somewhere, and maybe a Dorcha and Seumas. Or was. Or will be. This is not only a different place, but a different time. Perhaps in this world the Picts are the civilised race? – maybe the Picts rule Oceania? Perhaps George is king of the Picts and Captain Cook a Pictish hero? Who knows.'

'George doesn't sound like a Pict name,' grumbled Seumas. 'It doesn't sound like any sort of name at all.'

'That's not my point,' Kikamana said. 'My point is that you can take the same elements that make up the real world, put them in a pot and shake them up, then pour them out and find *this* world. Do you see what I mean?'

'No,' replied Seumas, 'and my head's spinning. Can we just leave it at that?'

They spent a cold night, shivering under their thin individual blankets. The following morning Chief Tuwhakapau appointed an elderly warrior as their companion. His name was Tangata. He was tall and very thin, his muscle tone beginning to flag, but he had an honest face. He explained what was happening.

'Maybe we kill you, maybe we don't,' smiled Tangata through broken and missing teeth. 'Chief Tuwhakapau is not sure whether or not it would be a good thing to kill the Captain Cookers just yet. Killing Captain Cookers might be tapu. He has consulted the tribe's two tohungas and one says kill you, the other says not to kill you. They argue a lot. In the meantime my advice is you must get our chief to love you, so even if it isn't tapu to kill you all, he lets you live because you're nice people.'

Tangata smiled again. His ancient leathery face, covered in blue-black tattoos the exact lines of which had disappeared into the creases caused by old age and the weather, had a kind of warm grotesque quality to it. With his thin grey hair, his wispy white beard, and his almost black eyes, he might have been someone's great-grandfather. He had the matter-of-fact, no-nonsense style of speech of the chief, and perhaps all Maori, and he left you in no doubt where you stood. An old, respected warrior, he would treat you right if you were genuine, but kill you instantly should you prove treacherous.

'What happens today?' asked Kieto. 'Do we break camp?'

'Yes, we go to the village of our enemies, where we make war with them.'

Boy-girl said, 'Why do you make war?'

The old Maori shook his head slowly. 'War is our destiny. Only in war can man find glory and honour. Perhaps you would not understand, being a stranger, but respect from other warriors is most important to us. And when we die, the great warrior goes to a shining paradise, where he will hear his praises sung by those he left behind to mourn his passing.'

'In other words,' said Boy-girl, in an aside to Kikamana, 'they don't need a reason.'

The Maori broke camp and the warriors went on the march. The six Rarotongans and their guide took up the rear. For them it was quite some feat, to travel overland at a near trot. It was a fatiguing journey. They went through bush and over grassland, into rainforest, up hill paths, along gorges, and finally in the middle of the afternoon Tangata pointed to their destination, a fortified hill village.

'The enemy pa,' said Tangata. 'They have seen us coming and sound their drums.'

To both the native Oceanians and to the Albannachs the pa was an astonishing sight, a piece of engineering beyond the experience of any of them.

The whole hillside had been flattened at the top and fell in tiers on all sides. A ring-ditch circled the outer defences, with a rampart and palisade immediately behind the trench. Along the outer palisade of sharpened stakes were fighting stages with ladders leading up to them. Behind the outer defences, on a higher level, was a second rampart and palisade, within which were thatched buildings, houses and store rooms. Placed at intervals along both the outer and inner stockades were posts of carved figures – ancestor gods – who along with the warriors of the tribe would help protect the village against invaders.

The defending warriors on the fighting stages looked down upon the approaching aggressors and seemed utterly superior. To Seumas, Kieto and the others their position appeared to be unassailable. To these visitors an impossible task lay ahead of the raiding party: overwhelming a foe in a position of such strength would take an army of thousands.

'It can't be done,' said Seumas. 'We chose the wrong side this time.'

The invaders ranged themselves on the plain below the fortified hill village and began a haka.

Warriors in serried ranks, Tangata among them, began to leap in unison first one way and then the other, at the same time letting out a deep resonating cry which curdled the blood. Their spears and clubs rose and fell in a perfect imitation of a breaker curling along a beach, so that they appeared not as many individual men, but as a single beast with a single mind. It was as if a monster were performing out there on that warm sunlit plain, a dark frill with white trimmings rippling along its front and flowing in waves back through its broad flat body.

Terrible screams came from the monster now, as the invading warriors alternated their deep bass notes with high blood-chilling shrieks. Fury foamed from every pore as they roused themselves to a fervour of battle-lust, their passion for killing evident in every brandish of a weapon, in every athletic leap of the body, in the rolling of eyes and the jerking of heads.

'Perhaps thousands of warriors will not be needed after all?' murmured Kieto, now thoroughly impressed. 'Perhaps these warriors will just flow over the fences like a giant octopus, sucking the life out of what lies underneath?'

On the ramparts of the village the defending warriors had gathered. Many of them were on the fighting stages, ready to cast rocks and spears down on the attacking forces. Others stood inside the palisades or behind the pa gate, over the lintel of which stood the tekoteko, an artistically sculpted statue of a demon possessing great magical powers of defence.

Once the haka was over, Tangata came running back to his six charges, to watch over them. If any treachery was to be done, it would be now, while the backs of the invaders were exposed to an attack from the plain. Tangata did not seem disappointed that he was unable to take part in the battle. He told them he had seen many wars, many such attacks, and having survived until a ripe age he intended to spend the rest of his years being a little more cautious in his fighting.

'What's happening now?' asked Kieto. 'Will there be a full frontal attack?'

Tangata was dubious about this. 'What we tried to do

was shame them into coming out and fighting us on the plain, but unless they're touched by the sun they won't do that. The village is too high to throw hot stones on the roofs of their houses, so we can't do that either. I think the young men will attempt to gain honour with a few rushes at the palisade, then we'll settle down into a nice long siege.'

The old man's words were no sooner out of his mouth when a group of young warriors, eager to gain respect and glory, ran to the palisade and launched their spears at the enemy. This action flushed a rash of spears from behind the ramparts of the fortified village. Most of the javelins missed their mark, but one or two struck flesh. A warrior on a fighting stage fell to his death. Three young men were either wounded or killed amongst the attackers.

One young attacking braveheart tried to rush and climb the palisade, club in his teeth, only to be crushed by a hail of rocks from the defenders, delighted to have a clear and available target for their missiles.

Following this foolhardy move the attackers sat down at a distance from the pa while one of their number strutted up and down, challenging the enemy to send out a warrior to do single combat with him. He shouted insults, boasted about his own prowess and skill at fighting, called those behind the wooden stakes 'babies' and 'little fish'.

His call was answered with alacrity by a member of the village and a hand-to-hand fight ensued between the two. The attacking forces gained the first victory and a great cheer went up amongst them. The next man from the pa was also despatched, but with less ease. Finally, on the third acceptance, the attacker's champion went down under a fierce blow and a groan went up from his companions. From the fort came the first cheer and the victor was allowed to return to his comrades behind the palisade to receive congratulations.

All this was pure sport to wile away the time.

Thereafter, the siege settled in and the attackers camped around the village, spending their time in eating and drinking and taunting the occupants. The hope was they could goad the warriors inside the village to come out and battle with the waiting besiegers, but so far the men of the village proved wisely invulnerable to this assault on their manhood. After all, Kieto pointed out, what was the point in spending a great deal of time and effort in building defences for a village, if you were going to abandon it for a handful of insults?

Kieto was extremely impressed with the pa. He saw in it great possibilities.

'It could be used as a fort, an encampment, when we set out to conquer the Land-of-Mists,' he said to Seumas. 'Have you seen anything like it before?'

'I have heard of such things amongst the Angles.'

'Then we will adopt this fortification too, and put it to our own use.'

The idea of a siege, starving or thirsting one's enemy into submission, was very new to the Rarotongan experience. Rarotongan battles were fought out in the open, with warriors dressed in their fine and colourful war garments.

The Rarotongans had, it was true, certain forms of organised warfare. There was the fatatia method where armies met face-to-face. Or the more sneaky aro nee where only they met the enemy on a narrow front and the larger flanks remained hidden behind trees or rocks, ready to pounce. And there was the aro ro where the army advanced in lines and when the first line had been battered or beaten, the second line moved up to take its place.

A more manly tactic was the paitoa, where the army was ordered to stand as firm as a stone wall, while the enemy hurled themselves against them.

In uura tama faarere no man was allowed to leave the battlefield alive before they had conquered the opposing force.

One method which might turn an enemy army around, if it had weak leaders, was the ropa tahi. In this the whole attacking army made it known they were concentrating mainly on killing chiefs and warriors of high rank. This tactic was enough to frighten the bravest warrior king, faced with a horde of fanatical hot-blooded young men intent on killing him alone, regardless of who might get in the way.

Kieto got to speak with Tangata.

'When we first approached your camp,' he said, 'your warriors came out in a tight formation – what do you call that?'

'This we call the *turtle*,' replied the old man, grinning. 'We will use it again – against *them*.'

He pointed to the forces behind the pa, which numbered around nine hundred men. The attacking force was in the region of fifteen hundred warriors. It was almost two against one, if it ever came to an open fight.

Tangata was quite happy to sit down and talk about the fighting methods of the Maori. He had seen much and was full of knowledge on the subject. Kieto took it all in, asking many questions, receiving information on strategy and tactics of famous battles. Tangata was a fund of fighting experience, which he was quite happy to share with his questioner, since it made him the centre of attention.

'What about sea battles,' asked Kieto. 'Are the Maori good at fighting on the water.'

'Not as good as on the land,' admitted Tangata with a show of honesty. 'The people of Hawaii are much better, I have heard. A ship called here not long ago telling us of a great sea battle there, between two kings.'

'Tell us about it,' said Kieto.

There had been news of a war between two cousins on the Hawaiian Islands. Kamehameha and Kiwalao, whose decisive sea battle off a beach known as Mokuohai had resulted in a victory for Kamehameha. The Hawaiian God of War, Kukailimoku – a fearsome deity with lustrous eyes and blood-red head – had ensured the felling of Kiwalao with a stone from a sling and one of Kamehameha's warriors had dispatched the chief by slitting his throat with a lei-o-mano. Thus the Hawaiian islands of Kauai, Oahu, Molokai, Lanai, Maui and Hawaii now came under the domination of one man.

As Seumas listened to the story unfold, once again he marvelled at the Oceanian memory. Each detail of the battle was recounted by Tangata and Seumas had no doubt it would be entirely accurate. This was a war which Tangata had not personally seen, but which had taken place thousands of miles away, at the farthest reaches of the Ocean. Yet the old man had committed to memory all that had been told to him by the visiting sailors from that land, whose own memories were as reliable as day following night. In turn, Kieto would have all these particulars locked in *his* memory.

The Oceanian's ability to retain minutia was phenomenal, making him one of the greatest navigators of all time, one of the finest oral story-tellers the world has ever known and unmatched by any other race at recounting personal and national history.

2

Ragnu had learned through his occult powers that the son of Seumas the Pict was now travelling with the Arioi and was indeed one of its number. This discovery was a revelation to the priest, who now saw further possibilities of wreaking revenge on the Rarotongans. To kill the son of Seumas would be to ensure that the goblin's line ended with his death. What more could a bitter man ask for than the total destruction of a family?

'Now I have you,' muttered the priest. 'I have you and I have your soul.'

The idea of killing one of the Arioi, a member who had risen quite high in its ranks, despite being a Hivan, fitted in with the priest's wider plans. He had long since become jealous of the rising power of the Arioi. Its Painted Legs were now regarded almost as equal to kings in rank. In fact, one of its Painted Legs *was* a king who had placed his duties and obligations behind him to join what Ragnu considered to be riff-raff.

Ragnu discussed his plans with his other priests, underlings who would follow their lord to the depths of the ocean if he so desired.

'To kill this creature, a Hivan youth called Kumiki, I must first be able to penetrate the ranks of the Arioi.'

'How will you do that, lord?' asked one of his priests. 'The Arioi might be a troupe of travelling singers and poets, but there are warriors amongst them – wrestlers, spearmen, others – who are quite capable of protecting their comrades. One hundred and fifty ships – that's a fighting force if necessary.'

'True,' said Ragnu. 'A hundred and fifty ships. In any other guise it would be an invasion fleet, would it not? But we have a navy to equal it. The last king feared invasion from the Hivans and so built a flotilla of ships which would meet such a need. What if I were to be given command of the Raiatean war ships and was sent out to attack the Arioi?'

The younger priests looked at their kahuna with mystified expressions on their faces.

'But who would give such an order?' said one at last. 'The Arioi are welcomed everywhere they go. They are a peaceful group. That's why they show their yellow sails, so that no island nation will attack them, thinking them to be aggressors. Who would order such an attack?'

'Our own king,' said Ragnu, enjoying unravelling his scheme for his followers. 'If he believes the Arioi to be something else – an attacking force from the Hivan Islands.'

There were nods amongst the other priests now. They had learned over the years not to underestimate their lord's intellect and magic. His sorcery was equalled by none. His knowledge of the secret ways was legendary amongst them. He could make beasts of the night, turn men into frogs, change the shape of the weather, destroy the indestructible.

'You must have worked out a plan,' said one of his students, 'for poisoning the king's mind against the Arioi.'

'Not *poison*,' Ragnu explained, his eyes glinting, 'but misrepresentation. The king will perceive a threat and I shall step forward and offer my services, to remove that threat. When the mistake is known, I shall be horrified, but who will blame me, since my own king has ordered me to attack?'

One of the priests opened his mouth to speak, but Ragnu continued by saying, 'I know what you're about to ask – how will I make the king perceive a menace where there is none? – but that must remain my secret for the time being. If I told you all, you would be as clever as I am, and that cannot be.'

This made the other priests laugh and even brought a smile to the face of the would-be questioner.

One young man, a newcomer to their midst, had one last question to ask.

'Will you be satisfied, my lord, with just *killing* the son of Seumas? I would have thought torture . . .'

'Yes, yes,' snapped Ragnu, waspishly, 'of course you would have thought torture more appropriate. Killing a man quickly does not salve the desire for revenge, does it? But when a man dies slowly and in great agony, this is as good as having him to oneself and killing him by painful degrees.'

Ragnu went to a shelf on the temple wall and took down an object wrapped in cloth. He laid it on the floor and unwrapped the item carefully, to reveal a horrible weapon called an airo fai. It was an implement invented by the devious high priests of Tahiti, kept hidden until a crucial point in any battle, then brought out and used to terrify the enemy. Used like a dagger, the sharpened bone with its flex-ible backward-sweeping curved spikes, went *in* smoothly and easily. It was when the instrument was wrenched *out*, with the backbone barbs opening like jointed spines, that the terrible damage was done.

Many of the young priests present gasped at the sight of the ugly weapon and one or two went pale as images entered their heads, of the weapon being used.

Ragnu smiled at their squeamishness and said, 'The ser-rated back-bone of a sting ray, fashioned thus into this long dagger, will inflict such terrible wounds on a man – rip his insides out, tearing the flesh ragged – that he will die in the most dreadful circumstances. He will suffer such pain as would cause a god to howl. He will drag himself from enemy to friend, begging to be clubbed out of his misery.'

The priests stared in awe at the weapon, knowing Ragnu's words to be true.

Ragnu picked up the dagger and began to walk amongst his men, as if musing on an interesting subject.

'Of course, one cannot use such a weapon without testing its capabilities, and fortunately it has come to my attention that there is a spy amongst us – someone sent by King Tangiia of Rarotonga to report on my affairs. That person will be a suitable testing ground for my Tahitian gift, will he not? Don't you agree? Do I hear murmurs of assent?'

He heard nothing, for the whole group had gone deathly still. Several priests had begun trembling, though this was not proof of guilt, for any man with even the faintest threat on his head might be forgiven for shaking in such circumstances.

Faces had drained of colour. Even those who were secure in the knowledge of their innocence realised they would have to witness a gory execution and were not looking forward to the prospect.

Up and down their ranks strolled the crooked figure of Ragnu, highest of high priests, his hand clutching the weapon the Tahitians called the airo fai. Sweat rolled from their brows as they stared straight ahead, unwilling and afraid to look their lord in the eye. The tension in the room grew with every second, until its silent scream could be heard by every ear, its tautness in every breath taken by the waiting men.

Finally, one youthful priest could stand the suspense no longer, jumped to his feet with a cry, and tried to flee the room in which the stress was unbearable.

Ragnu was quick as a spider across the floor. He reached the youth, spun him round with a swift hand, and buried the airo fai in the young man's stomach. The youth gave out a terrible scream. Ragnu twisted the weapon half a turn in the wound, then tore it out, pulling with it on its many hooks of bone part of the priest's stomach and intestines. The grey, bloodied innards dangled like a gory umbilical cord from a hole no bigger than a man's eye socket, while the victim fell to his knees and tried to push them back inside again, screaming incessantly as he did so.

Ragnu made his priests sit where they were and witness the victim's slow death as he convulsed and shrieked – the air reeking of blood, gore and human excrement – taking as long as the great fire in the middle of the temple to finally die.

When the ashes of the fire were cold, and the young traitor had finally breathed his last, Ragnu allowed the others to go, knowing the scene would have impressed them beyond any words he could have uttered. Of course the youth had not been a traitor – there were no such creatures amongst the ranks of Ragnu's priests – but it did no harm to occasionally make an example of one of them, just in case.

3

Finally, the goading of the attackers drew the young manhood of the defending force outside the walls of the pa. The Rarotongans, still under guard, watched from a nearby hill as the two armies clashed with great ferocity on both sides. Kieto was eager to be down there in the mêlée, but the Maori chief forbade it. The Rarotongans were still under suspicion.

The quality of the fighting was superior to anything Kieto had ever seen before. It was clear to him that the training and philosophy of the Maori youth resulted in a warrior who was of the highest excellence when it came to warfare. Even Dorcha, the person least impressed with violence, acknowledged the fact that she had never seen such accomplished fighters as the Maori.

As with most open-plain warfare amongst Oceanians, the battle swayed back and forth, despite the disparity in numbers. When a bad omen appeared in the sky – a cloud shaped like a lizard – the attackers took flight and ran towards their distant home, even though their numbers were vastly superior. It was not cowardice to run, it was proper battle form. A few moments later the fleeing army decided there was nothing to fear from the gods, since no further bad portents appeared, and they turned on their pursuers, whose valour had now dissipated. Suddenly hunters became hunted, running in the opposite direction!

In the end, as the day died so did many of the defending force, and the remainder retreated into the pa. The following morning negotiations took place, with envoys like birds flying between pa and invaders' encampment, and finally some agreement was reached between Chief Tuwhakapau and the chief of the pa. Seumas, Dorcha and the others never did find out what the original argument had been, but it seemed to follow Tangata's explanation: warfare for its own sake, in order that men might gain respect, glory and fame amongst their kind.

It transpired the defending force had recently been wasted by an epidemic of some kind (brought to them, said Tangata, by Captain Cookers) and an earlier war with a tribe in the next valley along. The pa was therefore a lot more weakly defended than it had first appeared and the families inside were fearful of being overrun by blood-crazed warriors who might burn and loot, kill and maim, in the heat of the moment, possibly to regret their impulsiveness later.

The reason the youths came out to do battle with the attackers was so that honour could be satisfied and the fire could be taken out of the invading force who had worked themselves up to a fever pitch for the battle. Once these two goals had been accomplished, the chief of the pa could take the unusual step of surrendering his village to the enemy, rather than face a long siege or the threat of fire.

Now that the war was at an end, on both sides there were ceremonies to purify the warriors. At the start of the war the priests had consecrated the fighters and that tapu had to be erased before the terms of any settlement could be negotiated. The drums of peace sounded within and without the walls of the pa.

Once these formal rites were over the defeated chief came out with a bundle of sticks and some leaves. These

were the materials for his own roasting, should the invading chief think it necessary to kill and cook him. It was an
old Samoan custom, no doubt picked up by the Maori chief
from some mariner, to take the sting out of the occasion.
The materials for the fire were symbolic only, a gesture, not
to be taken seriously.

Chief Tuwhakapau was magnanimous in victory however and exchanged bonds of friendship with the defeated
chief.

'You were great in your generalship,' said the pa chief.
'You deserved to win.'

'No, no, my strategy was of little account,' the victor
demurred. 'The weather was good to us, the wind was in
the right direction for the flight of our spears and we
probably surprised you with the suddenness of our attack.'

It was good form for the victor to make excuses for the
failures of the defeated army, to give them back a little of
their honour. It was all right to boast before the battle, but
afterwards the winners were expected to be modest. They
had, after all, seized the day, and had nothing more to
prove.

Once terms had been agreed, the pa chief went back to
his village to prepare for the entrance of the victorious
chief, his nobles and priests. Instead of opening the gate to
let him in, a section of the stockade was lowered, for Chief
Tuwhakapau was now a special guest and the right courte-
sies had to be shown to him. The pa chief needed to show
he was going through a certain amount of trouble to receive
his guest.

Kieto asked the old man Tangata whether they would be
allowed to accompany the nobles to see the inside of the pa.

'I shall ask the Chief Tuwhakapau,' said Tangata. 'No
doubt you are considered lucky for him since he has won
the battle and you have shown no treachery. Had he lost,
you might be roasting on a fire now, but since he
won . . .'

The chief said he would be pleased for visitors from sacred Hawaiki to form part of his retinue.

The group of six found themselves the objects of much curiosity from the inhabitants of the pa. It was a strange time, for there was mourning in progress, for the dead warriors on both sides, yet there was festivity in the air, because the war was over and honour had been satisfied. Kieto and his band had to be cautious in what they said and to whom they spoke, so that no tapu was violated in any way.

Dorcha was amazed at the quality of the carvings on the houses of the Maori.

'Look at the designs on the walls too,' she said, after viewing the wooden figures which made the house posts, 'and the patterns on the ceiling!'

The interior of the meeting house was indeed very beautiful, no less than the exterior. When she and Seumas walked around the village they found other houses, not quite as artistically wrought as the meeting house, but with carvings and patterns of high quality. A storehouse was among the most attractively carved buildings and it sported a carved figure on the point of the pitched roof which had something similar to the topknots of the giants on Rapanui perched on its head.

Seumas, however, was more interested in the fortifications than the artistry of the carvings.

He walked along the palisade in the early morning while the sun glinted on the dew-covered sharpened stakes and wondered about his own people in Albainn. Dorcha walked beside him, occasionally looking up into his worried features. She knew he was battling with his emotions and she knew too that she was important enough to him for her advice to mean something.

'What are we to do?' he asked Dorcha 'When it comes to the point where we must choose whether or not to join the expedition to Albainn, what are we to do?'

'What does your head tell you to do? Forget your heart.

We both know that even if we hated our birthplace, it would still give us pain to see it conquered. What you must do is put your feelings aside and think about the best course of action.'

'Am I to be concerned about being called a traitor, reviled by my clan?'

'You should not let it influence your decision, if you have a greater good in mind.'

He nodded thoughtfully.

Dorcha knew that Seumas had grown in mental and spiritual stature since he had been amongst the Oceanians. When he had arrived on Raiatea he had been a headstrong Pict, full of the vanities of manhood, whose fear of peer opinion dictated his actions. In those far-off days, he had to act like the man he was expected to be. Now his wisdom had matured, he had grown away from that bull-headed Pict and had a much more thoughtful and sensitive nature which he was not ashamed to display, knowing it made him no less a warrior for it. He made decisions himself and no longer automatically fell in with general opinion.

'It must be,' he said at last, staring over the fence at the grassy plains beyond, where the shining river wound its broad flat back, out of the distant mountains, 'that I at least will go with Kieto when he attempts his conquest of our homeland. You shall come too, if you wish, of course – but I will not persuade you to do that for which I have little stomach myself.

'I will not take part in any fighting nor assist either side in any way, but I must be on hand to smooth the path to peace. Whatever happens Kieto will go with his Oceanians to the Land-of-Mists and my refusal to join him will make little difference to the outcome. If I am there, however, I shall be available as a go-between, knowing both sides as I do. Someone who understands both Oceanian and Albannach *must* be there, to explain any misconceptions, so that unnecessary bloodshed can be avoided.

'Think what a Scot or a Pict would make of a man running away on the battlefield! By his own code he would be entitled to consider that man lower than dirt and to be shown no mercy. Think what an Oceanian would make of men who ambushed him! By his code he would be entitled to believe those men cowards and worse than beasts in their behaviour. Someone must be there to explain that under the rules of their own kind, both are legitimate actions and not to be taken as an insult.'

Dorcha put an arm around the waist of her man. 'You have more wisdom in you now, Seumas, than I would ever have believed you capable of in the old days. You know that if the Oceanians lose, or if you get captured, the clans will burn out your eyes, cut off your testicles – and then, when they think you are numb with pain, they'll quarter you with horses.'

Seumas sighed. 'I know it. They won't understand my position. It's impossible to expect them to make the leap that has taken me half a lifetime to achieve. I will be an abject traitor in their eyes – less than pigshit. Their hate for me will be very deep. They'll feed my remains to the crows.'

'But you have to go.'

He nodded, his eyes on hers.

'I have to go.'

'And I shall go with you.'

'You don't have to. I know how it'll distress you. When it's all over, I'll come back to Rarotonga. I wouldn't live very long in those winters, not now, now that I know a different weather. I want to end my years in the sun.'

She shook her head. 'And what if you *don't* come back – because you can't, I mean? I want to be there with you, when you die – if you die. It's right I should be there.'

'It might be the death of you, too.'

'So be it.'

He turned and studied the landscape around him, admiring the shape of it, noting the contrasts. Here, in the Land of the Long White Cloud there were many scenes. There were the hot springs, the geysers, the forests, the volcanoes, the grasslands, the braided rivers, the hills and mountains, the plains – and Tangata had told them of an island below this one, where there were glaciers whose snouts reached the sea, and high mountains covered with snow, and areas of perpetual rain. It was an interesting landscape, a coat with many different cuts.

'I could settle for this land, except that it's not in our world,' he said.

'We must go back.'

'Yes, we must.'

He stared at her for a moment and her features were caught in the light of the early sun. He touched her greying hair then looked away from her, quickly. She caught the gesture and mistook it.

'I know, I'm not as young as I once was.'

'It's not that,' he said, turning back, his eyes shining. He looked close to tears. 'I was thinking – I was thinking how I wronged you once, and how much I love you now . . .'

She said, 'We were never to speak of that again.'

'No, not me. You said *you* would not speak of it. Dorcha, I killed your husband – killed him in a fight over a sword. You hated me for it long enough, even when I'd learned to love you, but then you put your hate aside.'

'I learned to love you too, Seumas.'

'And you are prepared to come with me, to the place where I took your husband from you. You're willing to return to the land where we hated each other. You know what your clan will say to you, don't you? They'll call you a whore, a slut, for bedding your husband's murderer . . . oh, I know it wasn't like that, it was a fair fight, but all that won't make any difference to them. Those Scots, they'll despise you for sleeping with a Pict, an animal, a man who covers his skin with pictures, a savage, one of the Black clan. Are you sure going back there is not going to arouse unwanted memories, bring back the bitterness, call up the hate we once felt for each other?'

She smiled and took his hand. 'Do you think I'm still beautiful, Seumas the Black?'

He looked serious. '*A kotuku is seen but once,*' he replied, using an Oceanian saying. 'You're the finest woman – Dorcha, I love your body so much it chokes me to look at you. I can't believe how lucky I am to have such a woman at my side.'

'Good enough, Seumas. Yes, I may think on my old life, on the man I once had when we were young, but that was a different woman then. I was with him three years. You and I have been together for over twenty . . .'

'It's not the time.'

'No, it isn't, but it is the *feeling*. We're going there together,' she said, 'and when we've been there, we'll come back home again – to *our* home.'

He seemed happy with that and they said no more on the subject. They would both accompany Kieto. They had seen the boy grow into a man. They loved him. He had been their guide in Oceania, to the ways of its people, as well as its secret paths, its hidden places. He would need them on his campaign, his crusade to take the gods and culture, the ways of Oceania, to the people of Albainn and Engaland.

4

The Arioi fleet had been at sea for a month. They had climbed the waves of the ocean, descended into its valleys, and now they were – almost to a person – glad to see the shores of Nuku Hiva, one of several Hivan islands they would visit.

The Hivans themselves, a tall, handsome people, were not supposed to be generally enamoured of the Arioi. They called themselves a warrior race who believed actors and singers to be rather effeminate creatures. However, there were many among them who secretly enjoyed a good show, who publicly scorned the travelling players but secretly admired them. Certainly there was a kind of suppressed excitement amongst them.

Thus, as with any island group visited by the famous Tahitian Arioi, the beaches were crowded with people. There were indeed warriors amongst them, men such as Kumiki had once been, with twisted horns of hair on their otherwise shaven heads and tattooed on their faces with forbidding solid bars. Dedicated to cannibalism more than any other Oceanians, Hivans were rightly feared by their neighbours. Workers in stone, their marae and ahu stood outside temples of hewn rock. They were a formidable race with solid foundations.

They stood and stared quietly, while around them women and young people chattered with excitement as the yellow sails of the Arioi fleet drew closer and the singing could be heard.

'We are the Arioi, full of colour and light.
'We come to entertain you with our dancing and
    song.
'Witness our acrobats, hear our musicians, listen to
    our singers!
'We have poets and storytellers, we have enchanters!
'The Arioi are come! The Arioi are come!'

The chants reached the shore and filled the waiting Hivans with great glee. Children ran back into the villages to rouse invalid grandparents, haul them down to the beaches to watch this wondrous sight. Grandsons carried grandmothers and grandfathers on their shoulders. People cleared a pathway for those so old that they were laden with a tapu, in order that they should not be touched, even accidentally. Fat dogs, some only hours away from the pot, caught the excitement and yapped and barked. Pigs squealed, running around their pens, wondering what all the fuss was about. Cockerels crowed. Clamour was the order of the day.

On board the pahi the entertainers were in full swing, letting rip with their voices in song, leaping and dancing across pahi, playing their various instruments.

On one of the front pahi were gathered the drummers, pounding out their various exciting rhythms, while at the mast stood their leader, for the moment not playing, reserving his greater talents for the entertainment of chiefs. He was a tall, proud man, a Painted Leg, the first drummer ever to reach this exalted position. His right leg, tattooed black, was thrust forward for all on the beaches to see, and when the watching Hivans stared into his face they saw three solid bars tattooed across his cheeks and nose.

A Hivan! The words went hissing down the beach with the speed of surf on a curling breaker. The Painted Leg was a Hivan, a man from their own islands! A surge of immense pride went through the crowd. Chief Api Api was sent word. One of his own people had become a Painted Leg!

No matter that travelling players were regarded with some disdain by Hivan warriors – that was when they were Tahitians, a rather foppish people in any case – here was one of their own kind now a king of song and dance, of singers and dancers. Here was a Hivan supreme amongst all the artistes of Oceania. In the whole world the Arioi were the best, the most talented and lauded of entertainers, close to the gods, and of their number the best of the Arioi was one of their own kind. It was incredible.

Chief Api Api listened in amazement, hurried down to the beaches with a guard and retinue of priests, stood waiting as the Painted Leg – who in any case seemed to be a drummer, which happily unlike dancing or poetry was a fairly masculine vocation when all was said and done – stepped into the surf and strode onto the shore, to stare about him in a haughty manner.

The crowd moved in, not close enough to touch the Painted Leg, for he was surely a tapu, but to stare into his eyes, to see if they knew him at all. One woman, whose mouth had dropped open in wonder, suddenly found her voice and informed the people of Nuku Hiva of the name of this great man.

'Kumiki!' she cried. 'It is my Kumiki!'

The Painted Leg's face lost its disdainful expression for a few moments as his eyes anxiously searched the crowd for the owner of this voice. However, before his eyes could lock onto those of the person who had identified him, the people parted, and Chief Api Api stood before him. Kumiki's face assumed its former cavalier aspect and he greeted the chief.

'My Lord,' he said, 'I am happy to return to my home island as a Painted Leg, an Avae Parai,' he thrust his decorated limb forward for all to see, 'honoured among the distant islands. I am your own Kumiki, a humble bastard prince of Nuku Hiva. I return in triumph to greet my Chief, Api Api, and bring him gifts of mother-of-pearl, sharks' teeth, greenstone carvings, wooden ornaments, weapons and other treasures . . .'

A bundle was brought forward and unrolled at the chief's feet to reveal these items, and more, under the solemn but barely contained gaze of the chief.

'Kumiki,' said Api Api, after clearing his throat, 'I accept the gifts you bring and add my own praises to those already heaped upon your young head. You have brought great honour to me and my family, to these islands of the Hiva nation, and we are proud you are one of our sons. Come, you will share my basket with me, and tell me all about your conquests.'

Kumiki, followed by his faithful friends, the Otiore dancer Linloa and Ramoro, an Harotea, went with Api Api. Linloa was sent by the Chief to eat with his daughters. Since she was an Arioi, where women were regarded the equal of men, she was actually allowed to eat pork and dog meat with the men, but she made no complaint which might have spoilt the day for Kumiki.

Both Ramoro and Kumiki were allowed to share from the chief's own basket. A very great honour indeed. Ramoro was not entirely at ease, a Tahitian who preferred men to women amongst the savage Hivan people (who knew of what they were capable?), but Kumiki was relaxed and glowing with immense pride. He had left this island a boy in search of a father and had returned a great man.

Chief Api Api had no idea who Kumiki was at first. Now he had been surreptitiously informed by his priests that this was the son of a captured enemy chief's wife. She too had been a Hivan, but from another island, not Nuku

Hiva. The boy had unfortunately been sired by a goblin when the Raiateans had briefly touched the island and killed many people in his father's time. Then, when the youth had reached his manhood, he had set out to find this goblin father and kill him, for raping his mother and causing so much grief amongst the Hivan people. There was more to the story than that, as the chief well knew, but he kept his secrets to himself.

'Have you completed your mission yet?' asked Api Api of Kumiki, as they gnawed on dog meat. 'Did you find the lustful demon who forced himself between your mother's plump thighs?'

Kumiki frowned. He was a sensitive man and he did not like the picture of his mother conjured up by Chief Api Api's words. It seemed to him that things could have been put a little more delicately. There were certain adjectives used here which trivialised his mother's terrifying, humiliating and degrading experience and might have been dispensed with given the circumstances. However, even though he was now a Painted Leg, and felt himself to be vastly superior to the grubby chief of a Nuku Hivan tribe, he could hardly call to task a man who commanded several thousand fierce warriors.

'I am afraid I have not yet had the pleasure of slitting the goblin's throat,' replied Kumiki. 'It seems the foreigner called Seumas is on a voyage with the great navigator Ru, on his way to find a new island. When he returns from his seafaring, I shall seek him out and dispatch him.'

Chief Api Api seemed a little amused.

'I have never heard of a man hunting down his own father before. One usually reveres one's father.'

'This is surely a father like no other,' interrupted Ramoro. 'This Seumas is a creature from hell.'

'And what does that make your friend here?' said the chief, sipping kava juice and allowing himself to become very slightly drunk. 'A son of the creature from hell?'

Ramoro said, 'A man cannot choose his own father. The seed of the goblin has been overwhelmed by the long line of Hivan forefathers held by the mother of Kumiki. This demon's seed was but a trigger, to activate the birth of Kumiki, whose talents as a drummer have shown him to be worthy of his ancestors, to be a culmination of their collective selves. He has gathered within him all the skills of his grandfathers, going back to Tiki, and the demon's seed has been smothered, lost, in the flood of pure Oceanian which forms our friend.'

Api Api nodded. 'I agree. There is little enough of the goblin in Kumiki – yet, it is still a strange exercise, to chase one's own father with murder in mind. Shall you eat him, when you finally cut out his heart?'

Kumiki, to whom the question had been addressed, stared thoughtfully into the distance.

'If his flesh is not tainted, not nocuous in any respect, then I shall roast him like a lizard on a stick and eat every vital part of him – brains, liver, heart and lungs. The rest I shall throw to the sharks.'

'Sounds suitable,' said the chief, nodding his approval. 'I would do the same.'

Later, after they had left the chief to sleep off the effects of the kava, Kumiki and Ramoro went to supervise the building of the great stage. It was important that a Painted Leg should be there, while the gods were being invoked for a good performance. Oro, the God of War and Peace, was their patron, and as the platform was being erected sacrifices of lizards, a pig and a dog were made in his honour. While the sacrifices took place a story teller informed the thousands of Hivans watching the building of the stage how dancing first came to Oceania, through Koro, son of Tini Rau, Lord of the Fishes:

'One day when the world was young and the sea so blue it hurt a man's eyes to stare at it, Tini Rau, Lord of the Fishes, who lived on the Sacred Isle, but sometimes stayed on Mangaia, went for a walk wearing a necklace made of pandanus seeds. At this time Tini Rau was indeed staying on Mangaia, near Rarotonga, enjoying a pleasant break from his normal duties. His son Koro caught the fragrance of the seeds, which perfumed the air all around Tini Rau, and decided to follow his father.

'Koro watched as his father shinned up the trunk of a palm tree and knocked down some coconuts. These he husked on a sharpened stake, then broke open the kernel and scraped out the sweet meat of the coconut, wrapping it in a pandanus leaf.

'Tini Rau then carried the parcel of coconut meat to a place on the shoreline, where the rocks met the sea, tumbling down into its depths and forming a kind of rough ramp. Tini Rau stood ankle-deep at the head of this ramp and commenced to scatter the coconut like ground bait on the surface of the sea.

'First came all the shoals of tiny silver fish, millions of them, with brightly coloured cousins. Soon the water was swarming with yellows, blues, stripes, and all the colours of the ocean as the small fry came in to feed on the food being fed them by the Lord of the Fishes. Then came the larger reef fish – parrot fish, trigger fish, angel fish, red snapper – and a thousand other kinds of largish fish. These were followed by big fish like sharks, dolphin, porpoise, whales. Then octopi, squid, sting rays, manta rays. Soon, to Koro's amazement, the whole sea was frothing with fish of every shape and size.

'Koro's awe at the number of fish was short lived, for an even more wonderful thing happened as the Sacred Isle itself came over the horizon and slipped over the reef of Mangaia.

'At this point all the fish in the lagoon came up the rocky ramp on to the Sacred Isle, some having assumed full human shape, and others remaining partly in the water but having taken on the form of mermaids. Once they were all on land, or in shallows, the Sacred Isle began to float away like a boat, while the figures on it danced and sang, creating a beautiful sight.

'Koro, nor indeed any other man but Tini Rau, had seen dancing before and it was a sight which took his breath away with excitement. Never before had he seen movement which was so exquisite. Once the Sacred Isle was out of sight, however, Koro's exhilaration dissipated and he was left forlorn.

'The following evening Koro climbed a palm and gathered some coconuts, spreading the meat on the waters of the Mangaia's lagoon and chanting the fangu he had heard his father sing.

'Fishes came from far and wide, and eventually, also the Sacred Isle, gliding over the top of the reef. There were the fishmen dancing on its beaches, in its shallows, and Tini Rau, smiling, waving an admonishing finger at his son.

'Tini Rau welcomed Koro on to the Sacred Isle, where the dancing went on for many nights and days, at the end of which Koro decided that this activity had to be given to all men and women, whoever they were, and having obtained permission from his father made sure all ordinary mortals knew how to dance.

'This is how paradise came to earth, when Koro taught mankind the wonderful art of dancing!'

Once the stage was built, Kumiki was able to leave the place and find a spot in the forest to rest. Linloa, his faithful friend and assistant went with him, making a bed for him out of dried grasses and standing watch while he slept. Kumiki slept the sleep of the weary until he was woken in the early evening by the sound of argument close by.

He opened his eyes to find Linloa restraining a local female and ordering her away from the place.

'How dare you tell me where to go!' cried the young

woman. 'This is *my* island. I go where I please. And I wish to speak with the Painted Leg they call Kumiki.'

Kumiki sat up and rubbed his eyes, before asking, 'And why do you wish to speak with me.'

The girl turned a shining face on him, her teeth gleaming like mother-of-pearl as she smiled.

'It is I,' she cried. 'Your own beloved Miro!'

Kumiki leapt to his feet in excitement. This was the woman for whom he had done everything: joined the Arioi, climbed its ranks, become one of the fabulous and rare Avae Parai. This was the woman he had left behind, but swore to return to in triumph one day and sweep her off her feet, away from covetous relatives.

'Miro!' he cried. 'It is all right, Linloa – this is my long-lost love, my own beautiful Miro.'

Linloa's face fell as she regarded the plump and shining Hivan woman beside her and the little Tahitian girl who had ministered to Kumiki since he had joined the Arioi quietly left the glade.

Kumiki, left with his excited Miro, was moved to kiss the woman of whom he had dreamed since he left Nuku Hiva. Her lips tasted like ripe fruit. His hands roved over her soft firm body, touching her round breasts, her fat thighs, exploring the secrets of her hidden garden. Suddenly, she giggled.

Kumiki was annoyed. 'What is it?'

'Nothing,' she murmured, playing with a necklace of seeds, and looking at his Painted Leg, the symbol of his greatness, 'but we mustn't you know, not *really*.'

His irritation grew and he was astonished. He had been away for many, many months, and now he was being told 'he mustn't'? It was ludicrous. He desired her and once they had made love he intended to ask, nay *demand* her hand from her father, who would not dare refuse a Painted Leg, beloved of the people, king of entertainers, friend of Chief Api Api.

'What are you talking about?' he asked. 'Speak, my beloved. Your father cannot refuse us now.'

'Why,' she said, slyly. 'I might let you do something to me, on this moss, but you must promise never to tell.'

'For what reason?'

'Because I'm *married*, of course,' she growled playfully, as if to a child. 'My husband would kill me.'

Kumiki was stunned. He took a step back from her and stared. Had he heard right? Married? It was not possible. She had promised to wait for him. There was a pact. They had sworn an oath to each other under the gaze of Hine-keha. How could she possibly be wed to some other man?

'Married?' he repeated, stupidly.

'Yes, but you can have me now, here, on the ground. I want to feel you inside me. Look, my legs are trembling with excitement . . .' She took his penis in her hand and began pulling him forwards by it, guiding it towards her vagina. 'Quickly, before someone comes – put your seed in my belly!'

Kumiki gave out a great cry of emotional pain, pulled his tapa skirt over his genitals, and pushed her away from him.

'Get away from me. Married? How could you be married? You said you'd wait for me. We both promised we'd wait for each other.'

She pouted. 'Yes, but you were gone so long. I thought you might have met someone else.' She said, 'You can't expect a person to wait for years you know.'

But that was just what he *had* expected. Now this, to return to his home isle in triumph, to be fêted by kings, only to find that the girl he had left behind had waited – how long?

'When did you get married?' he asked, dully.

She told him. It was only a few months after he had left her standing on the beach. He sighed, realising he could not blame her. It was he who had sailed off over the horizon. She would have been happy had he stayed and forgotten his so-called father. Now all his dreams had been felled like trees, all in one day, one hour, one moment. And it was his own fault. He could not blame her for that.

'Leave me,' he said, wearily. 'Go back to your husband.'

She looked annoyed at this. 'Aren't you going to make love to me? I want to tell all the other women I've been with a Painted Leg. They'll be so jealous.'

'Go back to your husband,' he repeated.

Her face screwed up into a vicious expression.

'You can't do this to me,' she snapped, 'I'm precious.'

With that she flounced out of the glade and was gone.

Kumiki sat down on the moss. His spiritual pain was beginning to subside a little. It was true he would never get over this terrible blow, but he had seen his beloved Miro in a different light today. Her demands had been for selfish reasons, for petty reasons, so that she could brag to the other women at the water place, not because she regretted her rash actions and still felt an overwhelming love for him. He considered himself lucky to have escaped so lightly. Had he married her instead of going off to search for his father, she would now be cheating on him.

There was a rustle of leaves and he looked up sharply, wondering whether the ghosts of one of his ancestors was spying on him in his grief. However, Linloa stood there.

'She's gone?' said Linloa.

Kumiki nodded. 'It seems she is already married.'

Something like a look of relief passed over the features of Linloa and her tone suddenly became almost lighthearted.

'Well, never mind, there are more women in the world. You are desired by a great many.'

'They are impressed by my drumming, by my Painted Leg,' he said mournfully, 'but who would love me for myself? Miro knew me before I became famous.'

'So did I,' said Linloa, looking at him steadily in the green light of the glade. 'I knew you when you were a flapper – I saw you the day you painted yourself with yellow clay and acted like a mad creature, to become one of us.'

He nodded, still staring away from her. 'Yes, it's true, I have good friends in you and Ramoro. You did not jeer at me like the other Tahitians. You did not make fun of my red-coloured hair. You were good friends to me.'

'We still are – and I, perhaps, am more than a friend.'

This was delivered in a hushed whisper and Kumiki looked up to gaze into the features of Linloa. What was she saying? What was she trying to tell him?

'Linloa?' he said.

'I love you!' the words came out in a rush. 'I love you, and you hardly know I exist. You prefer girls who wave from the beach, to me. You do not find me beautiful. You prefer women who would go with any man, if he was an Arioi.'

'Linloa? I didn't know. I mean, I thought we were friends.'

'Friends, yes,' she said, sadly. 'That's all we ever will be I suppose, since you do not find me attractive.'

He felt chagrin. 'I never really thought about it. I mean, we rehearse together, we do so much – you're just always there. I'm very, very fond of you.'

'I'm grateful for that.'

He studied her now. He had always seen her as a very pretty woman. She was small and waif-like, with slender hips and narrow shoulders. Her hair hung down to her waist in rivers of black. She was as light as a feather to look at and he knew he could pick her up with one arm. Compared with him she was one of the Peerless Ones, a forest fairy.

'In fact, I think you're quite beautiful,' he admitted. 'It's just that, well, I haven't thought of you in that way before. It never occurred to me . . .'

'Does it occur to you now?'

As she spoke she released her waistband and let her skirt

fall to the forest floor. She was caught in a shaft of golden sunlight from Ra's lips, which pierced the canopy above. Her slim, delicate form glowed palely against the background of green misty light from the ferns and broadleafed plants. She trembled a little, vulnerable in her nudity, allowing his eyes to roam over her diminutive figure. Indeed she was one of the Peerless Ones in human shape. He wanted to gather her up in his arms, safeguard her fragility with his male strength. Her presence awakened in him all the protectiveness of the male of the species.

Within moments they were making love and he was whispering promises in her ear, telling her he had loved her all along without even knowing it, saying she was the most beautiful creature in the world and that he wanted to spend the rest of his life with her by his side.

When it was all over and they lay on the damp moss in each other's arms, he told her, 'I want to look after you.'

'I know,' said she, 'that is my strength.'

'Your what?'

'It was my intention that you should feel this way – that's why I did it.'

'Did what?'

'Spoke as I did, stood as I did, made myself look small and weak, so that you would feel strong.'

Kumiki had the distinct feeling he had been manipulated, but he actually didn't care. He knew he had found his life's love in this glade and none of those things would ever matter again. Linloa was his for ever, and she loved him passionately, he realised that. What did it matter that she had deliberately set out to make him want her? All was now well.

'I love you,' he said.

'I love you too,' she murmured. 'And we must be careful how we break this news to Ramoro. I don't want him to feel betrayed by both of us. I don't want him to feel we have conspired behind his back. It has been the three of us together until now. We must be gentle in the way we tell him, not rush out and say isn't it wonderful, let's all rejoice. I shall tell him we have gradually developed feelings for one another which have just made themselves evident, that we haven't been sneaking off, making love behind his back, hoping he would go away so we could be alone. Let me deal with it, in my way.'

Kumiki was impressed by her thoughtfulness. It was not that Ramoro would be jealous of him, Kumiki, because of his good fortune, but that Ramoro might think he had been the odd one out, while the other two enjoyed an intimate relationship. It was important that Ramoro should know he was being informed from the very start of the relationship, that nothing had gone on previously, that their joy was to be shared with him from the outset – indeed, that their joy was his joy too.

'Yes, you're right. I shall leave it to you.'

Once the stage was ready the show began and people came flooding in from the hills and valleys to see the marvellous Arioi. There was an emphasis on re-enacted battle scenes and heroic recounting of legendary exploits for the benefit of the Hivan population, who being made up of martial clans liked blood and gore more than they enjoyed singing and dancing.

This gave Kumiki full opportunity to use his drums in a martial role, adding drama to the actors' efforts during the mock fights and producing a slow funereal beat when the war was over and the dead were being counted. Kumiki could use each note to its best effect and his performance as always was excellent. He had a high profile during such exhibitions, which satisfied this particular audience's desire to see the Painted Leg who was one of their number, one they could claim for their own.

As usual, Linloa was energetic in her efforts to assist Kumiki during his performance. She was selfless and tireless, even though she had her own acts to perform. It was at one point in the evening, when the sweat was streaming from Kumiki's back as he leapt from drum to drum, thundering out a magnificent roll, when one of the audience leapt to his feet.

'Die, you wife-stealer!' cried the Hivan warrior who had a javelin in his hand. 'Adulterer!'

No sooner than these bitter words were out of the man's mouth than he launched his spear at Kumiki. The Painted Leg was trapped behind his instruments, unable to leap out of the way of the missile. Linloa saw in an instant that he would die if she did not do something. She threw a small drum she was carrying, like a disc through the air, and it struck the spear in mid-flight, causing it to be knocked from its course. It glanced from the corner of the stage and stuck in the trunk of a nearby palm tree, where it quivered.

When the warrior saw that he had failed to kill the drummer he gave a cry and leapt up onto the stage wielding a club. This he swung at Kumiki's head. This time however Kumiki was able to duck from the waist. The stone club whistled over his right shoulder. Kumiki then came up from under his drums and struck his adversary across the side of his head with a drumstick as thick as a man's wrist. The Hivan warrior dropped to the stage as if his legs had been boned. There he lay, still.

There was pandemonium amongst the Hivan audience. Warriors jumped to their feet, threatening to storm the stage. They had no idea why one of their number had attacked the Arioi drummer, but they didn't like the fact that he had been clubbed senseless. Only the intervention of Chief Api Api's personal body guard prevented any further violence from taking place.

The chief came to the stage and questioned Kumiki.

'Have you seen this man before?' he asked.

'Not to my knowledge,' replied the Painted Leg.

'Then why was he trying to kill you?'

Kumiki shrugged and Ramoro said, 'Never before has a Painted Leg been attacked during his performance. It is disgraceful. I thought the Hivan peoples were civilised.'

Api Api said angrily, 'We are civilised. Something must have been done to goad this man into his attack. Some insult, or long-standing dispute. Are you sure you do not know him?'

'I tell you . . .' cried Kumiki, angrily, but suddenly out of the corner of his eye he caught sight of Miro, standing amongst the women, glaring at him. Her eyes fell occasionally to the inert body of the man on the stage. 'Wait a minute,' Kumiki murmured to the chief, 'who is this man's wife?'

Api Api, who could not be expected to know every warrior's family personally, shrugged his shoulders and looked for assistance from his priests.

'This is Akamiku,' said the high priest. 'He is married to a woman called Miro.'

'I thought so,' said Kumiki, angrily. 'This is the husband of the woman I was once to marry. She failed to wait for me to return to these islands, however, and when I refused her favours – because she is married – she swore to get even with me. I expect she taunted her husband with untrue tales of our liaison so that he would attack me.'

'Lies!' shrieked Miro, from out of the crowd.

'In that case,' Kumiki said, calmly, 'we shall have to wait for this Akamiku to revive so that we can ask him.'

'You raped me!' screamed Miro. 'I told you I was married, but you took no notice.'

'It is you who is the liar,' replied Kumiki.

There was silence now, as the crowd observed both partners in this argument. An accusation had been made and refuted. Even under normal circumstances there was a difficult judgement to be made, one which lacked proof on both sides. A woman claimed she had been assaulted by a man. The man denied the assault. Without witnesses, unconnected with either party, there was no way of proving innocence or guilt with any degree of certainty. What usually happened in these circumstances was that a high priest, chief or king made a decision based on his own feelings, given the known circumstances of the case.

The high priest spoke to Chief Api Api.

'There must be a trial,' he said. 'You must preside.'

Ramoro stepped forward on hearing this.

'There will be no trial,' said the Arioi. 'The accused man is a Painted Leg. His status is at least as high as that of a king, perhaps almost as lofty as that of a god. Never has an Avae Parai had to defend himself against the petty accusations of an ordinary person. If that were necessary Painted Legs would be spending all their time defending themselves, because there are many who envy their talents and are jealous. No, it cannot happen. An Avae Parai is above the law.'

There were murmurs of agreement from the whole troupe of Arioi and even from amongst the Hivan crowds. What Ramoro had said was true. No one would dare accuse a king without proof and a Painted Leg was at least as elevated as a king.

Chief Api Api raised his eyebrows in the direction of his high priest, requesting guidance in the matter.

'Under normal circumstances, I would agree with what you say,' said the high priest to Ramoro, 'but here we have a case of a woman who was betrothed to a Painted Leg, before he became exalted amongst us. This is not just a member of the population trying to become famous by attacking a god. This is between two people who are known to one another, who have had intimate relationships in the past.'

'Nevertheless,' replied Ramoro, 'there is no proof of any misconduct. If the woman wishes to provide proof, that might be a different matter.'

'Do you have any proof?' asked the high priest of Miro.

Miro looked sulky. 'My body is my proof. My damaged reputation is my proof. My feelings . . .'

'These are not proofs,' said Ramoro. 'They are simply words.'

Chief Api Api shook his head sadly.

'This is a very difficult problem.'

Suddenly, Kumiki himself spoke up.

'The accusation of rapist is particularly abhorrent to me, since this is how I came into the world. My life's ambition is to eventually find the violator of my mother and make him pay for his crime against her body and soul. Yet here I am, accused of the same offence! I know I am totally innocent in this affair and that is why I'm willing to stand trial – but not a trial presided over by mortals – one which is conducted at a higher level – one which is decided by our ancestors.

'We shall leave it up to spirits. There is a game we play here on Nuku Hiva, called spear-stick. If I remember correctly from my youth, we push five sticks into the earth, in a line. The contestant has five throws at the sticks and has to knock down as many of the five targets as he can. The opponent may attempt to thwart the thrower, by running across the target area as the throw is being made, but of course this is dangerous for the runner, who may be speared by accident.

'I suggest we each choose a champion, this woman and I, and leave it to them. If the gods favour her champion, then I will bow to my punishment. If my champion wins, then she must withdraw her accusation and publicly apologise.'

The high priest nodded at these words and said, 'I think this is a wise and fair way of deciding the truth. However, accusing someone of a crime as terrible as this has its consequences. Only a chief can decide the punishment for the Painted Leg, if it transpires he is guilty, but if the woman loses, she forfeits her life, for false accusation.'

'Good,' said Api Api, 'now choose your champions.'

'I choose Chief Api Api!' cried Miro, quickly.

A murmur went through the crowd as swiftly as a shoal of fish sweeps through a lagoon. The chief was the best spearman on the island. His fame as a marksman was renowned throughout all the Hivan islands. In fact, he had never been beaten at spear-stick. Not only that, his psychological advantage over any opponent was strong. Who would not feel intimidated, throwing against the chief of Nuku Hiva?

Perhaps a man might be a little surer with a spear than Chief Api Api, but it was like a son throwing against a father: there were other factors to consider. There was respect for superiority of position, reverence for status, fear of a powerful but angry loser. These were difficult obstacles to brush aside. They manifested themselves in hesitancy, trembling arm and wavering eye. As with all such sports, success depended as much upon what was in the head as the skill in the hand.

Chief Api Api nodded his assent.

The high priest called across the heads of the crowd.

'And who does the Painted Leg choose?'

'I choose Telufo the Tongan,' said Kumiki, 'one of our troupe.'

There was a gasp from the thousands of people watching this drama unfold as an elderly man, grisled and grey, thin as a stick insect, stepped forward on the stage and nodded.

'A Tongan?' cried Chief Api Api, wondering whether he was being insulted here. 'What is this?'

'My chief,' said the high priest, 'I have heard of these people. The Tongans play a similar sport to our spear-stick. They place a short post in the ground and throw the spear so that it drops down onto the post. I have heard they are very adept at this variation of spear throwing.'

'But this Telufo is an old man.'

'Old, but still skilful, lord,' said Telufo.

'Do not presume to make a fool of me, Painted Leg,' said Chief Api Api. 'I want a good contest.'

'The ancestors will decide,' replied Kumiki. 'This is not a contest between two men of unequal rank and age, for your throwing arms will be guided by unseen hands – those of the divine ghosts of our forefathers. There will be no shame in losing, for this is a judgement on me and on Miro, not a test of your individual mastery at spear-stick.'

'So be it,' said the chief, removing his clothing and standing in a simple loin cloth. 'Bring the targets and the spears. Let the judgement commence. One set of five throws each – no more – and the one with the most sticks lying flat on the ground is the winner. Agreed?'

'Agreed,' said Telufo.

A large space was cleared and two thick marker posts were driven into the earth. Between these posts, using them as a line of sight, five sticks were thrust vertically into the ground. Straws were drawn and Chief Api Api won, electing to throw first. Telufo went down to the right of the line of sticks, to run across the target area if he so chose, in order to disorientate his opponent.

The chief threw his first spear without any interference from Telufo. It struck the first stick in the line, furthest away from the Tongan. There was a great cheer from the crowd, while the Arioi shuffled and looked apprehensive. Chief Api Api was clearly a good spear thrower and had not been given an honorary title simply because he was a ruler.

The second spear was thrown, then the third, and each time a stick went down. The crowd was silent now, some of them glancing at Kumiki. Linloa had taken his arm and was waiting as calmly as the Painted Leg himself for the outcome of the contest. There was a worried look in her eyes, but she did not transmit this to those around her, possibly for fear of influencing Telufo, for whom the pressure to win was already strong.

The fourth spear was thrown, with the same success as the three previous throws.

Chief Api Api was handed the last spear. Still Telufo had not moved from the spot. He watched with the glinting eyes of an elderly man as Chief Api Api, now completely absorbed in his own skill and success, drew back his arm. It was clear that the chief had been lulled into a state of pre-occupation. During the first two throws he had anticipated some sort of intervention from Telufo, but the old man had not moved, and now the chief had forgotten his existence as he stood quietly on the sidelines, as still as rock, just another one of the forest shadows that fell over the scene.

A split second before the spear was launched a shade detached itself from its fixed position and flitted across Chief Api Api's line of vision. The spear flew from the chief's hand, but the unexpected distraction was enough to spoil his aim ever so slightly. The javelin went through the air and passed through space between Telufo's arm and his skinny chest, grazed the last standing stick, and skidded along the ground into the forest beyond. The final target remained standing, albeit slightly skewed. Api Api had failed in his final throw.

However, Chief Api Api had laid flat four out of the five sticks: a great achievement. There were not many spear throwers in Oceania who could match this score.

The chief grunted in disappointment, but once he had got over that initial rush of annoyance for not felling all five and making a legend of himself, he stepped back in satisfaction.

'Your turn, old man,' he said. 'Good luck.'

With that the chief strolled out and stood in front of the replaced targets, a smile upon his face. Miro, standing to the left of the row of sticks, looked very smug. Her champion had proved himself with a brilliant display of spear throwing. Now the old man had to do something even more brilliant, which was very unlikely, and since Api Api's habit was to expose himself to danger by standing directly in the line of fire, ready to dodge the spears as skilfully as Rarotongans who were adept at evading spears thrown at them in quick succession, it seemed that Telufo stood little chance of matching the score, let alone beating it.

Telufo might well have been intimidated by Api Api's presence in front of the targets. If he struck the chief with a spear and injured or killed him, he would be executed and roasted by the Hivan population. Somehow he had to knock over the sticks without harming the chief in the process.

A spear was handed to Telufo. He weighed it in his gnarled hand. It seemed he at least knew how to hold it.

'A very nice spear,' he said. 'My congratulations to the man who shaped it. A good balance.'

He inspected the stone head of the spear.

'Well-crafted point too. Excellent workmanship.'

While the crowd was thus captivated by his soft speech, they were hardly expecting his next action. With a sudden swift movement, which took everyone by surprise, Telufo launched the javelin at the first target. King Api Api hardly had time to spin away from the target. The spear missed the first stick by a hair, burying itself in an earth bank beyond, leaving the target quivering like a sapling in the wind.

'Missed,' said the chief, recovering from his shock. 'Now you have to hit all the remaining four.'

'I expect so,' said Telufo.

The chief's priest cried, 'You *expect* so? We know so. Painted Leg,' he turned to Kumiki, 'prepare yourself for your punishment.'

Kumiki however, was talking to Ramoro, and he hardly acknowledged the high priest. There was a flick of the hand, no more. It was as if the Avae Parai did not *care* about the outcome of the match. Linloa stood at his side looking a little more anxious, but there were no signs of hysteria, as well there might be, given the task ahead of the old man.

'A little off target, I think,' murmured Telufo. 'A shade from the left.'

This time Chief Api Api was ready for the throw, as he danced nimbly in front of the target, always prepared to get out of the way but hiding the stick while the thrower took aim.

The spear flew. The chief was agile in avoiding it. Again, the javelin missed its mark by a fraction.

'That's it!' cried Miro.

Her husband had now recovered and was holding a cold compress to his wounded head.

'Kill the Painted Leg,' he growled. 'It was agreed.'

Chief Api Api shook a finger at the man. 'I sentence transgressors, not you.'

'Excuse me,' interrupted Telufo, 'but the contest is not over yet.'

He took up a third spear and threw it. Then a fourth. Both missed their targets by the merest dog's whisker. It was true they formed a neat line of their own, the four spears, each at the same angle and precisely in line. However, that was not the object of the game. The aim was to knock down as many sticks as possible with five spears. So far all five sticks were still standing.

'Enough,' said the chief wearily. 'It is time for me to pass judgement on the Painted Leg.'

Telufo smiled politely and bowed a little.

'But, if you please, lord, I still have one spear left.'

It was true that the game was not over until all five spears had been thrown.

'Then throw it and get it over with!' snapped Api Api, not at all pleased that he had to pass on punishment to one favoured of the gods. 'Quickly.'

'Perhaps you would like to protect the target?' said the old man, cordially. 'But since there is only one of you and five targets, perhaps your priests would stand in your stead? One priest could cover one target each.'

'Is the old fool mad?' cried the high priest.

Api Api sighed. 'Do as he says. Let's get this over.'

Five unwilling priests were pushed towards the line of sticks. One could see why they were apprehensive. With so many of them out there, they might bump into each other as they tried to get out of the way of Telufo's last spear.

Miro poured scorn on the spear thrower, saying he was a senile old turtle, who could not hit a tree while standing on the root.

Kumiki simply watched through narrowed eyes, his expression entirely enigmatic.

Telufo waited until the five priests had covered a target each. Then he tested the wind with a few blades of grass to determine its direction and strength. Finally he wet the fingers of his right hand, drew back, and launched the spear at a marker post some three lengths to the right of the line of sticks, well away from the target area.

Miro let out a squeal of laughter.

Her glee was premature.

The spear struck the right marker post, which deflected it at an acute angle. It passed *across* the normal line of flight and struck the first target stick. The spear continued its flat, almost level trajectory, to take the other four sticks out of the ground. With a single spear Telufo had removed all five sticks and was thus the winner of the contest.

The watchers, several thousand of them, were stunned by what they had seen. Surely this was magic? Or more likely assistance from the spirit world? There were gasps of wonder and everyone began talking at once. Chief Api Api stared in astonishment, unable to believe what he had seen.

'Is this possible?' he asked.

Telufo bowed and said, 'With the help of our ancestors.'

'No!' screamed Miro. 'It's a trick.'

The high priest took her by the arm.

'The rules required that the sticks are removed by a throw of the spear, that is all. Clearly, from what we have seen, you are falsely accusing a Painted Leg of raping you. Do you confess to these untruths? The chief may be lenient with you, if you admit your guilt.'

Miro fell sobbing to her knees.

'It's true,' she wept, 'I accused him falsely.'

'Such accusations denigrate those of women who have justifiable complaints against men,' said the priest, severely. 'Your sisters will not thank you for this.'

'Take her away and kill her,' murmured Chief Api Api. 'Bring me her heart.'

Miro shrieked in terror as the priests grabbed her arms and began dragging her towards an ahu.

'Wait!' cried Kumiki. 'I beg for leniency. The woman was wrong in falsely accusing me, but I do not want her life on my hands.'

'Why not?' asked Api Api, genuinely surprised. 'It is a worthless life in any case.'

'Still, I would rather she lived. I loved her once and it is only my consuming need for vengeance which separated us. Let her live and I will do an extra performance.'

Chief Api Api looked at Miro, sobbing in the grip of two young priests, and then shrugged.

'So be it, the woman shall live. And you, Lord of the Drums, will entrance us once again with your flying sticks! But tell me, the old man, Telufo – he was once a great spearman?'

Kumiki glanced at Telufo, who was grinning.

'Once? He still is. It is part of his act for the Arioi. He does that trick with the five sticks every performance. Had not our show been interrupted, you would have seen it anyway. It is his speciality.'

Api Api raised his eyebrows. 'And it always works?'

'Well, perhaps not every time,' admitted Telufo, still smiling. 'I remember once, several years ago . . .'

PART EIGHT

Kurangai-tuku,
the ogress

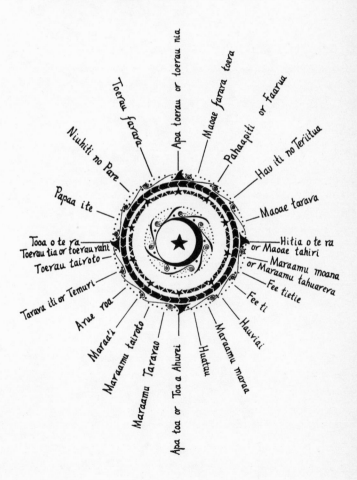

Toerau farara

Apa toerau or toerau nia

Maoae farara toera

Pahaapiti or Faarua

Niuhiti no Pare

Hau iti no Teriitua

Papaa ite

Maoae tarava

Tooa o te ra

Hitia o te ra
or Maoae tahiri

Toerau tia or toerau rahi

Maraamu moana
or Maraamu tahuarera

Toerau tairoto

Fee tietie

Tarava iti or Temuri

Fee ti

Arue roa

Hauviai

Maraa'i

Maraamu maraa

Maraamu tairoto

Huatau

Maraamu Taravao

Apa toa or Toa a Ahurei

1

The party of Rarotongans remained with the Maori for many days, enjoying the coolness of their climate while Kieto learned all he could about the art of warfare and the building of defences like the pa. There seemed to be three groups of pa: pa with terraces only, promontory or ridge pa with short transverse ditches, and finally, ring-ditch pa. Each was best for a certain type of terrain. Kieto spent his time examining the engineering, asking questions about the methods, and generally gathering knowledge from the Maori of the most effective way of building.

In the meantime, the other Rarotongans began to wander further and further out into the wildernesses of the Land of the Long White Cloud. They were uneasy, concerned that they had been gone too long from their own world, that Ru might have given up on them and put to sea again, thinking them all lost. Kieto, however, would not quit Aotearoa until he had all the knowledge he needed safely stowed away in his mind. He told the others that if Ru was gone they would need to build their own craft to sail back to Rarotonga, though how that was to be achieved in such a hostile environment as Rapanui he did not explain.

Boy-girl, who had entranced the Maori with her singing

and consequently was followed everywhere by a band of
suitors who were totally unaware of the dubious nature of
her gender, expressed a desire to accompany Seumas on a
hunt. Normally she scorned such activities, finding them
'tragically boring' but the attentions of her beaus were driving her distracted and she said she would do anything to get
out of the pa for a few days and into the tranquillity of the
countryside.

'Come on then,' said Seumas, grabbing a spear. 'Let's go
and kill some birds.'

'*You* kill the birds,' said Boy-girl. 'I'll just watch.'

However, before they had left the pa a young chief,
seeing the two preparing for an expedition, came to them.

'You will bring her back again?' he said to Seumas. 'I
forbid you to take her away.'

He was of course talking about Boy-girl.

Seumas raised his eyebrows. 'Of course, I intend bringing
her back again.'

The young man stared passionately at Boy-girl.

'She will stay with me for all time,' he said, nodding his
head slowly. 'If anyone tries to take her from me, I shall kill
them. If any harm comes to her on this expedition of yours,
I shall kill *you*, Captain Cooker. If she refuses my advances
when you return, I shall kill her. So be it.'

With this little speech the warrior strode away.

Seumas heaved a sigh. 'Now what? You've got half the
young warriors in love with you, and this one wants to cage
you like a bird. You deserve all you get, Boy-girl, but you're
putting us all in jeopardy.'

Boy-girl said in all seriousness. 'There's going to be
trouble – we'd best deal with it later.'

They left the fort and went out into a region between
lakes Rotorua and Taupo, bordered by the Waikato river, a
district which the earthquake god ruled and kept in perpetual restlessness and bubbling activity. It was a place
which seemed full of magic, yet so far in this Land of the

Long White Cloud the Rarotongans had experienced no magic whatsoever. Seumas was beginning to think that there was no such thing here, in this Otherworld, and had begun to relax about such things.

The Pict began impaling some of the large edible birds which ran around the bushes, using a long thin flexible spear which had been fashioned for the purpose.

'Are you sure you don't want a try at this?' he asked Boy-girl. 'It's not difficult.'

'No thank you,' she said, playing with the ribbons which dangled from her long black curls. Seumas had made her remove all the seashells from her locks, because of the noise they made. Boy-girl said she felt naked without them. 'I'm not sure I should have come on this expedition. I'm just as bored here as I was back in the pa.'

'Nonsense,' said Seumas. 'Enjoy the countryside. The views are beautiful. This is a land made for the gods! The volcanoes make it interesting, there are wonderful mountains, and the lakes are like pieces of fallen blue sky.'

Boy-girl sighed. 'Yes, you're right, it is a wide and pretty land, but still I'm bored.'

'We'll go back soon,' promised Seumas. 'Just let me spear one or two more birds. You can help me preserve them in their own fat in calabashes, once we get back to the pa.'

'I'll look forward to that,' grimaced Boy-girl.

Seumas stalked a bird which landed on a large bush. He crept up to the bush and was about to spear the creature when it was suddenly speared from the far side. Curious, he crept around the bush to find himself staring at an enormous woman, who continued to spear birds while he watched. She had no weapon in her hands, but was shooting out her lips, impaling the prey on their pointed tips, then retracting them so she could remove the quarry with her hands.

Seumas was astonished and gave out a little cry.

The ogress turned and saw him, her eyes opening wide.

Fearful that she would spear him with her lips, Seumas began to run. The ogress dropped her birds and chased after him, catching him easily because she had wings on her upper arms which assisted her flight and though massive and bulky, she appeared very light on her feet. Seumas struggled in her grip, calling for Boy-girl's assistance, but failed to break free.

Boy-girl came running around the bushes on her long slender legs and came skidding to a halt when she saw the ogress, whose features were incredibly ugly.

'In the names of the gods!' she cried. 'What's this?'

'Two of them?' growled the ogress. 'Who comes to hunt in the territory of Kurangai-tuku? Do you not know these are private hunting grounds?'

Boy-girl must have realised she could do nothing against this enormous woman, so she turned and ran, hiding in the bushes nearby, watching to see what would happen to Seumas.

Seumas said, 'We had no idea this was a private place. We're newcomers to this world.'

'You will come back to my cave with me,' said Kurangai-tuku, 'where I shall decide your fate.'

Seumas struggled in the arms of this ugly ogress, but she was so large his feet were well off the ground and he could get no grip on her fatty flesh. She took him underneath her right arm, pinning his own arms to the side of his body. He yelled and kicked to no avail. When he would not stop striving to escape, she slapped him around the head, a stinging blow which half stunned him and made his ears ring.

Kurangai-tuku then went back for her string of dead birds, shooting out her lips into bushes as she went, probably in the hope of spearing Boy-girl who was now hidden.

Seumas was taken to a nearby hillside where there was a cave. Kurangai-tuku found some woven grasses and bound him tightly, putting him in a dark corner full of spiders and insects which crawled over his face and into his nose and mouth. There were other creatures in the cave: domestic birds, tame lizards and other creatures. Still a bit stupefied from her blow, Seumas made no more protests, but simply watched for the chance to escape.

Kurangai-tuku plucked and scraped the birds she had killed, and those Seumas had speared, and began eating them raw. She was a disgusting eater, spitting out the bones into a pile by the exit to the cave. When she had eaten enough for herself, she gave out a loud belch which echoed through the cave, and then came and tried to push raw bird meat into Seumas's mouth.

'No, no,' he spluttered, 'I'm not hungry.'

'If you don't eat, you'll die,' said Kurangai-tuku.

'I've eaten today already,' said Seumas. 'I don't need any more yet. Later, and you'll have to cook it for me. We humans don't eat uncooked meat.'

Kurangai-tuku, who stated she was always hungry, said she did not understand this, but left him alone.

'Once,' she told him, 'we had a big bird running through the bush, one of which was enough to satisfy me for a meal. It was called a moa. But the Maori people have killed them all.'

'I expect you killed your fair share,' said Seumas, for which remark he received another hefty slap around the head.

Later in the day, Kurangai-tuku had run out of birds to eat and left Seumas in the cave to go and hunt.

While she was gone the other creatures in the cave, Kurangai-tuku's pets, came to investigate her most recent treasure, nuzzling up to Seumas and inspecting every part of his body. He yelled at the creatures, and thrashed his bound body as much as he could, but they still came back.

Seumas was hoping that Boy-girl had followed him to the cave, but she made no appearance, and after a while he realised it was because Kurangai-tuku was hunting in the region all around the cave entrance. He realised he would have to persuade the ogress to go further afield and waited until she returned from her hunt.

'That's a poor show of birds,' he said, nodding at the string of prey she had brought back. 'Can't you do better than that?'

'Of course I can,' snapped the ogress, 'but I have to go a long way from here to get fatter birds.'

'Well, I noticed some really plump pigeons,' remarked Seumas, 'in that range of hills behind where you found me. Not the hills *immediately* behind, but two ranges back from there. Fat wood-pigeons they were. They looked delicious.'

Kurangai-tuku narrowed her eyes in her ugly face and stared at the Pict.

'You are a funny kind of Maori. You have strange hair and there's no tattoos on your face. I don't know whether or not to believe you. If you're lying to me I'll break every bone in your body, then eat you slowly. I'll eat you alive, bit by bit, so you last me several days. Are you lying?'

'No, it's the truth. You've never seen such a flock of pigeons in your life. They're so fat they can hardly fly.'

Kurangai-tuku nodded thoughtfully. 'I shall go and spear some of these pigeons with my lips.'

She left the cave and through the exit Seumas could see her striding across the countryside, using a karakia to assist her.

'Stretch out, stride along,' she was crying. 'Stretch out, stride along.'

These words seemed to lengthen her step, so that she was covering the plain in fewer than a dozen paces, and stepping from peak to peak when she came to the first range of hills, creating a great wind by her movements over the land.

When she was out of sight Seumas called for Boy-girl, hoping she was within earshot.

'She's gone!' he yelled.

However, instead of Boy-girl, someone else entered the cave. By his appearance it was a young man, a Maori, and he stared about him feverishly.

'Is she gone?' said the young man.

'Who are you?' asked Seumas, trying to sit up.

'My name is Hau-tupatu,' said the youth. 'I was once a captive of Kurangai-tuku like you, but I used a karakia my grandmother taught me and escaped into a rock.'

'Why have you risked coming back?' asked Seumas.

'To get this.' The youth crossed to a corner of the cave and picked up a beautiful cloak of red feathers made from the underwings of kaka birds. 'I have always coveted this cloak – and now it's mine.'

At that moment a ruru owl let out a hoot of alarm, no doubt calling for Kurangai-tuku. Hau-tupatu felled the bird with a blow from his club. But then another, a tiny grey bird called a riroriro, flew out of the cave exit. It flew off over the hills, no doubt to warn the ogress that she was being robbed.

'Let me free, quickly,' said Seumas. 'Before she returns.'

'I have no time for that,' said Hau-tupatu.

With that he ran out of the cave leaving Seumas still bound and helpless. It was only a short time later that Kurangai-tuku came bounding home, demanding to know what had happened.

'I heard the riroriro calling me,' she said. 'I thought you had escaped, but I see you are still tied.'

Then she let out a terrible cry and rushed to the corner of the cave where her cloak of red feathers had been. She found her cloak of thick dogs' fur and an ornamented cloak of glossy flax, but no feathered cloak. A loud wail escaped her.

'Where is it?' she shrieked. 'Who has stolen my beautiful cloak?'

She spun round and stared out of the cave exit, to see the youth Hau-tupatu running over the plain. Flapping from his shoulders was the scarlet cloak. With her wings on her upper arms beating fast she ran after the thief. Seumas, frustrated and helpless, simply had to lie there and witness this drama, wondering if he was ever going to get free.

'Boy-girl,' he yelled. 'Where the devil are you?'

To his relief Boy-girl appeared from outside. She looked anxiously over her shoulder and then entered the cave. Once her eyes became used to the darkness, she saw Seumas, covered in lizards and spiders.

'Ugghh,' she said, fastidiously.

'Never mind *ugghh*,' cried Seumas. 'Get me loose. That woman will be back again soon. She's a monster. Quickly, loosen the rope.'

Boy-girl came to him and began fiddling with the knots, finding them too tight to undo.

'I need something to cut them with,' she said, looking around. 'Or burn them through.'

Finally, she found a piece of sharpened flint that Kurangai-tuku used to scrape the feathers from the birds she ate, and with this managed to saw through Seumas's bonds. Once he was free they rushed from the cave together and climbed the hill. They followed the ridge of hills and eventually, before the evening swept across the landscape, they reached the pa.

'Where have you been?' asked Dorcha. 'I've been worried about the pair of you.'

'This is one of those places,' said Seumas, wearily. 'I thought we had left magic behind us, in our old world, but this place has it too. We ran into an ogress, a creature called Kurangai-tuku, who used her lips like a spear. She caught me and kept me tied amongst her pets. Boy-girl finally managed to let me loose when a youth who called himself Hau-tupatu came to the cave and stole the woman's red feather cloak.'

'Hau-tupatu has been through here, wearing that cloak,' confirmed Dorcha, 'just a short while ago.'

Boy-girl was alarmed at this. 'We'd better tell the Maori – so they can defend the pa against Kurangai-tuku.'

Dorcha shook her head. 'According to Hau-tupatu, the ogress is dead. He used the theft of the cloak to lure her into a boiling spring called Te Whakarewarewa. She died horribly in the scalding waters.'

Seumas shook his head. 'That's the last time I go hunting with Boy-girl – she's bad luck.'

'Me?' cried Boy-girl. 'I've never been so frightened in all my life.'

That evening, while Seumas was washing himself in a stream outside the pa, he heard the plaintive cry of a small grey bird drifting over the landscape.

'*Riro riro riro riro*,' came the mournful sound.

When darkness fell, the cries of the bird ceased, and the land moved into a deep silence.

At last Kieto got what he wanted, a full-blooded battle with the Maori.

A messenger came to Chief Tuwhakapau and the chief of the defeated pa to say there was a great gathering of clans from upper Aotearoa near lake Taupo, where the lower Aotearoa clans were massing for an attack. Kieto requested to join Chief Tuwhakapau's warriors and this was granted. Seumas and the others elected to remain out of the fight, not wishing to risk their lives unnecessarily.

They marched with Kieto and the other warriors, those who had defended the pa now being allies of those who had attacked the pa, towards Lake Taupo. There, near the hot springs, they found hundreds of other tribes encamped, all preparing for a massive battle the following day.

Seumas was astonished at the number of men. They were like a dark sea over the plain. There were thousands on thousands of them, all excited and primed ready for a fight. That night their campfires covered the landscape like stars. There was much praying to the gods, men communed with their ancestors, spear points were sharpened, club edges were honed. One or two of the chiefs had thunder sticks left them by Captain Cookers and these were cleaned and polished. These thunder sticks were marvellous magical weapons which apparently could kill at a great distance, if the user had good eyes.

Kieto was allowed to inspect a thunder stick but pronounced it unfathomable.

'It's just like a hollow bamboo stick made of cold stone,' he told Seumas. 'A very *hard* cold stone. It shoots a pebble – who knows how? – which hits the warrior and kills him, as a piece of flint launched from a sling will kill a man.'

'That sounds like an iron weapon to me,' Seumas replied, when the material was described to him, 'not stone.'

'Do the Angles, Picts and Scots have thunder sticks?' asked Kieto.

'No,' replied Seumas, truthfully. 'They do not.'

The following day Seumas and the other Rarotongans stood on a hill and watched the battle. It was a glorious affair with great sweeping tides of warriors gathered to rush down upon one another in a massive display of death and destruction. The dancing and singing beforehand was impressive enough and filled the valleys and mountains with sound. Once again Seumas was awed by the haka, which chilled him almost as much as the sound of the bagpipes scared the Oceanians.

Then, when the two sides ran at each other, and clashed, there was a mighty crash which echoed over the land. Spears filled the air like swarms of elongated birds. Clubs cracked on heads. Swords hacked at limbs. Daggers plunged into torsos.

Now and again there was the crack of thunder and a puff of smoke as one of the chiefs used his magic weapon. Somewhere amongst the thousands of warriors presumably a man fell with a pebble lodged in his head or body. Seumas was not impressed with the weapon, thinking he could have killed half-a-dozen men in the time it took to prepare the thunder stick for another crack. Still, it was feared more for the way in which it did its business, rather than for the amount of havoc it wreaked.

Upper island clan turtles were formed, bristling with spears, and these tried to force their way through the centre, but were driven back by hastily constructed spear-shaped columns of the enemy, who attacked the turtles on a narrow front, driving like a wedge into the packed mass of warriors.

Next, the upper clans tried sweeping phalanxes of warriors, running down a slope and clashing with the enemy like wave on wave from a limitless ocean. This tactic almost worked as the lower clans fought to keep any ground they had gained, trying desperately not to give way. However, they were made of strong stuff, these tribes from below Lake Taupo, and they withstood the onslaughts like a cliff of solid rock.

The lower clans' ranks refused to be broken and this began to tell on the upper clans, wearying them.

There was the smell of gore and blood in the warm air, mixed with the scent of vegetable oil. The warriors had smeared themselves all over before the battle, to make themselves slippery and difficult to grip. They shone in the sunlight with great beauty, their muscles gleaming, their tattoos standing out starkly against their brown bodies.

The whole plain reeked of the odour of sweat too: fear sweat and sweat from physical effort.

Thousands of feet drummed on the earth as the battle swayed back and forth, causing trees on ridges to shimmer and shake.

The tide of men hacking, jabbing, stabbing, cutting, swayed back and forth over the noonday. Finally, the tactics of the lower clans were successful. A panic began to set in.

One side started running, those of the martial clans whom Kieto had joined, and Seumas and the others found themselves having to flee also. The battle had been lost to the tribes of lower Aotearoa. Those who had taken flight were pursued with some alacrity and glee, chopped down as they fled. The land was littered with oiled bodies, gleaming in the pleasant sunlight, and Seumas asked himself more than once, 'What for?'

Kieto happily survived this major battle with the Maori, breathless and sweating, high as a hawk on adrenaline. Shreds of flesh dripped from his whalebone club. Hanks of hair hung from his lei-o-mano. He was happy. He had been a hero amongst heroes and had discovered a love of battle within himself.

'War *is* glorious,' he said. 'No doubt about it.'

'But did you learn anything?' asked Seumas. 'Surely you were too much in the thick of it to see what was going on around you, generally.'

Kieto put a hand on the Pict's shoulder.

'I leave the tactics to you. You must explain them to me, as you saw them. You were watching it – what happened?'

'You were outflanked,' said Seumas. 'They sent a force – fleet of foot – around your right flank and these warriors drove your ragged edge into the middle of your line, causing great confusion there as they crowded with the centre.'

'See,' cried Kieto triumphantly, washing himself in a stream, 'I knew I could rely on you, Seumas.'

'Did you?' said Seumas. 'And you enjoyed yourself?'

'Immensely,' replied Kieto, his shining face dripping with water. 'But I'm sorry we lost. If I had been the general I would have strengthened the right, because their left had the best warriors they could muster. It was all too simple, wasn't it? We gained some experience there.'

'Yes,' agreed Seumas, 'I suppose we did. But we've got something else to think about now, you know. A young

Maori chief has fallen in love with Boy-girl. He swears he'll have us all killed if we try to take her away with us, when we leave. I'm sure he means it, just as I'm sure he has the power to command enough warriors to do the job.

'We're going to have to think of some way out of this.'

2

Finally, it was time to leave the Maori and the Land of the Long White Cloud. They had been away from Rapanui for three months now and surely Ru had set sail? If Kieto was worried he did not show it. He seemed to believe he was beloved of the gods and that nothing would stand in his way of eventually taking an invasion fleet to Land-of-Mists. And if he were to do this, then of course he had to live to return to Rarotonga.

'How are we going to get Boy-girl away?' asked Seumas of Kieto. 'The young chief is just as enamoured of her as he ever was.'

'Boy-girl says she'll get him drunk on kava, then we'll have to make a run for it,' Kieto replied.

On their last evening Polahiki schooled Boy-girl in the manner of the dance of the tropic bird, which is a speciality of the Hivan islands. The tropic bird is one of the most beautiful creatures in Oceania: an angel in earthly form. Pure white with a long slender red tail the tropic bird's courtship dance is a heavenly display. Dressed in a white tapa cloth, with red feathers in her hair, Boy-girl gave the Maori one of the most moving performances they had ever seen in their lives and the silence which greeted the end of her dance was profound. The audience was so affected they could utter no sound.

The young chief who was in love with her prepared to lead her away to his hut afterwards, and Boy-girl turned and said her loud goodbyes to her old friends, saying she would be happy to remain amongst the Maori, a great warrior race.

Cheers greeted this speech.

Polahiki then asked to remain amongst the Maori as well, rather than go back to his own world, since he loved the wide open spaces. He planned to go off by himself into the wilderness, find a lake well stocked with fish, and live there out of sight and sound of the rest of humanity. There were sweet potatoes in abundance in the Land of the Long White Cloud and if there was one vegetable which found its way to Polahiki's heart through his stomach it was the sweet potato.

'What a pity the young chief did not fall in love with Polahiki,' said Seumas in an aside to Dorcha. 'Then we wouldn't have to worry.'

'I can't imagine anyone, short of that ogress you killed, *ever* desiring Polahiki's body for any purpose,' said Dorcha. 'Though no doubt he would have made a meal for the unfussy Kurangai-tuku, however unpalatable he looks to us.'

To Polahiki himself Dorcha said the rest of the Ru party would be quite grateful for his unselfish act of remaining behind, since they would not have to smell Polahiki's unwashed body when the wind was in the wrong quarter, nor have to watch him cracking his lice between chipped dirty fingernails, nor have to avoid brushing against him for fear of being soiled.

'Rarotongans young and old will benefit from this generous act,' she told him, as he scowled into her face, 'and will be eternally thankful.'

On the other hand, the party returning to their own world would not be short of numbers. Tangata, the old Maori, was dreadfully curious about this similar Oceania on the other side of the cave, and wished to see it for himself.

'You may never be able to return here,' warned the Farseeing-virgin Kikamana. 'Do you leave any family?'

'No one,' replied Tangata. 'I am an old warrior without sons or daughters and my barren wife is dead. We were not blessed with children, so I am alone. Of course, I have brothers and sisters, and cousins, but they are not close to me in my old age. I want to do this one last thing – see this world from which you come – before I die.'

'So long as you know what you're letting yourself in for,' said the priestess. 'We do not wish to be responsible for your unhappiness.'

The next morning the party was ready to set out to return to the cave which led to Rapanui on the opposite world. At dawn Seumas crept to the hut of the young chief and called for Boy-girl. He received no answer. Thinking she had probably drunk kava along with her lover, he looked inside the hut with its elaborately carved door posts, into the gloom.

Boy-girl was there, looking distressed. She put a finger to her lips and pointed down, at something attached to her right leg. Seumas was horrified to see she was manacled, with an iron chain running to a central post. The manacle must have been left by the Captain Cookers, when they visited the Land of the Long White Cloud.

The young chieftain was asleep on the mat beside her, snoring noisily, dried kava juice rimming his lips.

'Where's the key?' mouthed Seumas. 'The *key*?'

Tears brimmed Boy-girl's eyes. 'Son of a pig has swallowed it,' she said in a normal voice, and gave the sleeping youth a savage kick in the stomach.

The boy jerked upright and was promptly sick on the floor. Seumas stepped forward and struck him a blow on the temple with his club, rendering him unconscious again. They searched his vomit with a stick, but found no key.

'I *think* he swallowed it,' said Boy-girl. 'It looked like it.'

'Wonderful,' murmured Seumas, gagging at the smell of the vomit. 'You *think*.'

'Well don't just stand there,' growled Boy-girl. 'Get me free!'

Seumas went out and got Kieto. Between them they dug away at the central post and then both men heaved on the chain. Finally the post gave way. The young chieftain groaned. Boy-girl gave him another kick and then dragged the post behind her, leaving the hut. They left the village with Seumas and Boy-girl carrying the heavy wooden post between them.

Tangata said, 'We must burn the post, or it will slow us too much.'

'No,' Seumas replied, 'we must get the iron off Boy-girl, or she'll be dragging the chain. Tangata, can you get one of those thunder sticks? Can you make one work?'

The old man grinned. 'I see what you mean.'

Tangata went back into the village, entering a hut. He came out again carrying one of the iron tubes. When he reached the others, he said to Boy-girl, 'I have loaded this thunder stick. Put your leg on the rock and turn your head away.'

Boy-girl, trembling in fright, did as she was told.

Tangata lit a piece of cord, then blew it out so that it glowed. He then placed the end of the thunder stick against the iron stud which pinned the two pieces of hinged manacle together. When he was satisfied with the position, he blew on the smouldering string to make it glow red again, which he then put to a small hole two thirds of the way down the whole weapon.

A terrible explosion made everyone's ears ring. Boy-girl screamed in pain and terror. Seumas started to run, a natural survival instinct taking over, then checked himself. He stared shame-facedly at Dorcha, who was white with fright. She had frozen on the spot, the other survival mechanism.

'It's done,' said Tangata, the only member of the party to be unaffected by the violence of the stick. 'Are you hurt?'

Boy-girl rubbed her ankle. There were powder burns all around it, leaving a pale band where the manacle used to be. It looked a little like a tattoo gone badly wrong.

'My leg stings,' she said. 'But I don't think it's broken – it's just bruised.'

'Can you walk?' asked Kieto.

She stood up and tested the ankle, finding she could. There was a slight limp, but nothing which would slow them down.

'Are we taking the thunder stick?' asked Kieto of Tangata.

'No we're not,' cried Seumas, gathering courage to pick it up. The tube was warm, where the thunderbolt had travelled through its length. He flung it far away from them, grabbed Dorcha's arm and said, 'Let's get out of here. The whole village will be awake now. We'll have to run.'

He was right, there was now a general call to arms. The young chieftain had come round and was yelling for his warriors to join him. A race began to reach the cave which led to Rapanui and the other world.

The sky was streaked with long wisps of cloud, against a deep red background. They ran over the broad landscape, each sorry for their own reasons to leave this beautiful yet mystical land. As they neared the cave entrance, the Maori came up over the hill. Spears began to fill the air, to thud into the earth behind the fleeing party. The Rarotongans entered the cave, just as the Maori found their range.

One spear hissed past Seumas's ear and he, being the last of the party, turned at the entrance to the cave and waved his patu club at the oncoming warriors.

'Good organisation,' he called, 'but this is a rabbit hunt – you've got to catch your prey before there's a fight!'

They were now close enough for Seumas to see the fierce tattooed features of the Maori. The warriors protruded their tongues and rolled their eyes putting on their war faces. The young chieftain who loved Boy-girl was hurtling down the last hill, right out in front of his warriors. Seumas took his slingshot from his belt, fitted a stone to the saddle, then whirled the weapon around his head.

The stone struck the Maori chief on the foot, sending him squealing, tumbling head over heels. He landed in a piece of boggy ground with a *splat*, his face going straight down into mud the colour of old porridge. Frogs leaped and jumped out of the way in fright, no doubt fearing the attack was directed at them. A wading bird rushed across the marsh, screaming blue murder, wondering what had fallen from the sky.

Slowly the chief rose, mud dripping from his features, the wading bird still screaming as it went over the next hill.

It was such a comical scene, Seumas could not but help laughing at the unfortunate man's somersaults. This had the effect of making the chief's own warriors laugh also. Finally the chief himself, having recovered his feet and wiped himself off, saw the funny side of things too. The Maori are big-hearted enough, confident enough, to laugh at themselves when they are involved in a ridiculous situation. Finally, all the pursuers were in a state of mirth, slapping their thighs and clutching their ribs. A laugh was as good as a victory.

Seumas gave them one last salute, before entering the cave and following his companions.

He received a cheer as his reward.

As he moved in the dimness of the cave's interior, he reflected on the Maori, on their greatness. They were a fascinating people with a true feeling for the artist, both in their wooden carvings, the quality of which the Rarotongans had never laid eyes on before this visit, and their buildings. In the science of war too, they were more advanced than the Rarotongans, with their magnificent pa and their tactics and strategies unknown to warriors of the small islands.

'It's a pity,' said Kieto, later, 'that we can't visit the Hawaii of this world too. It sounds as if we could learn much about naval warfare from them. That sea battle Tangata talks about sounds remarkable . . .'

The party eventually reached the cave and passed through it, encountering the clashing rocks and the armies of the dead, but well able to deal with them. This time too they had taken enough provisions, so they did not have to eat clouds of dry moths. Finally, after a long and gruelling journey, they reached their canoes. They emerged from the mouth of the cave on to Rapanui and paddled to a landing point just below the volcano which the short-eared villagers had called Rano Kau. On meeting fresh air again they found the island in turmoil. Open warfare had erupted. The whole place was seething with violence.

Seumas and Kieto stood on the rim of the crater and stared down the length of the island.

There were ranks of red stone giants ranged against white stone giants, battling it out in great numbers. The air was full of the sound of stone on stone as the monsters clashed, topknots flying, rock bodies crashing to the earth with an impact that shook the landscape, dust billowing. Some giants had fallen into specially dug traps – deep pits – and were being buried alive up to their shoulders in the ground.

On the human front, even more horrific scenes could be witnessed. Down one end of the island the Short Ears had dug a huge trench, right across the Poiko Peninsula, just beyond the Rano Raraku crater. Within this ditch they had piled brushwood and logs, which had been set alight, so that a river of fire crossed the landscape from beach to beach. Into this horrible flaming trap the Short Ears were driving the whole Long-Eared population like domestic livestock, burning them alive. The screams of the Long Ears could be heard from the crater lake of Rano Kau, at the other end of the island.

'This is ugly,' said Seumas. 'This is open warfare for you. Do you want this, Kieto?'

Kieto stared at the dreadful scene. 'If it is necessary for victory,' he replied, 'then so be it.'

Yet Seumas, whose stomach heaved at the sight, knew Kieto was also affected by the suffering. It seemed that the young would-be general's ambition, predestined perhaps and thus unavoidable, outweighed his compassion. Kieto had so long been in the grip of his dream of conquest, a sight like this, however harrowing, was not enough to wrench him free.

Kieto was one of those men in history who look on colonisation as necessary to the progression of his people. The Oceanians were by nature migrants: as their nations grew they spread outwards, seeking new lands, where necessary wresting them from their present owners. Colonisation was in their blood. If the land they found was uninhabited, so much the better, but if sparsely inhabited by another race then that race must stand aside for the over-whelming numbers of settlers.

Kieto was also hungry for recognition of his intrinsic and learned talents as a general. To be a great man amongst the Oceanians was to be either a great navigator or a great warrior. Here was a chance to be a warrior on a scale never before envisioned or possible. Here was an opportunity to conquer a land the size of the country which the Maori had found and colonised. What dreamer of fame and glory could pass over such a chance to become the most famous general in the history of the world?

Not Kieto.

'We must discover if Ru has been prepared to wait for so long,' said Kieto, turning from the massacre. 'We'll need to take the path around this side of the island to avoid both the giants and the battle between the humans.'

'To avoid the slaughter, you mean?' said Seumas.

'If those are the words you wish to choose.'

The party, including the elderly Maori, Tangata, circumnavigated the island until they came to the beach where they had been put ashore by Ru. Sure enough, anchored off the coast they could see *The Princely Flower*. Kieto ordered the lighting of five small fires in a row and shortly afterwards *The Princely Flower* came gliding over the water. Dirk was there, standing on the bows of the craft, with the cock Lei-o-mano perched on his back. It seemed the two had consoled each other while their owners were gadding about in an Otherworld.

Soon everyone was aboard and Ru set course for Tooa o te ra on the windflower.

Once the pahi was on its way, with a misty spray drifting over the bows and drenching the score of maidens which made up the crew (among which Kikamana was of course numbered), Seumas and Dorcha began to relax.

Dorcha took out her bamboo-shell chart and added the dimension which included Rapanui, while Seumas went back to his old hobby of studying the efficiency with which the naked complement of mariners, glistening with fine-spray moisture, went about their seamanship. He simply sat dreamily watching the women, with his arm around the neck of Dirk, who was demonstratively pleased to see his master back on board.

There was a softness to the air, out on the briny, and overhead a pastel blue was restful on the eyes. Out on the great ocean the waves were large graceful beasts, rolling as a mighty herd across the seascape. Dorcha felt a surge of contentment go through her as she worked with the slivers of bamboo and small money cowries, completing her chart of voyages of Oceania. She felt closer now to Seumas than she had ever done before in her life.

There was a Seumas she hated, a figure in the past, but he was now gone, faded away. They had done so much together, upon this second great voyage in the middle of their lives. Their earlier seafarings had been done alone, with he a wild storm in front and she following like a furious wind behind him. Now they were intermingled, almost as one, and had made this voyage together. Now their pioneering spirit had merged and she was feeling great satisfaction in loving and being loved by her constant companion, the Pict.

Once her task of completing the chart was done she joined Ru at the mast.

'Thank you for staying for us,' she said. 'It must have been a long wait.'

Ru looked at her and raised his eyebrows.

'Not so long,' he said. 'You were only gone a few days.'

'But we were in Aotearoa for well over a month!' she exclaimed.

Ru shook his handsome head. 'A few days, that's all. Admittedly events on the island boiled over into bloodshed and chaos while you were gone, which made our wait *seem* that much longer, but in fact the days were only seven altogether.'

'In that case, time must have passed more quickly in the place where we were. At least four of our days for every one of yours.' She considered this more carefully, before adding, 'So that's why we grew so hungry on our journey through the middle of the earth. It makes sense now.'

'You amaze me with your words,' said Ru. 'I have not yet spoken to Kieto, but I must learn from him what wonders you beheld in the land of the Maori. I see you left the dirty fisherman behind. Was he killed?'

'No, he elected to remain there.'

'Their loss, our gain,' grunted Prince Ru. 'And you returned with one of their number?'

'Yes, his name is Tangata, an old Maori warrior. Isn't he magnificent?'

Ru studied the grey-haired gentleman in question as that man rested with his back against one of the deck huts. He seemed bright and alert, watching all that went on around him, studying the sea with a keen yet cautious eye.

'He tattoos his face, in the way of the Hivans, yet the tattoos are not of the same pattern. They are much finer and more artistically wrought. Is he a mariner?'

'I think not,' replied Dorcha. 'So far as I know he hasn't been to sea before in his life. He comes from an inland place, where there are great lakes, but his tribe was not a sea-going people. His was a martial clan, whose warriors lived for fighting. We saw them in battle. The glory of war seemed to be their sole reason for keeping fit and healthy.'

Ru shrugged. 'Each to his own. I prefer to pit my wits and strength against the ocean. The elements are tough enough adversaries for me. Speaking of which there have been strange goings-on amongst the gods while you were away. We had a dozen electrical storms in the first three days alone, which seemed to be trying to force us away from our anchorage and leave you behind.'

'Are you sure?'

'No,' replied Ru, 'but it appeared that way, for in the outer ocean there was a good wind – we could see it in the flights of the birds – and it was a clear sky. Only around the island was there thunder and lightning, dry storms without rain. If we had left Rapanui I'm sure we would have found excellent and safe sailing.'

'Tawhaki and his creation Uira? What could we have done to upset the God of Thunder?'

'Whatever it was, I think it is settled, for the electrical storms disappeared after those first five days.'

It was true that in his frustration to rid the world of Kieto's party, Tawhaki had overstretched himself. Tangaroa wanted to know why there was so much thunder and lightning necessary around Rapanui, when Ua and Maomao were not present to herald in the noise and lights which normally accompanied a howling rainstorm. Ao, the God of Clouds and Tawhaki's unwilling co-conspirator, finally broke away from the God of Thunder and confessed to Tangaroa that there was a plot to thwart Kieto and his party. Tangaroa complained to Io, who lives on the remote twelfth plane, away from the squabbles of the lower gods, and Io duly sent messengers to Tawhaki, chastising him and warning him not to interfere in the affairs of men.

The God of Thunder was much displeased with both Ao and Tangaroa, but had no choice but to cease stamping around the heavens and releasing lightning from his armpits. He went away to the far corner of Oceania to bother the Hawaiians for a while, to vent his annoyance on their ships and to stir an old friend of his to action, Pele, Goddess of Volcanoes. The navigator prince Ru would not be bothered by thunder and lightning again, not on his present voyage into the unknown waters of Oceania.

That night Ru sighted a fatigued bird on the horizon. When it drew closer to the pahi he saw that it was a white-bellied sea eagle and it was carrying something in its claws. As it flew over *The Princely Flower*, the sea eagle released its cargo. A calabash landed amongst some ropes and failed to break open. Titopika was the first to pick up this object, since it landed almost in his lap. He recognised some symbols carved on the seed pod. In triumph he followed the instructions of these symbols, twisting on the glued stopper to the calabash.

The stopper came out like a volcano plug with all the pressure of the Goddess Pele behind it, shooting up into the sky and killing the sea eagle which had transported it.

True to his nature, Ragnu wanted no living witnesses to his deeds, even should that observer be a bird. A kahuna with the powers of Kikamana might force that bird to speak, to reveal the name of the sorcerer who sent it. So the creature was betrayed by its own master and death was its reward for a duty performed with diligence and efficiency.

Out of the now opened calabash came an earsplitting rushing sound as if all the demons of hell had been released.

Ragnu had at first intended to fill the calabash with poisonous gas, so that everyone on board the pahi would be killed. However, Ru himself was especially loved of the gods and there were all Ru's family and relations to consider. Ragnu decided in the end that while he felt no real concern over cold-bloodedly murdering a whole canoe full of people, whether they were princes or paupers, it might bring him unwelcome attention from the gods.

Thus he had filled the calabash with storm winds.

It was one thing to kill people with a deadly gas, quite another to present them with a situation like a storm. If Ru's vessel went under because of poor seamanship during bad weather, or because it was driven onto reefs or rocks, that could be attributed to the capricious nature of the ocean. A storm was a test to be passed or failed, depending on the captain.

When Titopika removed the stopper to the calabash, a hurricane was released. This mighty wind immediately filled the sails and drove the pahi far from its course. Waves grew monstrously high and lashed the decks of the ocean-going canoe. There was a white fury in the air, which smothered the ship. Those on board found it difficult to breathe, since the air was so full of stinging spray they swallowed sea water with every gulp of oxygen. Two men and a woman were washed overboard, never to be seen again. Pungarehu, still grieving over the loss of Wiama the night-girl, was one of those lost.

Dakuwanga swam in the midst of the storm, having just missed swallowing the sau of one of Ru's relatives as it made its way through the confused air to the entrance to Milu's kingdom. It was happily passed into the hands of Limu. Pungarehu's soul also fortunately escaped the jaws of the shark-god and he and the woman made it safely to the purple road, and down into the underworld. There he met his beautiful Wiama, to whom he was married in spirit if not in fact: she proclaimed herself his wife in order for him to safely pass the terrible Nangananga.

As the furious hurricane tossed the pahi around like a toy, throwing it this way and that in its petulance, Titopika himself was killed. One of the masts snapped and struck him a skull-cracking blow on the head. His brains spilled out like milk from a split coconut and were washed overboard. His body slipped into the sea, later to become food for the sharks and barracuda, and the little nibbling carrion. His sau went up into the ether, buffeted by Tawhiri-atea, the Storm-God.

Dakuwanga, having been thwarted of three of his potential prey, was especially alert. His sharp cold eyes spotted the sau of Titopika, struggling through the blinding storm, and descended upon it just as it was about to tread the purple road. Milu was waiting, ready to answer the usual question asked of him ('Why, on the point of death, am I aware of the meaning of life?') and to testify as to the unfairness of it.

Titopika's soul was not destined to become an atua however, for Dakuwanga's ravenous jaws closed around it just an instant before it touched the purple road. Titopika, silently screaming his last scream, was swallowed by the Shark-God. There would be no life beyond life for the tohunga. He was now on his way to becoming incorporeal excrement, to be scattered on the winds, over the seas, and never to know awareness again.

Milu shook his head sadly and returned to the Land of the Dead, for he could foresee no other souls descending.

Titopika left behind him a grieving wife, the princess who fell for his dashing looks, his élan. The poor woman had gone from bride to widow in a few short weeks. She went to a sympathetic Dorcha to learn her fate. She told the Scot she was pregnant. Dorcha used her occult powers and discovered that the woman's son would one day become a great chief on an island yet unnamed. He would raise his mother high in status and the pair of them would rule with great wisdom.

When the storm abated, *The Princely Flower* found itself in a part of the ocean where the air was sultry and the wind sluggish. Those on board knew the signs well. They recognised the putrid nature of the waters around them, the lifeless weed and floating coral. There were rotten palm logs floating away on a desultory tide. Strange ugly fish fed off their own decayed dead.

'We stop at no island in these waters,' said Ru. 'I want no more of monsters, or deadly fairies, or giants. We will ignore any enticements. Dorcha, Po'oi, help me find my way amongst these new stars up there in the roof of voyaging . . .'

For once the dark magic of strange islands was not allowed to delay them and after only a few days they had found their way out of the doldrums. They entered a sea, still unknown to them, which was sparkling and clear. Fresh breezes, surely from Hine-tu-whenua, took the craft in a skimming motion over the back of her sister Hine-te-ngaru-moana.

Many of the stores they had gathered on Rapanui had however been washed overboard in the storm and it was imperative that they stop at an island to replenish them.

Indeed, a likely-looking cloud was seen at noon, under which there would be an island. By evening the next day they had reached the outer fringe of the island and passed over the reef. Once in the lagoon Ru dropped anchor and studied the palm-covered beaches with satisfaction. Here there would be food in plenty.

'I can see coconuts and breadfruit,' said Ru, 'and we may find yams and bananas, if we're lucky.'

A party was formed to explore the hinterland made up of Seumas, Dorcha, Ru and Tangata the Maori. Dirk was to be permitted to accompany his master, since he had been pining for him while Seumas was in the Land of the Long White Cloud.

'See you behave yourself, mind,' said Seumas sharply to his hound. 'No running into the bush, looking for smells. There'll be enough for you without you charging off.'

Dirk wagged his tail and looked suitably responsible.

Dorcha sighed. 'You talk to that dog as if you think it'll understand you.'

'It knows what I'm about, Dorcha, even if it doesn't understand the words. I'm the one who trained it after all. It knows by the tone of my voice what I'm about. You women never did understand the bond between man and dog. I think you females are jealous of the closeness between a Pict and his hound.'

'Are we now?' teased Dorcha. 'This closeness? Is it the same kind of closeness that a shepherd feels for his sheep I wonder? I know how the cold nights can improve such a relationship, up in the damp hills of Albainn. I've heard of stories . . .'

The prim Seumas was as shocked by her insinuation as he was meant to be.

'You know I don't mean it that way,' he said, prudishly. 'I mean in a spiritual sense.'

'Oh, chaste is it? Well, make sure this pure relationship you have with your mongrel includes discipline. I don't want to have to spend my time on that island chasing a stupid dog.'

They were able to wade ashore from the pahi, through the shallow waters, leaving Kieto in charge of the vessel. Ru's family and relations gathered coconuts on the shore-line, breadfruit from the fringe of the rainforest and shellfish from the lagoon. Others made rods, baited their hooks, and angled for reef fish all along the coral lip.

The party of four proceeded into the rainforest with caution. Too many times they had blundered on to a seemingly uninhabited island, only to find it crawling with monsters, or infested with hostile tribes. This time they were going to be ready for anything unusual or threatening.

The group were surprised, however, for the deeper they went into the rainforest, the more pleasant became their surroundings. There were beautiful tall trees, their buttress roots as high as a man. Thin waterfalls jetted from high rocks, down on to mossy platforms, into fern gullies many shades of green.

Butterflies filled the dazzling air of sunlit glades. Dragonflies and damselflies hovered over moist banks. Lizards dropped from leafy boughs, to scamper through the undergrowth. There were all kinds of exquisite birds, with colourful plumage and elegant songs. Even Tangata the Maori was impressed, saying that Aotearoa had a wonderful variety of birds, but not as rich and plentiful as this small island.

Finally they came to an area where there was a huge pool, in the shadow of a volcanic rock overhang.

'Look how it sparkles in the sunlight,' breathed Dorcha. 'It invites me to bathe.'

Seumas looked around him. 'Not yet – you don't know what's in there.'

'What could be in such a pretty lake?'

Ru said, 'Seumas is right, Dorcha. We have to be careful. The pool might be attractive for a reason.'

Tangata, who was carrying a tall spear, bent down to look into the crystal waters. They promised to be thirst-quenchingly sweet. He was about to dip a hand into the pool to taste the water when he saw his reflection on the surface. With a startled shout he drew back and then jumped to his feet.

'What is it?' cried Ru. 'A creature?'

'No, not that,' replied Tangata, 'it is my own self – I have changed into a boy.'

He dropped his spear and ran his hands over his face, feeling his features. Then he looked down at himself, to find the same wrinkled limbs, gnarled hands and pot belly he had woken with that very morning. He was still a senior warrior.

'I don't understand it,' he murmured, going down on his knees again. 'There is an eight-year-old me in the lake, yet here on land I am still old Tangata.'

While Seumas gripped the nape hair on Dirk to hold him back, the others genuflected. They stared down into the pool and let out similar expressions of shock and surprise.

Dorcha said softly with nostalgia evident in her voice, 'A little girl – oh, I'm a little girl again.'

'A young boy,' muttered Ru. 'I recognise myself – it is definitely me.'

'Let me see,' said Seumas, unable to bear it any longer.

Still holding on to Dirk, he bent down and stared into the clear waters. The reflection was that of a male child, too young even to have tattoos. A junior Seumas. He smiled at himself and the boy smiled back. It was a miracle. Something wrenched at Seumas's heart – a feeling of lost childhood found again – and he sighed deeply.

Was this possible? Could they look back to the past, see themselves as they were, mourn for the innocence of infancy? It was a sweet-sour exercise, gazing at something which was locked in the past, unobtainable, yet so beautiful in its guiltlessness. A lump formed in his throat and a kind of yearning was like a pain in his chest, as he stared at himself as he had been, oh, at least a thousand years ago.

Seumas glanced across and saw an immature and artless Dorcha, a pretty little girl with matted black locks and black eyes, looking back up at him. He reached for the image with a small cry, as another kind of pain explored his breast. This was the child Dorcha might have borne, had they been able to have children. *His* child. These two, in the water, were their lost children, their unborn progeny, wistfully staring up at their parents.

Before his hand broke the surface it was gripped by Tangata, who despite being an old man was immensely strong.

'No,' said the old man. 'This is a magic pool.'

Seumas drew back, realising the Maori was right. Perhaps these images were bait to lure them into the pool? A hand might be clutched from under the surface and the owner dragged to his doom. There were goblins who lived at the bottom of stagnant ponds, who enticed victims into the water, then cut them up into pieces and hung the bodily parts from hooks. True, this water did not look torpid, but perhaps this was deceiving, maybe the impression of sweetness and clarity was false?

'Why . . .?' began Seumas, but at that moment Dirk wrenched free. The pool had been maddeningly inviting for the hound, who wanted nothing more than a swim in its cool-looking waters.

'Look out!' cried Dorcha, but before they could stop him Dirk had plunged in.

He swam around in a circle, his nose just above the surface, then climbed out onto the bank to shake himself. To the astonishment of the humans, Dirk had shrunk to about a fifth of his normal size. There was a youthfulness about him too, which became more evident with every moment, until finally, as he stood there wagging his little tail, they realised he had regressed.

'He's a damn puppy again!' exclaimed Seumas.

They gathered about the transformed dog in wonder, feeling his limbs, body and head.

Ru said, 'It's true – he is a puppy.'

Tangata stood and stared at the pool.

'I know what this place is,' he murmured. 'It's the Pool of Life.'

'I know it too,' confirmed Ru. 'You have the legend of these waters in your world also?'

Tangata nodded.

Seumas and Dorcha were at a loss.

'What does it mean?' asked Dorcha.

Tangata explained. 'When mankind was first put on the earth by the gods, they argued amongst themselves as to whether mortals should be allowed to live for ever.

'One god believed that a mortal's life should resemble a flaming torch, so that it could be relit many times, before finally burning down to the stub. Thus if a man was killed in battle, or died of some disease, he could be lit again. All men and women would live for ever.

'Another god suggested that a mortal might be fashioned in the way of snakes, and simply shed their skins when they grew too old, and thus replenish their beauty.

'A third god went ahead on his own and created a Pool of Life. He suggested that there should be one of these on every island in the world, where mortals could submerge themselves when they reached old age and come out a young child again.

'The fourth god, however, was full of bitterness and envy for everything which did not further his own importance. He maintained that to give mankind any sort of immortality would be a waste of time. "Let men and women just die when they are killed or fall fatally ill, and never return."

'Just at the moment this god spoke there was a heavy

rainfall and the gods wanted to get under shelter, so they all cried out, "All right, let it be so." And thus, because of a shower we mortals are doomed to die an everlasting death.'

'But,' Ru added, 'this one pool, created by the third god, still remains here on earth. And this is it. We have found it. It has been lost to mankind until now. Many claim to have found it, in various places, but they always lost it again.'

'Maui was very angry with the gods,' said Tangata, 'for robbing mankind of eternal life. He tried to reverse their decision by stealing eternal life from Hine-nui-te-po, but as you know, she trapped him when he tried to pass through her body.'

Seumas stared at the puppy which was frolicking on the grass bank of the pool.

'So, this is it,' he said, 'the Pool of Life? We can all relive our lives again, do it over. I remember how it was when I was young – I was happy then.'

'Were you?' asked Dorcha.

Her voice had a strange tone to it and he turned and stared into her eyes. Some of the nostalgic fervour went out of him then. He began to recall, truly now, how he was a poor starved waif, risking his life on the cliffs to collect fulmar eggs. In those days his arms were hardly strong enough to hold him to the cliff in high winds. Several times he had almost fallen to his death. Even when he had the eggs, most of them would be stolen from him by brutish men, or women with the eyes and claws of eagles. Yes, in those days he ran around in rags, avoiding beatings only by staying out of sight and sound of his father.

Had he been happy then?

'Well, I was a free spirit. I had only myself to account to – and anyway, it would be different here.'

'I wasn't a free spirit, I was a drudge,' said Dorcha, firmly. 'I worked like a slave for my father, then when I married I worked like a slave for my husband. And my emotions were in a turmoil. I don't want to go back to that again, to a time when I was so miserable I couldn't think straight.'

'But it wouldn't be like that here, in Oceania,' insisted Seumas. 'We could grow up here amongst these people, *really* become one of them.'

'We shall never be Oceanians completely,' she argued. 'We will always be outsiders. You have a vision of how you would like things to be, not how they will be. Go on, swim in the pool. I have no right to take this chance away from you. If you want your youth back, then you have the opportunity now to find it once more. Take it. Be a boy again.'

Seumas stared again at the shining pool.

'It would be stupid not to take advantage of such an opportunity. It's the dream of every man, to return to the time when he was young and strong. If I don't do it, how long have I got left, before my body betrays me? – before my joints seize and my back aches? – before my eyes fill with yellow sap? – before things inside me begin to fail? How long before I actually die? Ten years? Twenty at the most. Yet now I have the chance to become young again, to become a boy.'

'Take it,' insisted Dorcha, 'but I shall remain as I am – shall become your mother – your grandmother – and in a few years I'll watch you choose a new wife.'

'You could do it too,' Seumas cried. 'We could grow up again together – live again as husband and wife.' He turned to the other two men, who had been whispering amongst themselves. 'We could all become children again. Think of what we could do with another life! With all the knowledge that we have gained so far and yet more to follow.'

'You don't know that,' Ru said, quietly. 'You don't know that you'll even be able to remember anything of the life you've led so far. Look at the dog.'

Seumas gazed at Dirk, now a floppy wide-eyed puppy chasing a breeze-blown leaf along the bank of the pool.

'Dirk,' he said, sharply. 'Heel, boy.'

The puppy took absolutely no notice and continued with its play.

'Dirk!' snapped Seumas, in his most authoritative tone. 'Come! Come! Heel, boy. Now.'

Nothing. Dirk did not even look up. He was totally absorbed in chasing the leaf. There was no automatic response to a command. The hound had been subjected to years of rigorous training and obedience was normally instinctive. Clearly the dog had lost all of the training instilled in him and was now an undisciplined creature.

'You're right,' said Seumas, quietly. 'The dog doesn't remember.'

'It's as if he's been born again,' said Tangata. 'A new life, with a new mind.'

Seumas turned his attention to Tangata.

'You, Maori man, surely you're going to go into the pool? You're an old man. What sort of life have you got left?'

Tangata smiled, his tattoos disappearing into the wrinkles on his lean face.

'I am an old man, yes, but I have led a good life. I'm a warrior. I have many victories to my name. It is a respected name. There are songs about me, Maori songs in which my praises as a warrior and a man are sung. I am assured of a place in a warrior's heaven.

'Perhaps, the second time around I will not do so well? Maybe I will fail? Who knows. Luck and the gods play important parts in our lives. Next time I might not be so lucky, not so favoured? I am happy to die a respected man, envied by the young warriors because of my achievements. Also I am weary of life now. I'm ready to go.'

Seumas was almost affronted by the Maori's decision.

'Even you? What about Ru?'

Prince Ru shook his head. 'Nor me. I have current responsibilities to fulfil. My people expect me to find them a new island.'

'And if you were not a navigator on a voyage?'

Ru sighed and looked longingly at the pool. 'It is tempting, but I think I would follow the example of Dorcha and Tangata.'

'I see.'

Seumas shrugged. 'Well, I'm not going to do it alone – not without Dorcha. Ru, what do we tell the others, back at the pahi? Shouldn't they be given the chance for a new life?'

'There are almost sixty people on that canoe, but I'm going to make the decision for all of them. We will say nothing to them about the Pool of Life. What they don't know, they can't grieve for later. What if some of them do take the plunge and regret it instantly? What if some *don't* take it and later wish they had? No, better we don't tell them.'

'How will we explain Dirk?'

'We met an old woman who transformed the dog into a puppy. She was a sorceress and we killed her. Once the provisions are on board we'll speed away from the island, in case there are more of her kind.'

Dorcha nodded. 'I think we're doing the right thing – I hope so.'

'I'm not so sure,' Seumas said. 'But you're the leader of this expedition, Ru. I accept your judgement.'

The group of four retraced their path, back to the beach, Seumas carrying Dirk. The other passengers and crew were amazed when they saw Dirk and some showed anxiety over the idea that there might be more witches on the island. The only one who seemed delighted by Dirk's new young state was Boy-girl's pet cockerel, Lei-o-mano, who had suffered much from being chased around the deck by a mature Dirk.

Now the tables were reversed and it was Dirk who had to run from the wicked claws and pecking beak of the rooster. Lei-o-mano wasted no time in getting his own back on the hapless puppy. It was as if the rooster knew that in a few months time things would be back to normal again and the hunter would become the prey once more. The cock was making the most of it.

Stores were gathered in quickly, packed into the deck huts, and soon the pahi was gliding over the reef towards open sea. Not so long afterwards, the island was a mere speck on the horizon, as the wind filled the crab-claw sails and drove the pahi onwards.

Seumas stood at the mast beside Ru, staring back at the dark mote, wondering if he would ever get rid of that deep but unignorable yearning inside him.

PART NINE

Ararau Enua O Ru Ki Te Moana

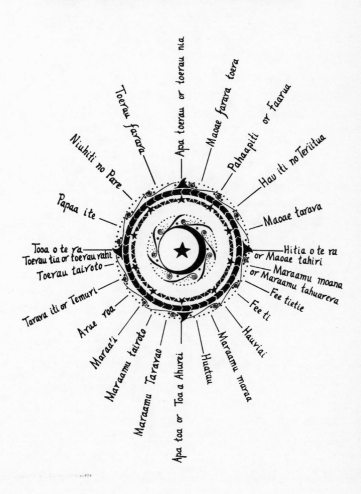

- Toerau farara
- Apa toerau or toerau nia
- Maoae farara toera
- Pahaapiti or Faarua
- Hau iti no Teriitua
- Niuhiti no Pare
- Papaa ite
- Maoae tarava
- Tooa o te ra
- Toerau tia or toerau rahi
- Hitia o te ra or Maoae tahiri
- Toerau tairoto
- Maraamu moana or Maraamu tahuareva
- Fee tietie
- Tarava iti or Temuri
- Fee ti
- Arue roa
- Hauviai
- Maraa'i
- Maraamu maraa
- Maraamu tairoto
- Huatau
- Maraamu Taravao
- Maraamu maraa
- Apa toa or Toa a Ahurei

1

Hine-tu-whenua carried *The Princely Flower* once more into a known and friendly sea. The surface was choppy, but there was a consistent swell which bore the double-hulled craft towards Rarotongan waters. Ru took this to be a sign that Tangaroa had taken charge of the craft and was leading it towards its destination, and the prince allowed the ocean to have its way.

Ru, like Dorcha with her bamboo-and-shell chart, had a record of the whole journey in a long length of knotted string, the device navigators used to prompt memory. It was not so much his own memory that needed the aid, but those navigators who would follow in his wake. Once the knowledge of the voyage became third or fourth hand, the captain of any pahi might need some sort of prompt to assist his knowledge.

The helmswoman was instructed to simply go where the currents took her, and not to force a direction.

Rongo-mai, God of Comets and Whales, sent a school of whales to guide the pahi. Kuku Lau, Goddess of Mirages, sent wavering forms to entice the ship onwards. The images Tiki and Marikoriko which sat on the deck seemed at peace with themselves.

At last all the omens were good and there was hope in the air.

One thing marred the anticipation of all on board: Tangata the Maori had begun to fade away. The further the vessel drew away from Rapanui, the more evanescent became the old warrior, until there came a time when he looked like a ghost. His body was almost transparent and those who stared at him could see the waves beyond him. When he walked in front of the mast, or rigging, these too were visible through his form. Also, his voice became thin and wasted, until one had to press one's ear to his mouth to hear what was being said.

'I think we're losing him,' said Boy-girl. 'I'm not sure what's happening, but one morning we'll wake up and he'll no longer be here.'

The Oceanians prayed to the god Ro'o to heal Tangata of his sickness, but still the old man grew dimmer and less tangible.

Then just before he disappeared altogether, his body began to darken in places. Patches like maps appeared on him, growing perceptibly stronger with each passing day. There came a point when Seumas remarked that he felt as if he were seeing double. There was a blurred secondary image, another outline, which seemed part of Tangata, yet somehow detached from him. It was as if an ill-fitting soul were trying to escape the mortal part of the old Maori and was struggling to detach itself.

Finally, the crew and passengers of *The Princely Flower* woke one morning, to find one of the figures, that part which had been fading, completely gone. The other shape, the form they had believed to be the soul, was growing stronger and more tangible. Now that the lithe, lean figure of Tangata had gone, they could actually recognise this materialising being. It was Polahiki, the Hivan fisherman, reappearing in his old world!

'What's happened?' cried Polahiki. 'Where's my cave?'

'You tell us,' said the astonished Kieto. 'We left you in the Land of the Long White Cloud, and now you manifest yourself out of the declining remains of Tangata the Maori. What have you done with the old man, that you should surface from his ghost to stand before us on the deck?'

Polahiki moaned and tore at the roots of his hair.

'I've come back,' he wailed. 'I was happy in my cave on the hillside of that Otherworld, and now I've come back.'

'But where is Tangata?' repeated Kieto.

'Why,' groaned Polahiki, 'he must be where I was living, in the cave that used to belong to Kurangai-tuku the ogress. It was a beautiful cave, right away from smelly humanity, and now I've lost it to that damned Maori.'

Seumas laughed on hearing this. 'I'm not sure Tangata wants to be in Kurangai-tuku's cave either.'

Kikamana said, 'It seems the winds of time and space will not allow a person to stay in the world in which they were not born and raised. Tangata and Polahiki have changed places again.'

'And to think we were rid of you,' said Dorcha to the fisherman. 'Now you're back and you smell worse than ever – I think we should order a bath.'

'Never,' snarled Polahiki, backing off. 'I'll kill the man – or woman – who touches me with water.'

But they managed to overpower him and get a line on him. They dragged his filthy body in the wake of the pahi, keeping a watch for sharks. He screamed the whole while, as the surf rushed over him, sometimes submerging him. Ru was merciless however and would not allow the line to be hauled in until he was sure Polahiki was in some measure clean. There on the deck they bathed him in sweet-smelling oils and perfumes, until he smelt as pleasant as a frangipani blossom.

They knew his nits would hatch again, and that he would be covered in fleas once more, but at least the worst of the dirt was gone from his body. Those who slept down Polahiki's end of the pahi remarked that the fresh air they had been enjoying until now remained to some degree clear of pollution.

The day after the washing of Polahiki a star was sighted in the roof of voyaging.

'There it is!' cried Ru, with great satisfaction in his voice. 'Under that star lies my island.'

Three days later a green glow was sighted on a cloud base. *The Princely Flower* was heading in the direction of Tooa o te ra on the windflower. Rarotonga was directly off the port side of the craft, in the direction of Apa toa, though many miles away. By noon they had sighted a hook-shaped island and by evening they were gliding through a huge and magnificent triangular lagoon.

'How have we Rarotongans missed this island, in our voyages across the ocean?' questioned Kikamana, in astonishment. 'It's almost on our beach.'

'Not more than twenty days sailing,' confirmed Ru, 'but I think the gods have kept it hidden until now, for me and my people to settle its land.'

Ru and his maidens carried Tiki ashore on their shoulders and built a fire on the beach as a sign that they had arrived at their new home. The great pahi was dragged up onto the sands where it was unloaded of all the tubers, seeds and shoots carried from Raiatea, these to be planted. There were pahua clam shells in plenty, in the lagoon, which quickly became a delicacy amongst the newcomers. The only dog still alive on board the pahi was Seumas's puppy, Dirk, so there were none to breed for livestock. Wild pigs had been found on the island of the Pool of Life and these would be domesticated.

Boy-girl's pet rooster was let loose amongst the few remaining hens, to become the father, grandfather and great-grandfather of all the new chicks on the island. He strutted and crowed as if he was actually aware of his unique status on this new Faraway Heaven, flashing his red and green feathers, shaking his sunset wattle with great dignity.

Sacrifices were made to the gods, especially Tangaroa, who had led them to the promised land. Ru officially named the island 'Ararau Enua O Ru Ki Te Moana' – *Ru in search of land over the sea* – but since this rather pompous title was too much of a mouthful for most of his people, it had a second name 'Aitutaki', meaning *to keep the fire burning*, because that was the maidens' function with the symbolic blaze while Ru climbed to the highest point on the island and surveyed his kingdom.

When Ru returned to the beach there was trouble, followed by tragedy. He had come down from the high place to say he had divided up the island into twenty sections, one section for each of the virgins who had crewed *The Princely Flower* from Raiatea to Aitutaki. This created dissension amongst Ru's four younger brothers, who immediately announced they would not stay and dragged *The Princely Flower* down the beach to launch it again, so they could set off on their own to find another island.

In their haste to get away before they could be stopped by Ru one brother fell under the rolling logs and was killed.

The bitter brothers and their wives and families were not prevented from leaving the island and they set sail for other climes. Ru, now king of Aitutaki, never did explain his reasons for not including his closest relatives in the distribution of land. Ru was and always had been an enigmatic man, not given to making excuses or explaining his actions.

The Rarotongans decided to leave King Ru to establish his kingdom. They built an outrigged sailing canoe, a váa motu, of sufficient size to carry them back to Rarotonga. There was Kikamana, Kieto, Po'oi, Boy-girl, Polahiki, Seumas and Dorcha, and the now maturing Dirk. These had safely completed what was to become one of the most celebrated of the legendary voyages. Pungarehu, the slayer of the Poukai Bird, and Rinto, had been the only ones to lose their lives amongst the Rarotongans.

Fully provisioned for a short journey, they set sail on a morning when the sky was red with promise. Dorcha and Po'oi were the navigators. The outrigged canoe, less than half the length of a pahi, skipped over the rich wide lagoon of Aitutaki and out into the open sea. They left the new island behind them, with its initial teething problems.

Kikamana still owned one twentieth of the land on Aitutaki, which she had offered to give to Ru's brothers. King Ru had forbidden the transfer, telling Kikamana that she must remain the owner, which led her to believe that some god or other had sent a message to Ru while he was on his solitary vigil and insisted that the twenty royal maidens be the ones to own all the land. So she left her section to be managed by an overseer and said she would return in the future to take possession herself.

'Well, we're on our way home again,' said Dorcha to Seumas.

Dorcha always referred to Rarotonga as 'home' whereas Seumas had difficulty in throwing off the feeling that home was actually Albainn and Rarotonga was a foreign land.

'I suppose so,' he conceded. 'Still, we've had ourselves an adventure, haven't we? I doubt there's a Pict alive who's seen what I've seen in my lifetime. It's been a full and rich life and I'm glad I've lived it.'

'You sound as if you're going somewhere,' Dorcha said. 'You're not feeling ill, are you?'

'No, no. It was that chance to return to boyhood which got me thinking again. I mean, I'm sure we made the right choice, by remaining as we are, but it still made me mull over my life and set me to wondering about whether I would change it. The only thing I would change, at this moment, is that thing . . .' he could hardly bring himself to talk about the fight which had resulted in the death of her man. The whole episode was still quite painful to him, not because of anything he personally felt over the incident, but because he had hurt her. 'You know, the death of your first husband.'

'We would not be married now, if it wasn't for that,' she said, pragmatically.

'I know, and that troubles me. I killed your husband and this resulted eventually in our marriage. I benefited out of a bad deed, which isn't right.'

'Look,' she laid a hand on his shoulder, 'you can't change the past no matter how much you think about it. Things happened we both regret, but now is now. You can't look back. We still have the twilight of our lives to look forward to and I'm not going to have that time spent in turning over events which can only cause us grief. Forget the past. I have.'

'Are you sure?'

'Of course I'm sure.'

In the middle of the afternoon Kieto sighted a fleet of pahi on the horizon. As they drew nearer the Rarotongans saw that it was the Arioi. On this occasion, when there was no hurry to get back to Rarotonga, Kieto felt they could board one of the Arioi vessels and talk to the troupe. The seafarers had missed the Arioi the first time around and everyone on board agreed that it would be exciting to see some of the acts.

The yellow sails drew nearer. When the first vessel was close enough, Kieto called and asked if they could come aboard. The answer was yes. Polahiki dropped the sail of the outrigger, a line was taken, and the smaller vessel was towed behind the lead Arioi pahi. Those on board the outrigger were soon on the deck of the pahi, full of interest and excitement.

On board a choir was singing, practising scales. There were tumblers running through their acrobatics. On the other pahi, around and behind the lead ship, performers were running through their acts. A canoe drew up alongside on which a drummer was leaping from instrument to instrument, rehearsing his show. Kieto was most impressed with what he saw.

'Who's that?' he asked the captain of their pahi. 'The drummer?'

'A Painted Leg,' answered the captain, with reverence in his voice. 'His name is Kumiki and he's from Nuku Hiva.'

'Brilliant,' Po'oi said, admiringly.

'That's why he's a Painted Leg,' replied the captain, laughing. Then he asked, 'Where are you people from?'

'We live on Rarotonga,' replied Kikamana. 'We've been on a long voyage – to an island called Rapanui.'

'I've never heard of this island. Would they enjoy seeing the Arioi?'

'They might, when they've settled all their differences. There's a civil war on there at the moment. You would do well to stay away until that's over. In any case, the island is in the far corner of the ocean, many months away.'

The captain grunted. 'I wouldn't want us to get mixed up in a war,' he said. Then he changed the subject. 'We went to Rarotonga some time ago. Did you see us there?'

Kieto replied, 'No, we left just as you arrived, and we've been voyaging ever since. Not that craft you're towing for us, but in a pahi much the same as this one. We went with Prince Ru of Raiatea to search for a new island.'

'And did you find it?' asked the captain.

'Oh yes, it's called Aitutaki and it's about twenty days sailing from Rarotonga, Apa toerau on the windflower.'

'Hmmm, we'll let them get settled then pay them a visit in a few years' time. So, you all went with Prince Ru . . .'

'Now King Ru.'

'Of course – but you all went with him?'

The captain was obviously fishing for names, but as it was impolite to ask directly he did not do so.

'Yes, there is myself, Kieto – Kikamana the priestess; Po'oi whose father was Kaho a blind navigator and feeler-of-the-sea; Polahiki a fisherman from the Hivan islands; Boy-girl, a hypnotist and ventriloquist, and finally Dorcha and Seumas, of whom you must have heard: they are people from the Land-of-Mists, the great country discovered by Kupe and myself.'

The captain stared at the couple about whom Kieto was speaking.

'Ah, that is the man called Seumas?'

'I knew you would have heard of him. That dog he's patiently training, despite all the noise going on around him, is the one he calls Dirk. We're not allowed to eat it,' laughed Kieto. 'He feeds it meat and uses it to hunt lizards and birds. Seumas is a strange man in many ways. You should get him to play his dead pig for the Arioi. A new act! He makes it wail in the most horrible way.'

The captain was affronted by this suggestion. 'Why would I want him to play in our troupe? We are a company of entertainers. We're not in the business of frightening old women and children to death.'

Kieto smiled and shrugged. 'Seumas says the music of the bagpipes – that's what he calls his instrument – he says it grows on you. An acquired taste. You might find your audiences clamouring for more, after a few years.'

'After a few years,' snorted the captain. 'You think we're going to allow him to screech and wail for a few years, chasing away our customers, in the hope that one day they'll become tone deaf and find his music acceptable? Not in my lifetime.'

Kieto laughed and later told Seumas about the conversation, which Seumas did not find in the least bit funny.

The Rarotongans were gathered around one of the masts, sitting in a circle, discussing all they had heard and seen that day. It had been an interesting experience, but not a full one. Obviously on board one pahi amongst three hundred, they could only watch one or two acts close up and a few others at a distance, but most of the pahi were too far away for the group to see or hear what was going on. Kieto had asked the captain his destination and found it to be Raiatea.

'We have no need to hurry back to Rarotonga, now our mission has been successfully completed,' said Kieto. 'Who would like to go to Raiatea once more? We could see the Arioi in full splendour, watch their performance over a number of days, then find a larger vessel than our outrigged canoe, and travel back to Rarotonga in style some time later?'

The vote was almost unanimous. Only Polahiki said no, grumbling about missing out on his fishing.

Kieto told Polahiki he could take the outrigger.

'We're sure to find a vessel going to Rarotonga from Raiatea – if you want to leave us, do so.'

Polahiki left shortly afterwards, the slovenly fisherman bidding everyone good riddance. The feeling was mutual. He was not the best of companions.

'It's a short voyage,' said Dorcha, 'but I don't envy Polahiki – stuck in that canoe alone with a dirty fisherman for several days.'

The others laughed at her joke.

Later that evening, when the group were preparing to go to bed, someone came on board from a neighbouring pahi. In the light of the torches, Kieto recognised the man as the drummer he had seen and admired during that day. The Painted Leg came with the captain and glared at the group, his eyes going from face to face, and finally resting on the features of Seumas.

'You are the goblin they call Seumas?' said the Painted Leg.

Up until that moment, Kieto had been awestruck by the fact that they were being honoured by the presence of a Painted Leg. He had been about to express his profound admiration for the man's talent at drumming. Now, however, a feeling of irritation swept through him at the Painted Leg's words.

'We do not refer to Seumas as "the goblin",' said Kieto. 'He is a respected Rarotongan, a warrior who has earned his place in our society.'

'You might not call him the goblin,' snapped the Painted Leg, 'but I do. In fact I call him worse. I call him a murdering rapist. Tomorrow, goblin, we will fight to the death, here on this deck. You and I. Prepare your mind for your last night on this ocean. You will not see another.'

Seumas climbed slowly to his feet and stared at the Painted Leg. He was now in his middle years and, though fit, knew that a match with a man half his age was a dangerous exercise. He had wily old tricks, certain skills which are only learned over a number of years, but he might not be a match for this super fit drummer, who spent his whole life leaping and dancing. Not if the drummer were as good at single combat as he was at pounding his instruments. Yet the Painted Leg was in years merely a boy, despite his grand title, and perhaps unseasoned in war.

'You call me names, Painted Leg, but I don't know what you're talking about. Kumiki from Nuku Hiva? Have I insulted you in some way, while we have been neighbours today?'

'You insulted my mother,' said Kumiki in a choked voice. 'You insulted her by raping her and leaving her for dead. She died in childbirth, giving me life. I am your son, for what it's worth, you ugly monster. I'm your *son*.'

Kumiki spat the word as if it were so loathsome and foul it tasted like bile in his mouth.

Seumas was genuinely bewildered and shook his head. 'I have never raped a woman in my life,' he said. 'You have the wrong man.'

Dorcha stood up and put her arm around her man.

'Listen to him, Painted Leg. He is trying to prevent you from making a terrible mistake. Seumas is my husband. If you kill him, you will have to kill me too. I know this man, and I know him to be honourable. He would not take a woman against her will. I am his wife. I know this.'

'I have the *right* man. Be here and armed tomorrow morning, goblin. If you are not I shall strike you dead where you stand. And anyone else who stands with you. You may all be armed, but I shall have *him*,' he pointed to Seumas. 'I shall avenge my mother and myself in the light of the dawn.'

With that, the Painted Leg left them, striding back to the dugout canoe where a paddler was waiting to take him to his own pahi.

Seumas stood there bemused. What was the Painted Leg talking about. It was a mystery to him.

'Have we ever been to Nuku Hiva?' he asked Kieto. 'When were we in Nuku Hiva?'

Kieto nodded, replying, 'We stopped there for a short while on our voyage with King Tangiia. It was where you, Po and Manopa, and some others were trapped up on a plateau. Don't you remember? You escaped by tricking the local people with a climb up to the peak of one of the mountains. Later, Manopa rescued you by coming back in a canoe with Wakana.'

'Oh, *that* island,' recalled Seumas. 'Where they forced me to eat long pig?'

He remembered now, having to chew on the flesh of a cooked man, the husband chief of the woman he was later forced to make love to in front of his Hivan captors. She too was a captive, from another island, and both had submitted to the act knowing they had no choice, but gaining little emotional pleasure from it. Yes, Seumas had raped a woman on Nuku Hiva, but at the point of a spear, and she too had been forced into the performance by a hostile and lustful tribe.

It was not as if he had attacked a local woman and taken her against her will. He had told no one of this shameful incident and those with him had held their peace too, having been forced to do the same. None of them wanted the details to be spread abroad. Now most of those men were dead – Manopa, Po, the young priest who had stolen the God of Hope from Raiatea – dead and gone. Certainly in the present company, Seumas was the only one who knew the truth of the incident.

'But that was so long ago,' murmured Seumas, more to himself than any other. 'It's not something I want to remember.'

Dorcha frowned and stared hard into Seumas's eyes.

'You did rape a woman?'

'Against *my* will, as well as hers. I was forced to do it. There was a club raised over my head – a dagger at my throat – I had no choice in the matter.'

Dorcha said, 'No choice? But you mean you were ready for it – capable of making love to a woman?'

'I know what you're thinking,' replied Seumas, angrily. 'But there was danger in the air. We were anticipating a struggle, a fight to the death, because there was no way I was going to submit to execution without a battle. The anticipation of deadly conflict does things to a man . . .'

Seumas went to his bed and lay on his back, staring up at the stars. It was as much a shock to learn he had a son as it was to know he might have to fight that son to the death. When he and Dorcha discovered, through time, that they were unable to have children, Seumas accepted the fact philosophically. He was not one to brood on such things. And now he had a son, a young man who had materialised out of thin air! And that son was a Painted Leg, a man supreme amongst his kind. Kumiki's achievements were something of which to be immensely proud. His son, an Avae Parai! He *did* feel proud.

They must have lied to the boy, his guardians on his home island. They had told him his father raped his mother out of pure lust. And because Seumas had been too ashamed to speak of the incident, there were few who knew the truth. Certainly this was the first time Kieto, Boy-girl and Kikamana had heard of it and they would be wondering why Seumas had kept it so secret. It made Seumas's story appear suspicious. Perhaps they too were wondering if Kumiki was speaking the truth? There was a man, a survivor of the group that went ashore with Manopa, Seumas and Po onto the island of Nuku Hiva, but he was back on Rarotonga, and could not speak for Seumas here.

Dorcha came to him and put her arms around him.

'I believe you,' she said, 'in case you're wondering if the whole world is against you.'

'I was thinking that, yes,' admitted Seumas. 'Did you see the way Kieto was looking at me?'

'It was just a shock that was all. Certainly it was a shock for me. Forgive me for my outburst?'

He kissed her tenderly. 'It was a shock to us all. How can I fight him, Dorcha? I don't want him to kill me, and I don't want to kill him? What do I do?'

'Refuse to fight.'

'You saw him. You saw his anger. He's been living his life for the moment when he could confront me. He's been feeding off his hate since he was a child. He won't take that for an answer. He'll simply cut me down where I stand.'

'Then you'll have to defend yourself.'

'I can't do that either.'

'Oh, Seumas, man.'

Seumas felt empty inside. Neither of the alternatives were acceptable. To stand and be killed, or to fight his own son to the death. It was an impossible choice.

'But he's a fine-looking boy, Dorcha, isn't he?' Seumas said, another feeling altogether surging through him. 'I can't help but feel proud of him.'

Dorcha sat up and looked at Seumas in amazement.

'You can feel fatherly love for the son who hates you on the eve of a battle to the death with him? You are crazy, Pict. That youth might have risen through the ranks of entertainers, but he has no maturity. Any sensible young man would have listened to your side of the story and weighed it against the tales he had heard from poisonous mouths. Instead, he charges in like a headstrong Albannach bull, not for a moment considering you might be innocent of the accusation.'

'True, but I can see myself in him. Was I not like that at his age, woman? You remember? A wild impetuous youth, hot-blooded and full of righteous vigour.'

She sighed. 'I suppose you were, but don't sound so proud of yourself. I thought you very stupid in those days, Seumas from the Blackwater, and I'm glad you grew out of it. If you hadn't, we wouldn't be lying here together now.'

Kikamana came to where they lay and asked to speak with Seumas.

'Are you going to fight this young man? If you win, they'll kill us all you know. He's a Painted Leg. They wouldn't be able to allow you to kill one of their greatest performers without some form of retribution.'

'What would you have me do?' asked Seumas. 'The truth is I raped his mother, though not willingly. What shall I do, offer to kill myself?'

'We can slip away now, in our own canoe. The captain of this pahi doesn't want the fight. He'll allow us to slide away during the night.'

Seumas had already thought about this.

'No,' he said. 'He'll continue to hunt me down, with all that hate festering in his heart. If he doesn't find me, it'll eat away his manhood and all the good aspects of his character. Bitterness and hate can turn the most talented person into a dry husk, worthless to the world. Let it stand.'

'But you can't kill him!'

'No, I can't – but I have to let him fight me, get it out of his system. Perhaps I can wound him seriously enough to stop the fight? Perhaps if he wounds me, it will not be fatal, but will be enough to cleanse him of his hate and anger? We shall see. Running away will not help me, or him. This confrontation has to take place sometime. Better now than later, when I'm a weak old man and he's twisted inside with fury and enmity towards me.'

'He's already twisted inside,' muttered Kikamana, 'but I accept your decision. I'll tell Kieto, Boy-girl and Po'oi. I'm sure they'll be behind you.'

'They – they don't think I'm lying?'

Kikamana looked surprised. 'Of course not, why should they?'

'I don't know,' said Seumas, miserably. 'I just thought they might believe the youth over me. You saw that hair. He *is* my son, no doubt about that. And I've never been open about this incident. I just thought – I thought—'

Kikamana interrupted, firmly. 'These are your friends, Seumas. They know you to be an honourable man. They trust and love you. Have no doubts on that.'

'Thank you,' mumbled Seumas, feeling uplifted. 'Thank you, Kikamana.'

Seumas and Dorcha tried to get some rest after that, but they were woken in the dawn hours by chanting from the pahi which kept pace with their own. There were prayers to Oro, God of War and Peace, patron of the Arioi, going up into the roof of voyaging from the mouth of Seumas's son.

Seumas wondered whether he ought to pray to some god too, but he had never been completely comfortable with the Oceanian gods. They were not his deities. He wondered if he should pray to his own god of war, whose name was buried deep in the back of his brain, but his own Pictish gods were back in Albannach and had no power here on an alien ocean.

Instead, he prepared himself mentally for an impossible task: a battle in which there were to be no winners.

2

Kumiki came on board as he had promised, bringing with him a woman. She carried his weapons: a lei-o-mano and a patu club made of nokonoko. The woman looked upset and Seumas guessed this was either his son's wife, or his betrothed. In the light of the day, Kumiki looked younger than ever. Seumas guessed the boy was not more than twenty years of age. This, coupled with the fact that he was Hivan and not Tahitian, made it even more amazing that he had managed to become a Painted Leg. He had to be a uniquely brilliant drummer.

However, this did give Seumas some hope. A boy so young, one who had concentrated on becoming a top entertainer, was not likely to have had much experience at war. In fact he looked green and unseasoned. It might be that Seumas could disarm the youth and gain a submission. On the other hand Seumas knew he himself was not as lithe and supple as he had once been, and would need all his learned battle skills to stay alive.

'Good morning son,' said Seumas, selecting a club for himself. 'Are you ready to kill your father?'

This opening greeting clearly disconcerted the youth.

'I shall do what must be done,' he snapped back.

Seumas's club was made of whalebone. Unlike Kumiki

he had deliberately chosen one which did not have tearing or cutting edges of shark's teeth or razor shells. He wanted to stun the boy, knock him senseless, and then call the fight a draw.

'Then be very careful,' said Seumas, as a space on the deck was cleared for them. 'I have powerful mana – my head is full of mana. My skill at single combat is renowned throughout all Oceania. I have killed many men, both in battle, and at contest. There are those who go in fear and trembling when they hear my name. The great magician, Ragnu of Raiatea, has long sought my death, but has been unable to bring it about.'

This bragging was an essential part of the psychological attack on one's opponent, before the actual fighting began, and it was significant that Kumiki neither took part in it, nor seemed affected by Seumas's taunting.

All he said in reply was, 'Normally, as a Painted Leg I am tapu, but the priest removed the tapu last night, in a special ceremony, so we fight merely as two men.'

'Nothing *mere* about me, son. I have beaten giants in my time. I have slaughtered Ponaturi with this very kotiate club. I have been chosen as an ariki by my tribe. Beware of me, boy, for I will take your head from your shoulders. If you manage by some freak of nature to kill me, my kabu will haunt you for the rest of your days, bringing terror into your life.'

Dorcha, standing on the sidelines with Boy-girl, Kikamana, Kieto and Po'oi, raised her eyes to heaven at these words.

However, his taunting was beginning to have an effect on the young woman who had carried Kumiki's weapons and she gave a little cry, burying her face in her hands.

'You are upsetting my wife Linloa,' hissed Kumiki. 'Stop talking and let us fight.'

'Your wife?' cried Seumas. 'Then she is my daughter-in-law! How do you do, daughter? My son has chosen well, you are a credit to him. Son, she is beautiful – plump and beautiful. If I had not a fine wife myself, I should envy you. That's her over there, by the way, your step-mother.'

Without meaning to, Kumiki turned and saw Dorcha staring at him with her black eyes. He swung back angrily, annoyed at having been tricked into looking behind him. Linloa however, was staring at Seumas in an agitated manner. Seumas smiled at her, hoping to put her at her ease, but instead it seemed he frightened her with his goblin's face and red-grey hair.

'Fight, damn you,' snarled Kumiki.

The two men went into crouching positions, one with a leg almost black with tattoos and bars across his face, and the other with no facial tattoos, but with strange elaborate designs down his tanned chest, shoulders and back. The Hivan tattoos made the youth's face look fierce, while the Pictish whorls and spirals broke up the shape of the older warrior, made it difficult for his enemy to see him with any clarity.

The Hivan youth's inexperience soon became obvious, as Seumas tried various moves. The blows were blocked, but not quickly enough, and Seumas knew that if he had swung more swiftly, as he was able, the parry would have come too late. Several times during that first encounter, he could have felled his son and cracked open his skull. The boy knew it too, for there was comprehension in his eyes.

'An old dog, eh?' he murmured to Kumiki. 'You need to be a little more athletic.'

At these words the boy changed his tactics completely, and began a series of astonishing acrobatic moves which startled Seumas and sent him into retreat. Now it was he who had difficulty in blocking the blows, but luckily he did anticipate each strike with accuracy. It was clear that the boy was extremely fit, knew how to weave, leap and somersault, and that Seumas would have to watch his back as well as his front.

'Clever, very clever,' he said to Kumiki. 'This old body has forgotten such tricks.'

The pair of them then went to it seriously, closing and engaging with ferocity, Seumas desperately trying to knock the youth down without killing him. The air was full of the sounds of clashing clubs. Neither man had drawn his lei-o-mano. Finally, Seumas managed to hook his club under Kumiki's wrist, and the youth's weapon went flying through the air like a black bird on the wing.

There was a gasp from the crowd and a startled cry like that of a bird from the girl Linloa.

Seumas could have felled the youth there and then, but he hesitated, looking for a clean swipe to the back of the head. While he paused in indecision Kumiki leapt forward, grasped his arm and wrenched it back, causing him to drop his own weapon. As he stooped to retrieve it, Kumiki drew his lei-o-mano and sliced Seumas across the upper arm, cutting into the flesh and severing a sinew. The Pict winced in pain.

Still, the kotiate club was soon in his hand and despite his wound he continued to defend himself, until Kumiki managed to force him back with his slashing dagger to the point where the youth could pick up his own club. With this larger weapon in his right hand he rushed at Seumas, causing the Pict to stumble on a pile of ropes. Seumas fell backwards, his own club raised in self defence. This was knocked from his hands and went spinning over the deck.

There was another cry from the spectators as the boy stood over the man, the patu club ready to split open the older man's skull. It was poised to deliver a killing blow, but it failed to descend. Seumas looked into his son's eyes and saw the anguish of indecision there too. The youth was fighting with something inside himself, some emotion which was staying his hand, preventing him from destroying his hated foe.

'Ahhhh!' moaned the boy, clearly trying to overcome his reticence.

To no avail.

He finally shouted in frustration, dropped the club, and rushed to his bride to bury his face in her breasts.

'I can't do it,' he sobbed. 'He's my father.'

It was so. One's ancestors were to be revered, not destroyed. A father was a father, however worthless. The gods would not approve of patricide, no matter what the cause.

The ropes were untangled from his feet and Seumas was helped up by the Rarotongans. Once he had regained his dignity, he went to his son.

'You fought better than I imagined you would,' he said. 'But you were mistaken in your beliefs, my son. The gods would not let you kill me because I am innocent. I never loved your mother, it's true. I never really knew her. Like her I was a captive of a hostile tribe and we were both forced to the act in front of jeering warriors. I had no choice.'

Kumiki turned and stared at his father bleakly.

'However,' continued Seumas, after catching Dorcha's eye and remembering an early morning conversation. 'I do think that your mother was a proud and stately woman, distinguished in her courage, and had we but met under different circumstances, I might easily have loved her. She was the wife of a great chief, the daughter of another great chief, ariki through and through. A noble woman who like me had fallen into the hands of conquerors. We respected one another, your mother and I, even as we performed for the scoffing warriors. You could say the union, which eventually resulted in our son Kumiki, was as dignified as it had to be in the circumstances.'

The youth continued to stare at him, but there was no longer any terrible hate in his eyes, only confusion.

Kumiki took his trembling young wife by the hand and

led her across the deck, to the dugout canoe. With her on board the small craft, he paddled away from the pahi to his own, where his friends and fellow performers were watching, hanging from the rigging, clinging to the mast. They had witnessed the whole fight from beginning to end and there was an air of respect about them as their Painted Leg's canoe approached.

When he stepped back onto the deck, they greeted Kumiki by cheering him as a victor, telling him his act in not killing his father was noble and worthy of a Painted Leg. And indeed it was a laudable act which had helped the young man rise above the less finer feelings in him. It had come out from within him, despite the driving deadly hatred, and surfaced at precisely the right time. Surely this was the spirits of his ancestors at work, guiding him to right and proper judgement? This was the work of more than just one man.

For his part, Seumas was happy that it was all over. He had not had to kill his son and the relief came through his pores in the form of sweat. Yet he felt cold. He sat on the deck with a cloak thrown round his shoulders, shivering and perspiring just as if he were suffering from a fever. Dorcha sat with him, her presence a great comfort to him. Boy-girl and the others remained a little way off, ready to assist if necessary.

'I didn't have to kill him, that's the important thing,' said Seumas.

'The important thing,' Dorcha corrected him, 'is that he's your son. You must do what you can now to get to know him. Now that he's aware of the truth, he may let you be his father, in the way that's best for both of you.'

'Perhaps he doesn't believe the truth?'

'Even if he still doubts you now, he'll come round in the future. He *wants* to believe in you. You're his father. Until now he's looked on you as an ogre, but I'll bet he's surprised that you're not such a monster after all. He'll want to get to know you too – you're his family.'

Seumas sighed. 'I hope you're right.'

'I'm right,' said Dorcha, in that infuriating tone she used which was full of confidence. This time he hoped she *was* right.

Over the next few days, as the fleet sped towards Raiatea, Seumas caught his son watching him from the other pahi. When he knew he was being observed, Kumiki pretended to be doing something with his drums, or helping the crew with the canoe, but Seumas knew that his son was inquisitive, and that curiosity was gradually softening the boy. Dorcha was right, as she usually was about these things, and Seumas simply had to wait.

A week after the fight Kumiki came on board again. He was treated like royalty. The captain of the pahi brought out a stool for the Painted Leg to sit on, while they both talked in undertones about the weather and any navigational problems the fleet was experiencing. Seumas kept one eye on his son, who did not look his way once, though the Pict had a feeling that the youth was aware of his presence.

'He's here to talk to you,' whispered Dorcha. 'I've heard from the crew that his wife has been urging him to make friends with you. She's got a good head on her shoulders, that one. Look at him. He's being too deliberate about not noticing you. Make an excuse to speak to the captain while he's there.'

'What?' said Seumas, panicking a little inside. 'What would I have to speak to the captain about?'

'Invent something,' hissed Dorcha. 'Use your head.'

It was not easy. Seumas was scared. What if Dorcha were wrong and his son simply ignored him, or worse, insulted him? What if that hatred had not dried and Kumiki was still seething inside, looking for an excuse to fight again? Seumas was worried that his son was still in a destructive mood, hoping for an opportunity to crush his father to a pulp.

Seumas eventually went to the captain and waited for the two men to stop speaking, before saying, 'I noticed the drinking water was brackish this morning – are we having to mix it with seawater?'

'We're a little low on fresh water,' replied the captain, surprised at this interruption. 'Does it bother you? There are drinking coconuts, if you wish.'

'No, no,' said Seumas, anxious not to be considered a whingeing passenger. 'I'm quite used to brackish water from my long voyages with Tangiia and Ru. I was just curious that's all, because it looks like rain. We can fill the gourds if we get a downpour. I just wanted to be ready.'

The captain raised his eyebrows at this extraordinary interruption, but the talk had its effect on Kumiki.

'You sailed with Ru?' cried the youth, enthusiastically. 'I hear he set out for an unknown island, but was swept away to the far reaches of the ocean.'

'Yes, I sailed with Prince Ru,' replied Seumas. 'He has now made his home on the unknown island, Aitutaki, and is a king. It was a long and dangerous voyage though. We did indeed get taken off our course and made a landing on the island of Rapanui, place of the red and white giants. On another island we met the People of the Night, who fade away when confronted by the light. We saw the armies of the dead, the Maori warrior nation, monsters, fairies . . .'

The youth's mouth was open in wonder, then he seemed to draw back a little and became slightly haughty.

'I have seen great wonders too, on my solitary voyages.'

'I'm sure you have,' said Seumas, 'and I would be pleased to hear about them. Why not come and share a basket with me and my friends?'

Kumiki stood up and nodded gravely.

'I should like to meet these people who sailed with Ru.'

Seumas tried not to smile and motioned for his son to go ahead of him, to where Kieto and the others were sitting.

'I must warn you,' said Seumas, 'that we eat with women, when we're travelling.'

Kumiki looked surprised. 'Eat with the women?'

'Yes.'

The young man did not pause in his stride however as he considered this unconventional behaviour.

'Well,' he said at last, 'I expect this is a custom you have brought from your own land.'

'I expect it is,' agreed Seumas.

He had reached the small group now and stood over Dorcha, a little too imperiously for Seumas's liking.

'Yes, this is Dorcha, who is also from my homeland.'

Kumiki suddenly flashed Dorcha a most charming smile and sat down beside her.

'What do we have to eat?' he asked her, boyishly. 'You must tell me all about this place where you were born. Is it hot? Are the mosquitoes bothersome? Who is your father and mother? Do you have pigs and dogs there?'

The questions poured from his mouth and from that moment Seumas knew things were going to be fine between them.

PART TEN

Moikeha and the winds

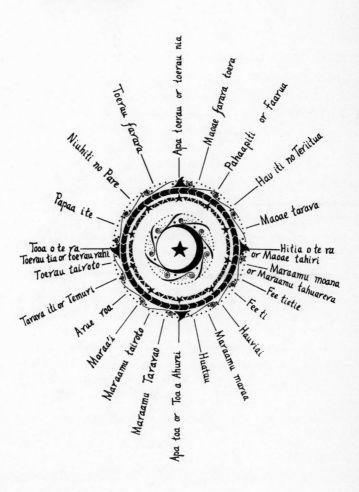

Toerau farara

Niuhiti no Pare

Papaa ite

Apa toerau or toerau nia

Maoae farara toera

Pahaapiti or Faarua

Hau iti no Teriitua

Maoae tarava

Tooa o te ra
Toerau tia or toerau rahi
Toerau tairoto

Hitia o te ra
or Maoae tahiri

Maraamu moana
or Maraamu tahuareva

Fee tietie

Tarava iti or Temuri

Arue roa

Maraa'i

Fee ti

Hauviai

Maraamu moraa

Maraamu tairoto

Maraamu Tavarao

Huatau

Maraamu Tavarao

Apa toa or Toa a Ahurei

1

So eager was Kumiki to get to know his father that he sent for his wife Linloa and the pair of them stayed on board the pahi carrying the Rarotongans for three days. However, at the end of those three days he suddenly remembered he was a Painted Leg and should be practising. He sent for several drums to be fetched from his own pahi. With these he gave the Rarotongans a semi-private performance, witnessed only by others because the night air carried the sound.

Seumas was amazed at his son's skill and pronounced himself to be very proud. He could not stop speaking of the youth to Dorcha, who continually nodded and smiled. Then Boy-girl caught Seumas's eye and had a quick word in his ear. The Pict's sanguine mood was mellowed a little by Boy-girl's advice. He nodded gravely at Boy-girl, going back to Dorcha's side.

'I keep forgetting,' he said later to Dorcha, 'that he's not your son too. I wish he were. He should be. Boy-girl told me I enthuse too much. I'm sorry.'

Dorcha smiled wistfully. 'It doesn't matter. You're excited by Kumiki at the moment – by the fact he exists. He's new to you. I understand that. Don't worry about me.'

'But I do,' he said. 'Your happiness is of the utmost importance to me.'

She put an arm around his shoulders. 'I'm glad of that. I hope I can regard him as my son too, and Linloa as our daughter. I like her. She has a sensible head.'

'A sensible head,' snorted Seumas. 'What's so wonderful about that?'

'Where there are men like you and your son, who have never managed to grow up completely, you need sensible women.'

'Huh!' Seumas grunted weakly, never knowing quite how to deal with this side of Dorcha.

After the performance, when the praises died down a little, Seumas and Dorcha had a long talk with Linloa, a beautiful young lady with fine manners and a shy disposition. Seumas could tell she loved her husband with a great passion. Her eyes never left his face when he was speaking. Seumas was not sure this was a good thing, for young men are apt to become a little conceited by such adoration, and begin to treat their wives uncivilly. However, Kumiki seemed hardly aware of his wife's devotion and occasionally plucked her arm to let her know he knew she was there and that all was well between them.

Over the past few nights, with the help of Dorcha and Boy-girl, Kikamana had been seeking to find a source of bad dreams. Now, while the group were engaged in conversation Kikamana had been communing with the spirits of her ancestors. They had passed on to her some alarming news.

'Someone's out to destroy us,' she said. 'There's a dark cloud coming from Raiatea. The cloud carries a poison meant to destroy us all. We must be vigilant.'

The buoyant mood of the Rarotongans was suddenly dampened as they stared over the sea ahead of them. Seumas knew of only one man who wanted them all dead.

There would be no peace for them until that man had been removed from the face of the earth.

'Ragnu,' said Seumas, quietly. 'It must be him.'

Ragnu had also been communing with his ancestors, asking them to act as his go-betweens. He had obtained from the ghosts of his forefathers the assistance he required in order to gain the attention of the gods. Hau Maringi, God of Mists and Fog, carried a thick blanket of damp vapour to the Arioi fleet and enveloped it. The miasma clung to the pandanus mat sails, dank and dismal, not letting Ra's rays reach them.

Over the course of a few days the sails began to rot for want of dry air. A black mould formed on the mats, eating away at the bright yellow colour, until the original ochre was no longer visible. When the captains of the pahi ordered replacement sails to be fitted, these too had formed the same black mould while the pandanus mats had been folded and stored in the deck huts. There was no other choice but to continue the journey with the sails as they were, hoping that they would not rot into tatters and force the fleet to use oars.

'I don't like the look of this,' said Kikamana. 'We must arm ourselves.'

'Against whom?' asked Kieto.

'Against an unknown enemy,' replied Boy-girl. 'I understand what our kahuna is saying. That fog is not natural – Hau Maringi is helping our enemy.'

The captain of the pahi was reluctant to inform the rest of the fleet about Kikamana's fears, concerned that he might look foolish, but Kumiki persuaded him that it was better to err on the side of caution, than to be caught out.

When individuals throughout the flotilla had armed themselves and were staring into the impenetrable mists,

a heavy swell came to rock the pahi fleet violently.
Although it was not a storm, for there was no wind, the
motion of the ships caused great distress. Many were sea-
sick, hanging over the gunwales and vomiting into the
ocean. All singing and dancing stopped and those who were
not unwell were comforting and assisting those who
were incapacitated.

For the first time in its history, the fleet was silent, its
crews and passengers simply wanting to be on dry land
again.

Then suddenly, as they approached Raiatea, the mists
cleared and the day was bright.

'A great flotilla of ships is coming,' Ragnu told the new
king of Raiatea. 'A fleet with black sails.'

'Black sails?' questioned the young king, who was not at
all experienced in international matters. 'What does that
mean?'

'You will remember,' said Ragnu, 'when King Tutapu
pursued Prince Tangiia over the oceans, his ships were
rigged with black sails. It was a symbol of war. Henceforth,
we understand those flotillas who carry black sails to be
war fleets, out to sack and pillage, to plunder innocent
islands. This island of Raiatea and its sister Borabora are
rich islands, my lord, and as such are likely to fall prey to
such marauders.'

'Show me this great fleet, with its ominous sails.'

The king was carried down to the beaches by his attendants and he saw the black fleet for himself. It was a silent
and dreadful flotilla, raiders who seemed bent on ravaging
Raiatea and Borabora. There were no friendly drums beating, no Tai Moana. Nor was there any singing and
chanting, as there would have been if these pahi had been
on a long journey and were glad to see friendly land again.
The king had no doubt this was a war fleet, probably sent
from Tonga. The Tongans were some of the fiercest pirates

on the seas, though they had never sailed this far in search of quarry before.

'What shall we do?' he enquired of Ragnu. 'We must defend ourselves.'

'Give me the Raiatean navy, lord, and I shall sail out to meet these impudent marauders on their own terms.'

Over the years of the last king a fleet of warships had been built for defence purposes. These were not sail-rigged ships, but pahi tamai: double-hulled paddled war canoes. They carried up to three hundred warriors. They were solidly built of strong hardwood frames: narrow craft with only an arm's length between stout twin hulls which stood high out of the water, so that those on board overlooked any much lower sailing vessel built for speed on the open sea.

The structure of these canoes consisted of transverse cross pieces and longitudinal girders. On the bows was an elevated platform where the warriors were gathered ready to do battle. The paddlers of these craft stood up to do their work inside the deep basins of the hulls. The king's banners flew from the prows, from which carved posts protruded vertically.

The king listened to Ragnu, but seemed indecisive.

'The only alternative,' said Ragnu, 'is for you to lead the Raiateans in battle.'

This new king was no great warrior, having gained his position through his bloodline rather than his courage. He was a good intelligent ruler, who kept peace amongst his peoples, but he was no admiral. Ragnu's suggestion had its desired effect.

'I give you command of the navy,' said the king. 'Go out and defeat this invasion fleet.'

These were the words Ragnu wished to hear.

That night, when Ragnu performed occult ceremonies for the favours of his ancestors, he learned of the presence of the Rarotongans on board the Arioi fleet. This was a wonderful bonus. He could now kill both Seumas and his son, the other Rarotongans, and destroy the Arioi all in one. Ragnu could hardly contain his elation.

Everything was going according to his schemes.

At dawn the Arioi fleet was within reach of the war canoes and with two hundred vessels, some sixty thousand warriors barbed with weapons, Ragnu set out to meet the oncoming ships. In case the Arioi had recovered from their seasickness and began singing, Ragnu had every drummer on every war craft pounding their instruments, to drown any sound which might reach Raiatea from the oncoming fleet.

The old sorcerer, streaked through with hatred and bitterness, stood on the bows of the leading war canoe looking like a monitor lizard about to catch its prey.

Kikamana, on seeing the war canoes launched from the beaches of Raiatea, knew that something was seriously wrong. It was true that the canoes were sometimes used ceremoniously, sent out to meet important visitors to the island, but she could see armed spearmen on the platforms, warriors with clubs in their hands, men wielding basalt canoe-breakers. Her instinct told her these men appeared agitated, as if they had worked themselves up to a pitch of frenzy, and she knew they were primed for battle. Her dreams, over the last few nights, had been foreboding. This flotilla of war canoes was the manifestation of her nightmares.

'Send up an alarm!' she cried to Kieto. 'We're about to be attacked!'

'Are you sure?' asked Kieto. 'Perhaps we're just being met?'

'Do as I say,' she snapped, 'or the Arioi will all be slaughtered by that fiend Ragnu.'

Kieto wasted no more time. He called to the captain that they were being attacked and to raise a signal to all the other vessels in the fleet. At the same time he woke Seumas and told him to arm himself.

'What's happening?' asked the Pict.

'Ragnu,' said Kieto. 'A war fleet.'

Seumas leapt to his feet, grabbing his whalebone club. Others were doing the same. His son Kumiki was already armed and ready for battle. The youth looked quite fierce with his battle face on, the horns of hair standing from his head. They glanced at each other, father and son, and gained spiritual strength from each other's presence.

Soon, most of the Arioi were ready for the onslaught, but Seumas knew they were not fighters. These people were entertainers – musicians, dancers, orators – not warriors. Of course there were those among them who knew how to fight, but they were untrained and unco-ordinated. They might fight as individuals, but the attackers were a cohesive force which would probably sweep through the Arioi and set the decks of their pahi awash with fire, blood and gore.

'Take heart, my friends,' cried Kieto. 'Stand together!'

The intention of those on board the battle canoes, now that they were closing, was plainly obvious. They were indeed prepared for conflict. Ragnu could be seen on the lead canoe, his thinning black hair floating on the breeze. His face was a mask of savage triumph as he bore down upon his enemies.

Maomao, the Great Wind-God, was angry with the Raiatean priest. There was a legend attached to Maomao, of which he was justly proud. In the early days of Hawaiian history there had been a mariner, a hero, by the name of Moikeha. Moikeha sailed to Raiatea, on the way back stopping at Kauai Island, where King Puna was running a sailing contest. The prize was the hand of Princess Ho'o Ipo, King Puna's daughter. The finishing post was the island of Kaula, one hundred miles distant. Chiefs and princes in sleek fast craft had gathered to take part in the contest, eager to gain a puhi for a beautiful bride.

Maomao disguised himself as an old man and requested passage with Moikeha, who in truth did not want the extra weight on board but out of politeness could not refuse the elderly gentleman. He took Maomao on board promising to transport him to Kaula, even if it meant losing the race.

Once under way, the princes and chiefs surged ahead of Moikeha's canoe. However, Moikeha's passenger had with him a calabash, full of winds, which he released and filled the sail of the small craft. Moikeha's vessel overtook those of his rival princes and chiefs, and reached Kaula first, winning a trophy of a carved ornament with which the Hawaiian hero returned to Kauai and claimed his bride. Ho'o Ipo bore him seven children and Moikeha ruled the island wisely until his death.

Now this story was well known throughout Oceania, but this upstart priest had copied the Great Wind-God's trick of releasing winds trapped in a calabash. This infuriated Maomao, who did not like to be imitated by mortals and was concerned that this repeated use of the calabash might outshine his own, or in some way become confused with it. Maomao therefore decided to punish the priest who had usurped his inventiveness.

Maomao blew the lead war canoe, containing the arrogant priest, far ahead of the rest of the navy, so that it met the force of three hundred sailing canoes – alone.

Suddenly, Ragnu's craft was swept ahead by a freak gust of wind, which whipped the paddles from the hands of his rowers and blew his accompanying warriors from the platform into the water. The fighting men were left behind, struggling in the waves, to be picked up by the rest of the war flotilla.

Ragnu's craft ploughed through the water and glided past

the first Arioi canoe. Seumas stood waiting on the bows of
the pahi. At great risk to himself the Pict leapt on board the
war vessel and confronted Ragnu on the platform.

Ragnu was resplendent in his battle dress. A feathered
helmet adorned his head. A huge cloak of kula feathers
swept from his shoulders. In spite of the fact that he was a
thin and wasted old man, he looked bulky and strong. The
priest's eyes glittered with triumph at being presented with
the one enemy he wished to have destroyed.

'Kill him!' cried Ragnu to the paddlers, deep in their
hulls.

The paddlers, however, were unable to climb up to the
platform swiftly enough to save the priest.

'Now,' said Seumas, gripping his whalebone club. 'Now
we meet hand-to-hand, priest.'

Ragnu, clutching a spear, whined, 'You would not kill an
old man? I'm a priest. Your soul will blacken and shrivel if
you harm me, goblin.'

'So be it,' replied Seumas. 'You have been too devious for
your own good priest – this is your last glimpse of the
world.'

Ragnu snarled and threw the spear, skimming Seumas's
shoulder in its flight.

The priest's next action horrified all those who wished
Seumas success in single combat. Ragnu had drawn a
weapon from the folds of his cloak. It was an airo fai, the
Tahitian dagger made of a stingray's backbone. The wicked
hooks of bone, sharp curved spikes, lay sleek and flat
against the blade like innocent feathers on a bird's back.
But Seumas knew that if he was stabbed by this weapon he
would have his innards ripped from him when the dagger
was retrieved and the hooks splayed open.

'What's the matter?' said Ragnu softly. 'Don't you like
what you see, coward?'

Seumas said, 'Let's get to it, priest.'

Ragnu laughed and lunged with the dagger, careless of

Seumas's club. Seumas's fight with his son had left him
with a shoulder wound that slowed him down. His club hit
Ragnu on the shoulder, ineffectively. With his left arm
Seumas tried to parry the priest's thrust, but only managed
to knock it higher. The airo fai struck him on the chest,
between two rib bones, and the point jammed there unable
to penetrate further.

Ragnu wrenched the weapon back savagely, tearing a
small hole in the muscle on the Pict's chest.

Seumas groaned and staggered back, the pain excruciat-
ing. Blood poured from the wound, running down to soak
his tapa skirt. Ragnu moved in, stabbing, stabbing, trying
to find a target on the abdomen of the Pict. Seumas's flailing left arm managed to divert the blows, but he was being
beaten back, towards the edge of the canoe. If he faltered
once, or tripped, the airo fai would be inside him, wreaking
wounds that would not heal.

The Rarotongans on board the Arioi pahi looked on in
dismay as they saw Seumas was off-balance. Their pahi
could not lock with the Raiatean war canoe, however, the
latter being more manoeuvrable having rowers instead of
sails. None the less, Kumiki could not stand to see his
father in such dire circumstances. The drummer took up a
spear, ran the length of the deck, launching the missile at
the distant Ragnu.

By some miracle of the wind the javelin was carried the
distance, but looked like falling short of its main target. At
that moment however, Ragnu saw his chance for plunging
his dagger into the weakened Seumas and stepped forward
for the final thrust. Kumiki's spear struck and pinned the
priest's foot to the deck of the pahi.

Ragnu screamed in pain, diverted for a moment.

Seumas gathered his strength and brought his club up in
a sweeping movement, hoping to knock the airo fai from
the priest's grip. Instead he hit Ragnu's wrist, driving the
dagger up under the kahuna's chin. The terrible weapon

was forced through the floor and roof of Ragnu's mouth and into his brain. The priest's eyes bulged. A reflex action caused his arm to jerk downwards, wrenching the dagger out.

With a shock Seumas saw the bulging eyes disappear as if sucked into his skull. It was a moment before the Pict realised the dagger's tiny bone hooks had caught on some muscles and had pulled the eyeballs down into the priest's mouth.

The dagger fell to the deck.

Shreds of eye muscle, mouth tissue and the dying man's tongue hung from the ugly weapon.

Ragnu coughed once and grey flecks of brain matter splattered the front of his chest.

Seumas stepped forward and with one swift blow knocked the priest sideways, tearing his foot from the spear. The Pict took up the body, held it aloft, then tossed it into the sea. It floated there, face down for a few moments, before hammerheads came swarming in to devour the bloody corpse, ripping it apart.

Dakuwanga was waiting for the ripe plum of all sau to pass into his multi-toothed mouth. Ragnu, ever devious, had a surprise for the Shark God. In life using his occult powers, the kahuna had swallowed the soul of a dog in anticipation of just such a predicament. This he now tore away from his own soul and tossed it to Dakuwanga, thus distracting the great spiritual predatory fish. The Shark God gobbled up the dog's sau while Ragnu laughed and made his escape.

'I am even trickier than Maui,' he praised himself. 'Even the gods cannot match my cleverness.'

Just as he was about to put his foot on the purple road, however, there was a whoop of delight from the clouds. Ragnu just had time to look up in horror to see a huge basket descending upon him. Amai-te-rangi, the angler god, scooped him up and carried him high into the clouds. The fisher god, eater of men and souls, had like Dakuwanga been appraised of the coming battle by certain ancestors of mortals, and was on the scene ready to snatch any morsels of food which fell from Dakuwanga's lips. Yet here was a complete sau, missed by the Shark God, and Amai-te-rangi devoured it gratefully, not forgetting to belch afterwards, in appreciation of a good meal.

Ragnu was to spend an eternity travelling through the gut of the giant angler.

Seumas turned to the paddlers in the war canoe and said, 'Take me back to your fleet, quickly. They are attacking the Arioi by mistake. Our yellow sails have turned black with mould, no doubt the work of that excuse for a man the sharks are eating – we have no intention of invading Raiatea.'

'It's Seumas,' cried one man. 'I know him. It's the goblin who went to Rarotonga with Prince Tangiia – he's an honourable man. Do as he says. Stop the war canoes before they reach the fleet and massacre the Arioi!'

'We have our orders from Ragnu,' complained another.

Seumas said, 'I give you my word, this flotilla is that of the Arioi. Ragnu is dead and the responsibility is now yours. What will you tell your king, if you slaughter a troupe of performers and players – artistes who have no training in war? Ragnu will not be there to take the blame. *You* will.'

There was a hurried exchange of words between the paddlers in which the second speaker was heavily outvoted, then the canoe set off to cut a line between the Raiatean navy and the Arioi flotilla. With great effort the rowers managed to put themselves between the two armadas. A great deal of yelling and shouting followed, until finally the Raiatean warriors understood that this was all a mistake, that the Arioi had come.

Anxiety and dread, which is in the mind of every man before a battle, suddenly turned to relief and joy. The Arioi were here! There was to be no death and destruction, only festivities. The war canoes accompanied the Arioi to the lagoon, where the king waited in some apprehension and puzzlement. At last the Arioi found their voice and began singing. Others began dancing. Musicians took up their instruments. Tumblers did acrobatics on the decks. Poets recited at the tops of their voices, trying to throw their words over the wavelets of the lagoon, to the people on the beach.

There was happiness and laughter in the air.

Kumiki found his father and spoke to him.

'If ever I doubted your honour and courage, I beg your forgiveness now, Father,' said the youth. 'I have greatly wronged you in the past.'

'Out of ignorance, not malice,' replied Seumas, magnanimously. 'You believed what you were told.'

'I should have consulted others.'

'What's done, is done. Let it be.'

Once on shore Kikamana explained to an uneasy monarch that there had been a plot to destroy the Arioi. The king was told that Ragnu, out of jealousy, had tricked the noble ruler into a situation which was now under control.

'Bring me this erring priest,' cried the king. 'I shall have his head.'

'Seumas took it for you,' replied Kikamana. 'It was necessary to kill the priest in order to stop the battle.'

'In that case Seumas the Pict is my honoured guest,' said the king gravely, 'for he has saved me much sorrow. I am embarrassed to be in his debt. Ask him what favour he requires as payment of this obligation on my part.'

Seumas, when asked, said he would like a gift: the cured hide of a pig. And also permission to play his pipes with the Arioi. The king had heard of this terrible screaming hog which the Pict claimed was a musical instrument and being rather timid in nature took some time in granting the request. Even so he made himself absent from the performance, making excuses for a journey to Borabora for a few days' rest, having had enough shocks for one month. He had been assured by his priests that the evil sound of the pipes could not reach him at that distance.

Seumas made his bagpipes, drilling hardwood for the chanter and using bamboo for the drones.

Three days later the Pict stood on the huge stage alongside his son and played the bagpipes: a dirge that brought tears to the eyes of Dorcha it was so beautiful, then a martial pibroch, and finally a lilting melody out of the hills. The tunes reminded her of the craggy mountains of her homeland, of the heather-covered hills, of the ptarmigan and hare, of the eagle and stag, of the wildcat, of the fir and the oak.

She could smell the sweetness of the frangipani, but she wanted to smell the pine. The gaudy colours of the hibiscus were in her eyes, but she wanted the delicacy of alpine flowers. The sound of parrots rent the air, but she wanted the howl and bark of the wolf and fox. Nostalgia took her heart in its fingers and caressed it, bringing forth a flood of feelings, some good, some not so pleasant.

For others around her it was difficult to find beauty in the sound. Some were clearly nervous and their eyes darted to those of their friends, seeking comfort. Others wore pained expressions, but kept their silence out of politeness. Others still looked longingly at their boats, clearly wondering if they could get up and go fishing without seeming ill mannered.

At the end of the recital Seumas bowed low to his audience and there was a kind of ragged cheer. Boy-girl maintained later that it was one of relief, that the performance was over. Dorcha however was convinced there were some amongst the Raiateans who appreciated the music of her homeland.

Kumiki got up from his position at his drums, took the hand of his father, and held it high, to show that at least one musician amongst them regarded the sounds as being that of euphony, however strange.

And who would doubt the judgement of a genius, a Painted Leg, a god amongst those who knew melody when they heard it?

After the bagpipes came the hura dancing and once more Seumas was embarrassed and shocked by the public display of sex.

'You would think they could learn to control themselves, wouldn't you,' he said to Dorcha.

'That's the whole point, I think,' she said. 'They become so immersed in the dance that they forget there's anyone watching. They forget about the world and go into a kind of trance.'

'Trance? They're as shameless as hares in spring. A trance is where you stare into space and do nothing. They're certainly not doing nothing. It's – uncomfortable.'

'For you,' she laughed, 'but not for everyone.'

'Humph,' he grunted. 'Well some of us have to retain a sense of decency.'

'You liked watching naked virgins run the sail up a mast.'

'That's different – that's sort of – natural.'

'And this isn't, you prude? I suppose you want to have the hura banned?'

He squirmed uncomfortably as the hura women in grass skirts began swivelling their hips faster and faster, keeping up the hot pace of the drums. The swishing of the skirts, the beauty in the faces of the women, the breasts bouncing underneath the garlands of flowers, all added to his discomfort. The rhythms became intense and he kept having to pull himself back from the edge of drowning in music and movement.

'I wouldn't dream of interfering,' said Seumas, 'any more than I would think of joining them. But one of these days someone's going to land on these islands and be very shocked and offended. Someone like that Captain Cook we heard about from the Maori. A man like him would put a stop to all this, you mark my words.'

2

When the performances were over and the Rarotongans were preparing to return to their home island, Hiro arrived back from his travels in distant lands. They had last seen him on his weather-beaten pahi in Rarotonga, before setting out for Rapanui, and he looked as strong and fit as ever. He was also very cheerful, greeting them with a wave and a smile on his salt-encrusted tanned face.

'Where's the king?' asked Hiro. 'I expected a lot of fuss as usual.'

'On Borabora,' replied Kieto.

'Good, I hate all that pomp and circumstance.'

Seumas said, 'Did you find it?'

'Did I find what?' asked Hiro, grinning. 'Oh, you mean the *writing*. Yes, I found it.'

They crowded around the adventurer, staring at him, looking for some kind of bundle: Boy-girl, Dorcha, Po'oi, Kikamana, Kieto, and of course, Seumas.

'Well, where is it?' asked Seumas, looking Hiro up and down. 'Is it on the pahi?'

'No, it's here with me now.'

'Show it to us then.'

Hiro laughed and picked up a stick. With this he drew strange symbols in the sand. They looked like tattoos gone wrong. Seumas could sense that despite his jovial mood, Hiro was excited. He wondered why.

'Is that it? That's the *writing*,' said Seumas, bemused and disappointed. 'Tattoo signs?'

'They're not tattoos,' replied Hiro. 'Wait a minute – I'll show you.'

He called to a friend who was coiling ropes on their pahi. The woman came wading through the clear waters of the lagoon and joined the group.

'This is Wheena,' said Hiro. 'Now, Wheena, we have to give a demonstration.'

Wheena, a large and jolly-looking woman, nodded and went away to a distance down the beach. Hiro in the mean-time found a piece of coconut shell and a chunk of charcoal from a fire. Then he stood in front of Seumas.

'Give me some words,' he said, 'any old words. Something perhaps that only you know. Not too many for the moment. This shell is not that large.'

Seumas thought for a moment, under the scrutiny of the others, then said, 'I have found my only child, a son.'

Hiro scratched away at a concave piece of coconut shell and then when it was covered in marks handed it to Seumas.

'Take this to Wheena,' he said. 'I'll stay here.'

Seumas took the shell gingerly and walked down the beach with his retinue trailing after him.

Boy-girl said, 'I thought writing was silent words. That's what Hiro told us it was before he left.'

'There's no such thing as silent words,' snorted Kieto. 'How can there be? Words are sounds.'

'Wait and see,' said Kikamana. 'It may be magic.'

'Yes,' Dorcha agreed. 'Keep your minds free.'

They reached Wheena and Seumas handed her the chunk of shell. She turned it upside down and then studied it for a moment. Then she smiled at Seumas.

'Congratulations,' she said. 'I'm pleased for you.'

A prickle of fear went down the Pict's spine.

'Why would you be pleased for me?'

'Because it says here that you have found your only child, a son.'

Chilled, Seumas took a step back from the woman and regarded her through half-closed eyes. Surely she had heard the words on the wind? Or perhaps some creature, a bird or a rat, had carried the message to her on its lips? This was magic, pure and simple, and beyond the reach of ordinary men. Of course, a signal could have been used, but for such an elaborate message, delivered word for word at the other end, and moreover a set of words which had only just left Seumas's mouth a few moments previously. How could they have worked out a signal for something he had not known he was going to say himself?

'What is this?' whispered Kieto. 'Is it magic, Kikamana?'

'I don't know,' replied the priestess, truthfully. 'It doesn't feel like magic.'

By this time, Hiro had walked up to them, still smiling.

'You want to try it again?' he said. 'This time I'll go off and one of you can send the words through Wheena.'

The pair of them did the trick over and over again, until gradually, Seumas allowed himself to be convinced that it was not magic.

'So you make the shape of the words with the charcoal?' he said.

'Just so,' replied Hiro. 'If I draw a pig, you know pig by the shape. Well, you can give words shapes too. That's what writing is. Spoken words drawn in shapes. When you see what the words mean, understand them, it's called *reading*.'

Kieto was the most impressed of the group.

'We can use this *writing* in battle,' he said. 'If I have a general who is out of earshot, I can send a message to him without worrying that the messenger will get the words muddled, or forget what to say in the heat of the battle. I can *write* my message and my general can *read* it.'

'I'm not sure it's the best use of writing I've heard,' admitted Hiro, 'since I'm not fond of war myself, but I agree, it's possible to use it for this purpose.'

Later, the Arioi had to set off to sea again, anxious to be out under the roof of voyaging. Seumas experienced a painful parting from his newly discovered son and daughter, who were of course remaining with the Arioi.

'I shall come and see you, Father,' said Kumiki, gravely, 'when next I can.'

'Do so,' said Seumas, 'and expect to see me at any time. One day, when I am through with voyaging and war, and you are ready to settle down to a farmer's life, we can live on the same island together, as a family should.'

Kumiki grinned. 'I will give you some grandchildren then – Linloa will anyway. At the moment we are not permitted children. The rules of the Arioi state that we must remain childless, or leave the group. But when we settle down, we shall have masses of them.'

Linloa laughed. 'Will we?' she cried.

The couple were about to board their pahi when Seumas took Kumiki aside one last time and spoke to him quietly.

'Listen, son, you – you don't do that dance – that *hura* thing – with Linloa, do you?'

Puzzled, Kumiki said, 'I'm a drummer, not a dancer, Father.'

'So you don't do it?' said Seumas, relieved.

'No – I play the drums.'

'Good, I would hate to think that my grandchildren were conceived in public view.'

The youth shook his head and smiled at his father's priggishness, then boarded his canoe.

Seumas's heart was full as he stood with Dorcha, his arm around his wife, and waved his son and daughter goodbye.

However, it was Hiro who dominated his mind, when there was leisure to ponder on the gravities and vagaries of life. This idea of *writing* was surprising, yet hardly as important as a wondrous new weapon, or the invention of a new kind of sailing vessel, or even a good fishing hook.

'I think Hiro makes too much of this *writing*,' he said to Dorcha, testing his own feelings by challenging the usefulness of the concept. 'It seems simple enough to me.'

'Then why were you so astounded in the first place?' she asked. 'Why have we never heard of such a thing before.'

'Oh, I've not heard of a lot of things, but that doesn't make them astonishing.'

Dorcha took his face in her hands and looked into his eyes.

'Listen to me, Seumas,' she said. 'You know I love you, so I always speak the truth to you. This *writing* which you pretend to scorn is probably the most important thing you'll ever discover in your life. It gives the user great power, even Kikamana said so. A man who can write is a man who can talk to others over oceans, without leaving his home. Think of that! It's miraculous. Words you speak now, write now, can be given to your unborn great-grandchildren, after you're dead. Writing crosses time and space, leaps oceans and centuries.'

Seumas was an egg-gatherer, a warrior, a lover, a bagpipe player, a man with many talents. He was still fit and able and could match any man in sport. He could probably outrun Hiro in a race, climb a mountain with more speed, hit a target more accurately with a spear. Yet he knew deep within himself that Hiro was a greater man than he, though he was big enough not to let this observation disturb him. If Hiro was a greater man, then Seumas could learn from him, without loss of pride.

'I will ask Hiro to teach me this *writing*,' he said, patting the head of Dirk, now grown to full size again, 'before we leave for Rarotonga. If Kieto and Boy-girl are beginning to understand it, I can learn it too. At least, I'll try. You should do it too, Dorcha, you're better at these things than me.'

Dorcha put an arm around his waist and hugged him.
'My man,' she said, proudly.
He laughed. 'My woman,' he said.
Together they walked along the sands to where Kieto
was talking earnestly with Hiro, drawing things in the dust
with a small twig, learning the great secrets of the universe.

Glossary

Adaro: Malevolent sea-spirit in the shape of a fish-man.

Ahu: Sacrificial platform, sometimes of stone or planks, sometimes of raised bark cloth.

Airo fai: Dagger made of a stingray's back-bone.

Aotearoa: Land of the Long White Cloud, New Zealand.

Arioi: Magnificent dance and song company formed in ancient Tahiti which cruised between the islands and dispensed entertainment to the masses.

Ariki: High-born noble.

Atoro: Fifth rank Arioi, one small stripe on left side.

Avae Parai: Painted Leg, top rank of Arioi, equal to a king.

Balepa: Corpse still wrapped in its burial mat which flies above villages at night.

Fanakenga star: Zenith star.

Fangu: Magic spell for various general uses.

Haka: Maori war dance.

Harotea: Third rank Arioi, both sides of the body marked with stain from armpits downwards.

Hawaiki: Mythical island birthplace of the Polynesian peoples, called the Sacred Isle.

Hua: Fourth rank Arioi, two or three figures tattooed on shoulders.

Hura: Erotic Tahitian dance.

Hivan Islands: Marquesas group.

Hoki: Group of wandering musicians, poets and dancers based in the Marquesas.

Hotu Matua: Legendary Polynesian discoverer of Easter Island and its people's first king.

Kabu: Soul with a visible shape, though not necessarily human form.

Kahuna: Priest, wise person, versed in the arts of black magic. (Hawaiian word, but used here to distinguish between a 'high priest or priestess' and a *tohunga*, a specialist in something, e.g. funeral rites, tattooing.)

Karakia: Magic chant to use against aggressors, as protection or as a weapon. It will also drive out the demons which cause illness.

Kava: Intoxicating drink made by chewing the root of a *Piper methysticum* shrub and mixing the subsequent paste with water.

Kaveinga: Paths of stars which follow each other up from one spot on the horizon. Polynesian sailors used these natural paths as a navigational aid.

Kopu: Morning Star.

Kotiate club: Hand club shaped like a stunted paddle with a bite out of one side.

Kotuku: Very rare white heron.

Kukui: Candlenut tree.

Kurangai-tuku: New Zealand ogress who used her lips like a spear, shooting them out to impale the prey.

Lei-o-mano: Dagger made of hardwood rimmed with shark's teeth.

Lipsipsip: Dwarves who live in old trees and ancient rocks.

Lotophagoi: Islands of Eternal Souls, where there is no day or night, the sun always shines, and no one is unhappy.

Mana: Magical or supernatural powers, the grace and favour of the divinities, conferred by them. A chief has great mana naturally, but another man must build his mana (carried in the head) by doing great deeds, by becoming a famous warrior or priest.

Manu's Body: Sirius.

Marae: Courtyard in front of a temple or king's house, a sacred place where sacrificial victims are prepared.

Mareikura: Heavenly angels, servants of Io.

Maru-ura: Sacred red girdle of kingship on Raiatea, made of scarlet feathers sewn into tapa cloth to form a history of the royal line.

Matatoa: 'Birdman'; an Easter Island death cult which evolved during the period of the island's clan wars.

Ngaro: Food of the dead.

Nokonoko, or aito: Ironwood tree, used for making weapons.

Omemara: Sixth rank Arioi, a small circle on each ankle.

Otiore: Second rank (one from the top) member of the Arioi, tattooed from fingers to shoulders.

Pa: Fortified Maori village.

Pahi: Large, double-hulled ocean-going canoe with a flat deck between the hulls, able to carry seventy or more passengers and ten crew for a month-long voyage without touching land.

Pahi Tamai: Double-hulled paddled war canoes.

Pareu: Sarong-like garment.

Patu club: Hand club shaped like a stunted paddle.

Pia: Arrowroot, which when scraped is white like snow.

Ponaturi: Sea-fairies, vicious and aggressive, often staging pitched battles with heroes of Oceania.

Poo: Seventh rank Arioi, 'pleasure making class', known as *flappers*.

Puata: Living monster conceived out of wood and clay, a boar-like creature but much larger than a real boar. A puata talks, and walks on its hind legs, but is stupid.

Puhi: High-born virgin, a maiden princess.

Putuperereko: Evil spirit with huge testicles.

Rapanui: Easter Island.

Sau: Spiritual puissance of a man or woman.

Tai-moana: Long drum carried on board a double-hulled ocean-going canoe – 'Threnody of the Seas'.

Taniwha: Monster of some kind, perhaps a giant lizard or a fish, or a creature which assumes the shape of someone's worst fears.

Tapa: Bark-cloth made from the inner bark of the paper mulberry tree.

Tapu: Taboo, sacred or consecrated, forbidden – it applies not only to the person or thing prohibited, but also to the prohibition and any person breaking the prohibition.

Tapu-tapu atia: Most Sacred, Most Feared.

Tapua: Goblin-like creature with a white skin.

Tarogolo: Evil spirit which seduces people of both sexes and cuts up their genitals to kill them.

Te lapa: Underwater streaks of light from active volcanoes beneath the surface of the sea.

Te Reinga: Land of the Dead.

Tekoteko: Carving above the gate of a Maori pa, either of human, animal or demon. A tekoteko had magical properties.

Tai-moana: 'Threnody of the Ocean' – a long drum carried on ocean-going canoes.

Ti: Cabbage-tree.

Ti'i: Wooden images used by magicians to assist them in their spells.

Tipairu: Race of fairies who love dancing and who descend on moonlit nights to take part in celebrations, always disappearing back into the forest at dawn.

Tipairua: Double-hulled ocean-going canoe similar to the pahi but closely resembling a war canoe.

Tipua: Goblins.

Tohua: Marquesan temple.

Tohunga: Priest who specialises in tapu, funeral rites and communing with the spirits of air, sea and earth.

Tu'i Tonga: Title of Ruler of Tonga.
Umu: Earth oven lined with stones to retain the heat.
Váa: Small paddled outrigger canoe.
Váa motu: Outrigged sailing canoe.
Vis: Blood-drinking succubus.
Wahaïka club: Hand club shaped like a violin.